Praise for N~~apoleon's~~

'This is an outstanding novel, ~~~~~~~~~~~~~~~~~~~~~~~~~~~ ts debut status. I loved it, from ~~~~~~~~~~~~~~~~~~~~~~~~ y textured, deftly woven, it ev~~~~~~~~~~~~~~~~~~~dence and a rare beauty – late eighteenth century England and France. The scene-setting is perfect, and laced with rich, juicy details. The dialogue is period-convincing, and spoken by meaty, believable characters. Hazzard is a tortured hero par excellence, a mixture of conscience, courage and martial skill, a man who can fall victim to arrogance and even cruelty.

'Better than Sharpe, gripping and intense, *Napoleon's Run* deserves to be a runaway success'

Ben Kane, *Sunday Times* bestselling author of *Lionheart*

'*Hornblower* meets *Mission: Impossible*. A thrilling, page-turning debut packed with rousing, rip-roaring action'

J. D. Davies, author of the Matthew Quinton Journals

'This book has it all. Combines great action with really good history, and an engaging and original character in Marine officer William Hazzard, who adds a satisfying dash of the swashbuckling Bombay Buccaneers to some solid scholarship. In many ways this captures the true – and surprisingly subversive – nature of early British imperialism'

Seth Hunter, author of the Nathan Peake novels

'A strong, fast-moving story by an author with a deep knowledge of the period and the narrative skill of a fine story-teller'

Andrew Swanston, author of *Waterloo*

Lords of the Nile

Jonathan Spencer is from southeast London, the great-grandson of a clipper-ship captain who brought tea from China. He served in the Canadian army, studied ancient and modern history, and has lectured at universities and private associations on the subject of Napoleonic Egypt. He speaks several languages, has trained with the former Russian National Team fencing coach, and has lived and worked abroad all his life. He currently lives in the Western Cape in South Africa.

JONATHAN SPENCER

LORDS OF THE NILE

CANELO

First published in the United Kingdom in 2020 by Canelo

This edition published in the United Kingdom in 2021 by

Canelo
Unit 9, 5th Floor
Cargo Works, 1–2 Hatfields
London, SE1 9PG
United Kingdom

A CIP catalogue record for this book is available from the British Library.

Print ISBN 978 1 80032 290 5
Ebook ISBN 978 1 80032 074 1

Look for more great books at www.canelo.co

Printed and bound in Great Britain by Clays Ltd, Elcograf S.p.A.

For my father, who knew the sting of the desert winds

The English informed them that the French had set sail from their country with a great fleet. 'Perhaps they will attack you and you will not be able to repel them... Sell us water and provisions according to their value, and we shall stay in our ships lying in wait for them. When they come we shall take care of the matter and save you the trouble.'

Al-Sayyid Muhammad Kurayyim declined their offer and said, 'We do not accept what you say... Begone, that God's will might be fulfilled.'

Al-Jabarti's Chronicle
Sheikh Abd-al Rahman al-Jabarti,
Muḥarram-Rajab 1213
June–December 1798

Crusader

The streets of Valletta and the Three Cities lay quiet and cowed in the grey pre-dawn mist, French patrols moving through the dim, empty lanes. The cool, damp air hung heavy with the tang of gunsmoke and iron, a memory of the terrors of the previous day – and the fleet of Napoleon Bonaparte riding in Malta's Grand Harbour, the lanterns on its forest of masts so many dancing stars on a brightening sea. The holy Knights of the Order of St John looked out from their lofty fortress battlements with resignation. Their Day of Judgement had come.

Sporadic cannon-fire thudded across the waterfront, shouted commands from French sloops and frigates in the harbour echoing across Valletta's bastions, so much crackling thunder. After the brief fighting on the outskirts, the new occupying troops began to spread throughout the city, beyond Cottonera and up into Gzira and Sliema, surrounding the Grand Harbour. Resistance had crumbled, Malta resting in a relieved if apprehensive peace – while the Knights agreed their pensions with the conquerors.

The damage to the capital on the first day of Bonaparte's invasion seemed minimal, but it had been enough. Torchlit donkey carts rolled slowly through the misty streets, the dead laid out on litters, loaded carefully by reverent Maltese, heads lowered, caps in hand, another stricken family left to weep. Some victims had been trampled among the panicking crowds, others crushed into the churches, or fallen in skirmishes with the French – militia and bystanders alike. Bowed clergymen watched, fearful of the days to come.

With the dawn had come the labourers to clear away the signs of defeat, their shovels scraping on the cobbles, the rhythm broken only as a digger paused to pick up an unexpected bonus, a trinket, a coin: on the first day of the new French Republic of Malta, there was little sign of regular local life – only the conquerors, the conquered, and the scavengers.

Far from the work-parties, a thin Maltese youth picked his way barefoot through the cold rubble at the end of an alley to a small church square, his toes clinging to jagged chunks of stone. He saw the glint of a rosary, and pulled it from the dust, hanging it round his neck, a good talisman, for protection – he looked next for a ring, a buckle, anything.

But when he bent over the next heap, he had something of a surprise, and no chance to cry out. Broad hands reached up from the debris and closed round his throat, as Marine Sergeant Jory Cook sat up, and rose from the dead, face blackened by smoke and dust, eyes bright, teeth bared. The terrified boy choked out a gibbering prayer.

Cook put a finger to his lips, '*Shh*,' then held out a gold coin. 'One word, mind,' said Cook with a smile, 'and I break yer thievin' little neck.' He mimed the action. 'Got me? Northeast. To the sea – *mareh*? Right?'

The boy nodded quickly, '*La mare, la mare*,' pointing, '*Iva, iva, il-baħar*,' his eyes widening as Cook clambered slowly to his full height, showering dust and debris everywhere. The boy swallowed fearfully and asked, '*Fransaya?*'

Cook looked sharply at him. 'Fransay? Not on yer life, mate.' He stabbed a thumb at his chest. 'Me Hingaleezee. Englishman, right?'

The boy smiled, relieved he had not fallen foul of the new conquerors. He shook Cook's hand vigorously, whispering with excitement, '*Ingliż...!*' He hesitated then asked hopefully, '*Massuldat l'aħmar?*' Then, in slow and hesitant Italian, '*Con soldato rosso...?*'

With the red soldier.

2

Cook caught his meaning at once.

Hazzard.

Once again he could feel the press of the crowd from that morning, hear their screams as the company of French moved into the square, calling '*You are free!*' A Maltese revolutionary was throwing grenades, and Hazzard charged into the midst of it all, in his bright red Bombay Marine coat.

Red soldier.

He looked at the shattered portico of the house next to him and remembered the whump of the grenade as it blew him and De la Vega off their feet, throwing him into the open doorway under a cascade of iron and masonry, his last view of Hazzard when he was hauled out of the square by a squad of French *chasseurs*, captured.

'With the red soldier?' he said. 'Aye, lad. That I am.'

The boy's face lit up. '*Iva! Ingliż, Ingliż!*' He tugged Cook's arm, urging him to follow, '*Biex tmur, iva, Ingliż?*' *We hurry, yes, English?*

A priest entered the far side of the square, two labourers following, leading another donkey cart, torches flickering. But there were no French to speak of as yet. He looked at the rubble nearby – it had felt like a hurricane at the time, and there was no sign of De la Vega. He thought about the flamboyant Spaniard, the privateer who had saved them all in the heat of battle at sea, giving his ship, his crew, and himself to Hazzard and the marines. It seemed a shambles.

Cook had come to his senses as he was pulled out of the doorway some hours after the grenade exploded and dragged into the darkness of the house. He remembered hands at his belt, taking his pistol and ammo pouch, then whispers and the sound of the looters running off, distant shouts in French, then nothing. He had passed out again, only to wake in the darkness of the abandoned house.

When he emerged, he saw civilians in the square, picking through the debris of the square, upturned carts, already looted, broken. Many called for missing relatives, searching, holding each other, then running for safety. He had searched for De la Vega, but found nothing. But before he could head back to the landing site under cover of night, a full demi-brigade marched past on the main road. Cook had stayed well hidden, and slept. Come the dawn he had bided his time – a tame scrounger was perfect for his needs.

'*Trove un altro?*' he asked the boy in rough Italian, pointing around him, into the alley, hoping the boy had seen De la Vega. '*Un capitano del mare?*' Find another? A sea-captain?

The boy understood but shook his head, sorry to disappoint, '*Leh.*'

Cook took that for a no, then froze: he heard French voices. He gestured to the boy, and he led Cook into the alleyway and out of the square. De la Vega had gone, he thought, either good news or bad, and prayed the Spaniard had not been piled onto a donkey cart. '*God save Bristol...*'

The boy led him through the backstreets, keeping to the shadows. At one point they heard the slow march of a French patrol and sheltered in a passageway, Cook watching them go by, listening to their muttered complaints, hoping none of them would turn or linger – even his sword-bayonet was gone, and he felt exposed. Although he was in civilian clothes he had no wish to be interrogated in either French or Maltese. Troops would be on the lookout for anything untoward. He had no doubts: Malta had fallen – and so had Hazzard. It was now up to Cook to get him back.

The boy beckoned him on again. Their luck held as they dodged through the lanes and alleys, and soon they approached the eastern limits of Sliema. Cook heard the cries of seabirds and could taste the salt in the air. They made their way through a warren of decrepit cottages and hovels, the inhabitants waking to the new day, opening their doors, lighting their fires, their harsh world now ordered by different rulers. Cook doubted they would notice any improvement. They reached a rocky shoreline, the sea crashing in tints of turquoise and green, and moved further from the city, in places the rock plunging straight into the water, then giving way to rough shingle. Long shadows stretched behind them as the sky lightened before them, streaks of silver mist on the grey sea giving way to pink and yellow, their course set by the white froth of the foaming surf.

After an hour of splashing through the shallows, they saw lamplight up ahead and came to a ramshackle stone cottage. Fishing nets stretched out on props, on the rocks, an open boat with a single mast rocking in the rising tide at a natural stone breakwater. To Cook it looked like home.

The morning was suddenly flooded with light as the sun rose on the horizon. A door opened and a woman and her daughter appeared. The boy ran to them, chattering excitedly, pointing back at Cook, and showed them the coin Cook had given him. The hesitant matriarch called him over.

'*Eeng-a-leesh?*'

Cook looked about. But for the waves and the knocking of the boat on the rocks it was quiet. They were unarmed. There seemed little risk – but he did wonder what kind of reward could be expected from the French for handing over an Englishman. He thought of the risks taken by Luca Azzopardo for Hazzard the previous day, running through the tumult of the French landings, braving the waterfront, and decided to take the chance. 'Aye, ma. I am, *Ingliż*.'

She looked out at the morning and blew out the lamp, and gestured to him to come inside. '*Vieni*, come.' He followed her in.

It was no more than a gloomy shack grown out of the rock of Malta by sheer will, slabs piled to make walls, a baking dry thatch overtop. She stepped quickly to one side and out of the darkness a cold muzzle touched Cook's ear.

'Who goes there then, matey?' said a voice in the shadows.

Cook stopped dead. 'Joan of Arc's fanny, y'arse.'

'Well blow me down, Madam Arc,' said Marine Corporal Pettifer in his rolling Cornish accent. 'Want some breakfast, Sarge? S'prob'ly fish, mind.'

Cook grinned and they shook hands warmly. 'I'll catch 'em meself if I has to, Pet.'

In one corner on a bedroll on the floor lay young Lt Wayland, his cutaway Marine scarlet jacket and gentleman's waistcoat folded behind his head, his once white shirt now torn and bloody from action with the French. He struggled to rise, a wounded hand wrapped in cloth, his lower left leg wrapped with a stained bandage. 'Sergeant Cook, thank God. Any others?'

'Just me, sir, so far.' He looked at Pettifer. 'No word?'

Pettifer shook his head. 'Not yet, Sarge. We're halfway to the landing site here, figured you'd be passin' eventually. That's Matteo,' he said, pointing at Cook's young guide. 'And that's Dolly – well, I calls her that anyways. Don't I, Dolly now, eh?'

All of eight years old, the girl smiled through a curtain of thick hair and hid behind her mother. Matteo nodded to Cook and pulled him towards Wayland, pointing, '*Ingliz, ingliz, iva?*'

'Aye, thanks be, lad.' Cook looked Wayland over. 'What happened, sir?'

Wayland looked away. 'We… we had some difficulty…'

Pettifer was bursting with pride. 'We was haulin' it fast down the coast road, when all hell broke out round us, Malt militia, civvies, and a whole ruddy column o'Frogs coming. He stood two ranks of us and the Malts across the road, Sarge, no messin', and gave 'em four or five volleys point-blank, while they couldn't even load their first. Put the whole damn lot flyin' for the hills. Bloody marvellous,' he said, then added quietly, 'Took a few cuts and burns to the right arm, one shot clean through the calf, but can walk.'

Wayland struggled to lift himself up. 'As I keep saying, Corporal, I'm perfectly all right—'

Cook held him down. 'Let's have a look, sir.'

Wayland gave in and sank back as Cook examined the bandage around his leg. 'We became separated,' said Wayland. 'Sergeant Underhill pushed the corporal and I down a slope as a host of French footsoldiers trooped past… When we emerged, the others had moved on and we were cut off.'

Cook nodded. 'He knew you'd make it better alone, sir.'

Pettifer nodded. 'Pure Underhill that is.'

Wayland watched Cook. 'It was... shocking, Sergeant.'

Cook looked up at him. 'Sir?'

'The... the action. We...' He corrected himself. 'I – I tried to... there were too many killed – I put us at risk, as well as the Maltese...'

Cook glanced at Pettifer. 'Losses?'

Pettifer shook his head. 'Not one. And them Malts was like ruddy lions.'

Cook knew what the boy was going through. 'Did you stop the French, sir?'

Wayland said nothing, merely looked down. 'Stopped them, yes, and, and butchered them... French officer could not believe it, the – the bodies, his men. The colour guard, a sergeant I think, had to run off to one side, his colours flying in their faces and they – they just couldn't see, or load... The Maltese militiamen were very brave.' He fell quiet again, then said loudly, his voice cracking, 'My, my pistol... went off in a man's face...' He blinked and said quietly, almost to himself, 'Our chaps had their blood up.'

'Then you did your duty, sir. An' damn them all who came up against you. For they got the wages o'sin.'

'Amen,' said Pettifer.

Wayland cleared his throat. 'Yes... yes, of course.'

Cook gave him the all-clear and retied his dressing. 'Wound looks fair, sir, but you can't be doing a constitutional 'cross the moors with it.'

'But we must reach Sar'nt Underhill and the others. The major will be waiting for us—'

'He won't, sir.' He tied a new knot and Wayland winced. 'Major Hazzard's been taken.'

Wayland blinked in the darkness. '*Taken?* But... what of Captain De la Vega? We must get them out...' He tried to pull himself upright and, but Cook kept him down.

'No, sir,' said Cook, 'Cap'n Cesár went down in the battle with me, but I couldn't find him nowhere. I reckon either he was pulled out quick or came to his wits and couldn't risk hangin' about lookin' for me.' He glanced at Pettifer. 'Or he was pulled out, and lies quiet somewhere, with the others.'

Wayland sagged visibly. 'Good God. It's an utter disaster.'

Cook got to his feet. 'Never give up the boat, sir – don't you worry. A hot scoff and all looks better. You rest easy here. Miah Underhill won't budge till we arrive, as ordered. As to the major, he knows what he's about. And leastways we know where he is.'

–

Isabelle Moreau-Lazare leaned for a moment against a gatepost at the palace of the Grand Master, her face flushed, her heart pounding, her hands shaking. Going ashore to see Bonaparte had proved a devastating blow, '*Ah, my dear, so pleased Talma could spare you from Toulon,*' his secretive smile, at least a familiar face in that echoing knights' hall, suddenly so full of generals and colonels and academics, all chattering loudly. When she had turned and seen Derrien and the captive officer in red, on his knees – the shock had been too great, too much.

William.

For that moment, she was Isabelle Moreau-Lazare no more, but instead was catapulted back in time to become Sarah Chapel once again, former fiancée of William John Hazzard of His Majesty's Marine Forces. Seeing him there, in that place, *in Malta*, had nearly stopped her heart.

Reaching some kind of sanctuary by the gate outside, she had almost fallen against the *comtesse* de Biasi, the older lady trying to hold her, keep her safe, her dazed mind barely taking in the concerned looks on the faces closing in on her: *Is she all right? Qu'est-ce qu'il y a? Isabelle? Belle? Qu'est-ce qui se passe alors?*

And quite suddenly she was filled with panic: she could not understand their French. It had become so much gibberish to her ear, and she looked at them, lost, alone, a trapped animal, utterly helpless. Isabelle Moreau-Lazare, actress and dancer at the *Comédie*, friend and confidante of Joséphine Bonaparte, had gone at a single stroke; instead, she returned with a shuddering crash to Sarah Chapel, the *Englishwoman*, from Suffolk, from Minster House – daughter of a squire, daughter of carriages and assembly rooms and gowns, and duty, *always duty* – a daughter *become an Admiralty spy*. She pushed them all away – and ran.

The streets tilting as she slipped and skidded along the cobbles, the tall, grand buildings bore down upon her, crushing her, and she ran from the *comtesse*, from Jeanne and from the *savant* boys Jollois and De Villiers. She rushed to the quayside, past the sentries, past the other *savants* still alighting from other ships, and tore up the gangplank of *Courageuse*.

Isabelle Moreau-Lazare had raced from Toulon for her life, but now she was hiding for her life as well, hiding her Englishness, her deliberately forgotten identity now screaming up at her from a dark, carefully constructed well, deep within her mind, *What have you done what have you done!*

She hurried from the portside rail to the quarterdeck and down the stairs, avoiding eyes, the eyes of the officers, the marines, sailors, *eyes everywhere*, nodding, bowing to her as she stumbled down another level to her cabin door. She was unable to breathe, a hand at her throat, at her breast as she wheezed, gasping, and slammed the flimsy door behind her and leaned against it, fighting for air.

William.

Shaking, she lunged for the little camp table by her cot, *the papers*, her special papers, her notes in the thin courier tubes, lessons of old, as she had been taught: her reports written in an infinitely fine hand, *9th demi in Gozo; no tropical cottons, wool coats in heat*, raw intelligence in illegible lemon ink, scratched transversely across banal greetings in French:

I do hope dear Brigitte will be better soon

9

no army water bottles
and does well in the spring with her new governess official and
navy arguments Adms Brueys, Villeneuve and Blanquet du Chayla
can visit me upon my return

Feeling the heat prickling on her skin, scalding her, she tore at the neckline of her gown, *must breathe*, the beads popping, rattling on the floor, tore at the laces at her waist, tugged at her sleeve. *Oh God, William!*

She had scarcely recognised him when he had been dragged away by Derrien, beaten, starved, but knew without hesitation, *knew*, it was him – *his eyes, his burning eyes*, locking onto hers, and the panic had tumbled through her mind: *How how how! They know they must know, they must.*

She stood still, her eyes closed, calming, trying to elicit some control over her fear, over her anger: all she had worked for, all she had pretended, *liar, spy*, to friends, to *everyone* – now possibly destroyed in a matter of moments.

She had driven Hazzard from her thoughts for so long, driven him from her fabricated world of neatly woven lies – yet, from nowhere, he had appeared. She had not been Sarah-Louise Chapel since July 1796, twenty-three months earlier. Two years living another life, a life so complete in its illusion it had seemed more real than her old one. It had been a life of terror, moment by moment, of watching every word, every thought, never to rest but for the tears choked back in lonely silence in one squalid tenement after another.

And she had fought for that world – it was not of anyone else's making, not her mother's, not her aunt's, not her peers', nor that of the whispering old dames who had tried forcing her into a *good* marriage, the lecherous gentry drooling over her in anticipation. Instead, *she* had chosen it.

Two cover legends, both the dancer-actress of the *Comédie* and the faceless shift-cleaner, who had eventually penetrated the government offices of the Tuileries Palace. No Admiralty agent had achieved the like – what London must have said of her plea for rescue at Toulon, and the loss of an invaluable source of intelligence, she could only imagine. *But they could never understand.*

Her flight from Toulon had been nightmarish, paying for passage to Naples with both gold and her body – *her body*. But she had done worse before, distracting the drunken Paris militiamen from a proper search, letting their hands travel up her bare thighs and take her against walls in rat-infested alleys, cooing to them how wonderful was their touch, how exciting – rather than let them discover the truth, the evidence concealed among the linings of her clothes and wigs. Yes, she had certainly done worse.

After her escape to Naples she had contrived an invitation to the Hamiltons simply by looking lost, street-map in hand, and knocking on the door of the Palazzo Sessa – pretending to Lady Emma that her English was so very bad, *je m'excuse, madame*. There she had met the maternal *comtesse* de Biasi at dinner. The kind and grand old *émigrée* had taken Sarah into her entourage with another, the petite Jeanne Arnaud, who had once been in the chorus at the *Comédie* as well. 'Every woman today,' the *comtesse* had said, 'is fleeing from something, my dear.'

When they had arrived in Civita Vecchia the *comtesse* had been welcomed as a trusted acquaintance of Bonaparte, and an informant from the court in Naples – though Sarah believed she was no such thing, her allegiance something of a mystery. Still, the *comtesse* had not cared what loyalties had motivated Sarah's flight to freedom. She knew only that Sarah needed shelter, and gave it without question.

As Isabelle Moreau-Lazare, Sarah had met the famous actor Joseph Talma, and subsequently been introduced to Napoleon and Joséphine Bonaparte, his greatest supporters. She had dined with them, laughed with their children at their home on the *Rue de la Victoire*. Over the winter months, the intense stares of the hero of the nation had not passed Sarah unnoticed, and wisely she had developed their strangely unrequited affair across the elegant salons and drawing rooms of the capital.

Her cover thus assured, Sarah and Jeanne had boarded the *Courageuse* with the *comtesse*, unaware they were at last among that great expedition of which Sarah had tried to warn London – the expedition that had nearly cost her life. When she saw the scale of the enterprise, the stores, the troops, the ships, she was appalled. But when she reached Valletta she sensed something worse, a creeping, nameless fear, of being trapped, being *caught*. Its source, she discovered, was the collector of counter-intelligence at the *Bureau d'information*, and dreaded spycatcher of Revolutionary France: Jules-Yves Derrien, known to all as Citizen *Croquemort* – the Mortician.

She had spotted him in Malta's Grand Harbour, and learned he had joined the convoy on a sloop from Naples. Instinctively, she avoided him, shivering at his serpentine stealth, his humourless dedication. He had come aboard *Courageuse* when they moored in Valletta, ostensibly to dine at the captain's table, but more to make an unofficial inspection. It was here that she recognised his voice. It was the voice from Toulon.

It was the voice from the home of Hugues Bartelmi – those quiet, measured tones as the Dutch grenadiers had stormed the house, killing, destroying. Immediately she knew it was he who had sent her leaping for her life from an upper-storey window and, so she heard later, tortured and murdered the entire family. Upon hearing that voice, she had set down her knife and fork, suddenly ill.

And now, seeing William John Hazzard in his clutches, she longed to be Sarah Chapel of Suffolk once again, to escape the terror of discovery, to run to him. But she knew she could not – not here, not among all this. And there was still too much to do.

She sank to her knees on the bare planks, and screamed into her bedding, her nails clawing at the blankets as she wailed in muffled silence, *what should I do, what should I do*. Moments later the door opened quietly, and she was lifted from the bed, the storm of her sobbing buried in the embrace of the *comtesse*, who said quietly to Jeanne, 'Shut the door, *ma petite*. Quickly now.'

After a moment, the *comtesse* leaned back from Sarah's tear-streaked face. 'You looked so unwell – and you have been for some time.'

'It is this man of hers,' complained Jeanne, peering at her curiously. 'She is always writing to him, dreaming of him. *Mon dieu*, your dress it is torn, *merde alors*, what have you *done*, Belle?'

Sarah clung to the *comtesse*, her old self returning, Isabelle, not Sarah, once more among her new-found family. She could speak again. 'It is just a dress, Jeanne...'

'I think she shall tell us only when she is ready,' said the *comtesse* to Jeanne, holding Sarah tight. 'Is it our Napoléon? Has he hurt you? If he has I shall give him the edge of my tongue – I have known our little Puss-in-Boots since he was a boy—'

'No...'

'Then what, *zut alors*, tell her,' moaned Jeanne. 'One of those officers? Taking a belt to you? We have had worse, *hein*?'

Sarah was on the verge of giving it all away. She wanted to, so very badly, for the relief, the relief of confession, the hope of absolution. And the anger sprang within her again. This was *not* how she had survived – this was *not her*. She had been *weakened* by seeing him, weakened by remembering who she really was – rather than holding on to what she had grown to become, and the strength she had gained.

'What then of your special one, the one you told me of? He is not struck down, is he? Have you had a letter?'

Sarah shook her head again. 'No, forgive me...'

'He is not dead then,' said Jeanne, then detecting a condemnatory frown from the *comtesse*, 'What?' she said in self-defence with a shrug, 'I am very practical in these matters. If he is dead you will be upset but maybe richer, hm? Good he is not dead, *eh bien*.'

No, but he had been, thought Sarah, *dead for two years, and now he lives, and I am becoming undone.*

'What did you see in the Grand Master's Palace?' continued the *comtesse*. 'We saw those peacock generals and their silly mistresses,

13

ah la la.' The *comtesse* laughed a moment then fell suddenly silent. 'But – there was another… a young man. With dragoons. I saw him.' She looked into her eyes, as if testing the truth of a small child. 'The prisoner of that monster Derrien. He was in red…'

Sarah looked at her. Jeanne did not understand. The *comtesse* did. She held Sarah's face in both hands then clasped her to herself. '*Mon dieu*. Oh *mon dieu*. We are in great danger.'

'But how can it be?' asked Jeanne, idly stroking Sarah's hair. 'Which one in red? Who? And what has he done? Something bad? Insulted that greasy *salaud* Derrien? Not difficult…' A thought occurred to her. 'I thought just the English wore red.' Then she understood. '*Merde alors*, 'Sabelle! *Un anglais?*'

'No, Jeanne,' said the *comtesse*, '*the* Englishman. The one they say fought off the 75th Invincibles before he was captured, and cut Derrien with his sword in Naples, *mon dieu*.'

'He cut the *Croquemort* with his sword? *Bon*,' said Jeanne, pleased. 'Then I am for him, *anglais* or no. Love, war, all is fair.'

The *comtesse* digested it quickly, nodding. 'Very well. The Englishman. Good that we know. We can plan. However,' she said, 'we are no longer in Naples, hm, are we? We cannot merely send the message to good Sir William Hamilton now, hm?'

Sarah stared back at her, her breathing light and fast, her pulse booming loud in her ears. The *comtesse* put a fingertip to her lips. 'No no no, say nothing, my dear. When a girl flees from Toulon to Naples, yet knows Napoléon Bonaparte, the *Comédie Française* and an English officer, *that* English officer, it can mean many things.' She smiled kindly, and to Jeanne. 'Oh *ça y est, mon dieu*. This is madness. Only the English and their Nelson can stop this fleet, stop this *brutality*.' She kept her voice low, 'We must help him. We must get him out.'

Sarah looked at her, confused. '*Madame…?* No, no, I *cannot* let—'

'Isabelle,' said the *comtesse* with stern care. 'We know that Malta is not the end, hm? Of all this? Of these men and their guns and horses? We know that this terrible fleet, it goes on to somewhere. And it will destroy the lives of thousands. *Tens* of thousands.'

'If you talk treason I do not care,' muttered Jeanne. 'If I am in a brothel in Dieppe or in London it is the same. Only to get to land somewhere and not feel so sick.'

Sarah shook her head, 'No, no, *madame*, you must not speak so, Napoléon would destroy you.'

'Nonsense, my dear, not me alone, but he will destroy himself and all of us without thought, be assured.' The old lady shook off her fears. 'I shall arrange something. Puss-in-Boots can refuse me nothing. We must all change, to *Orient*.'

Jeanne perked up. 'The flagship? With that *délicieux* Captain Casabianca? I'm ready to go now, *tout de suite*.'

'I am sure you are, Jeanne. The closer we are to Napoléon the safer we shall be – he does not get on well with the monster Derrien, and we can learn what he plans for your poor *anglais*.'

Sarah felt that not only had she failed in her duty to stay hidden, to stay silent, but she had also implicated her only two friends in her dread world. 'I cannot allow you to place yourself in danger, *madame*, forgive me.'

The older woman looked at her sadly, and embraced her again. 'You are the strongest I have known. And I care nothing if your name it is this, or that, or mere fancy   only that you are *good at heart*, and I *know* this. And that is all that matters.'

Sarah closed her eyes, part of her feeling it was over, now that she had half confessed. But she knew it was not. 'We must pack our bags.'

The *comtesse* nodded. '*C'est ça*. I shall see to the purser and the officer of the watch on *Orient*. They have empty cabins – some of the senior officers, they stay here on Malta. Will you be all right?'

'I can look after her,' said Jeanne.

'You could look after us all, little one,' agreed the *comtesse*. 'But now we must take care.' The *comtesse* stopped at the door. She gave Sarah a last look and said softly, 'We all have a special one. I wish I had reached mine in time, before he was taken from me, by all of this. And I shall never forgive them.'

She opened the door and hurried down the corridor. The passage fell quiet but for the shouts and noises of the decks above.

Out of the shadows stepped Citizen Masson, Derrien's lumbering yet dogged deputy – in his hand a small notebook, in which he had scrawled as much as he had overheard, or could understand.

–

Two days later, William John Hazzard was roused by an old Maltese bringing him breakfast in his new quarters in Fort St Elmo. Bonaparte had been true to his word. Hazzard was no longer manacled in Derrien's private dungeon, but billeted on a bunk in an old guardroom near the infirmary. A fleet doctor had cleaned his wounds, applied ointments and salves and bound them, and ordered him to rest. His shirt and tunic had been laundered and he had been shaved and allowed to wash.

Hazzard's nightmares now featured Derrien: in the backstreets of Naples, unable to lunge far enough to reach him, De la Vega's Toledo rapier whispering past Derrien's chin time and again, Hazzard calling '*Murderer!*' In the deep of the night, Derrien's shadow would steal in silently to stand over him, a dark demon, vanishing when Hazzard jerked awake in a sweat – though on the first occasion he woke to hear slow, fading footsteps, his door left swinging, like a hanged man.

He had learned much from his captors. The French junior officers were fascinated by their new charge: a small group of them escorted him around the fort, trying to practise their English and, so they believed, teach Hazzard French, while he carefully filed away the details of the various demi-brigades to which they all belonged. Naturally their conversation drifted towards the young beauties of Malta – and their new famous guests from the *Comédie Française* in the Civita Vecchia fleet, specifically, Sarah. Mistress, so it was rumoured, of the *général en chef*.

'Really? My goodness, lucky fellow,' Hazzard would say with a friendly lack of interest, his heart churning. She was the *belle* of the *Comédie*, they said, now billeted on the *Orient*, the friend and companion to Bonaparte and his wife – along with the woman he had pursued since Naples, the *comtesse* de Biasi.

As he was dragged from Bonaparte's presence after seeing Sarah in the Grand Master's Palace, his imagination had run pelting through the horrors of her last two years, where she must have been, what she must have endured. He knew her French had been impeccable, absorbed faster even than his own when they had both been at Grenôble, all paid for by Hugues Bartelmi. But that she could affect such a disguise in Paris society, at the very heart of the Revolution itself, seemed impossible to conceive.

Part of him could still not believe he had found her – and at what cost, he asked himself: a cost to everyone else, the marines, the men lost on their shattered and sunken brig, the *Esperanza*, Rivelli, and De la Vega, who had risked his all for him.

And Cook. Marine Sgt Cook, the old oak. Six years together, from India to Africa.

Jory.

Hazzard could hardly bear it. He knew it had been selfish and foolhardy to attempt infiltration from the unpredictability of the square, but at the time he could see no other way – like a green lieutenant from the depot in his first action. *No excuse.* He had run wild with the prospect of close-quarters with Derrien, heaving his way through the crowd in a bloody rage. His memory of the melee with the *chasseurs* was now but a series of flickering images: Rossy's startled face, the giant Pigalle, and the older, more experienced Caron, who had shouted at them to take Hazzard *en vivant* – *alive*. He had since learned their names and who they were: the famous *chasseurs à pied* skirmishers of the 75th Invincibles, the *Alpha-Oméga* – the best.

He shook with the cold realisation of his actions. After his capture, Derrien or some other authority could have had him shot out of hand, or thrown into a deeper dungeon with the other slaves and forgotten. But he had hoped that gossip about 'the Englishman' would have been too heady for soldiers to resist, and Derrien would soon have heard and investigated – especially after their clash in Naples.

Thereafter his only hope was for that same gossip to rise to the top, as it had. In acting the persecuted gentleman-scholar with

Bonaparte, Hazzard had sidestepped further confrontation with Derrien and French security: Bonaparte had been his unwitting saviour. Hazzard wondered whether Bonaparte would call upon him as he had said he would. Then all he needed to do was get Sarah out of Malta, find the marines, and call in Nelson. His answer came within the hour.

A full *Chef d'escadron* of cavalry and four iron-shod troopers of the 20th Dragoons led him out of the fort, not in chains this time, but upright like a free man, and escorted him through the streets and squares of fortified Valletta to the Barrakka Gardens. Hazzard squinted in the June sunlight, passing through a blur of blooms, palms and orange trees until they came to a halt. He could hear gulls among the noise of the fleet in the surrounding harbour, and felt the freshness of the sea air like a tonic. The *Chef d'escadron* murmured to an aide, who spoke to another, then stood aside, graciously ushering Hazzard forward.

On a folding seat before a tinkling fountain sat Napoleon Bonaparte. Long hair lying over the braided collar of a long, dark blue coat with the sheen of fine cotton and silk, he sat leafing through a small illustrated volume. Five paces behind, a slight young man in civilian dress took a deferential step back when he saw Hazzard, and bowed. Bonaparte looked up, his dark eyes fixing on Hazzard for a moment.

'Leave us,' he said to the dragoons. The cavalrymen withdrew some way down the path, but not completely. Hazzard noted two others to the right and two to the left – but for a distance of some fifteen yards he was alone with the general and the interpreter. Though Hazzard had been dressed in uniform, he had nothing that could be improvised as a weapon. However, his wrists were unbound – he need take only a few steps and swing the knife-edge of his hand to kill the man before him. He still had the slow-burn within him to do it.

How would their lordships react to that?

But he could not. He knew that much of himself. The idea was repugnant to him. It would be murder, pure and simple, not the cut and thrust of a fighting-deck on a ship in battle: it was raw, primeval – dishonourable.

But something far beyond his morality and chivalry prevented him. Instead of the general, he saw the confused look on Sarah's face in that echoing chamber of marble and gold when she had seen him and he had seen her, as she had greeted Bonaparte. From that moment, something pale and cautious had stolen into him, and raised in him that most painful desire: *hope*. Having seen Sarah alive he could no longer be as reckless with his own existence as once he had been – he now had something more precious to lose. Now he wanted to survive. Needed to, *for her*. Hope had stricken him lame, leaving him as hobbled as if still in fetters.

'I need men like Citizen Derrien,' said Bonaparte, looking through the engraved plates in the book before him, 'but I do not like them.'

The civilian interpreter translated into English. 'It must be… difficult,' said Hazzard with a very poor accent.

Bonaparte snapped a finger and a Berber, possibly a former slave, now a devoted servant, moved to a small table in the shade of a parasol near the guarding dragoons and prepared a tall glass of water for Hazzard. It had slices of lemon and lime and, somehow, was cold. Hazzard sipped at it and felt his throat open with relief.

'I understand you have accepted the terms of *parole*, Captain?' asked the general.

Hazzard had not planned to run. It was important to get inside the machine, at first to get at Derrien to extract Sarah, but now to use Bonaparte as an ally. He had to give the general the upper hand. He must let Bonaparte *win*. 'Yes, sir, with gratitude.'

Bonaparte grunted, satisfied. It was a minor victory – over whom was unclear, but Hazzard suspected it was over Derrien.

'If you have no objections, your sword will be returned to you when we encamp, for your protection. But I do have this…'

He held out the small figurine of St Jude on its long leather lace. It had been taken from Hazzard on that first day when he had been stripped and beaten.

'The gaolers were advised to return it, by certain of my men. The same men who safeguarded your sword.' He glanced at Hazzard. 'I was unaware the English had saints and relics – or Toledo blades. Do you follow the Roman faith?'

'No, sir, none but the Church of England. Though my uncle is a rector – much like a parish priest. It is a... family memento.' Hazzard looped it round his neck. 'I thank you.'

'I knew very well it was you who had written that essay,' said Bonaparte. 'It was not the Sorbonne, but Grenôble. I do not forget things. I know also that you are a scholar and you have clearly studied in France.'

The interpreter seemed just as surprised as Hazzard. Hazzard replied in broken French and poor accent, 'Not since a long time...' *Pas depuis longtemps*, then in English to the interpreter, 'The monograph was translated by a friend, before I returned to university in England.' It was an old lesson learned well in India: *never reveal that you understand their language.* Though Derrien might have learned the truth, Bonaparte evidently wished to make up his own mind.

The general was pleased at the discovery. 'Then you really are one of those Englishmen who live in draughty stone colleges at Oxford.'

'Cambridge, if at all, sir.'

'*L'université de Cambridge, dit-il,*' said the interpreter, with a complimentary bow to Hazzard.

Bonaparte nodded, pleased that essentially he had been correct. 'But you are, are you not?'

'No longer, sadly.' Hazzard thought of his family friends, of Edward Clark, John Cripps and Jesus College. It was strange to summon their spirits in such a place. 'Once. But now I study alone. An *amateur.*' He then thought of De la Vega: 'A good French word.'

Bonaparte almost smiled. 'Is this the English modesty of which I have heard? I have met the Irish, but you are my first *English* officer in close discussion. Tell me. I am curious.'

Hazzard had no answer for him. 'It would be for others to judge, sir.'

'So. Modesty indeed. A scholar. A *savant*, like our own. We are our very own mobile Institute it seems, the best of France floating at sea, now thrown ashore on this prehistoric rock.' Bonaparte closed his book and turned to him. 'I am a student of Caesar. What are your thoughts on his invasion of Britain? Was it his only failed enterprise?'

Hazzard knew that if his plan were to work, Bonaparte must win, but he must also be *intrigued*. Therefore, Hazzard argued with him.

'If it were an invasion, then true, sir, it failed.'

'How so?'

The question was a test. It was a common point of debate for novice historians of Caesar and ancient Britain, with no certain answer. 'He had too few men,' said Hazzard. 'Ergo, it was not an invasion – but a raid.'

Bonaparte gave a thin smile. He picked his way through the comment then replied. 'Perhaps he intended to recruit a new army from among the Britons he would conquer, swelling his legions.'

With every word Hazzard was aware of the man before him: a man from a fallen noble Italian family, outcast, feared by both peers and superiors, a self-made officer who had led from the front, and made brigadier-general by his mid-twenties. Worshipped by his men, he had been granted sufficient power to consume nations. Without doubt, thought Hazzard, Bonaparte saw himself as Julius Caesar.

'What then would he do with this new army?' Hazzard remembered the complacent assertions made by Sir John Acton, the Prime Minister of the Kingdom of Naples, and wanted to test them. He watched Bonaparte's reaction to his next question, 'Would he stay in Britannia? Or go back to Rome perhaps, where his true enemies lay?'

Bonaparte raised his chin and looked up with a frown, possibly aware they were playing the game. 'Did he have enemies in Rome?'

'One such as Caesar always has enemies in Rome,' said Hazzard, 'envious of his success, his popularity. Cato, Pompey Magnus, the Senate.'

'Perhaps,' conceded Bonaparte. 'Or was conquest itself sufficient for him? A conqueror,' he said, looking away, into a memory, 'must conquer. Else he too could be conquered.'

'Both perhaps. To venture further than the Republic had ever gone. And, in so doing, take Rome from afar.'

Bonaparte looked up at him and compressed a slow smile. 'We talk at last.'

Hazzard wanted him to believe he was winning the debate, satisfied that Hazzard was no threat but nonetheless stimulating. 'I would say you have come as Claudius, not Caesar. The true invader, not the raider.'

Bonaparte considered this a moment. 'I prefer Caesar. He was the statesman.'

'Claudius reigned longer. He was the better statesman.'

'But not as *great*,' said Bonaparte, a good riposte. 'And that is how history measures us.'

Hazzard looked out at the city, the harbour and the fleet. 'This enterprise,' he said, 'is more than enough to take back Rome.'

Bonaparte looked out over the ships, the spiked masts reaching into the blue of the horizon. 'I ask myself if he ever questioned whether he should return, having gone so far. Alexander lost his path, falling upon India...' In the same faraway voice he asked, 'Do you know the Quran?'

Hazzard thought of Dr Mohammed at the British Museum, his scrolls and books, the flowing, delicate script. 'Only what Christians tell me about it.'

Bonaparte nodded. 'Quite. We see only through such a filtering gauze, through the glass darkly, hm? At times I find Europe is swaddled in darkness. Ageing, corrupted. Europe is a molehill. It is nothing to me now.' He looked at the ground, lost, thought Hazzard, in his own manifesto. 'True power, *true* glory can be found now only to the east.' He looked out at the sea again. 'I have such dreams, Mr Hazzard. For all men. And Fate, like the Quran, is with me.' He looked back at him. 'I wish to be free of it all. As perhaps you did once, hiding in those draughty stone colleges. At Cambridge.'

Hazzard smiled. Not Oxford. He had remembered.

Bonaparte flapped open his book, glanced at the flyleaf, than clapped it shut and set it down on the bench. 'Excellent. It is a sad thing that I must come to this blighted place to find scholarly conversation with an enemy.' Bonaparte rose from the seat and moved away, the escort troopers moving in. He stopped on the path and turned, 'I trust you now have better quarters as befits your station, Captain. We shall speak again, and dine.' He nodded at the small volume, left behind. 'Enjoy the book. I make you a gift of it.'

Hazzard watched him go. This time, Hazzard's dragoon escort waited. One stepped forward and handed him the book, bowing his head in sharp salute. Perhaps his gambit had worked, he thought, and he had touched the thoughts of the conqueror. He opened the book. It was a copy of Caesar's *Gallic Wars*, in French. Inside was an inscription:

For practice – Bonaparte.

—

Jules-Yves Derrien, Bonaparte's *de facto* head of security, was also chief collector of the blandly named *Bureau d'information* – the deadly counter-intelligence arm of the Ministry of the Interior – and had a deep-rooted personal interest in Hazzard. He watched the exchange from the shadows of a palm-lined avenue by a bastion of the palace. He scarcely noticed the heat in his austere black frock coat. His dead, blank stare evinced nothing of the fury boiling within.

It was now impossible to own Hazzard, to control him as Derrien had so many others. And he had been *so close*, in his interrogations in the baking cell of Fort St Elmo, his frenzied beatings of the manacled Hazzard leaving him exhausted – a satisfying repayment for Hazzard's sword-cut in Naples, which still burned on Derrien's chin. He could have *used* him, broken him over the days to come.

But that moment had passed. After this meeting with Bonaparte Hazzard was inviolable. He cursed Caron and the Alpha-Omegas for their interference, telling the general – for that must have been what had happened. Derrien watched as Hazzard shook hands with the dragoons and the interpreter. They chatted, old friends. They gave him more lemon ice-water.

He would keep the *comtesse* de Biasi under close surveillance – Masson's notes had not been as accurate as Derrien would have liked. Fool. But he now had proof they had discussed the 'soldier in red', and guessed he was an Englishman, an *anglais*. Even if there were some strange collusion with Hazzard, he could not be surprised at their discussing such a sight – the general staff had been wittering on at him about it endlessly. 'A matter of state,' he had told them, and it had been enough. It usually was.

And he would keep the celebrated and beauteous *Mademoiselle* Isabelle Moreau-Lazare to himself. That vision of her at the palace gate, her softness, her sensuality, the taste of her skin as he had kissed her hand, had transcended anything he had ever imagined. And more than that: inhaling from that kiss the delicate scent created by the late *parfumier* Ablondi of Toulon – the same scent he had detected on an Admiralty cipher from a bloody corpse in Paris, and in a rainswept boudoir in the upper storey of Bartelmi's Toulon home.

Spy.

Mine.

The citizen general's mistress.

For a moment, something jarred in Derrien's mind. He detected a feeling, an emotional reaction he did not expect. It was unfamiliar.

Jealousy.

In the distance Hazzard and his escort strolled through the gardens. Another officer joined them, a pair of hunting dogs at his heels, and they spoke, formal introductions, Hazzard bowing, then patting the animals. As he bent, his step faltered a little, from his wounds no doubt, a hand to his back, one of the dragoons quick to support him, give their commiserations, a brief laugh among old soldiers – a private club to which Derrien could never belong.

Instead he felt only disgust for their hypocrisy, contempt for their sense of 'honour' and movable morality. Given the chance they would have killed Hazzard in the streets of Valletta, and now they bent to minister to him, their gallant foe. What chivalry. How fatuous.

Derrien watched Hazzard but did not see him, his mind elsewhere.

She must be kept safe. Yes.

No, she must be made to feel *safe, a difference, yes.*

At the gate, her bodice, open at the throat, her décolletage. Her scent.

Her scent.

'Maintain surveillance of the *comtesse* and the Moreau-Lazare woman,' said Derrien.

Citizen Masson, his *Bureau* deputy, nodded beside him. 'Yes, Citizen.' He stared out at Hazzard in the distance, his bull neck straining at a plain white collar, beads of sweat forming on his bulging forehead. When he looked at Hazzard he almost growled.

'They have been moved to the flagship,' said Derrien. 'To a cabin beneath the officers' wardroom.' Previously occupied by three officers of the 9th *demi*, he recalled, sent to Gozo in the first wave – two of them had not survived. Derrien did not make idle threats. So much for the muddied major of the *Orient*, he thought with satisfaction. 'If any of those women prove false, I want them in the lions' den. Where there is no escape.

As to Hazzard,' he said, 'I want him to regret every moment of his life.'

Masson stared out at Hazzard. 'Yes, Citizen.'

The French fleet was nearly revictualled, ships lining the northern arm of the harbour, squatting at the quaysides. Four thousand troops formed companies on the landings, then battalions, then demi-brigades, conflicting shouts of *sergents-chefs* and *chefs de bataillon* echoing across the harbour.

After rising early, Hazzard met with Bonaparte's aide, young Captain Jullien. Dark-haired, quick to smile, Jullien reminded Hazzard of Wayland. He found him by a stone archway in the fort, waiting with a group of officers. In his hands was De la Vega's sword, the Toledo *espada ropera*.

'*Capitaine*,' Jullien began, then hesitant, in broken English, 'it does me the honour, to present your sword,' he said, somewhat embarrassed by the import of such an honourable occasion. With a bow he held it out flat in both hands. '*Je vous en prie, Monsieur le capitaine.*' Please, Captain.

The gathering came discreetly to attention, heels clicking, and Hazzard took the sword in the same spirit.

'I thank you,' Hazzard said, just as formally, in bad French, to please him, 'It was a gift... from a good friend.'

'It was, *sauvé*, saved, yes? *Gardé?*' said Jullien, 'By, er, the men, you did fight with.'

Hazzard held the *espada ropera* with care. He had thought it lost, as he seemed to have lost everything else. 'Sergeant-Major Caron.'

'You remember.'

Hazzard nodded. 'I shall never forget. Give them my thanks.'

'*Suis heureux*, er, I am happy,' he replied, 'that they bring to us the honour.'

'They have. And they restore mine.'

Jullien nodded, pleased he had brought pleasure and good news, and shook his hand with genuine pleasure. Hazzard buckled on the sword and fell in with him and the other subalterns as they marched off down the corridors. '*Tout à fait*, it has been the madness,' said Jullien in heavily accented English, 'Very hoccupied, *oui*? *Vous savez*? Busy? *Occupé*?'

'Ah *oui, bien sûr,*' replied Hazzard, badly, *bienn soor.*

They passed through to the winding outer walkways of the fort. The army had been gathered on the foreshore and the decks of the waiting ships. Bonaparte addressed the troops. Hazzard heard snatches as they marched.

'Where are we going?' asked Hazzard.

'I think it please you, hm?' replied Jullien with a smile. He seemed to enjoy Hazzard's company. 'For the, er, *savant*, the Man of Learning, *d'histoire*, yes? *Le savant anglais? Oui?*'

Bonaparte's words carried across the bastions, '*...the blow you are about to give to England will be the best aimed, the most painfully felt she can receive...*' There were cheers but the speech faded in and out as they turned through the stone passageways. Hazzard wanted to stand still and listen.

'*...the Mamluk beys, who favour exclusively English commerce... whose extortions oppress our merchants, and who tyrannise the unfortunate inhabitants of the Nile, a few days after our arrival will no longer exist! We shall bring the Revolution and freedom to a new...*'

But Hazzard missed anything further, the words drowned by another tumultuous cheer. 'What does he say?' he asked Jullien, then in a poor accent, '*Qu'ess-il dit?*'

'*Qu'est-ce qu'il dit,*' corrected Jullien politely. 'What-is-this-that-he-say! *Mon dieu! Quelle langue!* What a *langooage*, as you say!' he laughed.

They passed through further arches, the sun bright on the ancient stonework just ahead of them. 'The general,' explained Jullien, 'announces the, er, destination, *Capitaine.*' Then, with some ceremony, 'We go to *l'Égypte! Formidable, non?*'

Hazzard nodded, playing the learned scholar, naturally intrigued at the news. 'How fascinating,' he said between clenched teeth.

'But, in the summer, *alors*! The months of *Messidor* and *Thermidor, mon dieu*. It shall be hot, *n'est-ce pas*?' He held up his hand, ushering him to the right. 'This way, *s'il vous plaît…*'

Hazzard obliged, his mind running like a ticking meter: *Where in Egypt? Artillery, horse, foot? All? Where will you anchor the fleet? Alex? Rosetta? Where!* He pictured Hamilton's study, with the smug Sir John Acton and his glass of Fiano, or Verdicchio, or whatever it damned well had been, his spies' tongues twittering in his ear – *they go to Egypt, don't they?*

And damn his eyes for being right.

'Yes,' Jullien stopped, embarrassed again. 'The *général*, he, he wish to put this to you, *lui-même*, himself, but, *très, très*, er, hoccupied, *oui*? As I say. He hope, er, you accept his invitation, to… rejoin, join us, in the *expédition*.'

Hazzard had suspected such but feigned surprise, 'Me? Why of course. *Très bien. Un grand honneur.*'

Jullien was delighted. 'Ah, *formidable! Merci! Mais, c'est historique, non?* We shall be the first of *civilised* men on the Nile,' said Jullien in fast French, brimming with excitement. 'Just to think! *Précisément – quel honneur* for all!'

Hazzard nodded, smiling. *By Christ above it's true. Wayland was right. Caesar wants the Nile again.* He had thought he might get the chance to slip away at night, to get back to the men, to warn Nelson or shadow the fleet somehow – but here he was being placed front and centre in the flagship, spearheading the invasion itself. He could hear Cook whisper in his ear:

Christ Almighty.

They emerged into bright sunshine. The streets were filled with troops marching in column, drums beating. The people crowded the waterside and shoreline to watch the boarding of the fleet, cheering. Among the army were a number of newly republican French Knights, as well as former galley slaves and prisoners, now freed men, who had sworn allegiance to their saviour Bonaparte.

Jullien led Hazzard to a stream of officers, adjutants and aides, petty officers shouting down the quays, checking orders, checking berths, and they joined the queue. Jullien talked about Egypt, the sand, the need for water, cotton uniforms at last – '*Je l'espère*, eh? I hope!'

Hazzard was only half listening as they mounted the gang-plank, a sense of a door slamming shut somewhere behind him, being cut off from Wayland and the *Volpone*, his loss of Cook and De la Vega – while Jullien chatted amiably, '*C'est plus mal*, er, worse? *Oui? Pour les dames, hm?* For the ladies? We have too many aboard, *alors! Les folies du coeur!* The heart, it is mad. But, *les anges*, the beauties, from the *Comédie*, are with us, hm? *Les belles danseuses…*'

Hazzard tried to sound only vaguely interested. 'The ladies are aboard the flagship? The ladies of the *Comédie*?'

'*Oui, bien sûr.* And some others. *Beaucoup* – er, plehenty, hm?' He shook his head, having forgotten something, '*Ah oui, je m'excuse*, I forget to say.' He extended a hand in display of the ship, '*Bienvenue à bord.* Welcome,' he said, 'aboard *l'Orient.*'

Hazzard looked up. She was a First-Rate giant, bigger than St Vincent's *Ville de Paris*, three decks of open gun-ports, row upon row of 36- and 24-pounder ship-killing muzzles run out in fierce display. But all he could do was thank the heavens above for this single touch of Fate: that within this enemy castle was all he had sought.

She was here.

Good God. Sarah, how did you come to this?

'Come,' said Jullien, pleased with his efforts, 'we have found you a *couchette*, hm? It was mine, *alors*, among the casks of wine. So now I have the, er, how you say, the henvy!' he laughed.

'You have been too kind. *Très gentil?*' offered Hazzard.

Jullien laughed, 'Ah! *Parfait, monsieur!*'

Just before he climbed the last steps to what could become his scaffold, Hazzard looked down the quayside, at the crowds, for what or whom, he knew not. Familiar faces? Faint hope? For Cook, for De la Vega? For hope they had survived and were there? For some way of signalling them, perhaps, were they alive.

But one glance at the foreign shore and he knew he was alone – but for Sarah, somewhere inside, within the belly of this great beast. Before he ducked his head into the hatchway, into the embrace of his enemy, he gave one last look at this old world, as all who sailed would have done, and wondered if he would ever see it again. He saw the work-gangs, pointing up at him, the only officer in scarlet. Then, without thinking, as if to convince himself he were not alone, he raised a clenched fist to them all, opened it, then clenched it again. It was an old hand-signal, a message in a bottle thrown without real hope into an indifferent tide:

Fortitude. Regroup.

–

The Maltese dockworkers had the best view of the ceremonies and parades, two of them lying by a heap of jute sacks, grubby robes pulled over their heads against the morning sun. They had all worked the holds of the *Orient*, *Franklin* and *Tonnant* for days, shovelling in horse fodder and shovelling out manure – but two of them in particular had always come out each morning to sleep in the sun. They saw freed Berber slaves and Turks, now volunteers, armed with their great *nimcha* swords and, among the newcomers, the mysterious man in red. They all watched him, one pointing him out as if he were a special knight, and others gathered round, arguing the matter.

A foreman saw them dozing and stormed along the gravel shore, waving his stick at them. '*Fuq saqajn tieghek u tikseb lura ghal xoghol!*' He whacked the first one over the head, beating at his flapping gown, raising clouds of dust, and the others laughed.

'*Oxhi! Oxhi!*' cried the beaten one in Greek, holding up his hands, '*Parakalo, effendi! Páo stin Kipro! Páo stin Kipro!*'

Somewhat baffled by this peculiar reply, the foreman kicked them back to their stations and they each took up a heavy sack, muttering oaths, waving their open palms and brushing their chins at him in the Greek style. When they approached the aft gangplank to the *Orient*, the one who had spoken the only basic Greek phrases he had ever known – *No, please, I go to Cyprus* – dumped his sack with others and marched straight past, down the quayside and into the crowds, whistling a snatch from 'The British Grenadiers'.

His companion meanwhile joined the lines of labourers carrying sacks of meal into the now familiar depths of *Orient*, mumbling, '*God save Bristol...*'

Within a few minutes Marine Sergeant Jory Cook was well ensconced in a dark corner of the cavernous holds of Bonaparte's flagship, and Corporal Pettifer was on his way to the rendezvous, with the news that at least he knew where they had to go next.

Departure

'You know of Citizen Monge?'

The wardroom table of *Orient* was crowded with civilians. At Bonaparte's request Hazzard was to meet the senior *savants* of the expedition's scientific Commission. They were the handpicked elite of French academia, and the invitation considered something of a privilege. In his Marine scarlet he stood out warlike in the gathering, and wondered if he were to be displayed as a rare new oddity in Bonaparte's private cabinet of curiosities.

As part of the parole, Hazzard had been allowed to move about the ship, albeit with an escort of two of Derrien's *Bureau* deputies at his heels. There was little room for them: some of the junior officers from Fort St Elmo had been posted aboard and still clustered about him with Jullien, a curious cadre of protection, had they but known it. He had seen Derrien only once that day – and only then at a distance before he disappeared below decks. Hazzard could no more have killed him than he could have killed Bonaparte.

He saw various ladies on the poopdeck and quarterdeck, moving through to the admiral's day room, but he did not see Sarah once. All the while his mind turned over endless questions about her past.

He sought peace in data, assessing the progress of *Orient* and the fleet. He moved through the troops on the crowded upper gundeck and fo'c'sle, threading his way through the stacks of cargo, trying to answer the questions posed by the young lieutenants, *Did you find any relics on Malta? Why did you retire from the Marines? When we reach Egypt shall we see Pompey's Pillar from the ship?* Jullien did his best, fielding and interpreting the questions and answers.

Meanwhile Hazzard observed everything, the captain's favoured spread of sail, their speed – but in particular the cramped conditions, the rumblings amongst the troops, their fights with sailors, the bo'sun arguing with army quartermasters, demanding room for his deckhands to man the ship, '*Lest we founder under your damned poilu merde!*' The ship required a crew of nearly a thousand men. There must have been at least another thousand troops aboard. No wonder there were fights, thought Hazzard.

He returned the soldiers' jokes with a stately bow of the head, an admiral walking his deck, and many laughed at *Milord Anglais*, Hazzard noting every collar flashing, every badge, every cracked cross-belt, every patched uniform, every sign of wear on their weapons and equipment. *Demi de bataille, light infantry, chasseurs. Charleville 1777 Pattern, .69 calibre. Italians, Swiss, Poles.* It was the army of an empire: Rome come to war. Bristling red beards and pointed moustaches, bright blue eyes, some with dark alpine skins, and the black faces of North Africans now free to join the expedition. All the while, the chattering young men and his gaolers believed he understood no more than two words of French. Or anything else.

The sky was bright, the wind perfect. He had assumed Captain Casabianca was taking advantage of a fair westerly, and would make a direct heading east-southeast to Alexandria, perhaps according to a set fleet plan. However, such a route could prove obvious and be easily intercepted. The danger of this was all too real to the helpless passengers around him: the soldiers stared out from the rails, as captive as he, on every lip the fearful whisper, *Nelson.*

Officer of the watch Lt Gilles Marais saw Hazzard and the group looking up at the network of rigging on the mainmast. He pushed past the two *Bureau* men watching Hazzard. The most senior, he gave a quick bow of his head to the others, '*Messieurs*,' and then at Hazzard. 'Major.' One hand to his hat, he craned his neck to look up at the rigging as well.

Hazzard had seen him coming from the aft rooms of the quarterdeck, but feigned surprise. 'Ah, Lieutenant. I was but a captain, you know, never made it to major.' He shielded his eyes from the sun as he looked up still higher, playing his part of the inquisitive visitor.

Marais nodded. 'Major when aboard a ship, hm – is that not the English way? But you know this I am sure. You know something of ships.'

Hazzard ignored this and kept looking up 'It seems very high...'

'Indeed?' said Marais. The top of the masthead was another 150 feet in the air. He shrugged, then stared at them boldly. 'It is, yes, too high for common soldiers to climb...' He looked away, the challenge clear to all.

Sous-Lieutenant Thierry laughed, 'I will ask you to support that assertion, Lieutenant...'

Marais shrugged again. 'Ten *livres*?'

Jullien intervened good-naturedly, 'Ah *non non*, this is not polite, gentlemen, he is a retired soldier, with honour—'

But the young men dug out their pockets. '*Fifty*,' said Thierry with triumph.

'Certainly,' said Hazzard. 'If he believes it is safe, of course...'

Jullien translated but added quietly, 'The risk, *mon ami*, there is no need, it is very high—'

Marais interrupted 'Perfectly safe. If you have, how do you say in English? A "head for the heights".'

The *Bureau* men tried to step in, but the others brushed them away, Jullien clearly concerned, but putting on a brave face, 'Then I shall climb up with you.'

There was a small cheer and growing excitement from the gathered crowd. 'Excellent,' said Hazzard. 'Shall we?'

Orient's ratlines were rigged with rat-board battens for steps all the way to the tops, and Hazzard was grateful – he was all too used to the endless twist and heave of rope footings. Marais stepped back and indicated the rail, his dubious expression evident to all.

Hazzard climbed up onto the ledge, the waves rushing furiously below. He reached one hand round to clutch a shroudline for balance, swinging a boot onto the first rung. Jullien did likewise. Hazzard then grasped the next foot-board batten with an overhand grip. 'Like this?'

Marais shook his head impatiently, '*Ah non non non, mon dieu*… like this… *comme ci*…' Marais reached up from underneath and demonstrated, taking firm hold of the vertical shroudlines with some exasperation. He checked Jullien, who followed suit. '*D'accord?*'

Hazzard looked at Jullien. 'Ready?'

Jullien looked up, uncertain, but shrugged, excited. 'I never am on such a boat before!'

To the calls of the officers and a growing crowd, they began to climb. Hazzard had to remind himself to move slowly, as if unfamiliar. Jullien puffed behind him, elated in the sunshine. '*Quelle journáe!* What a day for this, *hein?*'

As he ascended Hazzard gazed out at the deep blue of the Mediterranean, already extraordinary at thirty feet, the fleet ships in line all around, their frothing wakes streaming, churned by the vessel behind. And Jullien was right, it was a perfect summer's day. Their cause could be forgotten, momentarily eclipsed by the sight before him.

Hazzard passed the mainyard and reached out for the adjacent ladder to the platform on the mainmast top, and the way up to the topgallant shrouds. The wind buffeted him at every move, but after Fort St Elmo he felt exhilarated. He looked down and called to Jullien, '*Ça va?*' Jullien did not answer, watching and copying Hazzard's movements with care.

Once Hazzard made the platform, he gave the gasping Jullien a hand up, '*Mon dieu…*' two rigging hands helping him, astonished that the pair had made it so far.

Hazzard looked out, sails billowing all about him, the mainsail huge below, the foot of the lower topsail arcing just overhead before them, the horizon visible through a web of whispering rigging.

'Can we go up?' asked Hazzard, pointing.

Jullien caught his breath and looked. Another climb into the sky, the ratlines growing ever tighter and smaller as they disappeared into the heavens. The group on the deck below were calling out and urging them on. 'I think you must,' said Hazzard, 'for the honour of the army.'

Jullien laughed. '*Eh bien*. So it must be…! But I do as you do, *mon vieux*!'

Seagulls whirled about them, floating alongside in the slipstream, the wind stronger. The ratlines narrowed, the battens giving way to rope footings, and their weight bounced against the play of the rigging, the roll of the ship straining at their arms, the horizon tilting one way then the other by mild degrees.

Within ten minutes they reached the topgallant mast and hung for a moment's rest near the topyard, tackles and braces rattling all around. Hazzard shouted to him, '*Mind the crossjack…*' indicating the vibrating yard, then in halting French, '*Careful here!*' He had seen reaching hands trapped in less.

Just above there was a crow's nest of yet more finely wrought carpentry, Hazzard noticed, with rails and fine finishes, though cramped. The lookout helped them up and made room, stepping into the rigging for them. He was an older, bearded, long-haired man of more than fifty, in ragged white denim canvas *culottes* and thin leather slippers; he was as dark as the oak of the mast and hard as the sea all round. '*Bienvenue*,' he said. *Welcome.*

The topgallant sail snapped above, bulging with the wind, the lines humming in the roar. There was the glow of bright canvas everywhere, signal flags whipping and cracking. They looked out at the scene before them.

'*C'est magnifique*,' laughed Jullien, and Hazzard agreed. Just over the flaring sails of the mizzentops astern, Malta lay far off, a pale brown and green smudge in the distance. The horizon rose all around them, blurring from a white haze of cloud to an infinite indigo, paling into the arc of the deep sky. To them alone the world was revealed for the illusion it was, an endless sea under a dome of blue, the domain of gods.

Jullien shook his head in wonder. '*Jamais! Jamais n'ai-je été aussi haut! Merveilleux!*' Too excited to translate, Jullien thrust his hand out to Hazzard and Hazzard shook it wholeheartedly – for he had 'never been up so high', and neither had Hazzard, truth be told. But for war, he thought, he would have been this young man's very good friend.

Out to sea, there was no Nelson, no Union Jack, only the red, white and blue bars of the Revolutionary tricolour as far as the eye could see. *Orient* sailed in the centre between the 80-gun *Franklin* up ahead and the *Tonnant* astern, the battle-fleet boxing in the vulnerable transports protectively, frigates in full sail on the outer lines, accelerating, dropping back, patrolling, ever watchful. There before him at last lay the four hundred ships he had sought.

He recalled the calculations he had made that night on the *Esperanza*: a fleet of such size, given the sea-room required, would cover some four square miles of the sea. As he looked from west to north, to east and south, he could see nothing but ships. For today, he admitted, the Mediterranean was indeed the 'French Lake'. *Yes*, he thought, *Xerxes would be impressed indeed*.

The old lookout watched Hazzard riding the roll of the ship. He took the unlit pipe from his lips and said something to Jullien, who called to Hazzard over the wind, '*He says, you are born for the sea! He can tell! Mes compliments!*'

Jullien laughed and clapped him on the shoulder, thrilled. Hazzard nodded back at the old seaman, who returned to his pipe and his watch, looking out over the endless blue, his wrinkling eyes narrowed by decades of wind and sun.

They heard cheering on the deck below, saluting Jullien, and he waved back at them. The enormous ship had shrunk in size and shape to that of a distant bulging cigar, surrounded by blue and foaming white. It seemed so small Hazzard wondered if he might fly out to sea if he fell.

As they descended, Hazzard felt a fraud. Although he had enjoyed Jullien's company and the beauty of the vista from the tops, he had gambled that few naval officers could resist the chance to humble a soldier on the ratlines. Hazzard had planted the seed in Marais with the cold-blooded determination to climb up and reconnoitre the fleet – and he had done so more perfectly than any seaborne night raid could have achieved. He now had an accurate idea of their number and tactical disposition – and had calculated how to send every ship to perdition.

–

Hazzard stood with Jullien in the glow of candlelight at the dining table as the introductions continued. The other diners had already begun, serving themselves from the many dishes placed at intervals between the candelabra. But Bonaparte waited at the head of the table, two silent Berber bodyguards behind him, devoted to their new lord who had brought them freedom from the *bagnio* prison of Valletta, and freed them from the clutches of the Knights.

Jullien made the introductions, the *savant* interpreter from the Barrakka Gardens whispering in Hazzard's ear. There were no other officers present, and neither was Derrien. It was to be a meeting of academics, Bonaparte playing his favoured role of Member of the Institute, rather than Commander in Chief of an army.

The silvering Gaspard Monge scowled back at Hazzard from his seat – with his broad brow and furious stare he seemed more a maddened poet or composer than the logistical brain behind the entire enterprise.

'And what is your field, sir?' asked Hazzard, knowing it would annoy him. 'I fear I am forever buried in Thucydides and Plutarch.'

'My "field", *m'sieur*,' said Monge, the interpreter translating carefully, 'is the *physical*. The optical. The sun. The Earth. Light. *Heat*. The furnace, the steam. Smelting, casting, the iron – *fire*. *Life, m'sieur*. These things,' he concluded gravely, 'are my "field".'

Bonaparte leaned back, proud of his ageing mentor, and several clapped their hands, *Bravo, bravo*.

Berthollet, of equal age and station to Monge, stood to shake Hazzard by the hand. 'A pleasure to meet a fellow scholar, *M'sieur Azzarre.*' The French often dropped the H and final D in his name, something Hazzard was used to, but which here he smiled at, as if charmed from hearing it for the first time. 'But my commiserations,' continued Berthollet, spreading his hands in apology, 'the fortunes of war have caught us all. You are most welcome at our table.'

'I am privileged, sir.'

'And may I present the *comtesse* de Biasi,' said Jullien.

Hazzard turned to find an elegant lady, with the grace of a monarch. She smiled kindly and lifted her gloved hand to him. '*Madame*,' he said, bowing to kiss, 'an honour.'

He knew his face was expressionless, giving away nothing, saying nothing of the wildfire of his thoughts: *After all this time, are you friend or foe? What of Sarah? Who are you?*

She was sixty if a day, he thought, but he saw a sharpness in her not dissimilar to Lady Hamilton in Naples. In a single glance she conveyed her support, her care, and her fears.

'It is all mine,' she replied in English and glanced at Berthollet, adding in French, Jullien translating for Hazzard, 'For we are all here at the mercy of Fortune, are we not, Claude-Louis?'

She was magnificent, thought Hazzard, and sensed at once that she was an ally – though how or why he could not say. 'It was certainly Mercy, and not Mars,' he replied, 'which led me to safety here, *madame*.'

There was a smattering of light applause led by Berthollet, who inclined his head with a sincere, 'Bravo, *m'sieur*, kindly said.'

'And *Madame* Dutoit…' said Jullien, indicating the pretty but vacant face in the glow of candlelight opposite. She could have been barely nineteen. She batted long dark eyelashes at him in lieu of a fan, perhaps in the hope of dalliance. She got nothing in return. Hazzard took her to be the mistress of one or several of the army officers. He looked to the next, introduced by the *comtesse*.

'One of my *protégées*, Jeanne-Marie Arnaud, *danseuse* from the *Comédie* in Paris.'

Jeanne had a frank, sensual look beneath her loose blonde coiffure, and Hazzard could tell at once she was tough as oak. '*Mademoiselle*. An ornament to the stage.'

Jeanne gave a lazy smile. '*Oh la…* If only there were more such men aboard this smelly boat…' Charlotte Dutoit tittered uncertainly and the gentlemen did their best to join in, protesting jovially.

'And my other *protégée, Mademoiselle* Isabelle Moreau-Lazare.'

Hazzard took her in with an interested look, as any man would. It was the first time he would speak to Sarah since she had left England two years earlier. Her hair was longer and darker than he remembered. She was more beautiful than ever. But with it had come a slightly drawn, gaunt look to her cheeks, the years of evasion and deception taking their toll. '*Mademoiselle*.' The word nearly caught in his throat. 'Another beauty.' He bowed. 'Your servant, ma'am.'

She nodded and looked away, bored, saying, '*M'sieur*,' as if he were anyone.

He turned back to Jullien, feeling bloodier and bloodier, his heart pounding, his muscles tautening, fury welling up inside him, with Admiralty Intelligence, with their treacherous spymasters in Room 63, Sir Rafe *bloody* Lewis and Commander Charles Blake and their endless lies, with the whole damned circus caravan before him – but also with Sarah herself, despite his best instincts, despite all he could imagine of the risks she had run, of her extraordinary courage: *How could she just sit there in front of me so?*

Jullien introduced Jean-Joseph Marcel, 'the printer and *Orient-aliste*', and Fourier, 'the mathematician and physicist', Poussielgue 'the diplomat', Geoffroy St Hilaire 'the zoologist', Le Père, 'President of Engineers', and Bourrienne, 'the diplomat of *reportage*'. Crushed together at a corner sat two very young men, boys of barely eighteen. 'And these, the youngest of our fraternity,' said

Jullien, 'Prosper Jollois and Edouard de Villiers du Terrage, of the School of Bridges and Highways.'

De Villiers rose and shook his hand eagerly, '*M'sieur, enchanté.* I have never met an Englishman before...' and sat, embarrassed as the interpreter did his work.

Jollois added, somewhat more ironic, 'Though you do not have any horns that I can see...' And they laughed, Hazzard among them, glad of any release from the turbulence caused by seeing Sarah.

'To be on such an expedition, you must be very talented.'

De Villiers went red. 'We are draughtsmen, *m'sieur*, and we shall record all that we see – the great temples, the monuments and sculptures.' He grew excited. 'And perhaps build a bridge on the Nile...'

There was light applause and amused laughter. 'Certainly you shall!' cried Monge, wagging a finger at him across the table. 'When you finish your exams.' The boy bowed his head, pleased, Jollois nudging him in the ribs until they both laughed. 'Your pardon, *m'sieur*,' said De Villiers, 'But yes, it is a great honour.'

'And they should be honoured to have you too,' Hazzard said with a bow. He hoped the boy would survive what was to come.

Between the Dutoit girl and Jeanne Arnaud sat another *savant*, some ten years Hazzard's senior, with curling hair and a dark, sullen gaze. Jullien murmured with some reverence, 'And this is Nicolas-Jacques Conté, the engineer, the *aeronaut*.'

Hazzard bowed. *Aeronaut.* An evocative term, he reflected, that truly only the French could have coined. 'I saw a balloon ascent in England once,' said Hazzard, playing the eager layman. 'It was magnificent, a work of art. Though it came down with a bump. Does this make you an engineer or artist, sir?'

Conté was in a foul mood, perhaps because of the voyage. 'I make men fly, *m'sieur*,' he glanced at another nearby, 'with science, *not* art.'

The man at the foot of the table laughed. 'Ah! You lie, for art makes us all fly, Nicolas!' He was nearly the oldest of the *savant* group, and Jullien's voice took on a sudden warmth.

41

'The painter, Vivant Denon,' he said. A strong, grand figure with quick eyes and easy smile, in flamboyant cuffs and cravat. He took Hazzard's hand with a sincere welcome:

'Vivant, *je vous en prie* – I, er, beg you to say.'

Berthollet apologised for Conté. 'More than aeronaut, *m'sieur*, Citizen Conté is also *magicien*. You have this word in English? For he makes the engines that move the world! And I am a poor man of the chemistry laboratory. We are, all of us, in this special Commission of the Sciences and the Arts, this new Institute of Egypt,' he said, with a broad gesture and a pointed look at Denon, 'men of science, *and* art, Vivant.' Denon raised his glass happily and the assembly gave Berthollet kind applause.

Jullien and Hazzard took their places, the young interpreter, a nervous Citizen Dazier, sitting between them, to give Jullien a rest. 'Quite an operation,' said Hazzard, glancing at Monge. 'I shall wager, sir, that you were the mastermind behind its organisation…?'

There was some merriment at this and Berthollet ribbed Monge, the pair like elderly schoolboys. 'Well yes, and no,' explained Berthollet. 'We did it together, but somehow became as one. Every ticket, every docket was addressed eventually to one person: a Citizen Monge-Berthollet!' They all laughed again but Hazzard pressed him.

'But what an undertaking. I cannot imagine how difficult it was.'

Monge leaned forward. 'Twenty thousand books, ten thousand bottles, thousands of tons of powder, cannons, carriages, table-cloths, pens, ink, bedding, hammocks, tents, medicines, buckles, bootlaces!'

Jollois called from the end, 'Sandalwood and rosewood and cedarwood floors!'

They laughed again, Bonaparte pleased with them, taking a silent pride in the accomplishments of his masterpiece – while Hazzard quietly calculated the stores and supplies they must have crammed in every ship.

'Although,' admitted Berthollet, 'there was one item nearly forgotten from the list…'

Monge pooh-poohed him. 'Oh do *stop*, Claude—'

Le Père of the engineers leaned forward to deliver a loud whisper, '*Citizen Monge himself…!*'

After the laughter subsided, Bonaparte chimed in, 'It seems the greatest obstacle to Citizen Monge joining us,' he declared, 'was *Madame* Monge.'

'One cannot do battle with one's wife,' said Monge.

'I had to convince her,' said Bonaparte, 'and appeared at their doorstep while Citizen Monge was occupied. She thought I was one of his students, in need of a good meal.'

The table rocked and Hazzard joined in, and thought no ill of them. Until his eye caught Sarah, and he thought of Bartelmi, and Derrien, and a sleeping nation on the Nile, unaware of the disaster soon to come.

'All for science and art?' asked Hazzard.

'Indeed, sir,' said Monge forcefully. 'We shall unearth a civilisation. Never been done before.'

'Forgive me for saying so, gentlemen,' said Hazzard, 'but after Malta you seem to be more men of invasion than art.'

There was an uncomfortable silence, the broad smiles on reddened cheeks slowly fading. In the hiatus, Hazzard flapped out a napkin onto his lap and busied himself heartily at the dishes before him. 'This looks delicious,' he said. Bonaparte watched him with an amused smile.

'Ah, no no,' corrected Monge. 'The soldiers, they do as in all nations. *They* invade. But *we*,' he said, with a firm nod, '*we* are the true explorers.'

Marcel the printer commented as he cut into his food, 'At least we are not mere readers of others' efforts, "*m'sieur*".'

Bonaparte came back to life at this and tucked into the fish course before him while an official refilled his glass with Chablis. 'Surely a nation of readers, Citizen Marcel,' said Bonaparte, 'would move the world, would they not? And you a printer. Tut tut.'

Marcel shrugged again. 'But do you not also say history is but a series of lies, constructed by victors?'

'Ha!' cried Monge, pointing at Bonaparte as if in a parlour game. 'You did! I recall quite clearly. Caught! Caught!'

The slightly chastened laughter died down and Bonaparte looked to Hazzard. 'Would you agree?'

Hazzard continued to eat. 'I feel obliged to remind you all,' said Hazzard, looking at his plate, 'that Herodotus wrote the first treatise about Egypt, without conquest.'

Denon laughed – '*Touché, haha!*' – but Marcel merely muttered his reply, 'Then we shall be the first to disprove him...'

'By all means,' said Hazzard, 'plant your banner, for what good it will do in a land that has swallowed armies whole, and watched countless banners blow into dust.'

Denon and Berthollet applauded and Bonaparte inclined his head in some respect. 'We shall see. We go not in conquest, like Cambyses, but in liberation, and discovery.'

Hazzard goaded them further. 'Rather a large fleet for so few explorers.'

Denon laughed again. 'And our twenty thousand bottles of Burgundy!'

'Not quite, Vivant,' said Berthollet with a tilt of his glass. 'Some is Bordeaux.'

Denon laughed and Hazzard added, 'Ah, you mean Claret,' he said. 'Made in Aquitaine. Which was English, if memory serves.'

They did not laugh this time. Hazzard continued, slicing into his cutlet. 'But discovery can be a treacherous business. What of Naples, for example? So many things there that one may *read* of, which reveal themselves in the end to be mere *falsehood.*'

He jabbed his fork into a mouthful and chewed, then looked at the *comtesse*, Jeanne, and Sarah. 'Would you not agree, *madame*? That one is inevitably disheartened after such long travels, loss and sacrifice... then not to find what one seeks?' He looked at them all. 'I hope this does not happen with you gentlemen. It would be such a shame. To find no one to liberate, I mean.'

Sarah looked down at her plate. The *comtesse* de Biasi put a hand on his arm. 'Oh, but surely, all places have their mysteries. And perhaps,' she said more directly, 'we all find what we seek elsewhere.'

Lies.

The word came to him again and again.

The Admiralty. Blake, Lewis – Sarah.

Lies.

'I met Sir William Hamilton, sir,' said Hazzard to Bonaparte. 'Did I not say?'

Bonaparte's head snapped up. 'No. You did not.'

'I am sure he would send his regards. A charming gentleman. His lady wife is remarkable.'

'Yes! Yes,' said Denon with enthusiasm, 'I do know them, lovely people. And excellent guides for travellers in those parts. He is a keen study of *le volcan* fire-mountain there. Extraordinary man. And such collections!'

Hazzard tore at the meat on his plate. 'Alas they could not help me in my researches.' He looked at Sarah. 'Have you met the Hamiltons in Naples, *mademoiselle*?'

She shook her head, looking away. 'I haven't.' *Je n'ai pas.* Bored, muttered idiom, uninterested, almost sulking – it was perfect, thought Hazzard.

'Yes,' said Hazzard, 'Rather what I thought.'

Lies.

Something in him wanted to scold her, hurt her. He could not stop himself. The dishes on the table were changed for the next course, the Berbers standing aside, junior aides and Maltese girls clearing away quickly.

'To discovery,' said Monge with a stern look at Hazzard, raising a glass. Everyone followed, Bonaparte watching Hazzard. Hazzard did not move.

'You would not drink to discovery, Mr Hazzard?'

Hazzard looked at the ladies again, at the *savants*. 'I would, but not at such cost.'

Bonaparte was curious. 'Such cost as what?'

Hazzard thought of their brig, the *Esperanza*, the battle with the corvettes, of dead men floating in the sea, or lying in the gutters of Naples, the rubble of Valletta – and what lay ahead for Egypt. 'At the cost of lives, sir.'

'Discovery and blood, *m'sieur*,' said Conté, 'whether shed by the explorer or the explored, is in the nature of Man, the nature of things.' There were murmurs of approval from the more aggressive at the table.

'Spoken like a true rationalist, sir, safe in Montaigne's tower,' replied Hazzard. 'Or perhaps in your fat little balloon, so full of hot air.' Denon laughed – *Ohoho! Another hit!*

He took a helping of mutton and *truffade d'Aurillac*. 'I hear liberators are also required to shed blood once in a while. You had best be wary.'

The interpreter translated and looked to Bonaparte, uncomfortable in yet another silence. But the Commander in Chief smiled.

'It is a sacrifice.'

'Really? Yours or theirs?'

Jullien cleared his throat. Though well out of her depth, *Madame* Dutoit spoke up, eager to shine among the surrounding stars. 'Tell me, "Captain",' she said with derision, 'you seem quite happy in captivity. Are the English always so, when *defeated*?'

She giggled victoriously and Jeanne mumbled, 'Silly sow...'

There was rising laughter and another '*Ohoho!*' from Monge.

Berthollet and Denon were clearly discomfited, as was young De Villiers, the delighted Jollois looking on, chin in hand, enthralled. But Jullien tried to save the moment.

'We need not press the captain so,' he suggested. 'It is not the way of the gentleman to affront his guest.'

'Nonsense, young Thomas,' said Monge brusquely, 'it is a matter of scientific *discovery*.' Monge fixed Hazzard with a browbeating gaze. '*Well*, sir?'

Hazzard lay down his knife and fork. He could feel Bonaparte's eyes on him constantly. He dabbed the corners of his mouth with his napkin.

'We English are a backward people,' he admitted, watching the *comtesse* and Sarah and *Madame* Dutoit as Dazier interpreted for him. 'We love our king, but despise his ministers. We love freedom, but bow to tradition. We are highly disciplined, but resent authority until it earns our respect. We deride the law, but loathe injustice.' He took up his glass of Margaux as the interpreter caught up. 'We can be an aggressive, dangerous people. Consequently, the English do not fear a war thrust upon them. On the contrary,' he said, 'the English enjoy it.'

He drank.

'Preposterous,' said Monge, but his certainty wavered when he looked at Hazzard.

'And defeat, Mrs Dutoit, merely lets us prepare for the only battle that truly matters.'

The diners looked to Bonaparte. The young general nodded. 'I admit I am puzzled, Captain,' he said. 'I fight all battles as I did my first. Much as Caesar, as we once discussed. Do please enlighten us. Which is the only battle that matters in a war?'

There was an expectant hush as they waited. Hazzard reached for his wine. 'Surely, the only battle that matters,' said Hazzard, lifting his glass, 'is the final one.'

The diners looked to the mortified interpreter. He swallowed, his voice scarcely above a whisper. '*L'ultime.*'

The table fell silent and all looked at Hazzard, but for Denon, who was thrilled and applauded, 'Haha! *Touché encore!*'

Bonaparte stared back at him, white-faced. Sarah writhed in anguish. Hazzard felt the *comtesse* take his hand under the table-cloth, squeezing it lightly, a gesture of support. He found himself shaking with quiet rage.

'And how do you suppose *that* comes about if you lie in gaol?' demanded Monge. '*Ha, m'sieur. Ha!*'

Bonaparte continued to watch Hazzard. 'I fear it is not possible to offend an Englishman, Citizen,' announced Bonaparte. 'Is that not so, Captain?'

Hazzard declined to answer.

Bonaparte continued. 'You can make the attempt but three times. On the first, he will laugh with you – pretending he has not heard correctly. On the second, he will claim not to have understood – still to give you the benefit of doubt.'

'And on the third?' asked Monge, jocular and expectant.

'On the third occasion,' said Bonaparte, looking directly at Hazzard, 'he will kill you.'

All eyes turned to Hazzard, the laughter and smiles gone, the group suddenly aware of some hitherto undetected threat in their midst.

Hazzard took another sip from his glass. 'Perhaps,' he said, then smiled suddenly, 'though with such excellent cuisine, possibly not tonight.'

–

Jules-Yves Derrien did not dine at the general's table that first night. Instead he waited for the Dog Watch, when most of the crew would be in their sweating galley, cooking and eating. He made his way to the middle gundeck and the cabin formerly of the unlamented muddied major of the 9th *demi* – the cabin of Isabelle Moreau-Lazare and the little *Comédie* whore, Jeanne Arnaud.

He closed the door behind him. He could hear the voices above, in the wardroom, the murmurs and sudden laughter of the diners. He began his search. He first rifled through their valises, bags, shoes, hats, dresses, shifts, linings, belts, ribbons, stays, corsets and lacquered soap-boxes, everything. He then started on the bedding. Derrien was particularly skilled at the secret search, leaving no trace of the process, replacing every item just as he had found it, angling each separate piece meticulously – so the victim remained utterly unaware they had been exposed.

He found a torn dress, discarded, and recognised it from that day – and stopped. His hand feeling the silk, he imagined her naked heat inside it, and held it to his nose and mouth, and inhaled, closing his eyes. *Yes*, there it was: the perfume from the dead Ablondi of Toulon, but also, far more intoxicating, it smelt of *her*.

'*Mon dieu...*'

He shivered in excitement at the thought of her a moment. He examined one of her wigs, a formal silver-grey, somewhat old-fashioned, and another in a silver-blonde – and then smiled.

He hurried back to his own cabin, a forward storeroom near the junior officers – close to the stairs and the marines' berths. He went in and slid the bolt he had fitted. His fingers trembled with anticipation.

With extreme care he withdrew from his pocket several of the narrow tortoise-shell tubes he had found in the wig. They looked like hair-curlers. He inserted a finger in one of them, and poked out a thin sheet of notepaper he had seen rolled tight inside, and nearly laughed with a strange pride: *her ingenuity*. Of course he would order a search of her cabin for the sake of protocol, but now it would reveal nothing; he wanted to keep her from Masson and the others. He wanted her to himself.

He unrolled the first sheet carefully, a personal letter, and read the salutations, skimming the contents, '*I do hope dear Brigitte will be better soon...*' He sniffed at it. He smiled. With a small tinderbox he lit a candle on the desk. He held the letter high above the flame, slowly lowering it, waving it in circles over the heat. After a moment the page rattled and crisped slightly, drying, then darkened, and a light brown scorching began to spread. Before his eyes transverse lines written across the personal message began to appear in burnt lemon ink:

> 9th *demi in Gozo; no tropical cottons, wool coats in heat*
>
> *no army water bottles*

navy arguments Adms Brueys, Villeneuve and Blanquet du Chayla

Vaubois i/c garrison Malta 4500 men

Powder magazines Fort St Elmo flooded

28'89'66 Red 14 34 59 3B

He felt another shudder go through his body, a tremulous pleasure, flashes in his mind's eye of the women in the dark waists of the ship, his sweating hands slipping on their skin in his pounding nocturnal frenzies, now as nothing compared to what lay before him. He *had* her, *with evidence of an Admiralty cipher.* With all of his victims he always sought more evidence, always more, for it was this that excited him most: not the violent consummation of power, but its potential, its sweet promise, and the terror it inspired.

For he knew her now: the scented beauty of Bartelmi's household; the desperate flight to Naples; the message from that courtesan slut, the *comtesse* de Boussard, of a new girl with the old *comtesse* de Biasi; all now made sense. And he knew Isabelle's skill at subterfuge, her cunning to lie a-bed *with Bonaparte*, of all men. This would be his one hold over the general, over them all: she would be *his*, and *his alone*.

His breathing grew faster. Quickly he undid his buttons and tore off his coat, tugged the cravat from his throat, hauling the shirt over his head. He fell to his knees on the plank floor, his altar the desk, the candle and the letters his offering, *her letters*, one hand reaching, feeling for it under the mattress on his hammock, finding it, and withdrawing it slowly: the rawhide scourge he had used on Hazzard that first day.

His breathing quickened. Lightly, just to test, he threw the frayed ends over his shoulder. He winced at the sting on his upper back. Then again, lower, his mouth and eyes opening wide with the unexpected pain and flood of warmth – then *again*, harder, and *again*, still *harder*, until his hand flashed rhythmically with the lash, *Hazzard*, as he punished himself for feeling such pleasure, for sensing her naked, *Isabelle*, vulnerable before him, in her scented slip, a bare breast exposed, *Isabelle*, her lips parting, smooth legs stretching on the cot behind her, *harder*, until he gasped – a paroxysm of pain and pleasure at his own sin, penance and absolution all at once, and he fell forward, whispering his own holy litany, 'I *am* the Republic... I *AM* the Republic...'

–

When at last the party broke up, it had already gone four bells of the Mid Watch, and Hazzard guessed it was one or two in the morning. Jullien escorted Hazzard down the ornate carven staircase to the lower decks, the boards crammed with soldiers in bedrolls, while just above them the slung hammocks of sailors swayed in so many snoring cocoons.

Jullien was drunk, and Hazzard was keeping him good company, the pair of them laughing at nothings, theatre, variety, satire. They stumbled in broken English and French until they reached the middle gundeck, the oldest friends. Hazzard liked him, and regretted what he must do to him, do to them all.

Jullien escorted him to his cabin door. Intended for Jullien, it was aft, with access to the senior officers. A marine stood sentry, another sat at a folding table with a lantern, and rose hastily when he saw them arrive. Jullien took hold of Hazzard to steady himself. He spoke quietly, waving a finger at him *non, non, shhh*, then laughing and stifling more laughter, only to fall suddenly serious, a strange half-smile on his earnest face.

'Think not too badly of us, *mon ami*,' said Jullien at length. 'When you go. *N'oubliez*... not to forget, that some of us, we loved the English poets...'

Swaying with wine, Jullien offered his hand and Hazzard shook it, a Gallic custom, offered only grudgingly in Britain, thought Hazzard, a kindness he missed from France. 'I think, *mon vieux*,' slurred Hazzard, 'I am going nowhere... for a very, *very* long time.'

Jullien smiled again as he got him to the door. 'Ohh, *mon ami*,' said Jullien, shaking his head slowly from side to side, arm round his shoulder, 'I think you will go, somehow.' He sounded as if he would miss him. He glanced at the marine behind them, then said suddenly, almost angrily, in English under his breath, '*I know it was you.*'

Hazzard stopped and stood dead still.

Jullien added in a rush of French, 'You saved a Maltese family from a madman throwing grenades in Sliema – then cut down four of the Alpha company of the 75ᵗʰ Invincibles with your sword, and two fusiliers of the 4ᵗʰ *Légère*. *Mon dieu*. I *know this*. You are *savant, oui*, but also *chevalier*, gallant *soldat*. Do not deny me this memory of your valour, *mon ami*.'

Hazzard watched his flushed face. Jullien was shocked by the tale of Hazzard's capture, fearful, bewildered that Hazzard had made nothing of it.

'Army gossip,' said Hazzard. 'A *trompe l'oeuil*. Trick of the eye.'

Jullien was disturbed by something, his self-conflict, his duty. 'I know you live by honour...' He made to move away, then clutched Hazzard by the hand again, 'I beg this of you. Do nothing that would blacken our names, or your own. And remember my sadness, that we are enemies.'

Jullien staggered back up the stairs, one of the marines following him with a lantern. Hazzard went into his cabin and fell onto the slung hammock, rocking violently, and began to snore. Disgusted, his guard banged the door shut.

Hazzard opened his eyes and lay still, a dim light from the passage glowing under the door; he stared at the wall, his thoughts rushing. His twin mission, for what it was, was half complete. He had found Sarah – though she was by no means safe. But Lewis's mission was still running: *Stop the fleet, Captain. Find them, sink them, kill them*.

He was now faced with two priorities: to wrest Sarah from the ship, and to carry out Lewis's orders. The sole objective that once had bound him to his duty to follow Lewis's orders was his personal determination to destroy Derrien. When he had believed Bonaparte's fleet had been yet another arbitrary threat from France, he had been prepared to pull Sarah from its threshing gears and get her *out*, and be done.

But something new had come into play regarding the Admiralty's command to intercept the fleet: he now knew the fleet was headed for Egypt.

He *wanted* to stop it. He had to.

He heard Sir John Acton's arrogant remark once again, '*It is a bold venture and will yield millions in revenue. Jolly good luck to 'em if it keeps 'em out of Naples.*'

Oh Lewis, you knew all along.

I shall burn them all down. Yielding millions or not.

He thought of Bonaparte, of the *savants* led by the forceful Monge and Berthollet. Were they unwitting pawns in Bonaparte's grand scheme, he wondered, or implicated in the horrors to come – counting the dead, French and Egyptian, contorted in their incomprehensible agonies, the drifting sands becoming their shroud, the eager scientists and magician aeronauts making their notes for posterity: *a natural consequence, m'sieur*, all for their noble academic endeavour.

If they had not grasped the true purpose of their venture, he pitied them, for it threatened their very lives. He thought of those young men, those thoughtless, excited, unprepared young men, who had seen nothing of war. *Nothing.* Yet they had signed on for the deadliest adventure of their careers.

And Bonaparte, luring his devoted troops to follow him into the desert while he dreamt of becoming an Oriental potentate greater than Alexander – no doubt festooned in robes and tassels with a Grand Vizier in his fantastical Babylon. *Do you know the Quran? I have such dreams, Mr Hazzard...*

Damn him and his bloody dreams.

And part of him was envious. How he wished he too were a young De Villiers of seventeen, off to Egypt to record the wonders of the ancient world. Ten years ago he would have given his life to be part of such an expedition.

And what was its intent: the *savants* aside, there was only one objective, or so the government of France believed, and without question that was India. Of all of them, Le Père had kept a quiet eye on him throughout the meal – Le Père, President of the Engineers. He and Hazzard both knew they were not going to Egypt to build bridges on the Nile or draw pictures. They were going to dig.

Suez.

And for that reason Hazzard would do it all, come Hell itself: get Sarah *out*, destroy Derrien, and set light to the brave new colony before it even landed – and damn Bonaparte's dreams.

He tugged out the note slipped into his sleeve by the *comtesse* de Biasi when he had first kissed her hand. She had proved more deft than his most light-fingered marine, Private Kite. It said '*Orlop, 2am aft stair*'.

He would get but one chance. He did swift calculations. Barely eight knots, he thought, say seven – with the sail area of the *Orient* it should have been at least ten, but she was riding low, heavily laden, and had to move as slowly as the convoy, *give it six to be safe* – over how many hours, *how many*, and he reached for his watch but remembered, *gone – everything was gone*.

It had been two bells when Jullien had talked of theatre, song, the *Beggar's Opera* and *Bartholomew Fair*, in their broken *lingua franca* – they had wandered briefly into the fresh air. The *Orient* had weighed anchor before they had called the meridian, nearly four watches earlier – sixteen hours then, at six knots, subtract two hours to assemble fleet formation, six knots by *fourteen* hours, the constellation of Cygnus off the larboard bow.

It could be far enough. And near enough.

Now.

He took a draught of the water left in the jug and splashed his face. He turned to the corner for the *espada ropera* – he had not worn it at dinner but left it propped behind two stacked wine-casks in the cabin. It was gone. He looked behind the casks, if it had fallen. It had not.

Stolen? By a common soldier?

That was too tempting to believe. *Derrien?* No doubt Derrien would prefer him unarmed while aboard, but the ramifications stretched out before him, reaching to the obvious conclusion: he had been discovered.

It was not enough to stop him.

So be it.

He opened the door. The marine at the table outside had time to frown and start rising from his seat before Hazzard gave him the heel of his hand into his chin. He fell heavily and Hazzard thought he might have killed him but he did not care, because he was thinking of Sarah now, and escape. He dropped him back onto his stool, his head slumped. From this point, there would be no return.

There was light from above along the middle gundeck. Unlike British ships, they had closed only some of the hatches, leaving the midships grilles open for fresh air. Even so it grew hotter and more oppressive as he descended. He heard footsteps above and hurried.

Using the 110-gun *Ville de Paris* as a guide, he located the aft staircases and went down to the lower gundeck on the port side. Glowing a luminescent white, bleached hammocks swayed against the mild roll of the ship. He listened and watched. Beyond a bulkhead further on came the yellow blaze of a lamp, shadows flitting. He ducked. It was a pair of marines doing their rounds. In the flashing shapes of the posts and beams he could make out the humped shapes of still more soldiers bunking on the deck in rows, between the cannons, the murmur of voices, the glow of a pipe here and there. The marines moved away, heading forward.

He found the steps and slipped down into the deep silence of the Orlop, the final level just above the giant holds of the ship. At the bottom of the steps was a low door, but no guard to be seen: no marine, no soldier, and no sound. He opened the hatch slowly, fearful of creaking hinges, but there was nothing. He stepped down into a black, woollen deafness.

The dark was thick, enveloping. He was below the waterline. As his senses adjusted he heard the sea: it boomed against the hull, not with the rush of spray at the bows on the surface, but with a slow, heavy pulse, the timbers cracking and lowing with deep, sonorous moans, echoing like whale song.

He moved forward, his hands out, a blind Teirisias feeling his way in the Underworld. He jerked back when he encountered the sharp splintering edges of storage crates and the stiff jute of sacks, at first shocked, then reassured that there was evidence of life here, the cargo absorbing his every sound, even his breathing in the heavy air. He moved past, then struck his head on one of *Orient*'s huge ribs jutting out between packages and packing-cases. He could detect the scurry of rats.

The traditional Orlop of his experience was a split deck, one side higher than the other, creating two long-jettied overlapping platforms the length of the ship – he had no way of telling if this were the case here, or whether a French First-Rate had a single deck. He was afraid he might fall into the blackness of the holds, at least a storey high, a lost, broken figure to be found only on disembarkation, if ever. The skin at the nape of his neck contracted at the thought, the soles of his feet tingling, already weightless in the imagined fall.

But once he rounded a bulkhead and its pile of stores he heard voices and the rhythmic working of a cranked machine. He wondered if the bilge pumps were being operated, but he could hear none of the usual grindings from above. A weak light began to suffuse the blackness and he could feel his eyes react, hungry for anything to define the darkness more clearly. The noise came from the hold below.

To the stern, he guessed, lay the purser's cabin, the slop room, and steward's room – but it seemed deserted in favour of the cargo. The powder magazines could be anywhere, perhaps amidships, or behind hanging curtains aft or forward, as on the *Ville*. These were crucial to his plan.

He moved further aft, hit an object, *staircase*, stopped, bumped something to his right and stepped round a post. He saw the source of light: an open hatchway. He moved toward the hatch and nearly bit his tongue when a silhouetted figure stepped out.

'Down in the Orlop again, lad?'

Hazzard choked back his shock as Cook put out a steadying hand, coming round into the light. 'Y'always did creep about at night didn't you, sir?'

'Jory! By *flaming* Christ—'

'Nah. He ain't here. I looked.'

'How? What in hell happened?'

'Got a bit of an 'eadache from that last bomb on Malta. Needed one of Porter's pillikies.'

Hazzard went limp with relief. 'Thank God. De la Vega?'

'No sign, sir. But no body neither.'

It was enough to give him hope. 'I *told* him—'

'Aye. But he didn't know y'was to walk into the arms of the Frogs now, did he, though he guessed.'

It was a rebuke. Hazzard accepted it. 'It was the only way.'

'And y'knew I'd bloody stop you.'

Hazzard nodded. 'I did.'

'And you'd a'been right.'

Hazzard accepted both the compliment and the complaint. 'The men?'

'At the rdv, sir. Mr Wayland walking wounded. I told Petty he was to execute your final order and get 'em back to Nellie or the *Volpone*.'

'What a bloody mess... Was it you who gave the countess that note?'

Cook pointed. 'In a way. Ain't got much time, sir. Look further aft.'

Hazzard peered round a tower of packing cases. The shutter of a dark lantern opened slowly, and the area was soon bathed in light. It was Sarah.

Hazzard stared for no more than a moment, then took her, held her, so she would not fly away, could not escape from him this time, burying his face in her hair, '*God above...*'

She began to weep, '*Forgive me forgive me,*' she repeated.

'Found you, at last,' he said, her tears hot on his neck, her hands forming fists, knotting his hair, holding him tight. 'How? How? My God... *Sarah...*'

He could say no more than her name again and again and she his, '*William.*'

Then he was shaking her, his frustration coming to the fore, his briefing at the Admiralty by Blake and Lewis, his chase across the Mediterranean, the loss of the *Esperanza* in battle, duelling with Derrien in the gutters of Naples, all rushed out of him and struck her instead, as if it were her fault. 'Where *were* you! You wrote a letter from Naples, *yet you weren't there*! Why did you *lie*?' He stopped when she broke down in his arms, his breath catching. '*Blake* – lied to me at the Cape, lied to me in London – I'll *kill* him for this, by *God*. Lewis as well. I'm going to make them *pay*—'

'No... Will, you do not understand...' She shook her head, trying to stop him.

'—took advantage, *pretended to*—'

'*Listen to me!*' She took a breath and whispered the truth of it: '*It was I who went to them.*'

He stopped, his hand touching her damp cheek, suddenly still. 'What?'

'I went to *them.*'

Hazzard stared. 'You went to *Blake*? The *Admiralty*? You went to that bloody place? Wh... *How*? Why?'

'After your return from the Cape. When I saw what they had done to you, all of them...' She looked down, remembering the feeling of it, 'I wanted the truth, of what had happened. You had done too much, and I wanted, needed...' She kept weeping but gave a strangled laugh, the months and months of loneliness suddenly unstoppered, at an end, and she closed her eyes. 'Say my name, William, say my name for me I beg of you...'

'Sarah...'

She began to sob, '*That is me, that is me...*'

He held her, feeling her body quake as she cried into his shoulder. 'I wanted adventure, did I not...'

No.

'I found it,' she said.

Christ, what have I done.

'I am alone, and have been for so long...' She looked at him steadily. 'You would not know me any longer...' And she told him what she had done.

Hazzard stared. He could not conceive of it, Isabelle Moreau-Lazare of the *Comédie Française*, former mistress of Joseph Talma, and possibly lover of a general who would be king.

The Admiralty agent.

Sarah.

He held her face, looked at her, could barely speak. 'It was *I* who left you...'

Cook moved forward. 'Sir. Footsteps. Best show a leg.'

Hazzard listened. They were still far off.

'Derrien,' he said, 'Does he know?'

She nodded, wiping her face. 'No. He nearly caught me in Toulon... but I escaped—'

'How?'

'Climbed down the drainpipe from the top floor and jumped, hid for the night then found a boat to Naples.'

'Christ God above...' He looked further aft, then back at the glow from below, from the hold. 'Jory, we are getting out. What's down there?'

'Bloody great printing press. Three or four civilians, working day and night, sir.'

'They're making these,' said Sarah and handed him a sheet.

Hazzard held it under the lantern. It was a single page. He recognised the script at once. 'This is Arabic.'

Marcel, the printer.

'They're also laying up a newspaper, like they did in Italy,' she said, 'and a journal for an Institute of Egypt, or some such.'

Bonaparte's words came back to him: *I am a mathematician but enjoy the sciences of whichever persuasion.*

Cook nodded. 'I've heard 'em, sir. Alexandry, Rosette, Jeeza. It's all they natter about. Very excited they are to walk in and take it all, like the Turks're a lot o'daft mollies. The Frogs don't know a piskie's tit about it.'

'They want Suez,' said Sarah. 'I've heard them.'

'Could they dig out the old canal?' asked Hazzard.

She nodded. 'Theoretically, either to the sea or across to the Nile – they keep debating. It's what I tried to pass to London, and Bonaparte confirmed it on Malta. The scientists, the *savants*, they have all manner of tools and surveying instruments, geological, geographical, engineering, everything. There are roughly a hundred and sixty-five of them, to compile a Domesday Book of Egypt, a record of everything they find. Here are their names.'

She thrust a tightly rolled sheet into his hands and he saw the names, many of them he knew from his own studies, *Malus, G.-St.-Hilaire, Le Père, Aymé, Raige*, and others in categories, *Section the First: Mathematical, Section the Second: Military Engineering*, and still more. Hazzard thought of Berthollet's comments at dinner, chemists, physicists and artists, Marcel to immortalise the results.

She delved into an inner pocket of her bodice. 'Here. I had wanted to pass it to you at dinner, had it on me all night. It's all I have so far, the divisions, the adjutants, demi–brigade generals...'

Hazzard opened another scroll of thin sheets. He read through them, and could not believe his eyes.

Armée d'Orient
Division Kléber. – (Adj-Gen Escale).
Gen de Brig: Damas i/c 2nd Light Demi. (c.1700 men)
Verdier i/c 25ᵗʰ (1700) and 75th Line Demi (1700) // (5100?)

Divison Desaix (Adj-Gen Donzelot?)
Gen de Brig: Belliard i/c 21st Light Demi (men dᵒ)
Friant i/c 61st and 88th Line Demi. (men dᵒ)

Division Bon (Adj-Gen Valentine).
Gen Brig: Marmont i/c 4th Light Demi (dᵒ)
Rampon i/c 18th and 32nd Line Demi. (dᵒ)

It went on, lists of divisions, their strengths, generals, battalion commanders, cavalry regiments, number of artillery and horses. At the bottom, a total: 38,000 fighting men and reserves. He looked at her, for the first time understanding the depth of her dedication. 'How on earth did you get this?'

'*Holy God...*' murmured Cook, reading the order of battle for the *Armée d'Orient* over Hazzard's shoulder. 'The 9th, 22nd, 69th, the *75th* – it's their feckin' army from Italy, been moppin' up the Austrians like bread in gravy. Turks won't stand a flamin' chance...'

Hazzard now thought only of escape. 'How many small boats do they have?'

'Most are lashed, stowed or slung, sir. But there's three strung out astern on a line, secured just below the short stays of the quarterdeck. No room for 'em up top. Reckon above a thousand troops aboard.'

Sarah put a hand out. 'I cannot,' she said.

'We are *all* going, Sarah, for God's sake...' Even as he said it he could see that she would not accept it.

'I can't leave the *comtesse* to the mercy of Derrien, or leave Jeanne—'

'Yes, you damn well can—'

'I *cannot*—'

'*I did not come this far to lose you again.*'

The footsteps were drawing closer. 'Sir,' said Cook, 'The ship's got three hanging magazines: for'ard, midships and aft. I've rigged a bang to the Number 2 for the 24-pounder ammo, just in case. Length of quickmatch behind us will give us enough time to scarper. Then we can take a line to a boat from the upper gundeck. Bit of a drop, but, we done worse...'

'Can we put a small charge into the hold? Scupper her so she sinks slowly?'

'Damn tricky if it hits the bilge and fuse goes out—'

'You can't mean to *explode the magazine*?' gasped Sarah to Hazzard. 'You would kill *everyone* aboard – *two thousand people*!'

61

The footsteps stopped. Sarah looked up at the ceiling, alert.

'Here,' she said, with shaking hands, digging out her final prize. 'The spare key to the Great Cabin, you can break in, take charts, whatever you need, but not *kill them all! William, for the love of God*—'

'*How else* can we stop them?'

De Villiers and Jollois.

You must be very talented.

Spoken while Hazzard knew he was going to blow the magazine.

Head of the serpent, thought Hazzard. *If Bonaparte were dead, would any man dare assume his mantle? Had they the authority? Or determination?* Half the general staff of France was aboard *Orient*.

Cook pointed at the ceiling. 'Sir. Marines comin'.'

Hazzard then thought of Berthollet. And Denon.

Fortunes of war.

She took his sleeve. 'You would kill all of the *savants*? All of those good brave young boys! What of the *women* aboard, the sailors' wives, the civilians—'

'For God's sake, Sarah—'

Jullien.

Do nothing that would blacken our names, or your own. Remember my sadness that we are enemies.

'Change of watch, might be,' said Cook, looking steadily at the ceiling, listening. 'Or we're done for...'

More boots, running now, and Hazzard took Sarah by the hand. 'Sar'nt, the quickmatch—'

'*William*,' said Sarah, 'if it comes to it you must leave me—'

'The devil I will—'

She tugged his arm hard and held him tight. 'If you try to light the powder magazine I will *run*, somewhere into the ship! I *will* stay aboard!'

'Don't be ridiculous—'

'Will, *you do not know me any longer.*'

Running boots banged down the stairs. He watched her. *Was she right?* Still he fought her. 'I will *not*—'

'You *must*. I can still gather intelligence!'

Cook got up, 'Sir. Now.'

Closing the dark lantern they used the glow from below and hurried aft just as the boots came thumping down the midships steps in the darkness. Cook pushed Sarah down against the crates in the darkness behind them, the quickmatch fuse coiled alongside, a post screening her, creepers of rope dangling from above, a jungle of deep shadow everywhere. Hazzard did not move. He heard musket-locks cocking. The shutter of a lantern clanged open, its light blinding. The Orlop leapt into bright focus, Hazzard caught centre-stage, kneeling behind a crate.

It was Derrien. Six marines behind him presented arms, ready. Hazzard remained at a crouch.

'Mr Hazzard.' Derrien looked about at the stores, the locked cabins. 'Raiding the provisions? Were you… what is that English word… "peckish"?'

'Only six marines this time?' said Hazzard. 'I hear your Dutch grenadiers at Toulon were easy meat.'

Derrien at first did not understand. 'These men, you mean? Oh, there are always more soldiers, Mr Hazzard, somewhere. Behind you, above you, all around you. Really you surprise me. Did you believe you had only one man watching your door? How ever do you think I acquired this…?'

Derrien opened his coat a fraction to reveal the golden hilt of the *espada ropera*.

Hazzard almost lurched towards him in his anger. He glanced at the marines, and spoke in French. 'So now you are a thief as well as a murderer.'

The marines glanced uncertainly at Derrien, the French unexpected. Perhaps out of pride, Derrien continued in English. 'And what are you doing, down here in the dead of the night? Did you not see how very easy I made it for you? No guards on the hatches, none on the steps – and down you came. Because I know what you are: *assassin, saboteur.*'

'And I know what *you* are,' he replied, still in French, 'liar, *thief. Traitor.*'

63

Derrien sounded weary. 'Really, there is no escape on a ship at sea, Mr Hazzard. This surely is obvious to a naval man such as yourself. You will come with me now.'

Hazzard rose, holding up a length of black fuse and the naked candle from Sarah's lantern. He continued in French, so that the marines would understand.

'Perhaps you can explain this. The aft hanging magazine has been set to explode with this fuse. It burns at a rate of one foot per second. The detonation of the initial charge will ignite two hundred tons of powder cartridges for the 24-pounder cannons of this vessel.' He let it sink in. 'The remaining ammunition in the forward and midships magazines will then explode. This ship, and everyone on board, will be blown to pieces.'

The marines looked at Derrien. They backed away.

'*Do not move,*' he snapped at them. They stopped.

Hazzard held the quickmatch fuse very still, Sarah's candle beneath it. Derrien fixed his eyes upon it. 'Your French is very convincing.'

'Better than your English.'

Derrien stiffened.

'You would not dare. You too would be killed.'

'In English one says "go to Glory".'

The marines were hesitant, looking to each other, no longer to Derrien, confused: was the Englishman now a Frenchman? Hazzard knew he could push them just that little bit further.

'*Soldats de France,*' he called to them, '*Je suis Capitaine St Juste, 30ᵉ Infanterie de marine* – on special orders from the Minister of the Interior! Citizen Derrien is an enemy of the state, thieving the wages of this fleet with the connivance of the purser. *He has set this trap for us all.*'

Derrien shouted back, '*Bougez pas, vous idiots!*' Do not move!

Hazzard pushed them to their limit, '*I give you this direct order! Arrest him at once!*'

A dishevelled figure in spectacles and shirtsleeves appeared at the top of the ladder down to the hold below, a large sheet of paper in one hand. It was one of the scholar printers. 'H-hello…?'

It was sufficient to distract. Cook hurled a 3-pounder round-shot like a cricket ball. It struck Derrien in the shoulder and he dropped the lantern with a cry, knocking a marine's musket to one side. It went off. As they staggered from the blast, deafened and choking in the cloud of burnt powder in the confines of the Orlop, Hazzard lit his fuse.

Derrien screamed. '*Non, non!* Stop him! The fuse!'

Hazzard seized Sarah and they leapt for the ladder just behind, the quickmatch fizzing and lashing in mid-air, a maddened serpent spitting with fire, Derrien shouting, '*The fuse, the fuse!*'

Hazzard and Sarah shot upwards, Cook hard behind. They reached the lower gundeck, lamps shining, men stirring, only a few hearing the heavily muffled report of the gunshot. They raced up the steps to the middle gundeck, Derrien raging out far below for no one to hear, '*Aux armes! Aux armes! Arrêtez!*'

Hazzard reached the top of the ladder on the middle gundeck, plotting the course to the small boats at the stern, and found Derrien's deputy Citizen Masson waiting, with a fist.

The loaded blow caught Hazzard on the left cheekbone, spinning him over onto several soldiers in their bedrolls on the deck who shouted out, '*Ehh, tiens, salaud! Qu'est-ce qui est!*'

Sarah tried to take Masson by the arm, '*Non! C'est pas lui!* It's not him, you don't understand!'

Masson threw her down with a curse and she rolled against an upright with a cry – and some of the soldiers did not like it. '*Eh – laisse-la tranqulle, salaud!*' Leave her alone, you bastard!

Masson swung his fist again and Hazzard went flying into the gloom, banging into a water-butt and two hammocks, their occupants crashing to the deck with curses.

'*Non,*' called Hazzard, trying the same tack as below, '*Écoutez-moi!*' Listen to me!

He swung a left and Hazzard dodged behind a post and heard the fist crash into it, and someone called in excited support, *bravo!* Masson swung again, losing his footing and hitting the bulkhead, swearing – the spectators cheered. Hazzard delivered his first hit to Masson's right ear, then his left into the sternum and there was another roar from the crowd.

Quickmatch coiled twelve yards from hanging magazine, he thought, *allow a yard per coil…*

Hazzard tried to weight the odds in his favour, '*Salaud de merde!*' *Bloody bastard!* and hit Masson again in the stomach, shouting in French, 'Taking a sailor's wages, cheating his family—'

The thick-necked Masson lunged for him, but Hazzard rolled away, spectators urging him on, their hatred of Derrien, Masson and the state easily stirred. They shoved Masson around between them but he drew a short dagger and swung it at them. He swiped it high and narrowly missed Hazzard's head. '*Ohhhh-lo-lo,*' shouts rose from the crowd again, '*Pas juste!*' *Unfair!* Someone called out '*Eh, prends ça…*' and an older sailor in tattered canvas denims tossed Hazzard a knife – it was the masthead lookout.

It bounced on the deck and Hazzard snatched it up, ducking another blow, and brought the blade up, slashing at Masson's wrist. Masson howled and dropped his knife, the crowd sensing a victory. Hazzard put his boot behind Masson's right heel and the deputy went down hard to still more cheers. Hazzard leapt on him, the knife raised.

'*Non!*' cried Masson, '*Je cède!*' *I give in!*

'*William!*' It was Sarah.

Hazzard raised the knife high, '*Compliments to Citizen Croquemort…*'

With all his strength he brought it down into Masson's palm, driving the blade through the hand and into the planks, pinning him to the deck. Masson screamed and the crowd gave a bloodthirsty roar with raised fists, *Hwaaa!*

He heard Cook – '*Sir!*' – and Hazzard launched himself at the steps, hands clapping at his back, soldiers pushing him up and away out of trouble, but all he could think of was the sound echoing all about him, *Boots again, marines, somewhere, everywhere.*

Sarah took his hand, pulling him up, his thoughts racing, *Upper gundeck, Jory said, take a line astern,* he looked behind them. '*Jory! Where is he!*'

Quickmatch. Run.

'He went up!' she cried.

Main gundeck.

All was quiet, the noise from below so far unremarked. The fresh night air hit him and he sucked it in, craving oxygen after the fight, the muscles tired as he dodged round the closed hatches, round the cannons and stores, pulling Sarah tight in his grip behind him. Boats stacked amidships, casks lashed in rows – *quickmatch, detonation of Orlop* – and he could almost feel the heave of the decks as the blast burst the ship at the seams, *no, not yet, still time.* He flew up the steps to the gangway, a marine running towards him, too far, Sarah behind, and he flung himself at the starboard rail, looking down.

'*There's one*—' he said, seeing a line, grabbing the sodden rope, but Sarah pulled him round.

'Will…' Her voice was low, calm.

He looked at her.

Of course, he thought, *it would have gone off by now.*

While he faced down Derrien and the marines, when she was in the dark behind him, a scrabbling sound: Sarah at work, snapping the brittle coil of quickmatch.

A dozen marines tramped unhurried across the darkness of the main deck below, lamps swinging. Several knelt and assumed firing positions, some standing, a pair coming from the quarter-deck along the gangway to Hazzard's left, some forward from the fo'c'sle. They formed up on all sides. Rigging hands looked down from above, pointing.

Trapped.

Derrien stepped out from the fo'c'sle hatchway, flushed with triumph, pistol in outstretched hand. 'Take him alive.'

A cry went up as Cook crashed into two marines on the gangway from behind, head down, arms out, and they fell to the main gundeck eight feet below. Muskets rose, the locks rattling, but no one fired. Cook shielded Hazzard and Sarah, waiting.

'Sir…'

'Sar'nt.'

'Can't make the boat from here, sir.'

'Mm.'

The darkness of the sea was pocked with the shimmering lights of ships' lamps all round, so many stars in a floating night sky. Masson exploded onto the deck below, nursing his bloody hand, his face clenched in pain and outrage. Derrien called up.

'You will come down, Mr Hazzard. Or Masson will come up.'

Hazzard thought of Berthollet at dinner. Young De Villiers, Jollois, innocents.

Fortunes of war.

There would be no mercy this time, Hazzard knew. He had broken his parole. *A cell in the belly of the ship and then – what? Shot for a spy in Egypt? And Sarah would have to give evidence.*

Never stop.

'Do they know, Citizen,' Hazzard called out in French, 'what innocent blood is on their hands already because of your crimes? Your theft, your murder of their daughters back home? In Paris? In Toulon?'

Derrien looked momentarily amused. 'The charade is over, Mr Hazzard. You have nowhere to go,' he said reasonably. But he noticed that the concentration of the marines had wavered.

A lieutenant appeared on the quarterdeck at the mainmast stays, four more marines behind him, officers coming to doors and ladders, roused from sleep, or a late game of cards disturbed. And the *comtesse* de Biasi, in her nightgown, cap and shawl, clutching at the lieutenant, pointing with a gasp at Sarah, then down at Derrien on the gundeck below, '*C'est lui! It is he! There, as I said, Citizen Derrien, he has run mad…!*'

The four marines commanded by the lieutenant aimed their muskets – but not at Hazzard: at Derrien. The others looked back at him, questioning.

'You will lower that pistol, Citizen,' warned the lieutenant, 'or fall dead to this deck!'

Derrien flicked a glance at him. 'You do not command me—'

'I am the officer of the watch, *m'sieur*, and, for this moment, *I rule the world.*'

Hazzard heard the clatter of latches behind him and saw a flare of light from the broadside hatch just below, above the flying spray. A head appeared, then another, looking up, sailors, soldiers who had watched the fight. Some of the other gun-ports opened, others looking up, pointing.

He spoke to Cook.

'Can't be taken again, Jory.'

'Sir.'

A door on the quarterdeck opened, more voices, the captain, pulling on his coat, Lt Marais behind. Bonaparte would come next.

He whispered to Sarah: 'Will you follow me?'

She looked at him. 'I broke the fuse.'

Quickmatch. Two hundred tons of powder.

'I know.'

Masson snatched the weapon of the marine to his left, someone called, '*Non!*' and he aimed roughly and pulled the trigger. Three muskets went off in quick succession, Masson spinning round, Derrien falling back, a bullet chipping splinters from the rail near Hazzard, a stinging claw raking at his shoulder.

Options limited.

'*Jory,*' he said, '*Go.*'

Hazzard dived backwards over the rail, the wet line slipping from his hand, Sarah reaching for him, her hands trying to catch hold of his neck, his collar, to save him, to stop him as he lost his grip on her – the officer of the watch rushing in for her, his hands reaching round Sarah's waist, *good man*, blood on her neck, her face uncomprehending, and a final cry: '*Will—?*'

His last view of her, her mouth open, the blood, her eyes closing as she collapsed into the lieutenant's arms. Cook's voice, '*Sir!*' jumping after him headfirst, Derrien shouting, '*Get him!*'

Hazzard's thoughts began to focus on odd details, the sting of the spray and salt scent of the water, the hum of the shrouds, the roar of the sea. Then his world was suddenly silent as he realised what had happened.

Sarah.

Hit.

He struck the waves over twenty feet below, Cook following.

–

At the open gundeck hatchway, the group of sailors watched as the two men crashed into the sea. '*Là-bas!*' *Over there!* One pointed at the frothing surface, the raging wake of the warship churning them over, '*Vite!*' and within a moment a net of kegs was thrown far out, and they watched them splash and bob on the waves.

'*Ce n'était pas juste,*' they agreed, *No, it was not right.*

Some crossed themselves, but the old masthead lookout in his ragged canvas *culottes* did not. He leaned out and looked up at the rail above, at the marines and officers searching in the darkness, holding up lanterns, muskets searching, and muttered, '*Salauds.*' *Bastards.*

He looked down at the dark of the sea, '*Père Neptune… en vos bras les hommes sont égaux. Protégez nos frères de la mer.*'

Father Neptune, in your arms, all men are equal.

Protect our brothers of the sea.

Neptune

The slam of the water on Hazzard's back drove the air from his lungs and he sank down another two fathoms, but his arms splayed out instantly and propelled him back to the surface almost at once. He burst through the waves.

The boiling eddies of the ship's wake tossed him violently, and he went under again. '*Sir!*' Cook surfaced, an arm raised, both of them rolling end over end in the swell, the roar of *Orient* fading and a fearful knocking in the back of Hazzard's mind: *watch out… watch out…*

He remembered and turned to see the 80-gun *Tonnant* bearing down upon them, the night sky a slate grey above a frothing sea, the ship a leviathan in silhouette, white spray flying from her rearing bows.

'*Jory…!*'

He dived and struck out but felt something on his legs, fouling, tangling, *get off get off*, tentacles wrapping round him, pulling him down. He sank, gulping, rose again and gasped, fighting it off, a mouthful of seawater and the hollow clunk of wood as it rode over his head, *forgive me, Sarah.* An empty cask, and another, a rope, a net, barrels, floating, not the underside of *Tonnant* – *not dead not dead, it's good, saving me…*

'*Jory! Here!*'

Cook splashed towards him and they each took hold of the net and the kegs, five of them and an open crate, a life-raft of bobbing wood between them as *Tonnant* roared past, its mass filling their ears with a storm of sound. No one saw them, no one called out – they had become flotsam, jettisoned with the refuse and scraps.

They hooked their arms over the nets, the floating kegs buoying them up.

It took another hour before the fleet lines passed them by. No frigate came, no sloop, no fleet boat. No one knew. They faced the darkness of the open sea, alone. His ribs ached and his shoulder burned with a deep fire. He wanted to sleep.

'*Dead man's float, sir... dead man...*' gasped Cook, spread-eagled on the surface, and Hazzard did likewise, turning over onto his back, hefting his knees over a cask. *Boots boots.* He kicked them off and they sank away, his stockinged feet lighter, free. His shoulder was stiff, a bite out of it, the sea numbing it, *Derrien's last shot? Masson's fists?*

Lying back, they floated face up on the tangle of casks and netting, able to breathe easy at last, *meagre offerings to Neptune*, thought Hazzard, grateful for his intervention – and he would thank him for a French sailor who had flown no flag, but knew only the power of the sea.

Watch for Cygnus.

With the passing of the fleet the dark bowl of the skies glowed bright with stars, the breadth of the heavens bringing them closer, smothering him in its infinity.

Silence.

A wash of waves.

Onset of vertigo, he noted, a gentle swinging left, then swinging right.

His head sank back and his ears filled with water, the dull roar of the engine of the Earth. The swell rising, then falling, calming, he lost himself in the swirling deeps around Polaris, and in his mind Sarah was more than hit, she was dead.

Cygnus.

The great swan of Zeus, flying above, wings outstretched, the sailor's guide, taking him home.

Now find Vega.

Orientate.

Ship making eight knots, no six, from 11°E... with the current, that makes...

'Better 'n the Indian Ocean, ain't it…' murmured Cook, far away.

Hazzard heard him, muffled, his voice carried more by the water than the air. The memory of their first ship going down, stranding them in the hot seas off old Dutch Ceylon. *Water like a Turkish bath, clear to a thousand fathoms… could see every fish in the—*

'Are you wounded?' gasped Hazzard, pulling his head out of the water.

Took a while to reply.

'Jory?' He tried to lift his head to look, but could not.

'No, sir…'

Blood in the water.

Cook understood. His voice rumbled hoarsely. 'No sharks in the Med, sir…'

Hazzard wondered who had told him that. *Bloody old wives' tale. Poseidon had transformed the kidnappers of Dionysus into dolphins – who, then, did he make into sharks? Generals and ministers of the Crown and their sucking-mouthed lamprey minions?*

They pulled each other in closer to the floating net bag, tying themselves together, old habit learned long ago.

'Be a mermaid along any minute, sir…'

The air burnt his throat, bubbling, and he coughed it out, then lay his head back on the tangle of rope in the water. The net of casks ran under their backs, and they rested their limbs on the floating bed of barrels, spent, exposed. But safe, under the dome of night.

Time passed, somewhere.

Barrels.

'Anything inside…' he said, his throat dry as a ship's rusk.

Cook looked at one. 'Smells like… gunpowder…'

They had their arms on a cask between the two, an old armchair at a club. It smelled to Hazzard more like salt fish. He remembered the French had it on the Île-de-France.

He had seen the lines trailing, a dozen of them, dragging through the water astern, and he had thought they could catch

73

one and get to the slung boats, cut one free. Sarah would have had difficulty. But he knew she would have tried. Jumped from a drainpipe after all.

Dead?

Left her to die.

He had to bow to her decision, in the end, no choice, her waist plucked from him by the French watch-officer just as he went over, her head crooked, confusion in her eye.

'She was in France,' said Hazzard, 'for two years… false name, false history…'

Spy.

'She was hit, in the back, or the neck, when I went over…'

Cook had turned to look at him, one eye half-closed, swollen, bruised. 'Take more'n that to put her down, sir…' He looked away again. 'Made o'ruddy iron, that one.'

They floated silently, the swell softly raising them up, then setting them down, a vast, soft bed. *So easy*, thought Hazzard, *to roll into its bosom, breathe in, and forget.*

'Could have knocked me down with a bloody feather,' mumbled Cook, 'when I saw that bastard Derrien again.'

A wave, lifting Hazzard gently, then sinking away.

A shooting star streaked across the sky like an Indian rocket. It flared with a hiss, and vanished… *are they searching for us with rockets?* The stars looked down, quiet, watchful. No one searching.

'Sir.'

Cygnus, Ursa Major… Polaris in the north – count degrees from horizon, forty-five minutes, then account for speed of current… too tired too tired.

He closed his eyes, as if to sear the image of the sky on his memory. *Which way now, Poseidon, or is it Neptune? Send us the kidnappers of Dionysus that they may guide us.*

'*Sir*…' More insistent. 'Why didn't the magazine blow?'

Hazzard floated.

Six knots, add perhaps two knots extra… why? Why not slower? Big convoy, always as fast as the slowest ship. Over fourteen hours, no,

74

too fast, too great a difference, too far out. Miss everything, hit open sea. Guessing.

'That fuse was broke 'fore you lit it. I saw.'

Hazzard admitted it. 'Yes...'

A good ruse, he thought, set off a tangle of quickmatch while you get out the back, let them scramble for it, not connected to anything.

Sarah had broken the fuse too. Both of them had, without the other knowing. Two busy little consciences, too parsimonious to kill off a few innocents like De Villiers and Jollois or the *comtesse*, had condemned Egypt to the heel of a fantasist who thought he was Julius Caesar.

I have such dreams, Mr Hazzard.

Bonaparte.

Tens of thousands.

Cook asked nothing more, knew not to, guessed Hazzard.

Sparing the *Orient* had brought another feeling along with it: although Wayland had been right about Egypt, and he had accepted it instinctively as soon as he had heard Acton say it, part of him would not believe it. Somewhere deep within he *wanted* them to land, to prove it all true.

So that Lewis and Blake would pay.

Lies.

He would tell Cook, explain somehow, one day.

But chiefly Hazzard did not blow the magazine on *Orient* because he knew, he *knew*, he would have to leave Sarah behind. He had sacrificed a nation to the murder and savagery of war for the sake of his own desire. And the conscious acceptance of this made him want to slip from the floating casks and sink slowly to the bottom of Poseidon's lair for ever.

–

The watch-officer and *Sergent-chef* of Marines had thrust Derrien and the wounded Masson into the first empty room on *Orient* that the lieutenant could find. Derrien threw them off, '*Leave me, you*

75

dogs!' and once they did so, he drew his screw-barrelled pistol, thrusting it into their faces, and the marines backed away. Masson whimpered, nursing his bloody hand and now his shoulder, his face chalk-white, sweat streaming from his brow.

'By the end of this escapade, Lieutenant,' spat Derrien, 'I shall have you commanding a *coastal galley-boat!*'

'You will be *silent, m'sieur*,' rasped the lieutenant of the watch. He held a wad of cotton to his own neck: it was he who had been hit by a splinter caused by Masson's musket-ball. To the lieutenant's regret, Derrien had escaped the marines' confused shots. 'You are called to the wardroom, Citizen *Croquemort*.'

'You will pay for this interference,' threatened Derrien, but the lieutenant merely yanked open the door and waited for him.

Derrien found a small audience waiting inside, Captain Casabianca, Admiral Brueys, Lt Marais and three other naval lieutenants, the chief ADC Colonel Junot, aides Duroc and Jullien, and Bonaparte. Brueys looked tired, roused from his bed, but Bonaparte was fully dressed, as if he had even yet to retire.

The marines withdrew and closed the door. For a moment no one spoke. Bonaparte seemed very calm, leafing through a booklet of bound papers. He did not look up.

'And so?'

Derrien took a breath. He was not moved by this assembly, this display of power. He had stood before Robespierre, and called him traitor. 'An incident, Citizen General. The officer of the watch overstepped his authority and called armed marine soldiers to the upper gundeck, causing confusion among the ranks. In this confusion one of the soldiers shot Captain Hazzard, possibly hitting *Mademoiselle* Moreau-Lazare, his...' he hesitated '...his hostage. He and an accomplice, a stowaway dockworker, fell overboard. With some good fortune, *Mademoiselle* Moreau-Lazare was retrieved at the last moment.'

He was determined that not even Bonaparte would learn anything more of Isabelle Moreau-Lazare than Derrien wished. Because she was *his*. Not Bonaparte's. And this would be his

76

official version of events. Anything further was a matter for Citizen Derrien and the *Bureau d'information*.

Bonaparte watched him. 'And?'

'When steps were taken to recover the bodies,' Derrien continued, 'there was no sign. He is presumed drowned.' He said nothing of the quickmatch in the hold, or the powder magazine. He would keep that in reserve.

Colonel Junot turned his cadaverous features slowly to Bonaparte, incredulous.

Bonaparte was not incredulous. He was incensed. He whacked down the booklet on the edge of the table. 'An *incident*.'

Derrien remained equally unmoved by this show of anger. 'Yes.'

'What you have *done*, Citizen,' he shouted, 'is beyond *belief*. When we know the English are after this leaden-footed convoy of transports filled to the *brim* with *my* guns and *forty thousand* of *my* soldiers, when we learn from one of our frigate captains that Nelson passed *no more than a thousand metres* from us in the night mist,' he breathed with outrage, '*you decide to fire a shot on deck!*'

His pale skin glowed brighter across his bony features. Derrien said nothing in reply.

'Have you any idea what Nelson would do to this convoy, should he find it? He would hack it to pieces at the cost of *every ship in his squadron*, do you understand?'

'Yes.'

'No, you do not understand. Only the naval officers understand. And we have discussed it. Nelson is a *madman*. A madman armed with a *thousand cannon* and the deadliest gunners in the world!'

The officers watched, enjoying the fall of Citizen *Croquemort*. Junot voiced their mockery, 'Did you learn anything of value from the Englishman, Citizen? What actual *intelligence* did you glean, what great secrets of Nelson?'

Derrien glanced at Casabianca and the naval officers. They did not look away. He then addressed himself only to Bonaparte.

'A considerable amount, Citizen General.'

Bonaparte glared back at him. 'Such as? For, even now, Mr Hazzard may have been rescued by the English, and could be informing them of our course, our strength and disposition. Jullien tells me he even climbed to the lookouts on the mast *and saw the entire fleet – everything.*'

Marais glanced at Jullien, then looked down, but said nothing.

'He was shot, Citizen General, and subsequently drowned—'

'*He was flogged like a Corsican mule by your dogs in a Maltese gaol, but look what he did to you and a platoon of our finest marines!*'

Derrien stared back.

Bonaparte waited. 'You have nothing to say.'

'I acted according to my orders.'

Junot could stand it no longer. 'Orders? From whom?'

'I would respectfully remind the Citizen General, and his staff, that I am not under his orders, but those of Citizen Directors Barras, Révèillaire-Lépaux and Rewbell, and the Ministry of the Interior.'

'I *beg* your pardon?' gasped Junot, shocked. 'You will retract this *impertinence*—'

'Neither will I divulge further details save those relevant to the General in Chief and the security of this enterprise.' He gave the naval contingent a bow of the head. 'Of value to the Citizen Admiral and officers of the fleet is that I have concluded the British squadron under Nelson will head direct to Alexandria, with such speed that they will reach it before we do.'

There was a brief silence as Casabianca glanced at Marais for confirmation. 'How could the British know for certain? And how could you know this?'

Derrien looked at Bonaparte. 'I must submit that the remainder of this report should be disclosed *in camera*, Citizen General.'

Bonaparte did not relent. 'Answer him.'

Derrien inclined his head. 'Very well. From the beginning Mr Hazzard was not what he claimed. The historical paper which he had indeed written was not from the Sorbonne, but the university at Grenôble, was it not, Citizen General?'

Bonaparte frowned, surprised at this unexpected riposte. Eventually he registered acceptance. 'So I later recalled. What of it.'

'I discussed the matter with our own specialists, one of whom also recalled it in his own research, and was aware of a copy in the library at the Vatican's Office of Propaganda. It was the work of possibly one of the foremost yet little-known scholars on the history of Egypt, Greece and Persia, who dined so modestly with the *savants*, learning everything about the expedition and their role within it, from chemistry to engineering, yet revealing none of his own expertise... save an educated gentleman's mild interest in Herodotus.' He looked directly at Bonaparte. 'As I insisted at Valletta, through interrogation I learned that he is half-French. Of a Bordelaise Huguenot mother. He is of course fluent in our language, as I continually reminded the officers of this vessel, and he was educated at the university of Grenôble under the patronage of counter-revolutionary Hugues Bartelmi – where he began his study of ancient cultures, including Egyptian hieroglyphics, and...' he said, pulling from his pocket one of Bonaparte's special printed flyers, 'the Arabic language. He had this in his possession before he fled.'

Junot snatched the sheet from him and glanced at its incomprehensible contents. 'He could *read* this?'

'I believe so, yes. Some of it, perhaps. It was for this reason he was sent by the British Admiralty to intercept, infiltrate and destroy this expedition.' He cleared his throat quietly. 'He is William John Hazzard, a contributor to the *Gentleman's Magazine* in England, a correspondent of Dr Samuel Johnson, and a scholar of Jesus College, Cambridge, and served in the British East India Company naval service. He is a master swordsman, who overcame six men of the 1st Company of the 75th Invincibles, and killed a Maltese revolutionary and two fusiliers before being captured. He is not just an ordinary officer of Marines.'

The assembly stared, astonished. But Junot was on him in seconds. 'And *you* let him escape?'

Derrien's expression was as blank as ever. 'I am not convinced that the Citizen General would agree entirely with that conclusion.' He took back the flyer and carefully folded it away into a pocket.

Bonaparte stared back at him, furious, the rebuke evident – that it was Bonaparte who had released a deadly spy from captivity and brought him into the very heart of their operation – and worse, that Derrien had warned him not to, but had gone unheeded.

Junot put a hand to his sword. 'How *dare* you…'

Bonaparte said nothing. But Derrien again seemed impervious to Junot's threats. 'It would not be unreasonable to assume,' he continued, 'that Nelson is more than aware of Mr Hazzard's mission, and will head for the region via Naples as soon as he is able. We must proceed on this assumption and continue to conceal our true course as best we can.'

After a moment of angry silence, Bonaparte nodded.

Brueys glanced at Casabianca. 'Heading of the British?'

'Uncertain, Admiral. Only one sail spotted, possibly with a British ensign, but it was dark of course. Possibly a scout, to or from Syracuse, or a Ragusan merchantman, we cannot say, but she headed away.' Brueys nodded. If she had been a scout and had seen them, she would have followed at a distance.

Bonaparte was not a man to admit errors easily. Instead he looked to Brueys and Casabianca. 'Admiral, how long to change course for the northeast, for Corfu and the Ionian Sea?'

Admiral Brueys thought it no great difficulty. 'We shall signal Admiral Decrès in the *Diane* to lead, bring in the flanking frigates and coordinate such a correction at once, General.' He glanced at Derrien. 'A feint to the north would not be unwise, given this new information. We can set a course for Corfu via the Bay of Taranto, and drop southward upon Alexandria from Crete when our scouts confirm that the port is clear.'

Bonaparte inclined his head. 'Very well, let it be so, I thank you.' His gaze hardened as he turned it on Derrien. 'I will, then, hear your full report, Citizen. Now, if you please.' He turned from the wardroom and a sentry snapped open the door to the passage and the chambers beyond.

'As you wish, Citizen General.' Derrien looked at the gathering. He nodded. 'I bid you a good night, Citizen Admiral.'

It was effectively a dismissal of the most senior officer, but etiquette demanded Brueys acknowledge his good wishes. He did so with a reluctant bow, then said to Casabianca, 'Captain, let us be about it, if you please…' They filed out, but Junot went last, his steady gaze focussed on Derrien with outright loathing.

Derrien followed Bonaparte into the corridor. Bonaparte turned. 'Junot is right. How *dare* you.'

'I did not wish to say, Citizen General,' said Derrien, hitting him with it finally, 'but I found Mr Hazzard in the holds of the ship. He had laid a fuse to the central powder magazine.'

Bonaparte stared at him.

Derrien added, 'I believe it carries some two hundred tons of ammunition.'

Of all the officers aboard, Bonaparte knew best how much powder was packed into the magazines aboard the *Orient* – and what would happen if they were detonated. 'Very well,' said Bonaparte. 'And?'

'I disabled it, Citizen General,' he said, 'interrupting his efforts.'

Bonaparte regarded him carefully for some time.

'So.'

Derrien knew not to press his advantage yet. He waited. 'Of the moment, Citizen General, it is Citizen *Mademoiselle* Moreau-Lazare that concerns me most.'

Once again, Bonaparte was wrong-footed. 'Why?'

'I should like to know why Mr Hazzard took her and no other. Her relationship to you might perhaps be of value to the British if she were to be captured.'

'What *utter rubbish*.' Bonaparte had hardly flinched, but his fury glowed white-hot. 'You will *not* come within arm's reach of *Mademoiselle* Moreau-Lazare, is that clear? She is a beloved *companion* to my wife, a *friend* to my children, and a mistress of François-Joseph Talma...'

Derrien did not falter. 'It is my belief she will need protection for the remainder of the voyage. Particularly from *Chef de brigade* Junot, should he come to the same conclusion as I.'

Bonaparte's eyes burned into his. 'Junot is my senior *aide de camp*. He does not *jump* to conclusions—'

'Nevertheless I should like to keep her safe,' said Derrien, 'in case I can be of assistance. She would naturally wish to follow you to Cairo and be at your side – but I wonder if she might rest more safely with the junior *savants* and others at Rosetta,' said Derrien.

Bonaparte was as ready as any other man of power to mistrust his closest advisers, but he had been knocked off-balance. 'None of this ventures any further, do you understand? Not a word.'

Derrien was more than satisfied. Once again, he had become the keeper of secrets. 'The ship's company will remain under close observation,' he said with a bow. 'I endeavour to serve, Citizen General.'

Derrien withdrew, leaving Bonaparte to consider his words. In the pursuit of his own self-interest and security, Derrien had outwitted the *ancien* naval officers, set the high command against itself, cast doubts in Bonaparte's mind over his mistress, and wrapped himself in the invulnerable cloak of the secret servant. Citizen *Croquemort* was still very much alive.

–

Bonaparte moved through the chart room to his cabin. Two marine guards stiffened at his approach. He saw his cabin door ajar, lamplight inside. He waved the marines off and they withdrew.

He pushed open the door, revealing the glowing lamp on his bedside table, the turned-down white sheets. Bourrienne stood in the middle of the room, looking uncomfortable.

'Louis?'

Bourrienne removed his spectacles and gave an oblique look to one side. Waiting uncertainly behind the door was Sarah, her face smudged with tears, looking down at her hands, busily tying a handkerchief into knots. Bonaparte stared at her a while, then glanced at Bourrienne. 'Anyone?'

Bourrienne shook his head. 'No one saw her come in. So, I trust,' he said, with a note of stern warning, heading to the door, 'no one will see her leave.'

Bonaparte smiled at his old friend. 'You need your bed.'

'I was in it,' yawned Bourrienne, 'swinging this way and that like an old sack till the world erupted.' He glanced at him with a gesture, as if to take care of her. 'Poor thing. I shall say goodnight.'

Bourrienne closed the door quietly and they heard him dismiss the guard, his voice fading as they tramped along the passage behind.

Bonaparte looked at her. She began to sob again and he approached her, and took her hand in his, holding her cold body. She trembled.

'There there,' he murmured, and she broke into tears. He held her close. 'What I cannot understand, my darling Belle,' he said softly into her ear, 'is why he took *you*, of all people.' He felt the ends of her damp, curling hair with his fingers. 'Why, why, why. I cannot understand...'

She clung to him, weeping, and he held her, '*Napoléon,*' she whispered, '*I was so frightened...*'

'Shhh,' he sighed to her. He became aware of her scent, her skin. 'You are so like Désirée. Nothing would frighten her.'

'Ci-Citizen Derrien frightens me,' she sobbed.

He shook his head, admonishing a child. '*Non non non.* He will not. *C'est rien.* Do you see? He cannot touch you.'

He slid a hand round her neck and held her tight – then kissed her. Her mouth pushed back against his, hard, as he pushed her against the doorframe, his hand in the small of her back, holding her, her breath catching as he raised her chin, opening her throat down to her bosom, his lips on her.

Abruptly he stopped. With one finger he traced a curving line over her skin to her shoulder. He saw the blood.

'His?'

She nodded. 'Or the lieutenant, who saved me...'

He closed his eyes, putting his forehead to hers. 'I found him an honest man. *M'sieur* Hazzard. Not a liar, or cheat. Not a monster.' He sighed. 'But I will kill him, most certainly.'

She did not move.

'I am so far from her, Belle,' he said, 'and think of her always, my Joséphine, though now she betrays me. So says the gossip. You are a memory of happier times, our home in the *Chausée d'Antin*...'

He kissed her deeply, his fingers in her hair, holding her fast and she sighed into him, the heat coming through her gown, her shift, every part of her, her fingers entwined in his long hair.

'But I must be ruthless,' he breathed, 'and if necessary... I will have Junot shot, or Citizen Derrien...' He kissed her again, and pressed himself against her. He held her suddenly firm and dead still. 'I will do the same to anyone, Isabelle.' He looked suddenly deep into her eyes. 'If I must.'

She froze. He pulled back from her. The threat was clear. He put a finger to her lips.

'Rest under my protection, *ma belle* Isabelle.' He smiled, an old joke. 'You need fear no one. Go to Rosetta with the *savants*, far from the army and the fighting, hm? I will see to it. Jérôme will be there too, at some point, never fear. For Eugène and Joséphine's sake as well.'

She nodded obediently. 'Yes, Napoléon.'

He watched her carefully, as if waiting. 'Hm? But...?'

'I wanted,' she said miserably, 'to go with you... to Cairo...'

His face gave away nothing, but his body tensed, locked tight, possibly at the thought of Derrien's prediction. He watched her, his dark eyes wide and shimmering in the half-light of the cabin. 'I must take that country in less than a month. It will be easier to do so knowing you are safe.'

He pulled from her and leaned against the frame of the door, suddenly bored, or exhausted, looking at the deck. 'Now, go, please.'

She moved past him and his grasp slid from her arm, to her wrist, her hand, her fingers, until finally she pulled away. A dark look on his tightly controlled features, he shoved the door shut with his boot.

In their embrace his roving fingers had not found her left hand, clenched tightly around her knotted sodden kerchief. Inside he would have found the small figurine on its torn leather lace, snatched from the neck of the man who had fallen into the sea, victim, like St Jude, of another lost cause. When she was clear of all eyes, she burst into tears, her sobs almost suffocating.

Along the passage on the stairs above, hiding in the darkness, Jules-Yves Derrien watched her as she moved below, weeping, his only thought: *Mine.*

—

The heat of the day had transformed the Maltese shoreline into a molten griddle of burning stones. Wayland could feel them through the soles of his boots as he and Pettifer sloshed through the shallow surf.

They had been gone for some time, skirting the French patrols in Sliema, heading out to the point and the inlet where they had left the boat from the *Volpone*. An evening sun streaked the sky.

'Rondyvoo...' Wayland mumbled absently, '*Rdv. Repondyvoo. Rsvp. TS. Toot sweet.* Always abbreviating things, the French... or us. Bloody lazy, dammit.' He stopped and pulled the wineskin off his shoulder for a swig of water.

'Not yet, sir,' said Pettifer. 'Nearly there. All the sweeter when we are.'

Wayland held the skin poised. With a sigh he lowered it and closed his eyes. He saw the Frenchman's face again, the eyes wide and burning in the blast from his pistol. His hand felt sticky again, the blood, the bits of scalp, *get it away*.

'Sorry, sir.'

Wayland slung the wineskin over his shoulder, untouched, and they carried on, picking their way through the pebbles. Their landmark was a thorn bush with a dead limb leaning out over the shallow water. After another half mile of relative silence they spotted it up ahead. Pettifer stopped. Wayland detected woodsmoke.

Pettifer put a finger to his lips. Wayland drew his pistol, fully alert. They moved further along the beach and approached the thorn. Using the muzzle of his musket Pettifer parted the bushes gently and peered through. Wayland looked over Pettifer's shoulder.

A hunched figure in dirty old robes and turban squatted in front of a flickering fire heating a small black pot hanging from three crossed sticks. They could smell coffee. The *Volpone*'s boat was beached on the far side of the rocky cove ten yards on, partially covered in brush. It was certainly where they had landed those days earlier, to witness the invasion of Malta.

Pettifer quietly clicked back the lock on his weapon and jabbed a finger at the surf to Wayland's right, making a circling movement with his hand. He then pointed to himself and made a circling movement in the opposite direction, from the landward side of the bush. Wayland nodded. He headed back to the shallows.

Wayland headed to the surf and went in up to his knees, the seawater filling his boot and stinging his wounded calf. He winced with the burning pain, and nearly stumbled on the stones, one eye on Pettifer as he disappeared into the bushes.

The Maltese at the fire had not moved, possibly asleep. Pettifer stepped out, the musket levelled. Wayland waited, hidden by the thorn at the water's edge.

'Stand and deliver,' said Pettifer.

'Bloody took you long enough,' said Kite, looking up from the fireside.

The adjoining hedgerow moved and the others appeared, muskets ready, and Pettifer swore, lowering his weapon. Underhill walked straight past him, a mug in hand. 'Sounded like a herd o'battalion mules, laddie.'

Pettifer sighed. 'Gon' to get you buggers one day.'

'Got me doubts on that...' said Kite, before a gentle cough caused him to jerk round. Wayland stood quietly, his red coat slung over his shoulder, pistol hanging at his side. 'Blimey, sir, I did not see you proper.' His face split into his winning grin. 'Pardon me saying but you're a right sneak, sir.'

'And you are a terrible liar, Private Kite,' said Wayland. They were all there – Kite, Napier, Warnock, Porter, Hesse, Cochrane and De Lisle, Underhill, but of course no Cook. He took a breath, his tone oddly dull. 'Report, please, Sar'nt Underhill.'

'Sir. When Lieutenant Alfonso had no word of his captain he vowed they would not leave till they did find his body, may he rest in peace.' He pointed at the landward thicket of brush with resignation. 'Couldn't stop 'em, sir. They went in search some two days gone, and the *Volpone* frigate moved off in support.'

'Returning when?'

'Unknown, sir.'

None of them seemed particularly perturbed. They drank their coffee. But it was another burden for Wayland.

'So we are to find Nelson, alone, in our rowboat. Superb.'

Cochrane glowered into his coffee cup, as if at tealeaves. 'And so did Jonah seek the whale...'

'Aye, sir,' said Underhill, 'But there is also this, sir. Knock-knock.'

Warnock was busily eating a large orange and spat a mouthful of pips to the ground as he got to his feet. He ducked into the bushes and dragged out a French soldier, red-faced, gagged and bound hand and foot, and threw him down where he rolled, fighting to right himself, guttural cries muffled by the gagging kerchief. His hands had been tied behind his back and then to his ankles, so that he was forced to sit with his knees up or kneel.

He could certainly not stand, run or walk. He stopped trying to call out, his wide eyes flicking from Wayland to Warnock and the others.

Wayland looked at him as if seeing a ghost. He had the same uniform as the column they had encountered. He had the same moustaches. The same equipment. Perhaps they were all the same, Wayland thought, all from the same place, born at the same time. 'Where did you get him?'

'Skirmish, sir,' said Warnock, not looking up from his orange.

'I found him, sir,' said Napier with pride. 'Nosin' round a farmyard, sir, while we were gettin'... well, gettin' uz dinners.' The boxer looked to Underhill for guidance. Warnock swore quietly.

'Were you looting, Private Napier?' asked Wayland.

'Foraging off the land, sir,' declared Underhill. 'Lad's a bit thick, sir.'

Wayland had not the interest to pursue it. 'What has he told us, Sar'nt?'

Again Cochrane mumbled, 'That we be bound for the land of Pharaoh and lotus-eaters...'

Wayland lost his temper. 'Oh for *God's* sake, if you have *nothing* to say, *shut up.*'

The group stood still. Cochrane stared into his coffee.

'Sir,' continued Underhill as if nothing had happened, 'Cocky is most correct, sir. That the fleet is headed to Egypt. That their officer commanding, General Bonypart, announced it afore they weighed anchor, he says, and that they garrison the island with four and a half thousand men, wounded being sent back to Toulon.'

Wayland had not moved, his pistol still hanging from his right hand. He felt no elation that everything had been proven true, only a greater sense of defeat, that even this dread event had come to pass.

If the French had headed for Gibraltar instead, he knew Admiral St Vincent and the Mediterranean Fleet would blast it and *bloody* Bonaparte to Kingdom Come. But out here, there was no St Vincent, no Mediterranean Fleet. Not even Nelson or Hazzard. There was only himself. He looked down at the remains of his shirt and waistcoat. They stank, as did he. He pulled on his red Marine coat.

'You were right, Corporal...' he said to Pettifer, doing up his jacket buttons. 'The major has been taken by the French,' he announced, 'aboard their flagship, the *Orient*. According to Corporal Pettifer, Sar'nt Cook has gone aboard after him in pursuit. Presumably stowing away in the holds.'

'Hard to say otherwise, sir,' said Underhill, without a flicker of reaction to the news.

'Thank you, Sergeant.'

'Just saying, sir.'

'Well *don't*.'

'Sir.'

They fell into silence, watching Wayland, exchanging glances.

'If you pardon me, sir,' said Pettifer, 'but reckon 9 Company is yours now, sir.'

Wayland nodded. Another burden. 'Then clear the landing site. All provisions into the boat, and prepare to get underway to find Admiral Nelson's squadron.'

'How's that, sir?' asked Underhill.

'*We head out to sea, Sergeant, and damned well look for him or swim to bloody Egypt. Is that clear?*'

'Clear aye, sir.'

'What of him then, sir?' asked Warnock. He jerked the tip of his knife at the French soldier, then bit into another segment of orange.

Wayland did not like his insolence. He sounded pleased with himself, as if he had something still to reveal. This was it.

'I mean, we can't leave him here, can we, sir?' said Warnock, as if it were sudden ingenious realisation. The others stayed very still, waiting.

'Beg pardon, sir,' said Underhill, slinging a pack into the small boat, 'but he would tell tales of a party of disciplined foreign soldiers dressed like Malts, sir, speaking the King's English. One of 'em in scarlet. I know I would, if I were he.'

'But whatever should we do, Sarge?' asked Warnock, still mocking. He reached forward and stuck his knife into a bit of driftwood, then spat out more orange pips.

'You bastard, Knocky,' muttered De Lisle.

'What? I'm just askin', ain't I?'

Wayland could feel their eyes upon him.

Porter looked at Warnock. 'Leave him be, for the Lord's sake—'

'You murderin' sod,' said Kite.

'You know, Kitey,' said Warnock, eating more orange, 'always wondered this about you. I 'eard you took eight Frogs prisoner at Cape St Vinno, makin' 'em stick their 'ands up and everything. Old pals or no, that's a difference 'tween you an' me, mate,' he said confidentially, 'when they sticks their 'ands up, I reckon it's a best time to drill 'em one.'

'Private bloody Warnock,' said Pettifer, 'I'll be warnin' of you—'

Warnock spread his hands out in mock self-defence. 'What, Corp? These are the requirements of actions in the field,' said Warnock officiously. 'Says so in the KRs. Even our Mad Billy Jack says so.'

'Do wot?' said Kite.

Warnock spat, angry. 'You 'eard 'is bloody sword lesson, Mickey! You was there! Disarm 'im, and *then you bloody kill 'im.*'

'Bugger you an' your King's Regs...' De Lisle drew his knife. 'S'all right, sir, I'll take care of him.'

Hesse had said little so far, absently twirling the points of his moustache. The Austrian got to his feet. 'No, it should be me.' He put his heels together for Wayland. '*Herr Leutnant*, I shall be quickest.'

Wayland knew they could not release the man nor keep him. He looked down at the ground, his neck burning from the heat of the day. He was so very tired, the dead man's face again bright, this time in flames. The two were so alike, the dead man and this live one.

'Five thousand four hundred and twenty-six paces...' he said, his eye on Warnock. 'Would you not say, Corporal Pettifer? From our last shelter?'

Pettifer took a moment to understand. 'Sir? Oh. Yes, sir, about a mile and a bit, sir...'

'That is what I said.'

Someone whispered, *He counted the ruddy paces...*

Underhill drew a pistol. The Frenchman started to cry out and scrabble across the sand and stone, his face a deep purple as he tipped over, trying to crawl and writhe away.

'Sir – *wait*.' It was Porter. 'The Valerian...'

Underhill put up his pistol. 'What?'

'I gave it the major for sleep,' he said hopefully. 'I can dose him, knock him cold for over a day...'

The Frenchman had stopped moving, his eyes switching to Porter, aware of some development.

'That'll never work, boy,' murmured Underhill.

'*Yes, it will*,' insisted Porter. 'If it can put a man down for a surgeon as I've done, it can put a man down while we get out...'

Underhill sighed. 'He's just a Frog. A poor bloody footsoldier like us.'

'...and we can souse him in rum, down his throat so he reeks of it...'

Warnock looked baffled. 'What daft bloody rot.'

'I don't get it,' said Kite.

Porter moved fast. 'Give us a tick o'the clock, sir, just a tick, I beg. This chap's going to have a kip for at least a day and a night, and when he wakes he'll have a splitter of a head and smell like Gin Alley.'

'You joking?' said De Lisle.

'No, it is of great sense,' said Hesse. 'He will be like a drunk, and no one will listen to his word...'

'Bollocks, 'Essy,' argued Warnock on his feet, shoving Porter. 'I never heard such a lot o'bloody cock and wind in all my—'

There was a loud report and Warnock cried out and fell backward, tripping over the Frenchman's bound feet, De Lisle spinning away, '*Jaysus shite!*'

They turned to look at Underhill. But it was Wayland who had fired, straight past Warnock, hitting the French soldier squarely in the centre of his forehead. The man lay still, his arms locked behind his arched back.

Wayland lowered the pistol and closed his eyes with relief. 'Clear the site and ready the boat.'

He sat down on a stone, unslung his wineskin and pulled out the cork. The dead Frenchman's burning face was gone. He paused with the wineskin, seeing Hazzard on the *Esperanza* in the light of a swinging lamp, raging at him as he thrust his sword into the hanging sack. But he knew it had not been Hazzard who had forced his hand. He drank. The memory faded, and he cared no more. The others cleared the site without another word, in no doubt, at last, who was in command. It was all so wonderfully quiet.

—

Seagulls. Screeching overhead. Blinding sunlight.

Stench of rotting fish, the wind from their wings, flapping close, vultures of the sea, spotting the two dead things floating in the water.

Wake up wake up—

Hazzard struck out blindly and tipped back under the surface, the water going up his nose making him cough and splutter and he swung his arms and hit one, a shrill screeching, the flash of a yellow beak. '*Get off get off!*'

He had opened one of the casks and found dried goat meat, judging from its spice, and dried fish. It had made them thirsty, made the gulls descend.

He had misjudged the speed and current. That was obvious. They were too far from the right spot, he knew that now. Soon they would drink the sea saying, '*Lo, haha, deep down 'tis not so salty after all,*' like too many seamen before them, and begin to die moment by moment.

There were cries from the other gulls and another, very close. The sun burning.

Wake up wake up!

He had faded again, slept, *too bright.* His legs had sunk some-what, dragging him down, and he lifted them back to the kegs on the surface, his head going back, his chest rising, and breathed more deeply. Light dazzling on the water, hypnotic. Then he thought about the gulls – *a port*, and he heard the other cries more clearly. Not birds.

'J'ry...'

Cannot speak. Lips swollen, salty, hard. Like the dried fish.

There was a splash in the water not far off, *sound travels on the water, could be miles. Must be.* He heard the hollow knocks of boathooks and floats against gunwales and excited shouts in Italian and the tug of the net round his shoulders and feet, *they've caught us...*

'*Inglese, inglese...!*'

Hazzard turned his neck stiffly to check on Cook. He was lying back, his ears submerged, his eyes closed, one hand on his chest. *Y'auld oak.* Behind him the rippling edges of a fisherman's net, a silver flash of scales close by as they were drawn in towards the boat.

'S'r'nt...'

'Ess...'

He saw the bearded, nut-brown faces looking down, gesticu-lating for a hook to pull them in.

Sicilians. The fishing fleet from Ragusa.

Cygnus transit 15°.

Course and speed not misjudged after all.

-

Two days later, off Cape Passaro, a fishing boat drew alongside the others that had emerged from a small Sicilian harbour to meet the

British men of war resting at anchor. They passed first a sloop, the sleek *Mutine*, and moved into the shadows of larger ships looming overhead, *Orion, Goliath, Swiftsure, Audacious, Zealous, Leander, Bellerophon, Majestic.*

At length one of the crew pointed, calling excitedly: *Vanguard.* A line was thrown and caught and *Vanguard* called down to ask what stores they offered.

Captain Berry appeared at the quarterdeck rail and shouted down. 'You want *what*, sir? Dash it, I don't speak Italian… What did he say?'

The answer came back, the fishermen pointing to their bulging net on a boom, ready to swing out for lading.

Berry called back, '*I fail to understand you!*'

Lt Hardy, captain of the *Mutine*, joined him at the rail of *Vanguard* and looked down. 'Fish, I believe, sir, for the brave English, he says. Rather jolly of him.'

'But we don't want for any dratted fish, Hardy. The men can't stand the stuff. We've replenished our stores already…' He called down again, 'Fresh *aqua, signori*, but no damn fish!'

But to the protests of the bo'sun and the mates, the boom swung out from the fishing boat, barely clearing the midships rail of *Vanguard*'s upper gundeck and narrowly missing the mainmast shrouds. The Sicilians began to bicker, hands raised to each other, gesticulating madly as to where the hatch for the hold was, and the net dropped and swung sharply, nearly fouling the stays, banging into the mainmast. Berry was livid.

'*Not on my deck, I said! Get it outboard at once, Mr Currie!*'

Under the shouts of the young midshipman of the watch, the deckhands of the *Vanguard* tried to fend off the swinging net but it dropped to the main gundeck, bulged, and disgorged much of its flashing silver bounty in all directions. Furious, Berry hurried down the steps from the quarterdeck. 'Mr Currie! Set the hands to clear this at *once*—'

But he stopped short when he saw two wet figures clamber out of the hanging net from the midst of the flapping fish, and fall exhausted to the deck. A cry went up with a rattle of musket locks, '*Hold hard! Who goes there?*'

Hardy watched fascinated as two filthy, barefoot fishermen struggled onto their hands and knees, one with a duffel bag over his shoulder – three marines and a sergeant were immediately upon them, muskets ready, the sergeant grabbing one by his soaked shirt, '*Gerrup, yew 'orrible littew man, yew.*' But one of the marines inspected the duffel bag – and pulled out a scarlet coat.

'Apologies… for the fish,' gasped one of the fishermen. 'Major Hazzard, Sergeant Cook, 9 Company, Marines…' Hazzard was still out of breath. It had been worse than he had thought. 'Permission to come aboard…'

'*Hazzard?*' said Hardy. 'My good God…'

A figure emerged from the wardroom doorway under the quarterdeck steps and approached. He looked down at them and stooped to offer his one good hand. 'Mr Hazzard?' he said, 'Sir William Hamilton was right. You do not disappoint, sir.'

34'18'89 – signal to Admiralty: Exploring Officer has made rendez-vous.

Nelson.

Hazzard looked into the lined, careworn face, and took the proffered left hand gratefully, and got to his feet. Nelson positively beamed as Berry joined them from the rail, 'Who the hell *is* that?'

'Captain Berry,' said Nelson, with a touch of pride, 'This is Mr Hazzard and Sergeant Cook. As promised, in Naples.'

Berry looked them over with disapproval. 'I'm not the slightest surprised, sir.'

'You two have been in the water, Major,' observed Nelson. 'For how long?'

'Two days, sir. We jumped from *Orient*'s upper gundeck.'

It took a moment for the gathered marines and officers to register his words. 'You *jumped* from Bonaparte's flagship?' asked Berry. 'A First-Rate in full sail?'

'I reconnoitred the fleet from the masthead, sir.'

Someone said, *God above*, possibly Hardy, thought Hazzard. Mugs of grog were put into their hands and cloaks slung over their

95

shoulders. Hazzard sipped at the rum and felt it burn, closing his eyes a moment, life returning. The Sicilians had done their best and got them home, back to the fleet. *God bless Neptune, and an unknown French sailor.*

Berry was incredulous. 'The *masthead*? How the *hell* did you—'

'Estimate three hundred and eighty or three hundred and ninety ships, sir, in three sections,' said Hazzard. 'Frigates on the flanks, *pinques* and poleacres, *avisos*, armed merchants and thirteen heavy ships of the line guarding the transports. All riding low and over-laden, making six to eight knots.' He looked out at the small squadron anchored around them, then back to Nelson. 'They covered the horizon.'

'*Good God*,' said Hardy, 'It's true...'

Nelson waited. 'And...?'

Hazzard nodded. 'Egypt, sir,' he said at last. 'They're heading for Alexandria.'

Nelson took a relieved breath. '*Knew it...*' He gave a hard-won smile. 'Well done, sir.' He turned to Berry. 'Cap'n Berry, can we set a course for Alex, if you please. Mr Hazzard,' he said, 'has called the tune.' He looked at Hardy, a note of hope tight in his throat, 'This time we've *got* them, Thomas,' he said hoarsely, with renewed determination, '...*by the scruff o'the neck.*'

Redcoat

Alexandria glimmered in the heat of a midday June sun, the domes and minarets of the mosques glaring golden white in Hazzard's eyeglass. Levantine ships of all shapes plied in and out of the harbour, sloping lateen sails gliding past, Turkish merchantmen, caravels, *feluccas*, large *chebeks* and peasant *djerms*. Tall square-topped fortresses dotted the castellated ochre walls of the city, and just behind hovered a shimmering white haze, a desolate expanse of desiccated inland seas. Hazzard knew very well what lay beyond – it was the edge of destruction, the distant desert.

He had been only twice in his time. The Alexandria he remembered was a city of Christians, Copts, Hebrews and Muslims, their temples crowded in fitful competition. As they drew closer Hazzard could see the mix of people, some pale, some dark – he focussed on each black African face he saw, hoping to recognise Sotho, Khoina, Zulu or Xhosa, but there were none that he could tell. Instead he saw Turks, Greeks, Italians, Syrians, Berbers and Levantines, in *kaftan* and *keffiyah*, fez, collars and tailcoats. He thought of the Cape and heard the mutterings again, *Makwerekwere, tata: foreigners.*

Cook watched the scene through narrowed eyes, the crows' feet at his temples crinkling in the sun like brown paper. 'Who the bloody hell'd want this? You can smell it 'fore you can see it. Worse'n Kal'kut.'

'Here.' Hazzard handed him the scope. 'Not a Frenchman in sight.'

'We bloody beat 'em to it is why. Told 'em they were only doing six knots at best...' Cook raised the glass and surveyed the unmanned forts and batteries. A few Ottoman troops moved around in the heat onshore, a Turkish ship of the line offloading stores and gun-carriages. 'Turks about... but not many. No patrol squadron to guard the place. Nothin'. Like they're just asking for it.' He took his eye off the glass and squinted into the glare. 'They on our side or theirs these days?'

'Hard to tell. Think they're friendly, but not allies.'

Lieutenant Hardy had requested they accompany him on the *Mutine* sloop to reconnoitre the harbour. The rest of the squadron stood offshore at a diplomatic distance, its gun-ports firmly shut, waiting. Hardy joined them at the rail. He raised his own glass as they slid slowly towards the port. 'Mr Batty, bring us round to the old harbour, please...'

The ship sliced gently round to starboard as the braces were trimmed. It was a good manoeuvre, thought Hazzard, showing an armed broadside and the red ensign before coming in.

Merchant traders began to run to the quayside, driving mules and carts to the docks, ready for sales. The Ottoman troops stared, then began to form up, an NCO whacking their backs with a crop, and a crowd gathered.

'Seems we are awaited with some eager anticipation, Mr Hazzard.'

'I wonder if the marines could be of service, sir,' suggested Hazzard. 'Just a bit of drill.'

Hardy smiled at the thought. 'Capital idea.'

A platoon of the *Mutine*'s Marine complement assembled on the main deck. Hazzard and Cook knew the company NCO, a Sergeant McMahon, an acerbic, thickset Ulsterman from Belfast. They watched as he drilled them to attention several times before their display.

'*P'rade! One two, one two, look lively there bye, ye blighted jackeen aejits...*'

The twin harbours of Alexandria were divided by a central spit forming a rough T-shape, separating the old western and new eastern harbours, the cross-beam of the T forming a protective screen and breakwater to seaward. Each harbour had its own fortresses, storage warehouses and basin, though this had sprawled since Hazzard had been there last. The western harbour was clear of traffic and *Mutine* nosed into the entry channel.

Hardy's first officer sidled up and asked quietly, 'Should we fire a salute, sir...?'

'I think not...' said Hardy circumspectly. 'We might frighten them into saluting back.'

The sloop was met by a pilot boat, a small oared craft crewed by three men waving their arms and shouting.

'Jolly friendly,' murmured Hardy guardedly. 'Douse sail and bring us in, Mr Batty. Ready the gangplank. Marines to the fore.'

McMahon nudged Cook. 'Want to see how it's done, Cookie?' They watched the crowd gathering on the quay. 'We drilled for the King o'Naples, y'know. Oh but he loved us, and signed on with fair King Georgie.'

Cook muttered, 'Your buttons're undone, Mick-Mack.'

McMahon glanced down at the front of his trousers. His ruddy features beamed back at Cook. 'Ah, but be a darlin' and do 'em up for us, eh, Cookie?'

The Alexandrians gathered to watch as *Mutine* slowed elegantly, boats pulling her in to moor. A drummer-boy stepped up to the rail and began to beat time as McMahon and his twelve marines marched down the gangplank, formed two lines and banged to a halt on the quayside.

The Alexandrians stared in fascination, the sun gleaming from the marines' brass buttons, white cross-belts and facings. McMahon roared out his orders. '*P'rade...! Shoulder – arms!*' The spectators jumped back as the marines crashed into their drill, the brightwork on their muskets flashing.

'Mr Hazzard,' said Hardy, 'I think you shall best be employed with me, if you don't mind.'

'Sir.'

The marines fixed and charged bayonets, shouldered and ordered arms, then slammed back into place with a final roar, '*Aye, sir!*'

It had the desired effect. The waiting crowd cheered as if at a theatre performance of acrobats, then quietened in awe as Hardy, Hazzard and Cook were piped down the gangplank, the spectators' voices rising with excitement at the sight of Hardy resplendent in his navy blue, flanked by Cook and Hazzard in Marine scarlet.

They were met by a group of well-to-do men in robes, waiting with some deference, the crowd moving aside for two who stood at their head, the elder possibly Hazzard's age, with dark moustache and beard, and alongside him a younger companion in his early twenties. They bowed in greeting to Hardy.

'*As-salamu aleikum, Kapudan.*'

'*Wa aleikum as-salam,*' replied Hazzard. Hardy glanced at him in some surprise then looked away, smiling to himself.

The younger Alexandrian asked, 'Are you English, sir?'

Hardy replied, 'We are indeed, sir.'

'*Eímaste Englézi,*' repeated Hazzard in Greek for the crowd to hear. Greek was still the common tongue in Alexandria, or at least it had been, he recalled, despite the Ottoman Turks, whose troops scowled from the rear. '*Erchómaste en eiríni.*' *We come in peace.*

'Well done,' whispered Hardy.

'Very impressive,' replied the older bearded Egyptian with a flawless accent, 'but would you mind awfully if we got a move on?'

'You're English,' said Hazzard with a start.

'No,' said the man, coming closer, 'but some of us chaps learn very good English in Austria,' he laughed. 'And go to jolly good schools in England.' He shook his hand. 'Joseph von Hammer-Pürgstall. Diplomatic envoy to our Viennese Consul in Cairo. I saw the red ensign and thought I should present myself to assist.'

'Thank God you did. Major William Hazzard, Marines.'

Hammer chuckled. 'Hazzard and Hammer. We sound like a pair of fearsome London solicitors.'

Hazzard introduced Hardy and Cook, and Hammer indicated his companion. 'This is Masoud ibn-Yussuf, my assistant. Speaks the *lingua franca* wherever he goes, an excellent interpreter.'

Masoud bowed, keen to be of service. 'I can help, if you please, Hazar-*effendi*.'

'What is the situation, Mr Hammer?' asked Hardy. 'We sent a message in for our consul but have had no reply.'

'Not surprising, sir. Your consul Mr Baldwin was recalled to London some time ago, "packed off home" you might say? Leaving you with no one but me, perhaps, and the rather distant threat of King George. I suggest we move with purpose.'

Escorted by the phalanx of marines, Hammer and Masoud led the party along the busy quay to the rock-lined redoubt of the harbour. Everywhere the hot wind carried the smells of the port, the cargoes, the livestock, and the taint of Alexandria's airless winding lanes. Barefooted children stared, the smoke from cooking fires drifting, flies floating on the breeze.

'Have they seen Englishmen before?' asked Hardy.

'Certainly, Captain. This is the hub of the world. And everyone has heard of Nelson.' Hammer smiled quickly but spoke with a note of censure. 'They might wear robes and tassels, you know, but they're not fools.'

'Whom should we meet?' asked Hazzard.

'Your best course is to deal with the Ottoman Governor of Alexandria, Al-Sayyid Muhammad Kurayyim. Do be careful. The name Al-Sayyid supposes him to be a family member of the Holy Prophet Himself.' His voice trailed off as he looked at another gathering on the distant dockside. 'Speaking of mountains and prophets... it seems he has come to you. Very unusual. Your message for Mr Baldwin must have alarmed them, Captain.'

From the great stone fortifications came a group in multi-coloured robes and turbans. In their centre was a spare, vigorous man beneath a broad canopy supported by servants, his advisers and followers clustering around him.

'Al-Kurayyim, *effendi*,' whispered Masoud. 'He comes.'

'Call him *Kurayyim Pasha*,' advised Hammer. 'It is not accurate but he will like it. Though it is a specific rank, "pasha" can be an honorific, much like the loose title "lord" in England...'

Hardy stopped at a respectful distance, McMahon forming the marines into a protective cordon to keep the onlookers back, porting their muskets, bayonets ready. Kurayyim raised his hand and his party came to a halt. Hardy and Hazzard removed their hats and bowed.

Kurayyim nodded, made a comment to his fellows and they laughed. Then he waved a hand, quickly touching his fingers to his heart, his lips and his forehead and spoke curtly in accented Arabic, rather than Turkish. '*As-salamu aleikum.*'

Hardy glanced at Hazzard, who prompted him with a stage whisper, '*Wa aleikum as-salam...*'

'Quite so, Mr Hazzard,' whispered Hammer.

Hardy cleared his throat and declaimed loudly, 'Wah alleykum el salahm, Koraim-Pasha.'

Kurayyim and the others were pleased by this and nodded in appreciation. Then Kurayyim called to them, '*Ma alladhi turiduhu minna?*'

'Masoud,' murmured Hammer, 'if you please.'

Masoud translated with some hesitation. 'Al-Kurayyim asks what business have you with him.'

'This is good,' said Hammer, 'his words are respectful. Give a show of friendly strength.'

Hardy spoke with some severity, 'I am Lt Thomas Hardy, Captain of His Majesty's Ship *Mutine*. We come at the behest of our great King *George*, and Admiral *Nelson*.'

After Masoud's translation many of the advisers whispered and nodded, commenting, '*Nelsoun, Nelsoun Amir... Amir al-bahr...*'

Hardy pointed out to sea, at the squadron standing offshore. 'He awaits on his great ship for the words of Koraim-Pasha, for he has heard of the pasha's wisdom and seeks to help him.' There was further excited whispering and Cook glanced at McMahon and the marines behind.

'Be ready, Mick-Mack...'

For all his bluff manner, McMahon was coolly keeping a close watch. 'Just say the word, Cookie...'

'Nelson seeks to warn Koraim-Pasha, and all of Egypt,' continued Hardy, addressing the crowd, 'that a great and terrible fleet is coming from France, to invade your homeland, and that you might not be able to repel them.'

Hammer shot a quick look at Hazzard. 'It is true then?'

Hazzard nodded. 'Yes. Under General Bonaparte.'

Hammer looked away but Hazzard heard him mutter to himself, '*Lieber Gott...*'

Masoud translated the warning for Kurayyim. There were calls of disbelief, the advisers shouting and waving at them, but Kurayyim hushed them. '*Limadha ataw?*'

'Why should they come?' relayed Masoud.

'They come, Koraim-Pasha,' replied Hardy. 'We have seen their ships. They will cover the seas, and fire a thousand guns upon Alexandria if they land their army. Sell us water and provisions at their value, and we shall stay to take care of this matter for you – for the French Sultan fears only one man: the great Admiral *Nelson*.'

'Very good...' murmured Hammer.

Masoud seemed relieved to convey the message and added a note of pleading. Kurayyim shook his head and wagged a finger at them, '*Hazihi khedaa...*'

'This is trickery,' said Masoud. Kurayyim continued and Masoud said, 'Thank *Nelsoun Amir al-bahr*, that is, amir of the sea, but you come here only for your own ends. We shall remain neutral in this...'

Then Kurayyim raised his hands to the sky and pointed at the sea dramatically. '*Faltazhab anta wa litamdi mashiat alrab!*'

There were cries from the crowd with raised fists, *Allahu akbar! Allahu akbar!*

'But he says...' Masoud looked fearfully from Hammer to Hazzard. '*Go, and let God's will be done.*'

Hardy took a breath. 'Good God...'

'Daft ruddy bastard...' muttered Cook.

Hazzard watched Kurayyim as he turned away, the interview concluded. Hazzard could only guess what Bonaparte would do with him. Hardy muttered under his breath, 'Fool. I doubt God will forgive him for what he has just done.'

Someone heard, detecting the tone, and a shout went up. Kurayyim snapped a look at Hazzard and there were cries of indignation from the gathering. Sergeant McMahon barked just the once. *'M'rines… charge bayonets.'*

The marines banged one foot forward, their muskets and bayonets to the fore, held ready. The crowd backed away with a low murmuring. One of Kurayyim's grandees stepped forward and bowed low to them.

'He mocks, but thanks us for our care,' said Masoud, his brow running with sweat, 'but once you have what you need… you shall be on your way.' He looked at Hammer. 'We must go, Hammer-*effendi*…'

'Now chaps,' said Hammer, 'back away like good English gentlemen…'

Hardy bowed, replaced his hat and said, 'Sar'nt McMahon, the marines will clear a path to the *Mutine.*'

McMahon saluted. *'Sah.* Comp'*nay!* About – *turn!'*

The people began shouting and waving their fists and the Ottoman troops tried to keep them back as the marines marched down the quay in two files, Hardy and the others in the centre.

'That did not go well, did it,' said Hardy.

'As well as it could, sir,' said Hammer, 'Kurayyim must impress his rivals in the *diwan* that he is a man of power and decision. Shooing you away shows this.'

'Yes, but at what cost.'

'He's about to find out,' grunted Hazzard.

Masoud hurried alongside them among the growing clamour. 'Sir, please, how many are truly coming? When?'

When they reached the gangplank some of the onlookers broke through, shouting in their faces, *Allahu akbar!*

Hazzard pushed back and a marine cracked one on the head with his musket but Hazzard called out, *'Stand off there, that man. No violence.'* He pushed through the crowd, 'A full invasion force, Masoud, any day now.'

'Can you stop them?' called Hammer. 'With only these?'

'We could make a merry mess of them,' replied Hardy.

'I am here, at your service, Hardeh-*effendi*, Hazar-*effendi*,' said Masoud, fear in his wide eyes. 'Will you come back to help us? Please?'

The crowd lining the dock heaved about them, whistling, jeering, *Kur-ay-yim, Kur-ay-yim*, but the marines ploughed through them, clearing the gangway to the *Mutine*, knocking several traders into the water. Hardy called out, 'Major Hazzard, quick as you can, if you please.'

Hazzard turned to Hammer. 'Is there a chance a delegation could get to the capital?'

'To the high Mamluk *diwan*?' Hammer nodded. 'It means a ride, a day and a half, less obtrusive than a boat upriver.'

Hazzard looked back at the *Mutine*. The squadron could wait offshore for the French for as long as it took, and then pounce. 'How soon could you organise such a journey?'

'Not difficult. Two guides and some horses.' He shot a glance at Cook. 'For the pair of you?'

'Perhaps.'

Hammer smiled. 'Then come tonight. Find a double-torch on the shore by the warehouses in the western harbour. We shall be there.'

Masoud shook his hand gratefully. 'May God be with you, Hazar-*effendi*,' the young Egyptian's wide, dark eyes burning into his own. 'Will you come back?'

'I will tell Nelson we must wait,' he said, halfway up the gangplank, already wondering if it would prove a lie. 'I will.'

They boarded the *Mutine* and cast off, and Cook murmured, 'What'll Nellie say about that then?'

Hazzard watched as they pulled away. 'I have no bloody idea.'

The Alexandrian traders waved in celebration as the *Mutine* set sail, Hammer and his small group heading off through the crowd, Masoud momentarily alone on the jetty, the sole mourner at an unseen funeral. Hazzard raised a hand from the rail of the sloop. Masoud raised his in reply, a lost expression on his face until Hammer returned to lead him away.

–

'Dashed ridiculous,' Hardy whispered to Hazzard over dinner on *Vanguard* that night. He swirled the wine at the bottom of his glass. 'Will, you've done more than enough, for heaven's sake.'

'It's not enough if the French are not *here*...' Hazzard stared at the table, the food dead in his mouth, his mind constantly working, wondering how he could have got her off, how he could get the men off Malta, knowing he could not. *Lieutenant Wayland, how are you faring...*

Hardy watched him.

'Surely you need rest. And our orders are clear – we did our best with that Koraim fellow. You can't go charging off into the desert.'

'How else can we warn them?'

Sir Thomas Troubridge reached over and took the decanter from Hardy to top up his own glass. 'Will, for God's sake...' He glanced at the other captains, and refilled Hazzard's glass, more for something to do as he spoke under his breath, 'You'll go too far. You've done it before. You've been on the brink for... for *weeks* – we all have...'

Hazzard gazed at the table, staring into nothing. Hardy tried to be jocular. 'Come, when will you let us take some of the brunt, eh? Up the damned masthead of a French flagship, by heaven, and over the side into the drink. We have gunners positively itching for their chance.'

There was a general chuckle round the table. At the head sat Nelson, watching them, saying little – ironically he reminded Hazzard of Bonaparte: closed-faced and watchful, somewhat humourless. He was surrounded by his devoted captains – several had stayed to dine after another conference. For weeks they had done nothing but plan; all had been drilled on their actions and reactions in any given scenario should they encounter the French fleet. Every contingency had been considered, including Nelson's death.

There was Hardy of the *Mutine*, Berry, Captain of *Vanguard*, Darby of the *Bellerophon*, Foley of the *Goliath*, Saumarez of the *Orion*, Ball of the *Alexander*, Thompson of the *Leander*, Hallowell of the *Swiftsure*, and Troubridge of the *Culloden* – a band of brothers indeed, thought Hazzard, the happy few. He could forgive Nelson imagining himself Henry V at Agincourt, facing insuperable odds.

'You've been hogging them for ages,' declared Darby brusquely. 'Time for us to have a bash.'

'Hear, hear,' said Saumarez. 'There'll be hell to pay if you don't make it back to his lordship in Gib. Said so himself, didn't he, Tom? Threatened to cut me sherry ration if I let 'im sink.'

Laughter at Sir James, a suave, easy manner, betraying none of the relentless aggression beneath. Hazzard well knew that each captain at the table would lead his ship alone into the middle of Bonaparte's fleet and blast it to Satan, or die trying.

'How long shall we wait in this godawful place, sir?' asked Darby of Nelson. He cast a doubtful eye at Hazzard. 'If the Frogs *ever* turn up, that is...'

They had been over Hazzard's experiences aboard *Orient* for hours – less about Bonaparte, but more about the ship, its standing rigging, its weaknesses, the water-levels on the hull, the pumps, distribution of guns, whether she listed at all, the number of officers and crew, their watch system, anything to get an advantage when the time came to attack – as it would, they each were certain. They were in no doubt of Hazzard; they were merely tired of chasing, and now, waiting – and tempers were fraying.

Nelson twirled the stem of his glass with the fingers of his left hand, then took up the port to pour himself some more. No one sought to help, to hold the glass or tip the decanter – it was a customary exercise for the one-armed man.

'If they are not here,' said Nelson, 'then we can but guess they have headed northeast, perhaps to strike the Greek Ionian isles. If you have Venice, as the French do, you simply must take Bari on the heel of Italy and Corfu across the strait, else you are bottled up in the Adriatic, it's imperative – and they have Venice, and some of the fortified isles. What then? Do we go there? Or perhaps they go to Constantinople itself.'

The others nodded their heads but Hardy glanced at Troubridge, puzzled. Hazzard could scarcely believe it. 'I do not understand, sir,' he said. 'We know the French are coming to Egypt.'

Nelson was irritated with this contradiction. 'Alas, Mr Hazzard, you know only what has been reported, or was allowed to be reported to you.'

The captains passed the port and examined their glasses studiously, only Troubridge and Hardy watching the exchange. Hazzard regarded Nelson with incredulity.

'Sir, Bonaparte announced his intentions to his army at Valletta, before my eyes. He confirmed it when I dined with him and his entire commission of *savant* specialists come to dig out a canal at Suez—'

'So they *said*, sir—'

'The general staff are working to a tactical battle plan to take the country from top to bottom in just thirty days. Why would he deceive on such a scale—'

'Yet he did, all the way from Toulon, sir. Not a soul knew, so we have heard.'

Hardy ventured to intervene but Troubridge did instead. 'Sir, did Major Hazzard not provide clear enough evidence? The Arabic leaflets, their own conversation aboard ship? The battle order of his army?'

'I cannot comment, Sir Thomas,' said Nelson, rather formally, though with some disappointment. Something troubled him.

Darby looked at Hazzard and piped up, 'All we can do is look upon the sea, sir. And there we find no enemy.'

'Men have lost their *lives*,' Hazzard reminded Darby, 'in battles that will never reach the pages of the *London News*. Our agent is still aboard the French flagship—'

'Who by your own account you got killed,' said Foley carelessly.

Hazzard turned on him. 'Who in hell are you to speak of such things to me?'

'Foley, sir, of the *Goliath*.' He set down his glass firmly. 'Would you like to know me, sir?'

'I am *Hazzard*, and by *God* you would *not* like to know *me*.'

Nelson remained calm. 'Mr Hazzard, you will keep your temper at my table,' he said. 'Captain Foley, you meant no slight, did you, sir? We shall have no wretched duelling.'

Foley sloshed back another glass of claret. 'No, sir. Forgive me.'

Hazzard could not have cared less. 'Men and women, from Paris to Toulon, Naples and Valletta, have gambled their lives to provide us with this intelligence, the number and organisation of their army, demi-brigades, commanders, disposition – and, above all, that the fleet is in full sail for *Alexandria*.'

'Do you seek to argue with the admiral, sir?' demanded Darby. 'The *tail*, so it is said, does not wag the *dog*.'

Hazzard knew very well what Darby's metaphor suggested. 'This red coat is mere decoration, Captain Darby. I am more than the Navy's bloody watchdog.'

Darby's face darkened and he half rose. 'How *dare* you...'

'Enough, enough,' said Nelson. 'Sit *down*, sir...'

Darby eased off but kept an angry eye on Hazzard. Nelson looked pained and banged the table. 'This is *frustration*, gentlemen, pure and simple, all of us. We have ploughed these seas to and fro, and *still* not seen them. Four *hundred* ships, by heaven! How could we *miss* them?'

'Then why leave, sir,' protested Hazzard, 'and risk missing them again?'

Nelson hit the table again. '*Because we must seek them, sir!* Lest they strike elsewhere!'

Hardy and Troubridge seemed resigned, while the captains glared at Hazzard for questioning their god.

Thompson of the *Leander* spoke up. 'Sir, *Leander* could scout past Crete with Hardy and the *Mutine*, while you wait here. We are but fifty guns and can speed like a frigate.'

'No, Thos,' said Nelson, 'a fine idea but I can't lose you as well. Our strength lies in our unity.' He sat tight-lipped, then announced his decision. 'Given fair winds tomorrow we shall retrace our steps. First to Crete, then Cyprus, to revictual, then Corfu. And give battle *where we find them.*'

Hazzard stared at them, at the florid satisfaction of the impatient captains longing for action. Red-faced, he threw down his napkin and put his chair back, his hands shaking. 'If you will excuse me,' he said with obvious disgust, 'I have another *appointment.*'

The break with protocol and etiquette too great for them to endure, Foley and Darby fairly burst from their seats in outrage but Nelson was too quick for them, and was on his feet first. 'Mr Hazzard, if you please, a word, sir. Gentlemen, you will excuse us.'

Taken aback, the captains all rose and bowed at Nelson's departure. Glowering, Hazzard followed him, Hardy and Troubridge watching.

They passed from the wardroom into the Great Cabin. Hazzard shut the door behind him. Nelson headed for his desk.

'You have done great work for your king, sir,' said Nelson, 'be in no doubt of that.'

Hazzard said nothing.

Nelson relented. 'Darby can be a boor. He speaks and thinks for no one but duty, action and Darby. His ship is known as the *Billy Ruffian* for good reason. They are tired. So are we all. We have hunted everywhere. By God, we have.' He thought of the past month. 'To Spain, Toulon, Sardinia, Naples, Sicily, worn ourselves to the bone. When I lost the frigates in that gale I sought the aid of Naples. Hardy reported that you had already done so. Sir William Hamilton thought you our one great hope. Acton was condemnatory. It was that which decided me on you.'

Hazzard had pleaded his case, reported everything, the losses, the *effort*, De la Vega, the *Volpone*, the *Lazzaroni* in Naples, the guide Azzopardo in Valletta, Sarah on the *Orient*. 'If you leave now, sir, I will have failed, and all thus far will have been in vain.'

'We cannot *wait* for them, sir. We must *act*.'

Nelson then reached for a folded page on his desk, a letter. 'Received at Syracuse, sir, but I ignored it, as you can see, and followed your lead regardless.' He flapped it open with a flick of the wrist. Hazzard took it. It bore War Office and Admiralty seals.

> *Given intelligence received at this office, the threat to the Sublime Porte of Constantinople appears all the greater than that to Egypt. The French intend progressive annexation of the Greek Isles as prelude to a swift attack on Turkey. Given relations with the Ottoman Empire, His Majesty's Government must intervene. Exploring Officer 34'18'89 to withdraw upon locating French fleet.*
>
> *Melville, Secretary of War*

Nelson looked as defeated as Hazzard. 'I was told by Sir William Hamilton that I should trust your word above all others,' said Nelson. 'But now, you see, we have no choice.' He moved to the port decanter on the desk, removed the crystal stopper and poured two glasses. 'Melville may be telling the truth. The Sea Lords have confirmed this fear. Therefore I must investigate.'

'I have not yet reported to London, sir. Lord Melville cannot know—'

Nelson banged down the decanter. 'I *know* he is wrong, sir. In my very *bones* I know that India hangs in the balance – hacking their way through Egypt to the Red Sea, to thrust a damnable French battle-fleet into the Indies is...' he put a hand to his forehead, 'it is *diabolical*...'

'Then what of the innocents lying a stone's throw from this ship—'

'We are *bound by duty*, sir! *Bound*.'

'Bound be damned! I speak of conscience!' Hazzard could scarcely conceal his anger. 'Can you not see, sir? He is gaming with *nations*—'

'And we are *England*, sir!' snapped Nelson. '*We determine the nations.*'

Footsteps in the passage stopped, and whispered voices diminished as listeners moved away. After a moment he handed Hazzard a glass of port. 'The log will show none of your part in this affair. Only my concern that we have missed the French yet again. And how I must tell my tigers out there to leave off their dinner...'

He was impatient, his nerves in shreds. Hazzard realised Nelson was not unlike him: *he cannot stop. He cannot simply wait.*

Nelson took back the note and moved to his desk lamp. He touched the page to one of the burning candles. The fine vellum flared for only a moment, floated and vanished.

This was the end, thought Hazzard. This was Empire speaking, and nothing would sway him. Hazzard put down his glass, the port untouched, light-headed enough from the sudden turn of events. In his mind flashed images of Hammer and Masoud on the dockside, and a city with no comprehension of the fate bearing down upon it.

'If England should thrive at such a cost, sir,' said Hazzard, 'then we are no better than Bonaparte, and the murder of their Revolution.'

'You refuse to withdraw, sir?'

'I do.' Hazzard's mouth was dry, his voice a husk. He put a folded envelope on a side table, his hand shaking. 'This is my report, about Malta's garrison under Vaubois, and a copy of the disposition of the *Armée d'Orient* provided by—' he stopped, his voice catching '—by our agent on the *Orient.*'

'Am I your messenger now, Mr Hazzard?'

'No. Sir William Hamilton is.'

Thirty days, only thirty, for Bonaparte to conquer Egypt.

There was nothing he could do to stop it. India rose bright and sharp in his mind, thoughts of fates and gods, and glib truisms about destinies and wisdom – *who was he to stop the machine? Damn them all.*

He turned for the door, then stopped.

'If you head north to Crete and Turkey as ordered, sir,' said Hazzard, 'revictual at Cyprus, then return here before heading west—'

'*No*, sir—'

'You would lose but a week, and so you may note in the log, but the French will not have been able to disembark all of their troops or cargo—'

Nelson was adamant. '*No*, sir. To the Sublime Porte of Constantinople, *then* out to the Ionian Isles *as ordered*. It is the only way, sir, and there an end to it, else we answer to the Lords Commissioners and Parliament for it, sir.'

'Very well then. *After* the Ionian Isles would you not need to revictual?'

Hazzard did the calculations: ten days, twelve, with favourable winds to Syracuse. Revictualling, several days, then eight, ten days to return to Alexandria on a good westerly. It made *sense*.

By which time – what? Egypt under the French heel?

But at least he would return.

'Quite likely, yes. To Cyprus—'

'What if you headed west instead, to Syracuse, to revictual, sir?' He thought it through as he spoke: *what was Bonaparte's plan after the conquest?* 'If they take Egypt in thirty days as planned, they would feel no urgency to unload their fleet...' Hazzard watched him. 'They might even delay until victory was assured.'

They regarded each other in silence, each aware of the other's interests and implacable refusal to withdraw. 'Syracuse...' Nelson watched him. 'It could be done.'

'But still, you will leave, sir.'

'Indeed, sir. For I must.'

Nelson stood by his desk, the lamp lending him an unhealthy pallor, or revealing it. Hazzard looked round the cabin, its instruments, its charts – it was the essence of *Vanguard*, of the Royal

Navy. It now appalled him. All of it did. His voice took on the dull tone of the vanquished. 'Then that is the recommendation of the Exploring Officer in the field, sir.' Hazzard put his hand to the door latch. He could hear the captains beyond, taking brandy. 'For your own referral, sir, I have written in my report that I intend to follow my original orders, as bidden.'

'And those orders were, sir?'

'To engage the enemy independently by any means possible.'

Nelson looked at the ash remains on his desk. 'Then no man can condemn you, sir.'

Hazzard very much doubted that. He opened the door.

'Mr Hazzard.' Nelson's voice brought him to a stop. 'If I do not find the French at Crete, or Corfu, or Syracuse, I shall follow my instincts, and return. With my tigers.'

It was a lifeline, thought Hazzard, tossed from the portside rail to a drowning man – but not enough.

'By then,' said Hazzard, 'it will be too late for Egypt.'

Hazzard went out, leaving Nelson and Melville's betrayal behind him. Troubridge and Hardy joined him at the door.

'William? What happened? You look like thunder.'

'*Come back*, Sir Thomas,' whispered Hazzard, feeling a rising despair, 'that is all I ask. For the sake of this wretched place and these poor damned wretched people.'

'We shall,' insisted Hardy, 'and I shall make some excuse, anything, and take *Mutine* to Valletta and get your men, damn it I shall.'

'Then come back – *make him*,' urged Hazzard. 'Tell him...' He wondered what indeed to tell him. 'Tell him... I will have a tethered goat waiting. For his tigers.'

'My dear fellow...'

Hazzard left them and moved down the passage to the stairs, hearing the crew singing to an old squeezebox:

...and if it's a boy he shall fight for his king,

And if it's a girl, she shall wear the gold ring...

When he reached his cabin, his hands trembled at the buttons of his red coat and he tore it off and threw it into the corner as if it burned him, contaminated him. He leaned his head on the plank wall, hoping it would somehow cool him in the endless heat. He put a hand to his chest, feeling through his shirt where the little figurine had once hung, left kindly for him by Ellie the housemaid, now lost, like Sarah, like everything, on *Orient*.

Lewis. Swine. Nelson and his sealed orders. And what am I now, what am I? Destroyer of nations.

Cook knocked and opened the door. 'Sir?'

'*Damn* them, Jory. Let them have their *bloody* war. Nelson's as bad as the rest of them, yearning for nothing but battle and damn the consequences. Let them blow their trumpets and trample infants underfoot and burn the whole *bloody* world down—'

Cook closed the door. 'What's happened?'

'Nelson's leaving. Tomorrow.'

Cook lowered his head, a nagging suspicion made real. 'God's *teeth...*'

'North to Corfu or across to Cyprus or Acre or some such cock and bull, and damn Egypt by their lordships' command, *damn everyone* by order of the bloody British Government.'

'What about the thirty-odd-thousand Frogs and that flamin' great fleet?'

'Navy thinks they'll find it if they sail round in circles long enough.'

'And the men back on Malta?'

'Nelson won't even send a sloop to pick them up – *nothing*. "Can't afford it, sir," he said. Hardy says he'll try with the *Mutine*, but God knows when, a fortnight, three weeks.' Hazzard turned on Cook. 'Haven't I always said? God above, you taught me that much, Jory. *Alone*. It's best. And look what's happened to them, thanks to the Royal bloody Navy... Sarah, Cesár, that poor little whelp Wayland and the men…' He muttered under his breath, 'Damn you for bringing them to me…'

'Me?'

Hazzard lashed out at him, driven by his own self-hatred. 'How did you talk old Jarvie into it, Jory? A half cripple like me with a gammy leg leading a jaunt across the high seas in a Spanish lugger? Admirals must have laughed themselves sick.'

'It weren't like that—'

'At least Lewis can say they tried. They can tell a Sea Lord or two they had a go, wash their hands of the whole filthy affair. *God damn them!*'

'*And damn yourself, boy!*'

Hazzard looked at him. The big man's face had suffused a deep brick-red.

'Lord Jack jumped at your name, sir. He wanted you back afore ever anyone said a word. And he knew you, he told me – pig-headed, he said, bloody-minded and all. And that he wanted blokes just like that, ones who wouldn't *stop*, just like you say, no matter come what. Well we got those blokes, and they're behind us, and they'll get here, too right they will. Then we done our bit, let Nellie and his buggers set this stinkin' place alight from tip to tail, just like you want – so don't you go damning them to me, no *sir*.'

Cook jerked open the door and nearly left him but Hazzard shouted, '*Stand still!*'

Cook was too old, too hard in the neck, to do anything but halt. He banged his foot down and came to attention, staring out into the passage.

Hazzard looked at his back. Cook stood waiting.

'How far could they be?'

It took Cook a moment. He turned. 'They're not on Malta no more, pound to a penny. Mr Wayland's prob'ly got his shirt rigged on a cutter's mainmast for a ruddy sail and be halfway here by now. E'en if they got to paddle with their bare hands.' He shook his head. 'Think that pup'd give up? Not on your life. And not on mine neither. Thinks the world on you. You taught him sword at the Academy, did you even notice? With your gammy leg and bad arm that near cut that Austrian champion to bits. Said he'd never seen the like. Ever since, he told me, all he ever wanted was to be like *you*.'

Hazzard watched him. Over the years they had long passed the point of who owed whom, debts both imagined or paid now in distant memory, but still Cook would watch over him, to the moment of his own destruction if need be. Hazzard knew this very well, as he would for Cook. In this way they had stayed alive together longer than many others. Which is why Hazzard had not involved him when he fell into French hands in Valletta.

Cook saw Hazzard's scarred Bombay coat flung in the corner. He bent down, picked it up and began folding it. 'And this is worth a damn sight more'n being chucked in a corner.'

Hazzard thought of Masoud, alone and afraid among the crowd. Melville, Lewis, even Nelson, had abandoned him. Abandoned all of them to Bonaparte and thirty thousand battle-hardened troops.

'They want to let them rot, Jory.' Hazzard shook his head. 'Lewis, Blake, the Admiralty. And Nelson's letting them.'

Hazzard and Cook would be the only shore-party from the British interceptor squadron – a squadron of some ten thousand men and a thousand guns. And the only aid coming to Egypt was two bedraggled marines.

Cook nodded. 'Don't seem right now, does it, sir?'

Thoughts of home, of his uncle the Reverend Hazzard, the parish church of St Jude.

For St Jude, patron of Causes Lost.

'No. Damn well doesn't.'

–

Just before midnight a jolly boat was swung outboard from *Vanguard*'s port side and was lowered away, with two oarsmen and a coxswain, and two red-coated marines. The rowlocks rattled as the oarsmen shoved off from the darkened broadside, heading for the lights of Alexandria, dipping and swaying in the July heat.

Hazzard looked back at *Vanguard*. Once, he would have associated a ship with home, safety, and felt a pang of departure – but this time it was different. He was no longer one of them and, he recognised, never would be again. He was glad of it.

As they pulled away, a silhouetted figure came to the quarterdeck rail, standing apart from the others. It looked down, the shape unmistakable, cocked hat, right sleeve pinned up. Hazzard thought of that first voyage from England to Cadiz, with the abrasive Tomlinson of the *Valiant*, and that wave of a final farewell, despite their differences. Hazzard felt Cook watching him. He wondered if they would ever see Nelson or his ships again. The figure did not turn, nor wave, but merely watched, growing smaller and smaller as they pulled away.

The tide carried them in, and they headed for the warehouses at the extreme edge of the western harbour basin. The twinkling lights of the citadel towers and minarets rose higher and higher as they drew near, turrets and domes glowing against a clear night sky.

Torches burned on the quaysides, lighting the slow passage of a *felucca* sliding into port. Hazzard looked for Hammer's sign but the long, sloping lateen sail of the *felucca* blotted out the shoreline. Hazzard held up a hand to the coxswain, who grew steadily more worried by the moment.

'*Sir, if we get spotted…*'

'*Wait…*'

The *felucca* glided past at a crawl, and there, by two ramshackle buildings, he saw them.

Twin torches.

'Bear to starboard,' he said, and the coxswain pulled the tiller, swerving towards the shore. Hammer appeared out of the dark with Masoud. The oarsmen fended off a half-sunken post from a collapsed jetty, and the boat ground on the shore. Hazzard and Cook jumped out with their packs, shoving the boat back to open water. The young coxswain touched his cap, *God be wi'ye, sir*. Hazzard watched them row gratefully back to *Vanguard* with a sense of finality. *Goodbye indeed*.

'*Al-hamdulillah*,' said Masoud, breathless with gratitude. 'Praise be to God you are here, Hazar-*effendi*,' he said, overwhelmed, shaking their hands. 'You came back… you both *came back*.'

'Put these on,' said Hammer, and gave them a set of clothes each, a long white *galabeyyah* shirt, a patterned *kaftan* and a dark split *binish* robe overtop. 'You might want only the *binish*, and keep those famed red coats of yours underneath. They may prove useful.'

'In this heat?' said Cook. 'You're barking.'

'In the heat of the desert sun, Mr Cook,' replied Hammer, 'the heaviest robes are the most prized.'

Cook had drawn a new uniform jacket from *Vanguard* but had removed the sleeves, as he used to in India on shore operations, leaving only shirtsleeves and a brass-buttoned and bastion-laced red jerkin – other than his white sailing ducks and boots, the robes covered the big marine completely.

Hazzard pulled the magnificent *binish* surcoat over his Bombay jacket, the scarlet sleeves protruding from just below the elbow, his white breeches and tall boots giving him the look of a wealthy Ottoman – and the robe covered an old '96 Pattern Navy sword obtained from the arms locker on *Vanguard*. Settling it on his hip, he thought of De la Vega and the *espada ropera*, lost on the *Orient* to Derrien.

Hammer examined the ensemble. 'It will do, and may serve to confuse, and therefore impress.'

Masoud helped them with a *keffiyah* headdress, producing a large folded triangle of thick white fabric. 'The *shemagh*,' he said, and positioned it on Hazzard's head, settling the knotted circlet of a black rope *iqal* on top and tucking up the end of the white cloth to cover his throat and chest. 'It was of my father,' he said. Cook wrapped and tucked his into a turban out of long habit from India. Masoud showed them how to tie the draped lengths of the *shemagh* over the face. 'For the sun, Cook-*effendi*,' he said.

'This neck don't get no redder,' muttered Cook.

Soon they were hurrying through the empty torchlit streets, their only company the occasional burst of Turkish or Greek chatter from an open widow, applause at a game as they passed by, the occasional group clustered round an open fire, a small cauldron and coffee-pot rattling on the coals.

From his previous brief visits Hazzard knew the harbour and foreshore area but had little knowledge of the winding lanes into the city. They passed along parched dirt roads lined with tall European-style houses crushed tightly together, rows of slum plaster dwellings and stables, rank and sour, heaps of rubbish in the alleys. Humped shapes of derelict sleeping Arabs lay in the lee of stone walls still warm from the sun, rats running in the undergrowth of spear-bladed palms and bush.

They reached a small cobbled yard behind one of the gate-houses in the city walls. Lamps burned in the windows and they could hear the murmur of voices, an argument, then sudden laughter, the sound then fading. A man appeared from the shadows and Hammer joined him.

Hazzard waited. The light caught a polished surface in the dull stonework of the wall. There, among the irregular lines of mortar, was a small tablet of inscribed hieroglyphs, a half moon, a stylised serpent, two feathers. The masons had used the ancient *stele* in the blockwork of the wall. Further down, another, covered in tight, swooping cursive characters. Hazzard touched them with his fingers.

Egypt.

Five thousand years of history. Maybe more. How did we come to be in this place?

The arc of the sky glimmered cool and indigo, heavy with soft stars. Hazzard looked out at the emptiness beyond the gates. The landscape sloped down and away, forming drab hillocks of scrub and dark sand, the distant desert to the southwest a dead flat line, almost white in the unearthly glow of starlight.

Cook stood silent beside him. Together they had looked out over the Indian Karnataka, the plateau of Decca, and the mountains of Jaipur in much the same way.

'Pilgrims in a heathen land, sir,' the sergeant rumbled.

'And we are the heathen.'

'Ain't it always.'

Hammer beckoned them to come quickly and the keeper let them through a low door in the large studded gate. It closed and locked quickly behind them, an iron bar swinging into place.

They hurried along the deserted road ahead, winding their way through the spreading wasteland. After half a mile they saw several men waiting with horses in the darkness of a thicket of palms and stunted trees.

'Awlad 'Ali,' said Masoud. 'An ancient people, the largest in these lands. Shepherds, traders... bandits, warriors. Descended from the *Blemi*. In many ways, they have been in Egypt as long as the old gods.' Masoud was an educated Alexandrian, and seemed uncomfortable at the prospect of dealing with such men. He summed up his feelings in one word: '*Bedu.*'

Hazzard had heard accounts of the Bedouin, the desert tribes whose territories stretched as far as their caravans could trade, or other tribes could contest – how they could ride fifty miles of desert in a day and stop for water only once, in a landscape that would consume anyone else, European, Persian or Turk.

He could see six horses and two men in dark robes. They wore black *keffiyah* headdresses, held in place by thick *iqal* rope circlets on the crown. A bandolier of cartridge pouches, a pair of pistols each, on one saddle a carbine and on the other a long Turkish musket. At their hips swung swords curved as gracefully as a crescent moon.

'*As-salamu aleikum,*' said Hammer and Masoud.

The Bedouin replied with a courteous bow. '*Wa aleikum as-salam, wa rahmatu Allah wa barakatuh, ya Hamar-effendi,*' he said with even greater blessing, and Hammer returned the bow. There were three others behind, servants or possibly slaves, thought Hazzard, holding the horses and waiting.

'Brothers Izzam and Alahum of the *al-Kalbi*,' Hammer said to Hazzard. The Bedouin bowed again as Hammer introduced Hazzard and Cook.

Izzam looked perplexed. '*Hazar?*'

Masoud translated it literally. '*Khatar.*'

Risk. Danger.

'Aha…!' They liked the names, and smiled broadly up at Cook, a full head taller. '*Ku'q?*'

Cook glowered down at him. 'That's right, mush.'

Alahum said something and laughed softly and Izzam's face lit up, 'Ah!' He spoke to Masoud.

Masoud interpreted, 'He asks if, truly, you are English, and if so, are you a lord and is he your servant?'

'Not bloody likely,' muttered Cook.

Hazzard showed his red sleeve. 'We are English, yes, and seek your help.' Then Hazzard said, '*Shokran. Nahnu momtannoun, al-hamdulillah.*' *Thank you. We are grateful, God be praised.*

Cook smiled down at their surprise. 'You should hear him do the Khanboli in Madras.'

'You speak the tongue of the Arabs?' asked Masoud, astonished.

'Only a few words, Masoud. *Qalilanaan.*' *A little.*

The Bedouin laughed, and Izzam spoke and bowed. 'Then God is truly great,' translated Masoud, and bowed as well. They readied the horses and Cook took the reins of a bay stallion. The horses were smaller than Hazzard had expected, with powerful legs and broad muzzles and wide, flared nostrils, each decked in ornamental tassels and leather tack.

Hammer murmured, 'These are pure-breed Arabians, Herr Hazzard. Will Herr Cook… be all right?'

Cook took the saddle in one step. 'I've rode with the Nabobs, sir, on Maratha ponies, so don't you fret.'

Alahum asked, '*Darb al-Hujjaj?*'

Masoud rapped something off quickly in the negative but they simply shrugged and smiled. He translated, angry with them,

'The pilgrim's road, he asks. He wants to take you to Jerusalem of all places, so he can charge you more *money*.'

Hazzard shook his head. 'No. *Al-Qahira*.' Cairo.

Hammer watched them carefully and said, '*Al Murad Bey*.'

Their confident laughter stopped.

'*Murad...?*' said Alahum, in sober confirmation.

Izzam mounted his horse, more business-like. '*Al-Qahira. Insha'allah*.'

'What did he say?' asked Cook.

'He made a brief prayer,' said Hammer. '*God willing*.'

Murad

The six rode south through the night, crossing Maryut, the dried inland sea Hazzard had seen from the *Mutine*, the waters of the adjacent Lake Maadiyeh held back by no more than a sea-dyke topped by a canal – Alexandria's access to the distant Nile. The ground shone white, the remnants of ancient salts glowing against the luminous deeps of the sky.

They did not take the route to Damanhur, a natural first halt on the road to Cairo, Hammer explained, with food markets and water, but rather swung southwest into the chilled scrublands of the desert, to avoid stray Mamluks and other *Bedu*. As they rode, Hazzard pictured Nelson setting sail and disappearing over the horizon, Blake, Lewis and Melville sitting smug in their offices – while Bonaparte urged on his invasion fleet with no one to stop him. Hazzard wanted to drive the horses hard.

They maintained a light canter, breaking only once, the Arabian horses imbued with a stamina unknown in his experience – he grew wearier of the thudding rhythm than they did, and he was left gasping. But before the sun crept over the horizon, they had covered nearly 40 miles of their 130-mile journey.

As the sun appeared, broad and red in the east, the cold of the night evaporated, swift as a waking dream. The *Bedu* urged on the pace before the sun climbed higher, when they knew their guests would be forced to slow and rest. By ten, Hazzard felt the light itself become a palpable force, pushing down on the crown of his head, driving them into their saddles, into the very earth. They slowed, riding through low, dry grasses and tortured brush, the sun climbing ever higher, their fatigue suffocating.

They passed a remote cluster of white mud houses, startling a herd of goats, dark figures beside them in the shimmering distance: the men in baggy white trousers and long blue and white *galabeyyah*, the women in black from head to toe as they struggled with loads upon their heads or under their arms.

'*Fellahin*,' said Izzam.

The *fellahin* paused to watch as the group rode past, as doubtless they watched the world and its changes go past, thought Hazzard. *How would they fare as Bonaparte's legions marched by?* An old man with a twisted leg waved a stick over his head, calling angrily at them. It seemed as good an answer as any.

The dust rose. Hazzard covered his face with the long hanging flap of the *shemagh*, tucking it into the side of the *iqal* rope circlet still snug round his head. Beyond the *fellahin* and another loose gathering of huts, heaps of smouldering ashen refuse spread at the side of the track, sending clouds of evil-smelling debris into the air. The pestilential flakes floated, mingling with countless flies, burning the eyes, and they kicked their heels in to gallop away.

Eventually they passed a series of deserted wells, so many stone-rimmed holes in the blowing dust, leafless brush leaning away from the ceaseless wind, stark, dead, the wells dry.

'The Nile in this last year,' explained Masoud, riding up beside Hazzard, 'it did not flood fully, *effendi*.'

'Half a league to our right, following the old well trail,' called Hammer over the wind, 'a man could die. He will not find the water he expects. Only the locals and the *Bedu* know the deepest wells. We go southeast now.'

'How much further?' asked Hazzard.

'Far enough.'

They reached a full well at just past noon, the terrain a bright dazzle, broken by rocky ridges and distant low hills carved by the wind. They dismounted, and Hazzard looked down at the ground. He saw no shadow. The sand was hot beneath his boots, burning through the soles. The Bedouin saw to the well, pulling up the bulging goatskins, and helped them fill their own, then watered the horses beneath twisted thorn and gnarled acacias.

Hazzard's eye settled on a distant escarpment, the horizon blurred into cloud and dancing light. 'What is that?'

Hammer shielded his eyes and looked. 'That is the beginning of Wadi el Natrun,' he said, then, with amusement, 'A great canyon carved in the rocks. How far do you think it is?'

Hazzard looked again across the shimmering heat-haze. 'Half a day away?'

Hammer laughed. 'Nearly twice that. In this barren place we wish not to be so alone. Our minds play tricks, and bring objects closer.'

The horses struggled through soft sand, slowing the pace, tossing their heads with frustration, prancing through the hillocks and low dunes until they reached harder ground on dry flats, lying between rising craggy rock formations which would suddenly end, providing no shelter, only glowing heat. They regained the time with a harsh gallop, glimpses of drab green in the distance urging them on, marking the edge of the fertile Nile fields.

Hazzard had forgotten how quickly light faded at such a latitude – twilight was short-lived, and they were soon dropped gratefully into a cool gloom. They stopped for the night, taking shelter under a stand of palms to the west of Alqam. The Bedouins built a fire, Izzam putting on the customary coffee-pot. Low swordlike shrubs studded the undergrowth, the wind whispering through the trailing fronds of the palms above. Small scorpions emerged from under nearby rocks, scuttling from the flames, and Izzam drove them away with his riding switch.

Alahum made Bedouin bread, baked in coals in the sand, but had with him several small melons for their guests. Hazzard noticed the *Bedu* did not eat any, and asked why.

Masoud translated the reply from Izzam. 'They do not eat much of the wet food, he says, *effendi*, preferring the dry, for the health.' Izzam said something more, spreading a thick layer of paste from a clay jar onto the flat sand-bread. Masoud added, 'All that is wet, he says, is consumed by the dry sands. Hence this good bread is dry. The thirst of the desert, he says, cannot be satisfied.

It will drink a man to nothing, leaving only dust. Better not to attract its appetite.'

Alahum showed Cook his Turkish musket. It was nearly six feet long, its angular trumpet-shaped stock criss-crossed by decorative multi-coloured wood banding. Cook surprised none more than himself when he loaded, took a shot and hit the tip of the desert shrub he was aiming for, even in the dark, to the delight of the Bedouin.

'Right ruddy luck that was,' laughed Cook. 'Should've 'ad a shilling on it.'

'Such things,' laughed Hammer, 'are very important to the *Bedu.*'

Overjoyed with Cook's marksmanship, Izzam tentatively offered him food from his bowl, a mixture of dried mutton and dates, uneasy that Cook might reject it. Cook and Hazzard were foreigners, and might not have the stomach for such things.

Hazzard murmured, 'As with the Mughals, I assume...'

'Quite so,' smiled Hammer.

'Aye. First two fingers and thumb o'the right hand, I remember. And give him a belch for afters.' Cook took a piece and muttered, 'Used to get a slap for that...'

The night spread overhead, a vast dome punctured by brilliant gemstones, clearer even than at sea, thought Hazzard. Hammer settled down next to him by the fire, an unlikely necessity, and they were grateful for it. 'You did well on the ride, both of you, for a pair of sailors.' Smiling, he watched him, then changed his tone, suddenly serious. 'You are familiar with this place.'

Hazzard looked out at the landscape in the moonglow. 'More with Egypt's past. My studies, some years ago.'

'Mm. Cambridge I understand.' Hazzard looked at him and he chuckled. 'We diplomats have our ways, you know. I have read various works of Kircher and ibn Washiyyah in Vienna,' he said with a laugh. 'When I had the time to. It is how I met the wise Masoud here – working at the libraries.' He looked into the deep blue distance. 'This must be like a return home for you, as it was for me. I think we are both a type of explorer.'

Hazzard wondered. 'I wish I were here only to explore.'

Hammer removed his headdress and ran his fingers through his thinning black hair, tired. He was certainly older than Hazzard, but still a vigorous man. 'And both of us understand the motives of the French academics you mentioned.' He sighed. 'I know some of those names, Monge, Marcel, Fourier—' he shook his head '—and especially Conté, he of the balloons. Extraordinary man. We cannot blame them for their excitement.'

Hazzard thought of the *Orient*, the darkness of the Orlop deck, the fuse.

Fortunes of war.

'No. But they're not coming just to explore. They're coming with one of the best armies in Europe.'

Hammer sat up. 'You do realise you must *convince* the Mamluks? This is not England. You must have an argument to support action, not just influence. You must convince the Ottoman Pasha, the Sultan's governor. And you must convince Murad, and Ibrahim, and the *diwan*, and they must convince their *sanjaqs* to send men to fight.'

'Are the Mamluks as divided as they say?'

'Worse. The Ottomans rule Egypt, technically, but the Ottoman Sultan cannot control them. The Mamluks have been here for many centuries, much longer than the Ottomans. Mamluks served under Saladin, remember. They are trained for war from childhood, the most formidable army in the East, and do not take kindly to interference. Insular, in a way, a law unto themselves.'

Hazzard wondered what kind of reception he could expect. 'They'll find their own argument when Bonaparte lands.'

Hammer laughed again. 'Oh, very good. Very oblique, very *Arabic*,' he said. 'They might well listen. Prophets always come out of the desert.'

'I am just a messenger,' said Hazzard, 'with bad news.'

He laughed again. 'So was John the Baptist.'

Alahum offered his bowl to Hazzard and he ate from it, pleasing him. Hammer whispered, 'Have you anything to offer him? A trinket as a keepsake? You will have exchanged then, and become more than strangers.'

Hazzard noticed Alahum's gaze, directed curiously at his Bombay Marine jacket under the *binish* robe, particularly at the brass buttons. Hazzard reached under the *binish* and pulled one of them off. He held it out for him to examine. Alahum looked at it, fascinated, then gestured, *For me?* Hazzard nodded, offering it again.

'Gift,' he said, glancing at Masoud.

Masoud translated for the Bedouin, '*Hadeyya.*'

'It will prove of value,' explained Hammer. 'The Mamluk often decorate their armour with their gold and silver – that way they always have money wherever they go. They become their own treasure chest.'

Alahum took it and showed it to Izzam. They watched the firelight flash on the anchor and chain motif, delighted, a prized token from the exotic foreigners.

On the second day they were hit by the heat, further south and too far west of the Nile to enjoy any cooling breeze, and it pressed down upon them as the sun rose steadily. Hazzard could not believe such a force could come without sound – the roar of a furnace or the booming of a drum – all was silent. In that silence the only sound but for the muffled hoofbeats beneath them was the hiss of every grain of sand as it tumbled, whispering. By eleven he had reached too often for the water in his goatskin.

The dust had embedded itself in every fine line and wrinkle on their faces and set hard in the oils and sweat of their skin. As Hazzard moved his eyes, the coating cracked and he could feel his skin crack painfully with it.

India had not been like this. Here the air was hot and dry, baking Hazzard's throat and lungs, and he knew a few sips of water would not cure it. The robes protected him from the pressure of the sun but the heat was everywhere, in everything. Hazzard looked over at Cook. He had wrapped his face as well, his normally brick-red skin coated in dust, as white as the sand.

The winds picked up and their course brought them curving closer towards the Nile, but the Bedouin had grown quiet and watchful, driving the pace harder and faster south rather than east, off the roads and into the sand, miles from the river in a more direct route to the capital. At one point Izzam held his hand out to the west and swept his arm across the horizon.

Hazzard looked. He had seen it on maps in London with Dr Muhammad, a great depression stretching across to Libya, of salt flats, *wadis* and stone towers, then nothing but a sea of dunes, where distances were measured not in miles or leagues, but in time, *two weeks to here, three weeks to there*. On the map it had looked like the ocean, but he knew its name.

Izzam nodded with a warning and lifted his chin, as if to say, *far out there*. '*Al-Sahraa...*'

Hammer pulled the mask from his mouth, a cloud of dust and sand blowing behind him, his beard powdered with white.

'*Desert, he says*,' he called, '*Sahara.*'

Nearly an hour later, the Bedouin slowed and eventually stopped. Izzam looked back at them and put a hand up to halt.

Cautious, Alahum rode on a short way further, then dismounted. He ran forward to a low dune and peered over the top. Cook and Hazzard pulled in the reins and stopped.

The horizon stretched all around them, white, blinding. Gusts of wind tossed the sand into clouds, the dried bushes nodding, then standing still. Everywhere was silence.

Hazzard peeled the scarf from his face.

'What is it?'

Hammer looked. 'Something.'

The Bedouin watched steadily. From his vantage point Hazzard could see nothing, only the endless scrub and rock-strewn sands. The glare was terrible. Masoud trotted up beside him and pointed.

'There.'

Still Hazzard saw nothing. Masoud pointed again. Cook looked out, his hands cupped round his eyes.

'Where?'

Hazzard stared, his eyes stinging. 'Got it.'

Dots.

'How many?'

They were moving.

A long line of them, the heat distorting the distance like waves on water.

'A caravan perhaps, *effendi*, from Siwa, the oasis, perhaps come through the al-Beheira sands.'

Some dots detached from the line. After several minutes, they grew larger.

Hazzard watched them. Five, and a sixth behind.

'Trouble?'

Izzam pulled his horse round and returned to them, pointing over his shoulder. '*Bedu*,' he said. He was tense, thought Hazzard. '*Mamaliq*.'

The five figures drew nearer, the sixth taking its time. They were on camels. Alahum and Izzam rode out and stopped. They waited.

'Herr Hammer?' asked Hazzard. 'Are we safe?'

'I think so. But let us be careful.'

'Sar'nt.'

'Aye...'

Cook thumbed back the cock on his pistol. The ratchet was loud in the tomb-like stillness. Hazzard cleared his robe from the pommel of his sword. They trotted their horses forward, slowing, drawing closer to Izzam and Alahum.

Hazzard saw there were five men, in voluminous *maghrib* headdresses, their dark faces barely visible, a variety of colours in their robes, their camels hung with heavy knots, tassels and adornments. They were possibly from the same clan or house, thought Hazzard. But the lone man riding behind was something altogether different.

He wore white, and held his riding switch and reins out to the sides, elbows out, showing flowing sleeves of silk, more Turkish than anything Hazzard might have taken for Egyptian. Covering his face was a mask of black silk, hung with fine sparkling chains strung with small gold discs or possibly coins, his chest similarly decorated, a type of armour, Hazzard wondered. On his head was a white turban wrapped tightly about a spiked conical Ottoman steel helm. On each hip hung a curved sword, their jewelled ivory mounts flashing as the camel approached.

It was a medieval Moor, he thought, ridden straight from the 11th-century tales of El Cid.

'This,' murmured Hammer, 'is a Mamluk.'

The Mamluk lowered his hands and the camel slowed to a halt with no evident command. The Bedouin escort called in a demanding tone to Izzam and Alahum, who answered aggressively, pointing back at Hazzard and Cook – they did not address the Mamluk, perhaps out of deference.

'What is the name of the man we need to meet in Cairo?' Hazzard asked Hammer.

'Murad. His proper style is Murad *Bey*. A bey is much like a duke. He commands the elite Mamluk cavalry. This man will know the name.'

Hazzard walked his horse forward. Cook followed. Masoud called, 'Hazar-*effendi*, please…' then trotted after him unhappily. The Mamluk turned his head slowly, noting their approach.

'*As-salamu aleikum*,' said Hazzard, slowly raising his open right hand in salute.

The Mamluk tilted his head, curious. After a moment he touched his fingertips first to his heart, his lips, and then his forehead. The gesture was measured, graceful, elegant. A deep voice replied, '*Wa aleikum as-salam*.'

Izzam and the others argued in terse snatches, the five escorts of the Mamluk riding round Hazzard in a loose circle, then round Cook, looking them up and down, then shouting a command at Izzam and Alahum.

To prove a point, Alahum then held out the brass button Hazzard had given him. One Bedouin rider snatched it from his hand, and the others crowded round it, looking. Then one of them made a comment and the others agreed but Izzam did not, and shouted back at them.

'So,' said Hammer from behind.

'Yes?'

'They demand you and Mr Cook as prisoners,' said Masoud fearfully. 'To ransom to the East India Company at Kosseir on the Red Sea. They are Maaza from the east – they are not Awlad 'Ali. They are on the wrong side of the Nile. Izzam is angry.'

With contempt Izzam said, '*Maaza…*' and spat.

They began shouting again and the Mamluk watched. One of the Maaza prodded Izzam with his riding crop then drew a large dagger, reaching out as if to take him by the arm.

Hazzard spoke. 'Jory.'

Cook fired his pistol. At the sound of the shot, the camels jerked their heads and roared, the riders calling in alarm as the man cried out and dropped from his saddle into the sand, clutching his arm.

'Only winged him,' said Cook. 'Must be the sun.'

'It'll do…' said Hazzard.

Hammer made to move forward. 'I had best speak to them—'

'No,' said Hazzard. He put his hand out to Cook, not taking his eyes from the Mamluk. 'Give me the pistol.'

'What?'

'Gift.'

Cook glanced at him. 'I liked that one.'

'Give me the bloody thing.'

Cook handed it over. Masoud rode up beside Hazzard. The Mamluk's camel reared its head, sensing a challenge, the tassels swinging from its heavy woven and embroidered bridle. Hazzard moved in front of Izzam and Alahum and they bowed their heads, withdrawing. The Mamluk noted this too, with another tilt of the head. Hazzard halted his horse, and bowed.

'I am Hazzard, a captain of the English.' He threw open the long *shemagh* scarf and *binish* robe, revealing the braided scarlet of

133

the Bombay Marine beneath, and the hilt of the Navy sword at his hip. The Bedouin escort fell silent and stared, forgetting their groaning comrade. The Mamluk studied the uniform curiously. Masoud translated.

'These are my guides, under my protection. They meant no offence.' Hazzard held out the empty pistol in the flat of his hand. 'Please accept a gift from a stranger seeking friendship among the Mamluk. A London pistol, made for my king.'

The Mamluk's face was entirely hidden, the vision slit in his black veil only shadow. He listened to Masoud's words, then walked the camel forward slowly. He reached out carefully and took the pistol. He weighed it in his hand, nodding with appreciation, examining the gold inlay. He held it up to the light and Hazzard guessed he was reading the gunmaker's mark, *H.W. Mortimer, London. Gunmaker to His Majesty.*

'We ride to Cairo,' said Hazzard. 'I seek an audience with Murad Bey.'

The Mamluk looked up from the pistol at the sound of the name.

'A large army,' continued Hazzard, 'led by a French Sultan, is coming to invade your lands. This French Sultan is the enemy of the English. I come as a friend to warn Murad Bey and help him defeat the invader.'

The Mamluk listened to Masoud's translation. He considered the words, then looked back at Hazzard. He looked down at the groaning *Bedu* in the sand. If the Mamluk drew either of his two swords Hazzard knew he would have only the briefest of moments to react – out of sight, his left hand gripped his sword-scabbard tight, ready. Again with a tilt of the head, the Mamluk regarded him silently.

After an eternity, he held up the pistol in thanks and bowed his head. He pushed it into a silk sash at his waist beneath his outer robe. He then spoke.

'*Azhab ila al-Shamal.*'

Masoud almost expired with relief. 'He says he goes north…'

The Mamluk waited until Masoud was finished, then added, '*Yumkinoka an taqul annaka sawfa tarkab be'ezn min al-Sheikh Ali Qarim.*'

'But you may say you ride in the name of Sheikh Ali Qarim.'

Hazzard bowed his head. '*Shokran, ya Sheikh Ali, raaka Allah.*' *Thank you, may God protect you.*

The Mamluk betrayed no surprise, but tilted his head again, then bowed in acknowledgement of the blessing. Masoud kept his head bowed and walked his horse backward out of respect. Cook and Hazzard held their ground. The Mamluk noted this as well. He shouted to his Bedouin escort, '*Besoraa, ya majnoun!*'

They gathered the reins of their wounded comrade, now climbed back into his saddle, bent over in pain, and rode back to the distant caravan. The Mamluk looked back at Hazzard. He pointed to the southeast. '*Al-Qahira. Maa as-salamah.*' *Cairo. Farewell.* He struck the camel with his switch, '*Hat-hat-hat,*' and it roared, trotting off.

Cook rode up next to Hazzard. 'I'm beginning to feel sorry for the Frogs comin' up against an army o'that lot.'

–

By mid-afternoon the wind had become a wall of dust and sand. It hit them with full force. The Bedouin shouted to Hammer and waved their hands for everyone to dismount.

'*It is just a short storm,*' called Hammer, '*but it shall be enough!*'

After the incident with the Mamluk, Izzam and Alahum had grown still more solicitous over Hazzard and Cook – they had no doubt the Englishmen had saved their lives from the Maaza. They hurried to take Hazzard's reins and dragged the horses to the ground with their backs to the wind, covering the horses' muzzles and eyes with bands of cloth and huddled in the hollow of their necks and forelegs, all in a tight circle.

Hazzard had to calm his mount, which kept struggling to rise to its feet, whinnying, its forelegs knocking him back, its hooves thrashing. Masoud shouted over the roar of the wind, '*The eyes, the eyes, effendi!*'

Hazzard lay on top of the beast and threw the ends of his *shemagh* headdress over its muzzle and eyes, and it calmed, his forehead on its broad cheek. '*There's a boy… easy…*' But Hazzard was left exposed and could feel the sand peppering his back and arms like hail, into gaps in his robes, his neck, his wrists and hands, and he felt the onset of thirst with the same familiar fear of drowning, *breathe, breathe.*

Izzam dropped next to him and covered him with an arm, propping a corner of his robe up with his switch to form a makeshift shelter. The sand rose slowly around them and they lay still, waiting, Hazzard feeling his head burning.

Within half an hour the storm passed, dying away as abruptly as it had come. Hazzard heard only a whisper, and could see only darkness. He had made a hollow for his mouth in the crook of his arm, the horse's breath loud and strong. The grains ebbed and flowed. The whispering continued, sand in his headdress, in his ears.

He felt Izzam move and pull at his shoulders. They emerged, the horse clamouring to get up, shaking itself. The wind had passed, the sky bright, the sun ravaging in a torrent from overhead, the hillocks in places higher and, in others, lower.

Izzam looked Hazzard over, and they shook the sand from their arms and necks. This time Izzam was not laughing. '*Na? Yais?*' he asked.

Hazzard nodded. '*Al-hamdulillah.*'

The Bedouin smiled. '*Hazar-effendi!*' It was the great joke, they said, that he would be buried in the sand for protecting his horse. Izzam looked about for a moment to orientate himself. Then, presenting it as a reward, he pointed over a low dune. '*Jizah…?*' he asked.

Cook said, 'Hang on, that's what the Frogs banged on about on the *Orient*. Jeeza.'

'*Jizah*,' repeated Izzam. '*Jizah.*' He pointed.

Hazzard looked left of the dune, then right, but could see nothing. He followed Izzam, stumbling through the soft ground, part of him wondering, then hoping, yet not wanting to hope too much for fear of disappointment. *Jizah?*

Cook came after him, the Bedouin calling out, and he reached the top of the rise.

Only a few miles away to their left the green lowlands of the Nile spread wide and long, tall palms mere sprigs marking the roads and fields, intermittent towns leading to the distant sprawl of Cairo. But he saw only the rising ground to the south.

Giza.

Across an undulating sea of low dunes, possibly half a mile in the distance, there rose an unnatural and unmistakable mountain of stone, out of place, thrust upward from the earth, as if in defiance of the desert all around.

Sphinx.

No more than a head, neck and shoulders, a broken face staring – and behind, almost invisible in the light of the sky, the monuments Herodotus claimed had once been at the edge of the sea, and had shone like silver.

Pyramids.

Hazzard stared in silence. He wanted to run to them, to plunge across the sand dunes, floundering his way over the dun waves of ochre *to see, to touch*. But he stayed still, and looked.

A great weight rose from his shoulders, flying from him. There had been so little time those past weeks, so little time to think, searching for Sarah, chasing Bonaparte, pushing him to this dry, empty world. But here, time ended. It had no place, no strength, no meaning. The need, the consuming urge to rush to Cairo fell away. The towns and cities of Man had become mere dust on distant sands. How many cities and kings had risen and fallen beneath the gaze of these stones – what difference could yet another ruler make, forgotten in another thousand years.

At last he understood the power of Fate in such a world – *insha'allah: God willing.*

'*Jizah. Giza.*' Izzam whispered, as if the Sphinx might overhear, even at such a distance, '*Aboul Haoul...*'

Masoud was not as afraid as the Bedouin, but said to Hazzard, 'The statue of the Sphinx is forbidden, and he calls it the "Father of Terrors".'

Staring yet sightless, no more than a pharaonic head, a terrible curse.

'Thought I'd seen it all...' muttered Cook. 'Christ lord above...'

'No Christ here, Sergeant,' said Hammer, gazing out beside him. 'This is the land of Pharaoh.'

'Why are they so frightened?' asked Hazzard.

'Not frightened, Captain,' said Hammer, 'merely aware. Evil spirits dwell among pagan idols.'

Perhaps they did, thought Hazzard.

'Tell them not to fear,' he said. 'Tell them, it is really the "Father of Mysteries". And that God knows even these.'

'Amen,' said Cook.

Masoud translated for the Bedouin. They listened, then Izzam bowed his head.

'*Al-hamdulillah, Hazar al-hakim.*'

Masoud bowed in reply to their compliment. 'They say praise be to God, *effendi*, and call you wise.'

They reached the Nile, passing through the villages and markets clustered along the western bank. The fields had been harvested but green leaf abounded along the swollen banks beneath stands of palms, thickets of alder brush. Teams of oxen and drovers turned the earth in silted mud shallows, goats in large herds cropping more distant stubbled fields. The river had flooded to some extent, but Hazzard could see some stretches of dried-out crops denied their water, even this far south. But compared to the area near Alexandria, it was lush.

'*Nahr al-Nil,*' said Izzam, once again presenting the scene, '*Marhaban fil Qahira.*'

'The Nile,' said Masoud. He bowed his head. 'He says welcome, Hazar-*effendi*. Welcome to Cairo.'

The river was vast. It snaked through the valley, a mirror to the sun beating down from glowing skies, casting the scene in molten bronze. It seemed broader than the Thames to Hazzard's eye, dotted with craft, some being towed upstream, others drifting with the current on lazy sails to the Delta. They followed a road to an antique bridge, crossing to a large river island, upstream of another, larger still. The arches of an aqueduct sheltered beneath tall, thin, tousle-headed date palms, beside a mosque and its towering minarets bright in the sun. Sycamores spread their shade, and the river breeze was refreshing. He began to cool, and could feel the sweat trickling on his skin again. He looked across the span of water to distant walls surrounded by clumps of trees, figures at its gates, at the riverside. He felt like a gawping visitor to ancient Rome. Cook rode up beside him. His mood was more prosaic.

'Eight French divisions coming in,' he muttered. 'They'll blow this place to Kingdom Come.'

–

Very protective of Hazzard, the two Bedouin rode close on the flanks, fending off beggars and traders, crowds of children hoping for food or employment.

More at home than ever, Hammer led the way, finding a path down Cairo's narrow streets. Some were lined with high buildings dotted with colourful awnings, crowding out the light overhead, robed women in doorways, some veiled, some working, sewing, scrubbing – at first looking up with suspicion, then looking away back to their work. Sudden squares opened before them, small tables at shopfronts, groups of men taking coffee, some with the simple *taqeyyah* cap on their heads, others in the Turkish fez, some in fashionable Ottoman linen coats with European cravats, most in kaftans and *galabeyyah*, sitting, smoking. The noise and smells were such an assault on Hazzard's senses after the silence of the sands he felt a dull roar in his ears.

They came to a wide road lined with gardens and terraced stuccoed palaces behind high walls, palm fronds lolling in the stifling heat. It was worse than anything Hazzard had felt so far. Poor, dispossessed *fellahin* and beggars sat in the shade of the walls, motionless with dead eyes, some lying fanned out in a semi-circle, their heads close together for talk, small monitor lizards and geckos scuttling through the dust.

They walked their mounts slowly, Hammer leading them to Ezbekiya Square. They found Mamluk troops everywhere, bare-chested spear-carriers in red turbans and sleeveless jerkins, gathered by their sheikhs, and on the perimeters barefoot youths with shaven heads and bronze armbands carrying bucklers and swords, packs, or tending mules braying in the heat.

'Slaves,' said Masoud. 'The Mamluk is a slave-warrior, *effendi*, from Turkey and the Russias. They have been in Egypt for many centuries. Paid soldiers for lords and princes. They rule the land but, traditionally, are still born as slaves to their sheikh. They too acquire slaves as they rise, earning their freedom only in battle. Do not look upon them, Hazar-*effendi*, it is dangerous.' Fierce black eyes followed their passage, but Hazzard accepted Masoud's good counsel.

Hammer sent Izzam ahead to give notice of their arrival – for identification Hammer had given him a note stamped with the seal of the Viennese Consul. By the time they reached the gates of Al-Elbe, Izzam was waiting.

The square was unlike anything Hazzard had seen in Europe or India: it was gargantuan, the size of a royal London park. More of an oblong, flat sections of lawn were cross-hatched by a grid of roadways leading to vast sandstone buildings of three and four storeys high, many with mature trees and gardens on terraces and balconies on upper levels, overhanging tall facades crowded with Gothic-style arches more than twenty feet in height. These in turn were dwarfed by the broad domes and minarets of mosques, which pierced the soft gold of the sky.

The square was packed with Mamluk forces. Troops in gowns and turbans assembled on the roads, horses prancing in review before pavilions and Byzantine canopies giving shade to amirs and sheikhs, their horse-tail standards and banners fluttering overhead.

Hammer slowed as they were met by a squad of moustachioed Mamluk guardsmen, easily the height of grenadiers, in bright red ballooning trousers and turbans. They marched ahead of them as escort through one of the tall arches, its vaulted ceiling bright with ceramic tile. Everywhere, eyes followed them. Their hoofbeats struck stone cobbles as they entered a paved yard, clattering, echoing, a spraying fountain in the centre. Hazzard saw a number of women in decorative gowns and shawls look down from gardens above, fruit vines and trees hanging from balconies and tall windows.

By the fountain was a group of men, some Mamluk cavalry, others in the flowing robes of noble rank. They parted as Hazzard and Hammer approached.

'Be careful what you say and say it through me, not Masoud,' said Hammer. 'My foreign accent allows me some leniency if our words cause affront. Murad has been a statesman and general here for some twenty years and is the most feared warrior in the East, his name known beyond Acre and Constantinople. With one stroke of his sword, it is said, he can decapitate an ox.'

They dismounted but went no further. A ferocious figure in black turban and dark robes stormed out to them, a crumpled note in his hand, a curved sword swinging at his side. He was the size of Cook, with broad moustaches and a thick beard beneath a large hooked nose. He roared across the compound in outrage. '*Hammar-effendi!*'

Hammer whispered, 'Murad.' He bowed and said aloud, '*Assalamu aleikum ya Murad Bey.*'

Murad fairly snapped back, '*Wa aleikum as-salam.*' He thrust a note into Hammer's hand. It was in both Arabic and German. It came from the offices of the Viennese Consul, Carlo Rosetti, Hammer's immediate superior.

Hammer read it.

He handed it to Hazzard with a sad bow of the head. 'I am sorry.'

It was a note relayed from a Turkish merchantman recently docked in Rosetta. It was short and to the point: *French ships sighted. Landing imminent Alexandria.*

Hazzard glanced at Cook. 'We're too late.'

Napoleon Bonaparte had arrived.

Strike

The call to prayer of the *muezzin* drifted from the minarets of the mosques across the palms and rooftops of Alexandria. Some continued to work in the waterways of the port and on the quay-sides, some knee-deep along the waterfront, loading the barges and large twin-masted *djerms*, while others heeded the call.

A cry went up, more strident than the *muezzin*. Some noticed an unnaturally heavy swell on the water; boats rocked and bumped each other, their sloping yards swinging. Weather-beaten faces looked out to sea. They stared, some unable to comprehend what they saw. The foreman of the dock turned and ran. Everyone began to run. The women on the nets by the grain jars, the fishermen, the traders, all began to run, the respectable men of town also began to run, their *reddah* robes tripping them up in their flight, old men, fat men, complacent men now in fear, some praying, some crying out for *Nelsoun Amir*.

'*Al-Bahr, al-bahr!*' *The sea, the sea!*

The Turkish troops at the dockside tried to restore order but their labourers stampeded. An elderly *imam* called for calm but was ignored, his hand taken by a Coptic curate and led to safety, beggars and cripples in tow, mouthing prayers to God – for the sea had become as land, and had come upon them, they said, and a thousand masts darkened the heavens, their banners blaspheming the skies with warlike pride.

The French Sultan, of whom Al-Sayyid Muhammad Kurayyim had been warned not days earlier, had come.

-

Sarah Chapel moved from the gathering of officers towards the portside taffrail at the lofty stern of *Orient*, towering high over the rushing water below. She looked out at the Promised Land.

Her eye sought anything familiar, much as Hazzard had done before her, but everything that greeted her eye was frightening. A foreign domed mosque glowed in the insufferable heat. Behind ochre fortresses of alien design, men and women in robes were running, everyone running, the harbour filled with Levantine ships and riverboats, their crews frantic, trying to make sail, blocking the channels.

Not far away, further along the rail, Bonaparte stood with his eyeglass raised, scanning the harbours, beside him Casabianca, Brueys, and several of his generals.

Admiral Brueys lowered his telescope and spoke, but she could hear little for certain, the wind and creaking of the stays drowning his words. '*I must press you again to let us land at Aboukir...*'

Sarah could hear no more. Bonaparte's stepson, Eugène, burst forward into her secret world, gripping the rail. '*There it is!*' called one of the junior officers beside him. '*The Pillar of Pompey!*' She looked at him and he smiled, thrilled. 'Will it not be magnificent, *Mademoiselle* Isabelle? Are you not simply overcome, as I?'

'Yes, Eugène,' cried Sarah, her heart collapsing within. 'Magnificent...!'

Jeanne and the *comtesse* joined her, the old lady taking her hand. 'It is so exciting, General,' cried the *comtesse* with enthusiasm, her trembling grip tightening, a secret indication of her fears. Generals Caffarelli and Kléber moved closer, the hard-faced Swiss on his peg-leg with the tall, dominating Alsatian.

'Now comes the more difficult part of it all, *madame*,' Caffarelli said with a tight smile.

'I disagree, Maximilien,' said Kléber. 'That voyage was utterly dreadful. This should be easy.' They laughed. 'Though you have brightened the journey, *mesdames*.'

The *comtesse* slipped her arms around the girls' waists and held them both close. 'It has happened,' said Sarah.

'Yes,' the *comtesse* whispered, 'and you must both head for safety to Rosetta with the *savants*, or the French Consul.'

'How, *madame*?' asked Jeanne. 'They said we all go to Cairo.'

'Isabelle knows how.'

Sarah looked at her. 'And you, *madame*?'

'I will be safe with Bonaparte's staff and *Madame* Verdier, but he must not suspect you, my dear, *must* not. You must go, and protect Jeanne.'

'I do not need protecting,' said Jeanne. 'But I can protect *her*.'

'Yes.' The *comtesse* sounded certain and hugged Sarah, whispering in her ear, '*If he is anywhere, my dear, he will be here, close to you. I know this much.*'

Sarah watched the generals file down the stairs to confer, their grand uniforms a blaze of colour and braid, their swords clanking. She closed her eyes tight and wished.

William – please… live.

–

They assembled in Bonaparte's stateroom. A young lieutenant appeared at the door, followed soon after by Derrien and a portly man in civilian dress, red-nosed with sunburn and agog at his surroundings, sweating and breathless from his journey.

'Consul Magallon, General,' announced Derrien. 'Arrived from the port.'

Since Hazzard's disappearance Derrien had struggled to maintain Bonaparte's confidence. To some extent he had succeeded, though not to his satisfaction. His mission of rehabilitation had been to alight at Alexandria and fetch the man who had called down the hellfire of France upon this far corner of the Mediterranean, Citizen Consul Magallon. It had been the work of a matter of minutes, as Magallon and several of his plump associates had been waiting stoutly at the quayside – with packed valises, as if ready for a short cruise.

Magallon overflowed with pride and took Admiral Brueys' hand effusively. '*Mon général – quel honneur.* I – I cannot believe that you are arrived!'

Someone coughed, '*Neither can we...*' Casabianca indicated Bonaparte nearby, who was not amused. Magallon repeated his greetings, with a deeper bow of apology. Bonaparte turned away to his maps.

'But we are here, Citizen. Owing to your letter, pleading for action.' It was not entirely true, but doubtless served Bonaparte's purpose to keep the man on his best behaviour.

Magallon was confused. '*Pardon, Général...?* My letter, you say?' he replied, then nodded, as if suddenly remembering. 'Ah yes, yes, of course, the, er, letter...'

Brueys and Casabianca looked away. Another rolled his eyes, '*Bon dieu...*'

'You did not warn us that we would be unable to dock in Alexandria,' said a disgruntled Lt Marais.

The overfed diplomat swallowed hard, and his sweat-soaked collar bobbed. 'N-no... I should think it is too shallow for the great ships... is-is that... correct?'

'So we have discovered, Citizen,' said Brueys. 'To our cost.'

'What news of Nelson?' asked Bonaparte.

Magallon looked uncertainly at Derrien, who answered for him. 'Nelson departed here two days ago and headed north, General. A Turkish captain has confirmed this.'

'Saw it myself,' said Magallon, 'Kurayyim sent him away, pish-tish!' He laughed but no one joined in.

'Yes,' continued Derrien. 'The English squadron might return.'

'How many ships?' asked Casabianca, alarmed.

'A mere half-dozen,' shrugged Magallon, 'I think...'

'Thirteen,' corrected Derrien. 'No frigates, each one a 74-gun ship of the line of battle, from their Mediterranean Fleet I should think.'

Brueys and Casabianca exchanged glances – small frigates aside, it matched their own battle-fleet almost ship for ship. Casabianca took a breath.

Bonaparte passed an eye over his map. 'Then we have little time to spare…' He looked to Magallon. 'What of the country between here and Cairo?' asked Bonaparte. 'Or am I to encounter Englishmen lurking there as well?'

Magallon's eyes flitted from one face to the next but none helped him. 'I, well, that is, the English East India people call at the Red Sea coast from time to time… Kosseir, far, very far from Cairo, across the, er, eastern desert…' He shrugged hopelessly. 'I know mostly of commercial activity at the Delta ports, General…'

Kléber boomed out at him, 'You mean you know *nothing* of the country between here and Cairo? What of the wells? What of water for the *forty thousand men* we have brought at your behest, you gibbering buffoon!'

'There are wells, yes, some, gentlemen, er, citizens, but the Nile, last year, it did not flood fully, and so far they may not be, er… full. But no, I do not *know* the countryside,' he cleared his throat, 'not terribly well, really…'

'*Putain de la merde…*'

Someone banged his fist against a wall and another cursed, but Magallon's failings were forgotten when they heard a call on deck.

There was a clatter on the stairs outside and an urgent knocking at the door. One of the young ensigns reported to Casabianca. '*Capitaine*, unidentified man of war sighted one league to stern. It could be the English.'

—

High at the taffrail of the poopdeck Bonaparte and Brueys peered astern through their glasses, the staff ranged behind doing likewise. Bonaparte's secretary Bourrienne joined him, searching through the fleet's labyrinth of masts and yards swinging in their view, wakes streaming into the distance. At last, they saw a distant flash of white canvas against the brilliant blue of the sky: a warship, giving chase under full sail.

Lt Marais had not waited but climbed with another into the mizzen tops far above, and called down, '*She is a ship of the third or fourth rank.*'

'Support vessels?' called Casabianca.

'*Non, Capitaine.*' He paused then shouted louder, '*Second sail dead astern!*'

'Another ship...' Bonaparte muttered under his breath to Bourrienne, 'Fortune will not abandon me now, Louis... Five days – *five days*... It is *all* I need.'

'We can still do it, *Général*. They are far off—'

Casabianca called out, '*Beat to quarters! Signals officer – compliments to the Tonnant and the Guillaume Tell: prepare to brace about!*' He looked to Bonaparte. 'General, we can come about and engage with all guns if you wish, or send in the rearguard under Admiral Villeneuve.'

'Wait for confirmation,' husked Bonaparte, staring through the telescope, trying to see if all were lost. Jullien and Junot looked to their commander, but Bonaparte had paled.

Bourrienne peered through his eyeglass and glanced at him. 'She is so small. It is a frigate – I would swear it is...'

'If he has a dozen ships...' murmured Bonaparte, calculating speed, odds, sea-room. 'Nelson could cut us into three divisions...'

'But what can so few English captains do to so many...?' asked Jullien.

Bonaparte watched the sea, then glanced at Bourrienne. 'They will be like the fox, Thomas, and forget they cannot consume us all – yet kill everything in sight.'

–

Down below, the stairs and ladders rang with boots as the troops assembled in their landing companies, the drums beating, sergeants roaring for platoons and sections to form up, *aux armes, sergents-chefs*! Soldiers and their packs colliding with the middle- and lower-deck gunners and powder-monkeys as they hurried to their stations, *Eh, passez-là stupide!* the threat passed from bow to stern: *Anglais.*

Nelson.

Sarah stuffed her shifts and dresses into the trunk she shared with Jeanne – if Nelson did come upon them they would get off, she did not care how, *jump like William*, and make her way to the British – with Jeanne, for her own good, whether she liked it or not.

The door opened and a figure forced his way inside from the chaos in the passage. It was Derrien.

'*You,*' she gasped. 'What is the meaning of this?'

Derrien spoke in urgent whispers. She had never seen him like this before. 'We have no time for games, *mademoiselle,*' he said, closing the door with a click. 'Or should I say, *Miss,*' he added, in English.

Sarah looked back at him, her face betraying nothing, out of old habit, but it shook her.

'*Comprends pas,*' she said blankly. *I do not understand.*

'Yes, you do,' he replied, again in English. 'You have been very clever to have come so far but it is *over,* and you are discovered and in great danger.'

'Danger? How?' she gasped, insisting on French. 'From *you of course—*'

'From *me?*' he retorted with some anger. 'I have been *protecting* you these three weeks past, have you not *seen?* If the general were to learn the truth he would *destroy* you, *mademoiselle.*'

'You *lie.*'

The calls and cries from outside, above and below somehow adding to his pressure, Derrien clenched his eyes shut, in frustration, desperation, she could not tell, and he held a fist close to her, biting back his own violence. 'Do *not,*' he hissed, 'do *not* say such things to me. Do not *pretend* so with me, *mademoiselle,* with Nelson coming upon us, this great ship perhaps to become our last chance. You met Hazzard in the Orlop deck, your interlined despatches with invisible inks, I *know* all of this, *do you hear me—*'

'*No, no, please…*'

'You *do not understand*. You do not *see*,' he rasped. 'The general is *not* in command here, Isabelle, it is I. *I was sent to watch him.* Out here,' he grated, '*I am the Republic.*'

She gasped, her hands at her throat, '*Please…*'

Derrien stopped. He was shaking her, his hand round the back of her neck, pressing her tight against the wall. He relaxed the tension in his grip, shocked at his strength, and she looked up at him, tears welling, the strain too much. He watched as she wept, seeing her submission, her fear. He released her, righted her, smoothed her dress, her gaunt doll's face smeared with tears, and he looked away, confused by ambivalent desires. 'How could they,' he muttered bitterly, 'how could they send one such as you. Stay here,' he said in a low voice, 'in the cabin, while the troops disembark. Until we return to Alexandria. I will come for you, and take you to… to safety. To Rosetta.' She looked up at him as he dried her tears. 'It will be the most comfortable for you.' His eyes looked away for a moment, into a dark past. 'This is my world,' he said, 'Not yours.'

He slid back the bolt and opened the door, less circumspect, uncaring who saw him now, drawing his pistol, his teeth bared, '*Out of my way, you damnable fools!*' and moved into the bustle of the decks.

Sarah slammed the door behind him and wiped her face, and banged the small stiletto she had kept hidden in her sleeve into the plank wall in anger. She caught her breath. She had come *that* close to using it, and it made her feel ill. Tears had served her well before, as they had served to confuse and distract here as well – yet still he seemed concerned for her. Unless he too were playing the treacherous spy as well.

She looked at the trunk and the clothes still to be packed, and hurried, uncertain which of them had been deceiving the other better. Whatever the answer, the tears and the doll's face were gone, and, she decided, she would get off the *Orient*, come what may.

A shout went up from the tops and Marais called down to Brueys, 'Admiral – confirmed! It is the *Justice*! She is French!'

Brueys raised his eyeglass. 'She was left behind, to scout.'

Casabianca moved up beside him. 'She must have followed from Valletta—'

The second ship disappeared off to the north, a merchantman, a Portuguese, someone called, and there was a cheer: Nelson was not yet at their throats. The fox was not yet among them.

Bonaparte released his fingers from the rail and Bourrienne lowered his eyeglass with a relieved smile. 'I said so, did I not? Small ship? You see?'

Bonaparte took a breath and they almost laughed. 'Yes, Louis, shall I appoint you Grand Admiral I wonder…'

Brueys approached. 'General, we shall be upon Marabout within the hour. Perhaps.' He hesitated before apologising but bowed his head, acknowledging the sword of Damocles which had nearly fallen upon them. 'As you say, we should get the troops off the ships as soon as possible. We shall signal the captains to prepare for disembarkation, as you commanded, at Marabout, not Aboukir.'

Bonaparte said nothing, but stalked away to his cabin, leaving the effluent wonders of stinking Alexandria far behind, Caesar and Pompey's Pillar all but forgotten in the demands of the day and how close they had come to utter annihilation.

—

The good news did nothing to quell the pandemonium aboard *Orient*. When they reached Marabout further along the coast, Sarah and Jeanne fought their way up the steps with the troops, their trunk bouncing, clutched tight between them. None paid them any attention, except to lift Jeanne over a man's head and up the last step to the deck, *Voilà, ma petite*, the trunk following after with cheers and laughter.

The captain's gig and nearly a dozen small boats had been swung outboard, several of them brought level with both the portside and starboard rails, some already down in the water, troops descending rope ladders, the sea pitching them in all directions. Company commanders and sergeants tried to maintain the sequence of boarding, *First and second company first battalion, stand ready! Second company will wait below! Clear the decks and get back down there, damn you!* Other transport ships in the fleet charged past, making for the coast, their boats splashing onto the surface, men rowing at once for the shore. The invasion had begun.

Sarah took Jeanne's hand. 'Quickly… *dépêche-toi…*' They struggled against the stream of soldiers, battling their way from the main gundeck up to the quarterdeck gangway. There were already several groups of civilians, the *commissaire* staff, *savants*, she guessed, some of them quite young, among them Berthollet, arranging the few women in a boat, looking away as they cocked their legs and skirts over the rails, *but of course, madame, just a short journey to the capital, we are sure*, a pleasure-trip – perhaps some believed him as they laughed.

The *comtesse* was nowhere in sight, and Sarah was pleased – she had not wanted to defy her wishes to go to Rosetta, but every moment Sarah stayed aboard near Derrien jeopardised the old lady's position, and her own life – of this she was certain. She ran to a boat and without waiting for permission threw in their small trunk.

'*Mademoiselle?*' An officer, a lieutenant of the 86th *demi*, tried to stop her. 'You will have to wait perhaps some time as the troops make preparations ashore to receive you…'

'*Très bien,*' she said, trying to sound as thrilled as the others. 'It is so exciting!' But she did not convince even herself, and she could see by the looks on many faces that she was not alone. Some soldiers, some civilians, women from the canteen, one sitting on a cavalry sergeant's lap as he held her tight, *Did I not say, eh, my wife, eh? With me you shall see the world!* Several academics, clutching bags on their knees, some older, some younger, sat holding onto their hats, clearly worried this would not be as simple a matter as the cavalry sergeant had claimed: *Ehh, m'sieur le professeur, stick with me, hein! Sergent François never falls off his mount!* He roared with laughter and slapped his wife's behind, but she turned and slapped him back hard, certainly lightening the mood for everyone. Sarah saw a place beside Charlotte Dutoit and pushed Jeanne inside.

'There, get in...'

'I'm not sitting with that simpering bitch—'

'Oh *mon dieu*, Jeanne, push her *over* then!'

She climbed in after, then heard a call far behind.

'*Isabelle!*'

It was Derrien, hemmed in by troops, calling out over the rail, '*Isabelle! Non! Arrêtez!*' He and Masson pushed their way through the men all along the quarterdeck gangway, knocking some aside, cursing them, 'Out of the way! *Vous idiots! Vous crétins!*' An anonymous hand shoved him and he stumbled, but leapt to his feet and whipped out his screw-barrelled pistol, Masson smashing the miscreant soldier in the face, then trying for a second time, his comrades pulling the bloodied man back, '*Non non non, pardon! A joke, pardon, m'sieur!*'

Derrien reached the rail too late. Sarah and Jeanne were lowered away, dropping in a series of sickening swings and lurches, until they smacked into the water, rocking violently. Derrien pulled himself along the rail, calling her name, *Isabelle! Isabelle!* Some of the nearby soldiers pointing at him, laughing. But moments later he threw himself at the ratlines and shrouds, his face twisting into a mask of incoherent rage as he shook the stays, *Isabelle! Isabelle...* an impotent, caged beast, the soldiers and officers backing away, no longer laughing.

Sarah shivered and Jeanne wrapped herself tight against her. The Dutoit girl opened a lace parasol over her shoulder, but her hands were shaking, and she pushed in on the other side of Sarah and they huddled together beneath its meagre shelter. '*Madame* Verdier goes with her husband the general, they say,' said Sarah, to distract them, to distract herself. 'Even into battle...'

Jeanne nodded. 'Maybe she takes a horse and not a boat then.'

The oarsmen pulled away fast, and *Orient* slowly retreated from Sarah's world, the vast bows rising up above them, great and terrible as if to crush them, then receding. All around them were jolly-boats, gigs and cutters, all racing for the shore. The boat heaved and Sarah lurched against Jeanne, the wind and the swell rising, the waves slapping the sides, the oarsmen before them straining forward and hauling back, calling the time, *'Tirez!'* Heave!

The clouds gathered overhead and the wind picked up, drowning the rhythmic calls of the soldiers, some paddling with the stocks of their muskets, *Un deux, un deux!* They passed other warships disgorging men on lines, some falling into the water, their arms waving as others pulled them in, some boats charging out immediately, wasting no time.

Eighteen and nineteen begin your sally and enter the fleet lines…!

Calls drifted across the sea, a cheer, and Sarah saw they were in the middle of the second wave of troops, the beach a tilting line of surf and breaking spray ahead, palms being lashed by the wind, dunes, scrub and tussocks of grass behind.

'Vive la Spartiate!' cried someone and oarsmen cheered, a boat passing. *Sergent-chef-major* Achille Caron hung over the side, the prow crashing into the battering waves as the *Alpha-Oméga* veterans of the 75th Invincibles rowed furiously with the oarsmen. *'Pull, pull for the shore, enfants!'*

'Putain!' called Rossy, *'Chef! We should be relaxing under the palm trees! I thought we were the elite!'*

Caron nodded, cramming his cocked hat tighter on his head. *'We are! That is why we have such comfortable seats, mon garçon!'*

'I am angry with this wind!' shouted the giant Pigalle, and moved forward in the heaving boat. He shoved two of the oarsmen away, taking both their oars, roaring as he pulled, battling the depths, the boat surging forward. *'I like not this holiday!'* The soldiers cheering: *Vive le Pig, vive le Pig!*

They rose on peaks and smashed into troughs, rowing for their lives, *Plus vite, enfants! Plus vite – faster –* and soon they were racing against the swell, against the coming storm, boats colliding and paddles and oars entangling, crushing hands, one boat capsizing.

The shore and the rocks danced before their eyes in a nauseating rhythm, the sky darkening still further and the wind whipping the waves into bursting spray. Caron wiped the spume from his soaking face and saw Sarah, her boat rising and falling, Jeanne hanging on to the gunwale, Charlotte Dutoit screaming in fright.

'*Putain*... madness, women in the line of battle...' Caron waved to their coxswain. '*Follow our line! Follow the wake!*'

Sarah grabbed at the shoulder of the nearest officer. '*Can you follow him?*'

He shouted back, '*Nom du dieu! We do what we can! Now sit still, mademoiselle!*'

She fell back with Jeanne, every wave lifting them and dropping them as deadweights to the hard boards. One of the *savants* vomited, retching over the side, Charlotte Dutoit howling again, the cavalry sergeant's wife holding her hand, *Hang on dearie, nothing can kill my stupid husband, believe me! I've tried!* She dropped her small valise and parasol into the waves, clinging to *Madame* François. Sarah held onto Jeanne, watching Caron, Caron looking back to them, his arm held high, giving her strength.

As close as they came to landing, the sea threw them back, time and again. '*Egypt does not want us, Chef!*' called one of Caron's men, until the boat shuddered and Caron fell against Rossy's sodden *boudin* bedroll on his pack as they scraped across submerged rocks with a splintering screech, panicked calls rising up, *Rocks, the rocks!* Although grounded, they were still forty metres out. Another boat hailed them.

'*Come to us! We can take you in!*'

Caron waved his bonnet at them. '*Away! Get away! Rocks!*' The boat began to grind and splinter underfoot, and he roared into the boat, '*Out! Out, garçons, and swim! Swim for your lives!*'

The giant Pigalle picked up Caron, put him on his back and stepped out into the water, a Titan oblivious to Poseidon's wrath, his feet finding firm ground.

'*I am standing on Egypt!*' bellowed Pigalle. '*Egypt is mine! For where I plant my boot, there shall I not be moved!*'

There were cheers from other boats, *Vive le Pig, vive le Pig*, and they rallied to him as he strode into the sea cutting a wake through the waves, the sea unable to pull him down, Caron high on his shoulders, the water rising up to Pigalle's waist, then his chest, then his chin, the shoreline rising and dipping with shallows and deeps. Caron launched himself forward, the other Alphas close behind, using their packs as floats until their boots felt the shingle, and they threw themselves ashore, retching, coughing, heaving up the sea. Caron saw the trailing boat, the women at the bows, and he waved to them. '*Come! Come!*'

Sarah held on to Jeanne. '*Ready!*'

'*I do not go if you do not go, Belle!*'

'*Then we go!*'

The boat leapt, the oarsmen falling back, oars thrashing in mid-air, men toppling out to starboard and calling, *M'aidez! Help!* They grounded and tipped, the swell crashing onto the occupants, Sarah and Jeanne flying into the water. The Alphas dived back into the sea to get them, Caron striking out for Sarah and Jeanne, an officer from the 85th helping him, *Pull them in, mon ami!*

Caron gasped, his long woollen coat dragging him down, soaking, a lead weight – then Sarah's hands wrapped round him and he pulled, getting to his feet, Rossy and Pigalle in the gloom, hauling in the women and the officer from the 85th half-drowned already. At last Caron fell back to the beach, his charges beside him. They lay spread-eagled in the surf, exhausted, gasping.

'You live,' he said to Sarah and she nodded, grateful.

'*Merci, papa...*'

She fell into his arms and he held her, then she pulled away, '*Jeanne*—' Their long skirts spread on the surf in a cloud of silk. Caron pulled them both away from the water's edge and sat a moment, Jeanne's head cradled in his lap.

'*Nom d'un nom...* she is younger than my youngest...' He shook his head sadly. 'What fool led you to this place, *ma fille...?*'

She looked at him. 'I could not say...' Sarah thought of poor Charlotte Dutoit, and wondered if she had survived the landing.

Men wandered everywhere, lost, looking for their NCOs – artillerymen with no guns, cavalrymen with no horses. Most were weak from the voyage, some supported by their fellows, some on their knees, vomiting, others lying or sitting stunned, staring out at the darkening water and the ships and the illusory safety they had left behind. Some had rowed over six miles, the winds still blowing.

Sarah, Jeanne and Caron peered through the eerie stormlight, the surf bright white, the skies scudding grey, then suddenly filled with luminous cloud. Somewhere inland they heard shots and a scream, then no more, a voice calling '*Bedouin...*' and a company came running past, a sergeant pointing and calling, '*There! There! The trees!*'

Caron took stock and gathered the nearest survivors with Sarah and the others, setting any troops he could find on one knee, facing the distant treeline and undergrowth, muskets ready as more and more stumbled ashore. He shook his head, muttering, '*What a shambles...*'

They heard Bonaparte shouting orders to *get the artillery ashore now*, with the horses *now*, or the officers responsible could swim back to Toulon for replacements. '*Am I to be foiled even now by your incompetence!*'

The sodden figures of Rossy and Pigalle joined them, then Antonnais and St Michel, used to the chaos of the army, from fighting in France, fighting on the Rhine, in Italy, everywhere and anywhere: Egypt seemed no different. They said nothing. Rossy scratched at his unshaven neck then chipped a salute to Sarah. They squatted together, for mutual protection.

'Some Bedouin came in, *Chef*,' said Rossy, wriggling a finger in his ear to get the water out. 'Captured a few officers with some of the women.' He inspected his cartridge-pouch for leaks, and held up a soggy bag of powder, shaking his head, laughing to himself, then threw it down. 'No more than five thousand men,

Chef, he murmured, 'at most. I hope the enemy are tiny little fellows who cannot shoot.'

'Everyone is tiny to me,' rumbled Pigalle.

'This is true, *mon ami,*' admitted Rossy.

Caron saw Caffarelli stumping along, his peg-leg sinking into the sand with every step. '*Putain.* Who has wine?' said Caron. 'It shall be my last in this place of deserts and demons…'

A goatskin was passed and Rossy handed it to him. They could all hear Bonaparte's aide, Colonel Junot, '*It is very simple,*' called Junot to the army, his words battling the howling wind, '*if we want to eat, if we want to drink, there is plenty awaiting us — in Alexandria! They will not be prepared! We march with our general! This is the desert! We march, or we die!*'

Caron held out the skin to Sarah and she drank, and handed it on to Jeanne. Caron looked around at the darkening beach. 'Let us go before the *Bedu* come back…' He looked out at the dazed men and women, the capsized boats, the palms thrashing in the wind, then took a swig and spat. It was water, not wine, and there was sand in it.

'*Putain,*' he muttered. 'Welcome to Egypt.'

—

Abu Bakr Pasha sat in voluminous robes, puffed hose and ballooned turban among cushions of fine cool cotton. As the ruling Ottoman governor, he was the representative of the sultan in Constantinople. Therefore, the Mamluk beys, amirs and sheikhs knew he was not to be trusted by the parliament of the *diwan* — for the sultan did not look fondly upon the Mamluk. However, Abu Bakr was a very practical man, and knew how to be guided.

All around him, on varying levels before the arched and pillared windows, sat the *diwan* assembly, called together at last to face the 'French emergency'. All of the Mamluk beys of Cairo had come, along with *imams* and *ulema* scholars, as well as the elderly Sheikh Abd'allah al-Charkawi of Cairo's revered Al-Azhar

Mosque. Hot breezes wafted through diaphanous curtains, the streets of Cairo below as clamorous as ever.

'The only reason the Frenchmen can have landed,' raged Murad at Abu Bakr Pasha, 'is because *you* and the *sultan* allowed them to!'

'This is not so,' retorted Abu Bakr indignantly. 'Besides,' he said, in that lofty tone favoured at the court in Constantinople, 'how can we know for certain they have landed? Could all be nonsense and tittle-tattle.'

Murad shook a fistful of despatches at him. 'Of course we know! As they were predicted so to do by the Englishmen!' He looked about the chamber furiously. 'We have waited for resolution for *hours* and still we sit and *argue* like old *women*.'

'Not so,' replied Abu Bakr, 'we have acted.'

Murad roared again, for he knew the pasha's 'action' had been to imprison a number of Europeans, including the Austrian Consul Rosetti, who had informed them of the imminent landing. He had also closed the European shops and cafes. 'Acted! I have called the cavalry and my *sanjaqs* from across the country! What have *you* done?'

'I have taken potentially seditious prisoners from the streets,' said Abu Bakr proudly.

'*Execute them!*'

'*Ransom them!*'

The High *Sheikh al-Balad*, Ibrahim Bey, sat some distance from the venerable Al-Charkawi, but inclined his head in his direction as if in deference – most knew it was a sham, a cover for his ceaseless feud with Murad. 'Murad the great warrior seeks to sharpen his sword at the first sign of conflict, without seeking peace...'

'Peace! You? What else must I do?' demanded Murad. 'Ignore a foreign army come to invade?' He rubbed his fingers together at him. 'And consider how to fill my *purse*?'

'That is not an argument,' replied Ibrahim carefully.

'I need no *argument*.' Murad held up his powerful hands. 'I will crush the life out of any infidel who would sully the land of Islam!'

His pale skin wrinkling across his elderly white face, Al-Charkawi listened, then raised a shaking hand. 'That,' he said quietly, '*is* an argument.'

Abu Bakr nodded. 'So it is. Do you say they come on crusade again? If so, our sacred duty is clear.'

Sheikh Al-Jabarti of the Al-Azhar replied to the ancient Al-Charkawi, 'According to their own hand they are Unbelievers, Sheikh Abd'allah. But neither are they Christian.' He held up a document for all to see. It was Bonaparte's proclamation, printed in the holds of the *Orient*.

Murad watched him from the centre of the floor. 'Well? What do you mean? How?'

Al-Jabarti bowed his head first to the venerable Al-Charkawi and then to the pasha. 'My lords. We of the mosque are disturbed by this, this miserable notice, which the French have distributed among the people. It declares them to be better Muslims than we, whom they call Mamluk, rather than Egyptian. Thus they seek to divide us.' He read from the page in his hands, 'It is a most peculiar proclamation: "*I am come to restore your rights, punish your usurpers, and raise the true worship of Muhammad. Tell them that I venerate, more than do the Mamelukes, God, His Prophet, and the Quran. Tell them that all men are equal in the sight of God...*" And here,' he continued, 'they then disown their Christian heritage: "*O, ye Qadis, Sheikhs and Imams; O ye Shurbajiyyah, and men of circumstance, tell your nation that the French are also faithful Muslims, and in confirmation of this invaded Rome and there they destroyed the Papal See, which was always exhorting the Christians to make war with Islam*"...'

Murad called out, 'How can this be? They are Christian Europeans.'

'Yet here they deposed the Pope-Sultan, their holy father...' said Al-Charkawi equably. 'What must this mean?'

'Yes,' continued Al-Jabarti. 'They do not understand that in casting down the Pope-Sultan they are not devout at all. They believe this makes them liberators of men's souls, rather than destroyers. By this note, despite its poor and ambiguous grammar, we see that they are godless heathen materialists, who do not believe in the Hereafter or Resurrection, neither that the world was created by God, but by their flimsy science, and irrelevant aspects of the moon.' There was derisive laughter. 'They do not follow the God of Abraham,' he concluded, 'They are therefore beyond God's law and must be resisted.'

Many of the *imams* and *ulemas* bowed as he sat, *God be praised*, and discussion rippled among the group. A *sanjaq* of Amir Mustafa al-Bakri spoke.

'The sheikh of the Al-Azhar is correct. A rider brought us one of these *firman* proclamations. These godless French sent men to the docks of Alexandria before moving west to land, and gave copies into the hands of the common folk, *fellahin* and such low men. The Awlad 'Ali and others have said they landed at Marabout in a bad gale. *Insha'allah* they get no further, for the Awlad 'Ali will attack them.'

'But it must be remembered,' continued Al-Jabarti, 'as it is stated by this man, this Bonaparte, what may follow. Here in his first article, that all the villages within three hours of where the French pass must surrender, and raise the French flag.' He held up his hands. 'Where must we acquire such flags I know not... Second, that any villages that resist shall be burnt down, and that the sheikh of each village must seal up all property, houses and possessions belonging to the Mamluks.' He waved the note about, flabbergasted. 'It would seem they do not understand what is Mamluk or not, nor whom they are liberating, truly – yet still they demand we stay in our sealed houses and fly their flag while they invade.' He shook his head. 'It seems they come to loot as well, and to praise a god they do not believe in while doing so.'

There was a rippling murmur and shaking of heads at this and Ibrahim Bey took his moment. 'Then it is true. They come seeking gold and wealth, as does any army,' he said. 'We should pay them and let them be gone.'

'Would that be possible?' asked Abu Bakr Pasha. 'It could be but a trifle compared to occupation and war.'

'It is a European army,' retorted Murad, 'unlike any before, with no talk of their prophet. They come for *conquest*, not *bribery*!'

The arguments continued. Outside the chamber, in a broad arched passage of polished white stone, Hazzard and Cook waited while Masoud listened carefully at the doorway, relaying as much as he could. Izzam and Alahum stood close by, as still as the Mamluk sentries. 'Murad Bey is angry with them all, especially Ibrahim...'

Hazzard joined him. 'Which one is Ibrahim?'

Masoud pointed him out from behind the cover of a linen curtain in the arched doorway. 'That one. If Murad is a lion, then Ibrahim is a cobra.'

Hazzard looked. It was not an inaccurate description. Ibrahim was lean and poised, a white turban with long headdress hanging beneath, much like the Mamluk they had encountered in the desert. A thin face, he thought, handsome, a fine line of black beard and moustache as if drawn with a pen, a man of wealth and status. He sat very still, only his eyes moving until he spoke in anger, then his head snapped forward to strike. Hazzard preferred the energy of Murad the lion.

'If they've landed,' said Cook, 'then we're too bloody late anyway...'

'Maybe not,' said Hazzard. 'They'll need a fortified position and Bonaparte would know better than to keep his back to the sea for long. He'll march inland to Alexandria as soon as he can, ready or not. We could catch him in the open with enough cavalry.'

'Then why can't this lot move their flamin' arses into their flamin' saddles...' muttered Cook, peering through the doorway.

Masoud put a finger to his lips. 'All decisions are taken by the *diwan*. They must be in agreement and the Ottoman Pasha must consent. It is the way of things. But Murad and Ibrahim hate each other – Murad once turned a cannon on his house it is said, and fired it from across the city...'

Cook turned away. 'Barmy as a ruddy rajah...'

They had been housed and fed, though virtually kept prisoner in their rooms, Izzam and Alahum sleeping at their chamber door, and waited yet another day for the *diwan* to assemble, Hazzard maddened with frustration. Hammer had gone to the Delta to spy out the coasts and ports, leaving Masoud behind as Hazzard's interpreter – the young Alexandrian spent most of his time calming the impatient Englishman.

There was a shout inside and they could hear Ibrahim and Murad, '*Then I shall go.*'

And Ibrahim answering, '*And when you have massed your cavalry, Murad, what then after your victory? Take power once again?*'

They heard movement and a Mamluk appeared, holding one of the curtains aside. They moved away across the cool stone corridor, waiting. Eventually Al-Jabarti emerged, his small form dwarfed by the palatial arch high above him. The Mamluk guards bowed as he passed and he joined Hazzard and Cook.

'I thank you again, Mr Hazar,' said Al-Jabarti in halting English. Masoud translated between them. 'This is proving difficult for the *diwan*.'

'As you said, Sheikh,' replied Hazzard. 'But when will they take action? They have hours, not days.'

'The *diwan* is always divided, power split between the great beys. Not just Ibrahim, but Osman, Hassan, Muhammad al-Elfi and Qasim Bey and more. But Murad commands the high-caste cavalry and is the most powerful.'

Another man, dressed much like Al-Jabarti in white robes and similar headdress, emerged from the chamber and joined them. He bowed to Al-Jabarti and looked to Hazzard and Cook. 'I am *Sharif* Nazir,' he said in flawless English, 'brother of Ali Qarim Sheikh, in whose name you rode from beyond Gizeh.'

'Sharif,' said Hazzard with a bow. 'Your brother was generous in the circumstances.'

'Perhaps so, but only if you speak the truth, Captain. Otherwise he is a trusting fool.'

He was angry, with the French, with all Europeans perhaps, and possibly with his brother for riding into such a storm with the Siwa caravan. There was no doubt Nazir knew the landing was real: riders with cries for aid had been coming in from Kurayyim since Hazzard had arrived, with shouts along the passageways, echoes of running boots and calls for more men, more horses. Murad had been sending out messengers to all parts of the Delta to confirm the reports and gather the cavalry.

'There is no question of their intention, Sharif. I stood on the flagship of the French fleet. There are over thirty thousand men coming to invade.'

Al-Jabarti stared back at him, his rich black eyes wide with alarm. 'Then why this *firman* proclamation? This Bonaparte-Sultan? He appeals to the common people and to our Ottoman lords as a liberator of Egypt, rather than conqueror – why, if he intends to invade in any case? I wonder, from whom does he liberate us? Ourselves perhaps?'

'The Mamluk is his declared enemy, Sheikh, not the sultan in Constantinople,' said Hazzard. 'He is aware of the power of the sultan and wants to avoid war with him. But he knows of the sultan's mistrust of the Mamluk in Egypt, and believes that he comes to do the sultan a service by defeating you. Be in no doubt, he is a clever man, and the most successful commander in Europe.'

'If that should mean so much,' scoffed Nazir.

'He has not yet been defeated on the battlefield, Sharif. He is believed fearless and virtually invincible.'

'So, not *completely* invincible,' said Nazir, as if seeking out the weaknesses in Europeans, watching Hazzard. 'Such pride, such such *blasphemy...*'

'Watch it...' murmured Cook, and shifted his stance. Izzam and Alahum did not like the sharif's tone and came forward a pace in support.

'Ha! It speaks!' said Nazir, 'The *sergeant*? And his, his *ruffians*?' He nearly spat. 'You dare speak to me?'

'He does, Sharif,' said Hazzard, 'He has been welcomed by princes more powerful than you can conceive.'

Nazir glowered at the insult, and Al-Jabarti spoke. 'Sharif, I entreat you, we need our friends.'

But Nazir mocked again, 'So. We need the great Red Pasha, but not Murad, or the army—'

Hazzard was confused. 'Red Pasha?'

'It is what the *Bedu* call you,' said Nazir with a deprecating gesture at Izzam and Alahum. 'Or do they not tell you so, for fear of God, for their vainglorious lack of humility? How absurd.'

Another roar from the *diwan* chamber announced the explosion of Murad Bey into the hall. He stormed from the assembly chamber infuriated, four of his armed *sanjaq* supporters behind him. He glared about, then saw Hazzard.

'*Hingleesh!*' He charged forward, his robes flying.

'*Jaysus an' all the saints...*' whispered Cook and moved one pace in front of Hazzard. Murad noted him and waved him away, muttering irritably, as if to allay fears.

'*Limuza atayta limisr ayyoha, al-Inglizi?*'

Masoud nearly fainted with fright but translated, 'Murad Bey asks, why have you come to Egypt, Englishman?'

Hazzard looked at Al-Jabarti who nodded. Clearly this was Murad's final avenue, to confer directly with the British strangers. He had a choice: stand back and advise, or promise support. Despite Nelson, despite the captains and their refusal to listen, Hazzard knew Bonaparte would crush all in his path, and decided: *damn them*. According to Lewis, Hazzard was His Majesty's Exploring Officer – and, as such could speak with the authority of an officer-parliamentary.

'I am here to offer our services as ally, on behalf of King George of England.'

'Hazar-*effendi*,' Masoud said deferentially, 'Herr Hammer is the one to interpret for you in such matters properly, not I...'

165

Hazzard shook his head. 'Herr Hammer left you in his stead because he believes you more than capable, Masoud.'

Masoud looked to Nazir but the sharif had turned away, arms folded, refusing to help. Murad listened to Masoud's interpretation, then flicked a glance at Hazzard, at Cook, at Izzam and Alahum, standing firm behind them in evident devotion.

'*Maza yurido al malek George min Misr!*' shouted Murad. Every utterance, thought Hazzard, was a challenge. He began to believe what Hammer had said about him.

Masoud swallowed. 'And what does King George want of Egypt?'

'Cocked and locked, sir...' murmured Cook. His left hand sliding to the butt of a pistol under his robes.

'King George wishes to destroy the French fleet.' He tried to convey the value of his offer to a desert warrior who most probably had never been to sea in his life. 'Murad Bey, we bring to you the captains of *Nelsoun Amir al-bahr*, and the warships of the Royal Navy. No man, not even the great sultan in Constantinople, commands such forces of destruction.'

'Too bloody right...' murmured Cook.

'And we offer our services as advisers in the fight against Bonaparte Sultan. He shall bring fire upon you in ways the Mamluk cavalry has never seen.'

Masoud was sweating and pleaded with Hazzard, 'I beg of you, *effendi*...'

'Tell him, Masoud.'

With a few uncertainties and corrections, Masoud translated. Murad gave a laugh, shaking his head. Hyperbole was a common enough pose, thought Hazzard.

Masoud turned to him, unnerved. '*Effendi*, what now?'

But Hazzard bade Masoud wait. Murad saw this too, and exchanged a glance with Nazir. The sheikhs behind waited, curious. Hazzard cast about for a convincing end to his offer, memories of Dr Muhammad in London, his antique books from the Moorish library in Cordoba, his dreams of the *Rubaiyyat*, and his earnest expression as he examined the manuscripts.

166

'I have heard it was written,' said Hazzard, praying Dr Muhammad had schooled him correctly, and added with some hesitation, '*Aadow aadowwi, howa sadiqi.*'

The enemy of mine enemy, shall be my friend.

Masoud bowed his head, backing away a pace. The armed *sanjaqs* behind Murad inclined their heads at this attempt, a fine compliment, and waited for their bey's reply.

The great man studied Hazzard, his sincerity, the truth within him. After an age, he nodded slowly and spoke through Nazir. Nazir muttered something but Murad snapped at him.

Reluctantly Nazir interpreted, 'Murad Bey has heard some say, before even the Father of Terrors, that God knows all mysteries.'

Izzam and Alahum had been speaking of their journey south.

'I too have heard this,' replied Hazzard.

Murad made his decision.

'Good,' he said, in English, 'Good. *Insha'allah, Hingleesh, sawfa nouwajeh adouanna fil maaraka bessayfi wa'nnar.*'

Masoud looked back to Hazzard, his head bowing in deep respect. 'Then, God willing, Englishman, we both shall meet our enemy in battle. With fire and sword.'

Al-Sahraa

Alexandria was in uproar. The ancient walled city had fallen in three hours. Houses had been confiscated as billets for senior officers and some of the *savants*, tenants politely ejected to the confusion of the streets, an army receipt for compensation clasped in their hands. Open spaces had been cordoned off for white canvas tents in tight, neat rows, sentries at every corner, muskets and bayonets keeping the newly liberated from breaking into riot.

After the initial assault from Marabout, the new garrison disembarked in luxury from the broad sweep of Aboukir Bay several miles to the east; columns of troops from the coast road poured into the city through the medieval gatehouses, and the Provosts set up checkpoints to direct the traffic: ancillary army staff, cooks, labourers, carpenters and farriers, as well as regular Delta traders trying to reach their commandeered cargoes in the harbours – and fearful families trying to get out.

A sunburnt Provost lieutenant in dusty grey coat, gorget and black shako fought off a shouting husband and his brothers waving documents in his face – '*Franssiyah, Franssiyah, eessi, eessi!*' He shoved them away, *Get back, damn you, enough!* Still he had the presence of mind to stop others, *You there! Passport! Oui, merci, passez par là*, pointing to a pair of press-ganged *savants* now demoted to clerical workers, then back to the family, *Non, allez-vous en! Away with you*, the clamour made all the worse by the ceaseless braying of donkeys and the bleating of goats. When he saw a pair of European women in the midst of the Egyptians, he knew they did not belong.

'*You there! Venez! Come, be quick!*' He waved an arm at them. 'Which brigade are you? Have you a ticket of leave or gate passport?'

The women were tattered and dishevelled, their once fine gowns torn and soiled, a simple army kitbag for a few provisions, army cloaks over their shoulders. For all the world they looked like dispossessed camp followers. It was Sarah and Jeanne.

Sarah shook her head. '*Non*,' she called back.

'You must have a camp number or passport to pass through the gate!' called the lieutenant. 'Which battalion?'

'We do not have one,' she replied, 'but I am to say *Sergent-chef-major* Achille Caron, and the 75th Invincibles—'

The officer stopped and turned, his full attention on them now. He knew the name of the Invincibles, and everyone knew the name Caron. He noted Sarah's sunken, black-rimmed eyes, her pale complexion, the *Parisienne* accent, and saluted. 'How may I assist you, *mademoiselle*?'

The crowd's shouts grew louder as the phalanx of Provost troopers parted and let the pair through, an NCO with a pickaxe handle pushing the Alexandrians back.

'We were to go to Cairo,' she told the lieutenant.

He took another passport and called over his shoulder, '*Oui, passez par là*,' then looked back at her, 'Cairo? Why are you not with the boats?' He broke off and nodded to an Alexandrian. '*Oui, d'accord* – they will be upriver at Ramaniyah by now.'

'The army kept us at the camp for nearly a week,' said Jeanne.

'I cannot allow you to travel to Cairo, *mademoiselles*. It is too dangerous. You must get to Rosetta with the others and wait.' He examined the ticket of a sergeant from a company of *sapeurs*, and shouted his orders over Sarah's head, but she persisted.

'*Capitaine* Jullien awaits us on the river…'

He shook his head. '*Suis désolé, mademoiselle*, I am sorry, but please listen, I cannot afford the men to escort you—'

He beat a pleading hand from his shoulder, *passpah, passpah, eessi, eessi*—

'Be off, I say, damn you! *Yallah, yallah, isri ya!*'

'What then?' shouted Jeanne. 'Should we fly off with your army balloons? Or shall we say *Bonaparte* to you? Or *Eugène*, and *Hortense*, his children, who have known us for years?'

The lieutenant gave her more attention now. '*Mademoiselle*, it is not poss—'

'Or the *Chausee d'Antin* where he lives?' continued Jeanne. 'Or that *Madame* Joséphine has the oval dining-room and puts her own flowers in her hall every morning? Shall we say this to you and remember the time, the place where *you, Lieutenant provôt*, said *non* to *Mademoiselle Isabelle Moreau-Lazare!*'

'*Sacre*, I do not have the men…' The lieutenant thought a moment. He turned to the NCO behind him. '*Sergent*, where is Yussuf?'

The call went up for Yussuf, over the heads of the mob. By a makeshift mule corral, tethered in the shade of nearby trees by the stone gatehouse walls, a number of Nubian goats stood bleating in the tumult. Cooing to them softly was a young Bedouin boy. He looked up at the sound of his name and dived into the crowds, making for the lieutenant. '*Jy viens! Jy viens!*' *I come, I come.*

'This is Yussuf,' shouted the lieutenant. 'He can get you to Aboukir Bay. He is Bedouin, *mademoiselle*, not too bright, but he has proved reliable. He will find you passage across the river mouth to Rosetta. It is the very best I can do, *je m'excuse*.' He turned away and called to the passing sappers, '*Keep moving!* Stop your damned gawping and gather for *appel* in the square and wait!'

They moved away from the gate and the Provosts. Barely sixteen at most, Yussuf bowed repeatedly to them, the habit of a life spent in subservience, *marci marci*, and took their bag. '*Pauver maddamms,*' *poor ladies*, he intoned sadly, as if to his goats, adding in broken French, 'I am Yussuf, ehh, how you say, *Joseph*.' He pronounced carefully for them. 'I take you, yes, take you? To the General Menouss in al-Rashid? The Rosette, *oui*? Come, come,' pulling them out of the mob and away from the gate, away to Rosetta and safety.

Sarah turned to Jeanne. 'Jeanne, go to Rosetta, to the *comtesse*, I beg you.'

Jeanne stopped dead. 'Why? Where are you going?'

Sarah took a breath. 'I must go to Ramaniyah, and Cairo.'

'*No*,' said Jeanne curtly. 'Where you go, I go.'

'*al-Ramaniyah?*' asked Yussuf.

'Yes,' said Sarah. 'It is very important.'

'Why?' demanded Jeanne. 'So you can find him? Find your *anglais*? He is *gone, alors!*'

'He is *not*, Jeanne!'

Because he intended to jump. She knew that. Because he knew he could escape.

'This is madness, a-a *folie du coeur!*'

'*Un Hanglais?*' asked Yussuf. *An Englishman?*

Sarah looked at him. The boy blinked back at them, perplexed. 'Yussuf,' she said softly, 'have you heard of, of any *anglais* coming here?'

'*Inglizi?* But yes they come, since days now, the great *Nelsoun Amir al-bahr.*'

Sarah kept her face a blank but within she felt a floodtide of relief.

Nelson. At last.

Jeanne looked away, muttering, '*Mon dieu...*'

But Sarah continued. 'And was there a man, alone... by himself, a soldier — in red?'

Jeanne hissed at her, 'Belle, *non, mon dieu*, not here, by the gate, you are *mad!*'

'Yes, yes!' he whispered. 'The Maaza *Bedu*, they say *al-Aafrit al-ahmar*, ehh... *le diable rouge*, hm? The Red Devil? The *Inglizi* with *Nelsoun Amir.*'

She wanted to put a hand to her mouth to stop herself from crying out, but she did not.

Oh God.

Yussuf went on excitedly, with pride, 'But we, Awlad 'Ali, say *Pasha al-ahmar*, the Red *Pasha*, a lord of power in the red coat, *rouge, oui*? He rides from the desert, from nowhere, to *le Caire*, and saved his *Bedu* servant with a pistol of a king, before a great Mamluk sheikh. *Nelsoun Amir* and the red man,' he declared, '*Hazar Pasha.*'

William.

Jeanne took Sarah's arm and hissed at her, '*Putain putain, Belle!* What do you *do* here, in this *mad* place in front of soldiers? Seek an *anglais*?'

'Yussuf,' she said slowly, 'we must go to Cairo, not Rosetta.'

Yussuf looked doubtful. 'Oh lo lo lo, *maddamms*. It needs the *monnaie*…' he said, 'for the man of the boat, for water, for the donkey-horse…'

'We have enough.' Sarah put a hand to a pouch slung on her hip.

Yussuf looked inside. More valuable than silver Ottoman *sultani* or *sharifi, piastres* or *scudi*, the purse was full of shining brass army tunic buttons, now become the prized currency. He closed it quickly, glancing over his shoulder for fear of sneak-thieves. '*Gardez-le bien*. Keep it well, dear cabbages, *mes chou-choux, mes choupettes*. I know.' He pointed south. 'We take little boat, on canal, come.'

They headed for the mule corral, Sarah unwilling to believe, yet her heart swelling in painful hope, in prayer.

William.

Alive.

–

Commander Blake opened the door to the chart room and entered. Admiralty staff officers had gathered to stand round the broad table, their figures dark before the tall, bright windows. At the far end, in powdered wig and navy-blue coat, was the First Sea Lord, the Earl Spencer, his normally upright posture bowed as he pored over a chart of the Mediterranean, his expression fraught.

Behind him, ever watchful, stood Lewis, listening as the staff presented their advice for action, '*Retire to Gibraltar, my lord, recall*

Nelson to Cadiz, prepare the Channel Fleet for a secondary assault from Boulogne...'

Spencer looked up as Blake entered, as if hopeful for some tactical reprieve. Seeing none, he looked down again. Lewis slipped away to join Blake.

Blake handed him a signal despatch.

'He did it, sir.'

Lewis took the message. 'Did what? Who?'

'Carried by Nelson to Sicily and then by Tomlinson of the *Valiant*, sir, through Gibraltar and Cadiz...'

Lewis skimmed the two sheets. 'Hazzard,' he said, and glanced at him.

Blake seemed to be indulging in a certain pleasure from Hazzard's achievement. Lewis read the signal once again more thoroughly – the first page was the enciphered original and the second its decryption from the cipher clerks.

> *34'18'89 landed Naples. Carriage attack on agent a hoax. Agent identified aboard French flagship Orient[120]. Fled Toulon with Cmtsse de Biasi and joined French fleet Civita Vecchia.*
>
> *Naples refused to give naval aid to England.*
>
> *Malta fallen to French 11 June. Action in Sliema, 9 Co. Wayland Lt, Ai/c, defeated French column, current whereabouts unknown presumed Malta.*
>
> *34'18'89 captured in Valletta to infiltrate French HQ. Taken aboard Orient[120] paroled prisoner. Reconnoitred fleet. Identified Adm agent.*
>
> *French fleet c.380 sailed Valletta-Alexandria 19 June.*
>
> *34'18'89 with CSM 1st Ft debarked Orient[120] night 20th inst. to rdv Nelson off Cape Passaro. Adm agent still aboard Orient[120].*

Nelson sqn arrived Alexandria 28 June ahead of French fleet. Treated w Alex officials but refused rights of station. Squadron dep^{td} Alex-Syracuse via Crete/Cyprus.

34'18'89 will execute original order.

Ends, Exploring Officer 34'18'89.

'Nelson was that close...' Lewis reread it. 'The fleets must have passed within a mile of each other.'

'Yes, sir. Mr Hazzard and Sgt Cook must have jumped overboard from the *Orient* in open water.' He put his kerchief to the side of his mouth carefully, his nervous gesture indicating there was more to come. 'I find his oblique reference to Miss Chapel somewhat chilling, sir. I should imagine it relays a certain bitterness of feeling.'

'His feelings, Commander, bitter or not, are irrelevant.' Lewis crumpled up the note. 'The question is whether Hazzard has cooperated with Nelson off the shores of Egypt and withdrawn as ordered. There seems to be something of a threat in his final comment.'

'There was no other appended by Nelson on the matter, sir. Indeed he does not confirm or deny Hazzard's presence, merely that he has intelligence concerning Malta. But we do have this from the Viennese Consul, Mr Rosetti.' Blake handed him another sheet. Lewis read it.

Two soldiers in red reported riding south to Cairo to parley with Mamelukes. Presume your officers. Both now under protection of Murad Bey.

'Good God.'

'I should imagine this must be Mr Hazzard and Sgt Cook sir.'

'I know what he damn well means – what in hell does Hazzard think he's doing?'

'Since Nelson was refused at Alexandria, they have ridden to Cairo to warn them of the coming attack, sir.' Blake had no doubt as to what Hazzard would do to warn the Egyptians of Bonaparte – and that he would do so despite being ordered not to. But he decided not to voice his opinion to Lewis. 'Anything further, I dare say, we shall discover only in some weeks, sir.' Blake paused, then asked, 'How then shall we withdraw our agent – I beg your pardon, Miss Chapel, sir?'

Lewis gave him an unambiguous answer. 'Hazzard has corroborated her information, Commander and reported to Nelson. Blown, captured, dead or alive,' he said with harsh indifference, 'she is now of no value.'

For some moments, Blake said nothing. Lewis looked at him.

'Comment, Commander?'

'Mr Hazzard will not see it that way, sir. Neither will their lordships.'

Lewis stood closer, keeping his voice low, aware of the assembled company. 'You will not play the innocent part in this, Mr Blake. We *want* a canal at Suez. All the better if the French dig it for us so we may take it from them later. Hazzard must simply *obey his blasted orders.*'

'To sink the French battle-fleet?'

'And nothing more.'

Blake looked at the despatch and added quietly, 'And the original order to resist the French by all means possible, sir? I believe I have a copy of it in the minutes...' Blake made a show of looking through his papers. It was a clearer threat than Hazzard's despatch.

'Do I understand you right, sir?' asked Lewis. 'Did you minute a confidential briefing in Room 63 without sanction, sir?'

'Merely an observation, sir,' said Blake blandly, 'that owing to their accountability for the activities of Room 63, the Sea Lords created Mr Hazzard an Exploring Officer in the name of the Crown, and thereby made him His Majesty's local *de jure* representative. We can have little authority over him without rapid communication. His orders in hand are to resist the French. By now he will have surmised that we suspected the target of the fleet was indeed Egypt and not England, and that we kept this from him. As such I should imagine he will have little interest in abiding by our wishes for him to withdraw.'

Lewis squared off to him, his voice low. 'If you have any warning, Mr Blake, that Hazzard is actively undermining our strategic aims—'

'Oh I would doubt that, sir,' said Blake. 'He might, however, subject them to, how shall I say, reinterpretation. According to the dictates of the moment.' He paused, then added, 'As we did, sir, with his fiancée.'

It was obvious to both that a gulf had opened between them – and that Blake had no intention of closing it.

'If stricken, Mr Blake,' said Lewis, 'this particular ship of state sinks with all hands. Is that clear? And if need be I would sacrifice a thousand Hazzards to prevent it. You would do well to remember that.'

Blake bowed, and withdrew silently, remarking with some pride how grossly Sir Rafe Lewis had underestimated William John Hazzard.

–

The marines bobbed on the waves in the blazing sun. Their stores had lasted two days, by which time their small cutter was well beyond Malta, its bleached, threadbare sail catching a hot westerly breeze. Between them they had nearly a century of experience at sea, but only Underhill, Pettifer and Kite had the vaguest idea how to navigate. They aimed roughly for the southeast. It bothered none that they might be headed to oblivion. It was better than dodging the French on shore.

'Water,' said Wayland with a hoarse voice, 'at quarter ration, Sar'nt Underhill.'

Underhill touched two fingers to his brow. His parade-ground rasp had declined to an even worse dry whisper. 'Aye-aye, sir. Quarter it is.'

The fish they had caught and eaten raw smacked of salt to such an extent their thirst raged. But they were shaded partially from the sun – they had improvised a small canopy from three of their baggy Maltese smocks, strung from a line rigged fore and aft, and they rotated a watch regularly in and out of the sun. Except Wayland, who sat stolidly at the stern, one hand on the tiller.

Sometime in the mid-afternoon, Porter noticed the boy had fallen particularly quiet.

'Sir? You've gone a mite pale...'

Wayland shifted, taking firmer hold of the tiller, and drew himself more upright. '*Ons'nse*—' he coughed. '*Nonsense*, Dr Porter...' They had called Porter 'Doc' for some time, Wayland using a more formal address to amuse them – though Porter had been but an apothecary's assistant, the quiet Yorkshireman knew more than most doctors of their experience.

Porter looked him over. Despite the sunburn his skin was almost grey, and there were dark bloodstains on Wayland's lower leg. Porter took hold of his boot. Wayland tensed and grimaced with pain, then slid off his seat into the scuppers in a dead faint. Hands reached to take hold of him.

'Quick,' said Porter, propping up his chin, checking his tongue. He nodded to De Lisle, 'Lil, lend us a hand... get that boot off...'

Porter supported Wayland's head while De Lisle took hold of his leg and gave the boot a mild twist. As it came off, it tore open a blackened scab. Wayland's calf wound had been weeping badly through its dressings, and must have been causing him tremendous pain, but he had told no one.

'God on high,' whispered Porter. 'Right. Lie him down flat.'

'Bloody hell...' Warnock helped shift him fully into the shade of the canopy. Wayland's forehead immediately began to bead with moisture. His head lower, Wayland came to and began to struggle.

'Will he lose the leg, Doc...?' asked Pettifer.

Porter peeled the matted stocking away. 'Not to me, he ruddy shan't.'

At Pettifer's suggestion they had harvested some floating seaweed and, though ridden with salt, they had found it good for eating. Porter took a handful of it, soaked it over the side then wrapped it tight round the wound in lieu of bandages. Wayland winced and gasped with pain. 'What's the rule, sir?' said Porter brightly. 'The sea's good for cuts got out of it, but not got within, i'n't that right, sir?'

Wayland sighed, 'You are... alas... no poet, Dr Porter...'

'No, sir,' he agreed. 'But I am Yorkshire, which is the next best thing.'

Wayland gave a feeble laugh and closed his eyes. They gathered round as Porter worked. 'If I can get the pus out, it might go a-right. Petty, give us your belt between his teeth... Clamp down, sir,' he called to Wayland, 'it might feel a tad smart...'

Wayland screamed as he bit down on the thick leather as Porter went to work, time and again, squeezing the poisons out of the torn flesh. Warnock looked down at him. 'Bloody hellfire. And me thinking he's just some molly kid...'

'You would, y'daft shite,' said De Lisle.

Napier nodded. 'He's a gent, like the major. They breed 'em tough as boots.'

'Bugger that,' said Warnock. 'He's hard as a coster's arse and no mistake.' He poured a ration of water into the cup and handed it to Porter.

Porter took it. 'He has had his ration for the afternoon, Private.'

'Go on, give it 'im and belt up. Say it's mine.'

Porter nodded. 'Duly noted in the log.' He tipped the water carefully between Wayland's pale lips.

Kite called back to them from the bows. 'Hoi – who's mindin' the shop? We got a customer.'

Dead ahead not a mile off, was the billowing sail of a man of war. They left Wayland to Porter and peered into the distant glare.

'What is she?' whispered Pettifer. He looked at De Lisle. 'Lil? A lost Frog?'

The waves slapped against the sides of the cutter. The rigging creaked rhythmically in the silence. Against the brilliant blue of the sky no one could identify the colours flying from her stern and mainmast.

''Talian,' said De Lisle. 'Bet yer a bob.'

'If she's a Frog,' murmured Underhill, reaching for his Shorter India, 'I bags the captain and the first officer...'

'Sure thing, Sarge,' said Warnock, 'just leave us a midshippie or two.'

Cochrane stared across the waves, his bony chin jutting like a defiant figurehead at the prow. 'If she comes about a-right, then we're done. And Jonah shall have us below.'

'Yer a bloody little sunbeam today, Cocky,' whispered Kite. He reached carefully for his musket, as if not to disturb Fate. The warship turned towards them.

'She's spotted us,' said Kite, and began to load and ram. 'Game's up. Well lads, 'twas most fine, our time on the high seas 'gainst the foe... but I intend to take a few with me, just to pay 'em back for generally givin' me the bloody hump.'

Underhill agreed. 'Prime your pans, and lock your bloody cocks, lads. We'll make a few holes in 'em afore we pays Davy Jones a visit.'

Each man began to load his musket and pistols. The ship bore down on them, spray flying from her sharp bows, the flash of its hull bright in the sun. As he loaded, Kite began to hum one of his favourites. Warnock and De Lisle joined in. *'I'm Jolly Jack... I'm Jolly Jack... I'm master of the fleet...'*

They watched the ship approach in the dazzling sun, taking note of her gun-ports. If they opened, they knew they were done for. It slowed, the bow-wave subsiding as the crew doused sail, the foremainsail reefed, the canvas collapsing, the tops furling. Kite levelled his musket, checking his sights. *'...But I never seen a belayin' pin... wiv bloody bollocks on... hoi.'*

The ship glided closer, its course aimed to pass them on the starboard bow. A challenge was shouted down from the rail. The marines sat ready in their boat, waiting.

'Here's to the major, lads, our mad, mad Bloody Billy-Jack,' muttered Kite. 'And let's hope he gets more'n a few to even the score...' Kite raised a hand and shouted back, '*Hoi, mate! Can't hear you, mon-soo-er! Come a bit closer, so's I can put one in your thick bloody 'ead! Voos savvy, eh?*'

'After the first volley,' said Underhill to them all, 'over the side, into the drink, and head for the trailing lines like the wharf-rats I knows you truly to be.'

'Aye, Sarge...' they mumbled.

A voice called down, this time louder.

'*Hola!*'

It took a moment for them to register the language. It was Spanish. Underhill got it first. 'It's bloody Dagos.'

De Lisle cocked the lock on his old four-barrelled turnover pistol. 'Sorry you ain't got your 'buss, Petty...'

Pettifer readied his musket. 'One at a time'll do me fine, Lil.'

They heard a choking sound from behind and Porter lifted Wayland's head. 'What's he say?' asked Warnock.

Wayland coughed, then waved them back. '*No – chaps... h-hold fire...*'

The frigate drew nearer, lines dropping over the side, two hands climbing down to meet them, shouts across the decks and rigging. High above them at the starboard rail appeared the familiar face of Alfonso and Ship's Master Handley. It was the Spanish privateer, the *Volpone* – their lifeline.

'*Hoi, Kitey! You lot on a Grand Tour then?*'

Kite's filthy sunburnt face split into a broad smile. 'Bloody matelot! We're Jollies, whelks an' cockles, alive-alive-oh, matey!' he called and Handley laughed down at him.

He was joined moments later at the rail by none other than their erstwhile saviour, *Capitán* Cesár Domingo de la Vega. '*Señores!*' He raised them a brief salute, '*Soldados of the sea you may be, hm? But sailors, perhaps no, eh?*'

Square

Early in the morning the mounted guard assembled in Ezbekiya and the crowds began to chant Murad's name. The Mamluk cavalry had come, the amirs' *sanjaqs* answering the call to arms, and all cried out for *jihad*. Word went about that over ten thousand horse and foot had gathered outside the capital.

'*Murad Murad Murad! Allahu akbar!*'

Hazzard stood with Masoud at a balcony on the second floor of the palace, overlooking the quad below. As well as the horsemen were Mamluk footsoldiers with their medieval panoply of arms, buckler, javelins, mace, axe, sword, a few with the long Turkish miquelet muskets.

'Not a line-infantryman in sight.'

Cook looked down. 'They'll be shot to bloody bits.'

Hazzard tore himself from this new frustration, feeling that he and Cook alone understood the engine of war that was coming to crush them all.

They had dined that previous night with Murad and his men, sheikhs and *sanjaqs* ranged around a hall on cushions and rugs amid wafting tapestries giving a draught of cooling air, vast tables laden with meats and fruits on huge ceramic platters and bowls, each carried in by Mamluk servants, a procession of heralds leading the way. Hazzard had not been able to converse with Murad directly or discuss tactics and strategy with anyone – they were isolated, Izzam and Alahum seated protectively either side of Hazzard and Cook, Sharif Nazir joining them at several points in the evening on Murad's orders. They were being entertained, but kept at arm's length, while the beautiful *awalim* danced to music, entrancing them all. The women of the assembly sat quietly, wreathed in veils of fine woven silks and linens, gathered in groups behind each lord, some watching Cook and Hazzard curiously, Masoud trembling with fear that any wrong move might spell disaster. To Hazzard the easy confidence in the palace was infuriating.

Some hours later they were escorted back to their rooms, Masoud exhausted by his role of interpreter, Hazzard feeling bloody and hopeless, imagining an unopposed landing by the French, battalions forming on the beaches and marching inland, no one to stop them – and no one in the palace, it seemed, was prepared to listen.

They followed their hard–bitten Mamluk guide down unfamiliar corridors and up stone staircases, arches soaring high above, the Nile breeze blowing in, Hazzard wondering why they had taken such a circuitous route. Eventually they came to a dark, broad landing of cool white stone. At the end was a gallery balcony overlooking the palace gardens. As they reached the top they stopped dead, Masoud in sudden stark terror. He took Hazzard's wrist tightly.

'*Effendi…*'

Before them, ranged across the darkness of the balcony, were half a dozen women in voluminous robes. With the flicker of distant lanterns and the glow of the moon through the trees beyond, the landing was wild with crazed shadow. Both parties stood in expectant silence.

Masoud bowed deeply, keeping his head down, 'Hazar-*effendi*, please look *down…*'

Hazzard bowed but did not look away, wondering who should speak first. Judging by her bearing, he recognised the one figure he had noticed at the feast: the foremost of Murad's wives.

Stricken with more fear than when he had met Sheikh Ali Qarim in the desert, Masoud hissed, '*Nafisa Khatun al-Muradiyya. Once concubine, now leader of the Mamluk harim and wife to Murad Bey. We are in such danger, effendi…*'

The dark figure approached, as if to pass by, and stopped beside him. As Hazzard's eyes grew accustomed to the darkness, he could see she wore a formal decorative *yelek* kaftan and flowing black cotton robes. This was topped by a long, fine black silk headscarf fringed with glittering gold trim; beneath it, a black and gold veil over her nose and mouth, the whole effect delicate, diaphanous, wafting slightly in the breeze, with a scent of Indian *patchouli*. Hazzard could see almost nothing of her, yet could detect the presence of extraordinary beauty. A pair of black-centred almond eyes looked back at him.

'*Al Pasha al-ahmar,*' she said.

The Red Pasha.

Masoud whispered, 'You must reply, *effendi.*'

Hazzard bowed again and spoke softly, 'Your servant, my lady. Sergeant Cook, and Izzam and Alahum of the al-Kalbi.'

Masoud translated, bowing. Nafisa spoke again and bowed her head briefly. '*As-salamu aleikum, ya Hazar Pasha.*'

Hazzard then guessed they had been led there by the Mamluk servant, hers presumably – he stood behind the group, one hand on a sword. Her eyes the only point of reference in the flowing silks, Hazzard watched them as they flicked up and down, sizing him up. She spoke, and Masoud translated.

'She asks, are the French coming, truly.'

'Yes, my lady,' said Hazzard, 'Ships enough to cover the sea, tens of thousands of footsoldiers, cavalry and artillery.'

Masoud glanced at him nervously, uncertain if he should impart such news. 'To the lord's wife, *effendi*, it is a grave matter to speak such things…'

'She asked for the truth. Tell her.'

Masoud nodded and conveyed his words. The younger women around her gasped and shifted in some fear. Nafisa calmed them, then addressed Hazzard again. Masoud gritted his teeth and translated.

'She asks, can the Lord Murad defeat them?'

Hazzard listened to her voice. It was gentle, detached, its lilt, in itself, beautiful. He exchanged glances with Cook. 'I cannot say, madam.'

Masoud squeezed Hazzard's wrist, his grip tight. 'I beg of you, *effendi… let us go.*'

She spoke once again, soft and plaintive. Masoud quietened, bowing to her words, and the feeling behind them. 'She says, then you must protect the Lord Murad. In doing so, you shall protect us.'

Hazzard lowered his head, the added weight of such an impossibility almost too much. 'How can I promise so, my lady…'

She looked at him, and he saw the fire, and hope, burning in her exquisite eyes. She had an answer for him.

'She says,' said Masoud sadly, '*Insha'allah*: it is all we can ever hope for.'

God willing.

–

After the fitful, hot night, Hazzard stared into the tumult of the courtyard below. Cook handed him a new shoulder-sling adapted from soft camel-leather. Hazzard tried it on and Cook passed him a Turkish pistol.

'Locked and cocked, courtesy of His Nibs downstairs himself. Not by Mr Manton or Mr Twigg, but does the same thing. Bit of a long nose on it but best we got. We going?'

'Saddle-sore or not,' said Hazzard, jamming the pistol into the holster and marching to the door. Cook snatched up a sword-belt and buckled it on, taking Masoud by the arm, 'Come on, laddie, you're Speaker o'the Delegation.'

They strode through the broad lofty passages, passing guardsmen, pikemen, squires and slaves. Alahum and Izzam fell in behind. Masoud worried, breathless, 'But what will you do, Hazar-*effendi*?' he asked. 'Against so many?'

'I have no idea,' said Hazzard. 'But I am not letting Bonaparte stroll into Cairo without a fight.'

They reached the quad. Footsoldiers and servants ran, carrying clutches of spears while others milled about, an Ottoman *Makrib* officer snapping orders at a squad of artillerymen, a sheikh surrounded by slaves pushing through the crowd to make way – there was no order, no formation, and Hazzard despaired for them against the Caesarian discipline of General Napoleon Bonaparte.

'There's our man,' said Cook, and pointed out Sharif Nazir. They forced a path through the crowd and Nazir saw their approach.

'Hazar-*effendi*,' said the Sharif. 'So. This is your triumph, I see,' he accused. 'The French have taken Alexandria and al-Rashid, just as you warned, and now approach al-Ramaniyah and the Nile. Are you thus pleased!'

'You damned yourselves, Sharif. Where are our horses?'

Nazir almost laughed. 'You could not possibly ride with the Mamluk. It would be an insult to their station! You may watch the work of the damned, *effendi*, from the flanks, guarding Hasim Bey.'

'I must warn Murad—'

'We have no need of such warnings, Englishman—'

'You arrogant *fool*.'

'And you blaspheme! For now this is holy *jihad*. How can we strike the infidel with *kafiri* Unbelievers in our midst! England shall *observe*, says Hasim Bey. And *learn*.'

A massed chant to God rose up in the square, the call travelling through the archways. From balconies above, women ululated with trilling tongues as the amirs mounted their horses. The great Murad was readied for battle.

'They're out of their bloody minds,' rumbled Cook.

'They just don't know, Jory.'

Someone called and he saw a squire waving. Standing back among a group of cavalrymen was a Mamluk in white robes, a veil of black silk covered in hanging gold discs, a breastplate made of chains of gold coins. Hazzard recognised him immediately: it was Sheikh Ali Qarim.

Hazzard pushed his way towards him, the others following, Nazir calling out, '*Hazar! There is nothing you can do, I say!*'

'Sheikh,' said Hazzard. '*As-salamu aleikum.*'

Ali Qarim bowed, returning the blessing.

Hazzard turned to Masoud. 'Please translate.' He looked at the sheikh behind his veil. He did not know where to begin. 'I am being prevented from warning Murad Bey—'

Nazir shoved his way through to them. 'Hazar! You will say *nothing.*' He stopped short when he saw his brother.

Ali Qarim removed the veil. As Hazzard had somehow expected, he bore a serene expression, his dark, weathered skin stark in contrast to the bright whites of deep, black eyes. A wide mouth was lined with a fine moustache and beard trimmed to a subtle point at his chin. It was the face of a philosopher, a thinking man.

Hazzard felt suddenly selfish in his desire to ride with them and advise, that he alone knew how to make war on France. Nazir made his greetings but in his anger left Masoud to translate. Ali Qarim spoke first.

'The French have heard of *al-Aafrit al-ahmar*,' said Masoud, 'Ali Qarim Sheikh says—'

'*Aafrit?*' Hazzard had no idea of the word.

Nazir waved a hand at the interruption. 'It is *nothing*, a way of speaking, a name given by *fools*. A spirit or *djinn*, a – a devil, *al-ahmar*, in red, that is all.'

'Red Devils?' muttered Cook. 'We've had worse.'

Ali Qarim continued quietly, Masoud interpreting. 'He says that three days ago he found many French captured by Awlad 'Ali *Bedu*, and even as far as the Khushmaan by the Red Sea, all have listened to the tale of two red sorcerers who rode with *Bedu*.'

'Good,' said Cook. 'Time the Frogs know we're comin' for 'em.'

One eye on Nazir, Hazzard took his chance, and said to Masoud, 'Tell Ali Qarim Sheikh that if the French give battle they will form into a large square – a formation defended by their bayonets, their spikes, four, five or even more rows deep. Like a fortress, or castle.' Masoud began to interpret. Ali Qarim's expression did not flicker; he listened carefully.

Nazir scoffed. 'A castle of men? A blasphemer's nonsense—'

'Each rank of two hundred men will fire a volley, Sheikh, that's two hundred bullets at a time, followed by the next rank, and then the next, and the next, each reloading and then firing again, one after the other, maintaining a *constant fire* across the field. This fortress can be defeated only by artillery. *Do not charge the squares with the cavalry.*'

The shouts and chants went up again, cheering as Murad mounted his horse and raised a hand to the amirs. A sudden silence – then Murad jerked his hand forward, his voice booming, '*Ilal amam!*'

The streets split into fresh jubilation. '*Murad Murad Murad! Allahu akbar!*'

The cavalry began to move off in file. Ali Qarim called for a servant. A slave-boy hurried forward, carrying a long object wrapped in dark cloth. The sheikh took it, and held it out to Hazzard.

'*Saif*,' said Ali Qarim. '*Shamshir*,' he added by way of explanation.

Hazzard unfolded layers of deep blue silk to reveal a gleaming ivory and gold-mounted grip. It was a curved Damascene sword.

Nazir muttered something to Ali Qarim, questioning his brother's judgement over such a gesture, but Ali Qarim silenced him with a sharp rebuke. 'He brings a *saif* for you, Captain, a sword,' said Nazir reluctantly, 'called *shamshir* in Persia. You English call it "scimitar", I am told.'

Hazzard pulled it from the cloth. The white leather scabbard was braided and decorated with gilt thread. He drew the blade several inches. The steel was like a mottled mirror, waves of pattern flowing like water, with Arabic characters inscribed just below the gold cruciform guard. It was perfectly balanced, the curve graceful, so natural the blade seemed ready to fly.

'*Hadeyya,*' said Ali Qarim, *gift*, then patted the pistol hung in pride of place across his chest, the one given by Hazzard. 'Martimar, Londan.'

Hazzard wished he could have given him something more useful than a single muzzle firing a single ball.

Ali Qarim spoke, then snapped a word to Nazir and the sharif obeyed, translating, 'They place artillery at Embabeh, the last village before Cairo, and thus to Bulaq on the other side of the river. The sheikh says, the soldier who can fight with cannons on water can defeat a fortress in the sands...' He had further terse words with Ali Qarim, but the sheikh silenced him. Nazir continued, with some resignation, 'He is asking, Hazar-*effendi*, when you return from guarding Hasim Bey, if you could advise with the defence of Cairo, of his homelands. These are the wishes of my brother, Sheikh Ali Qarim ibn Salah.'

Ali Qarim waited.

'This is truly a great honour, Hazar-*effendi*,' said Masoud.

'It will be an outrage to some,' added Nazir, 'but the sheikh's word carries much power.'

'*Atlobo minka haza almaarouf.*'

Nazir looked away, as if ashamed to translate. 'He says, I *humbly* ask you this favour.'

Hazzard regarded the calm face before him. In the back of his mind was the suggestion that Ali Qarim knew the Mamluk cavalry would fail, and that Embabeh would be Egypt's last chance. It was the request of a dying man. Hazzard could not refuse. He looked at the men on horseback, waiting, watching.

'We shall,' said Hazzard. 'Farewell. *Wa aleikum as-salam.*'

Ali Qarim smiled for the first time. '*Asbaha as-salamu ghariban huna.*'

He replaced his veil and mounted his horse, and led his troop and footmen after the train of cavalry. He looked back at Nazir and Hazzard, his eyes once again mere shadows above the gold and black mask, and then was gone.

Hazzard asked Masoud, 'What did he say?'

'Peace, said the sheikh, is now a stranger here.'

The excitement of the crowds in the square rose. '*Murad Murad Murad! Allahu akbar! Murad Murad Murad!*'

'Riding straight into bloody guns...' muttered Cook. 'Bloody barmy.'

'We do it.'

'Aye. But having a flamin' great ship round you makes a difference.'

'Bonaparte won't feel even a pinprick,' said Hazzard. 'Sharif Nazir,' he said, 'I beseech you. Let me prove to you what the Mamluk will face.'

Nazir watched his brother disappear into the parade. 'You will observe and guard with Hasim Bey?'

'Upon my honour. And for the sake of Ali Qarim Sheikh.'

Nazir turned and looked him in the eye, then cursed. 'You do truly have the *devil* in you both, English.' He looked for a groom to fetch their horses.

—

At al-Ramaniyah, Bonaparte's divisions staggered in from the waterless desert for rendezvous, the officers mutinous, the gloss of liberation long worn off. Whitewashed adobe hovels glowed in the heat, the army scattered in battalion camps, the men lying in the shade, propped against walls, many flat by the riverside, some gorged on the watermelons, some still eating them while up to their waists in the Nile, some drank greedily, some drowned in their eagerness.

Further down the embankment three adapted gunboats waited at their moorings. The flagship of the small flotilla, the *Cerf*, stood bright against the brilliant waters and dazzle of the blue sky – it was a *chebek*, a large, oared Levantine coastal trader, with two masts rigged with long, sloping lateen yards, now become an armed riverboat with an Egyptian crew, *fellahin* labourers hauling army field-guns aboard.

The two other improvised gunboats rode low and long in the river, cannons mounted awkwardly on the midship rails round a central shaded superstructure, a mortar since replaced with baggage and equipment. The flotilla was to follow the advance southward, cool on the Nile while the army sweated on the long march to Cairo.

Bonaparte stalked into his command tent. Monge and Berthollet rose from their chairs. Desgenettes, the surgeon-general, set down his glass of water, preparing for a confrontation. The death-march through the desert had raised his grave concerns.

'Is there a problem, General?' asked Monge.

'Problem? Mutiny *again*,' Bonaparte snapped. 'His grand five foot ten inches will not save Damas if I have anything to do with it! *Damn* the man!'

'I did warn you, General,' said Desgenettes.

'You did,' said Bonaparte, cooling, looking absently at the maps on his desk. 'What with my senior officers spouting seditious bile before their men, my junior officers being captured and buggered by amorous Bedouins, and everyone struck down with this, this idle, *slack*-jawed *lassitude*, this…what do they call it?'

'*Cafard*, General,' said Desgenettes. 'It is the lack of salt and water.'

Bonaparte threw down a divider onto the map before him. 'It is *not*, Surgeon-General. It is a lack of *gumption*, born of lying about on silken pillows in Italian villas. I should never have used the Army of Italy…' Bonaparte sighed. 'Are the boats ready?'

The naval commander, Perrée, stepped forward. 'Yes, General. With the *savants* and, well, the civil concessionaires, and their ladies of course, we are very cramped but the *Cerf* should be big enough to act as a viewing platform—'

'I am not staging a spectacle for an audience, Captain. All non-combatants, including those in the cavalry *who have no damned horses*—' one of Bonaparte's junior aides, Lt Desvernois, handed him a glass of water and he drank '—will go aboard the *Cerf* or the gunboats to support the army from the river. No excuses.' He waved a hand irritably.

Perrée inclined his head. 'General, your pardon. General Andréossy awaits your pleasure aboard the *Cerf* should you wish to inspect.'

'Should think he's glad to get his feet out of the sand and onto a boat... And the transport barges?'

'Yes, General, all arranged. They shall follow the gunboats.'

There was a commotion outside and after a moment a soldier put his head in and had a word with Desvernois. The young aide whispered in Bonaparte's ear and the general took a steadying breath. 'Very well.'

Waiting outside were two Bedouin messengers. Seeing Bonaparte emerge, they bowed low.

'*As-salamu aleikum, ya Sultan al-Kebir.*'

Bonaparte nodded impatiently. 'What did he say?'

One translated for the other. 'We say peace be upon you, Sultan *al-Kebir.*' He bowed again, his hands outstretched. '*Great* Sultan.'

Bonaparte gave nothing away but the generals exchanged glances. They could only guess at his pleasure.

'Very well,' he replied. 'What have you for us?'

'*Mamliqiyyah.*' One of them pointed up the Nile.

The other man spoke. 'The Mamluk come, Excellence, to Shubra Khit, like the host of Allah upon you, by water, by horse, by foot, led by Murad, *Amir al-Hajj*, Lord of the Pilgrimage. He comes with the Sword of Ali and a storm of fire.' Their message concluded, the Bedouin bowed low again.

Bonaparte closed his eyes in relief. *Thank God.* He nodded to Desvernois, 'Give them food and water. Send word to General Berthier to issue the orders, and fall in the army for an address. We march south through Minyet Salam,' he said. 'To Shubra Khit.'

His expression gave nothing away, but his eye had lustre once more.

The baggage trains moved with the field artillery, clouds of dust kicked up by horses in harness, urged on by the whips and cries of the Dragoons and *Chasseurs* galloping down the thoroughfare, frightened locals watching from darkened doorways. Platoons gathered their arms and equipment, everything that could move, everything that could be carried.

A platoon of the 25th with a dozen goats in tow stopped a mule on the packed desert road, two bowed figures on its back, a haggard young Bedouin leading on foot. A corporal snatched the rope halter from the Arab, but the boy shouted back in French, his voice a husk, '*Non non, allez, allez…*'

Exhausted, Sarah Chapel peeled the improvised *hijab* from her face, the sand and dust cascading over her shaking hands. She coughed at the corporal, '*We are French. H-have you water?*'

The corporal stared, incredulous. Lolling against Sarah's back, Jeanne lifted her head to peer at the soldiers over the bands of her headscarf. The corporal called out, '*Des bidons! Vite!*' *Water bottles, at once!*

Soldiers gathered round and they were lifted gingerly from the mule. '*Mademoiselle*, come, this is no place for you, *venez*,' and they were led to the side of the road, the corporal calling over his shoulder, 'Get him out of here and take that mule to the *sapeurs…*' He swung a switch at Yussuf. 'Off with you! *Yallah yallah! Allez-vous en!*' and began to swat him over the head and neck.

'*No.*' Sarah caught at Yussuf and would not let go. 'He is our guide.'

'*Mademoiselle*,' cried the boy. '*Mes choupettes…*'

Goatskins and water bottles were put into their hands and the corporal watched as Sarah gave a skin first to Yussuf. He tried to intercept it. 'It is for *you, mademoiselle*—'

Sarah struck his arm sharply. '*Leave him!*'

'Corporal Roy! Bring them this way,' said a young *sous-lieutenant*, waving them down the crowded road. They followed the officer, Yussuf keeping his head bowed for fear of being struck,

Sarah holding his hand. She could see the bright blue of the Nile, the twin-masted *chebek* rising in the distance. Through the mayhem of troops and horses they could see civilians, commissary staff, and a group of *savants* gathered on the deck in their top hats and frock coats, chatting, admiring the sweep of the river, examining the vegetation, the fruits, the soil, excited.

'It is bound for Cairo?' Sarah asked the officer. Jeanne gripped her hand tightly.

'But of course, *mademoiselle*.' The subaltern put a hand up to a lieutenant and ran to him, calling, 'Lt Vertray! Two more, *je vous en prie*, for *Le Cerf…*'

They were jostled by squads of men looking for their platoons, their companies, moving in all directions, *sergents-chefs* calling above it all, shouting orders, choking clouds of dust rising in the wake of galloping cavalrymen. Sarah fell against Yussuf, the *sous-lieutenant* catching her, *The heat, water… more water*, he said and in the commotion she whipped a hand to her breast and yanked the pendant figurine of St Jude from her neck. She thrust it into Yussuf's hands, whispering urgently to him, '*Go, Yussuf*, to Cairo, understand? *Qahira?* Take this to the Red Pasha, or one who knows him. *Find him. Understand?*'

Yussuf's young, pitted face crumpled in sadness. 'No no no no my cabbages, *mes choupettes…* I stay with you—'

'He will protect you, I promise.'

Lt Vertray handed a chit to the *sous-lieutenant* and called out, beckoning them, '*Mesdames, we are soon to depart—*'

'Please, Yussuf, *please*,' she repeated, squeezing his hand tight over the figurine.

'For you, *ma choupette*,' he promised, and Sarah watched him disappear into the crowd, looking back, fear in his eyes, swallowed up by the shakos and black helms and plumed bonnets and packs. Sarah and Jeanne were pulled along by the officers to join the *savants* and board the *Cerf*.

'You will be quite safe upon the river, *mademoiselles*,' assured the *sous-lieutenant* earnestly, shepherding her to the watermelon fields, down to the riverside and the busy gangplanks – little knowing how very mistaken he was.

–

The men of the 25th *demi de bataille*, 2nd *Légère*, and the 75th Invincibles marched through the village of Shubra Khit and out onto the level ground to the south, a battalion commander bawling, '*En carré! First Division will form square! First and Second Battalions the 25th to left marker, 75th to right marker, marchez!*' The line infantry rushed forward to assemble in their hundreds, their once gleaming leather helmets dusted almost white.

Caron led the Alpha-Omegas to their rally points and looked out over the terrain. The low rising sandhills to the south betrayed the approach of Murad Bey's cavalry, a towering dust-cloud in their galloping wake, a pillar of fire.

'*Sacre…*' Caron called to them, '*Alpha et Oméga, Premier et Dernier! Pig, mon enfant!*' he called to Pigalle. 'You shall be right marker for the 75th! Fifty metres and the division will form upon you! Show the *général* where you stand, *mon garçon!*'

A musket in each ham-like fist, the giant Pigalle charged roaring into the soft sand, a spreading arrowhead of cheering men racing behind. At fifty paces he rammed his heel into the earth and slammed down the butt of a musket, shaking the other over his head, '*I am Pigalle! And where I plant my boot, there shall I not be moved!*'

The colour guard dug the standards into the sand behind him, and the battalion cheered, *Vive le Pig! Vive le Pig!* Rossy, St Michel, Antonnais and the other Alpha-Omegas formed up behind him, the ranks of the 75th filling behind, line after line numbering off as they fell into formation, two ranks, three, four, each man crashing into the shoulder of the next, packs and *boudin* bedrolls jamming tight together, scarcely able to move, shoving the man in front, five ranks, six, muskets ordered before them, each platoon, each company, each battalion punctuating their formation with a massed shout: *Fermez! Hwa!*

General Damas galloped through the dust clouds to the centre, the staff forming their mounts into troops, nearly trampling some, as the 2nd *Légère* filled in the rearward walls. The 25th *demi* fell into position to become the driving engine of the armoured machine they had all become. The artillery horses hauled 12-pounder guns to the corners, sand and dust flying from their thrashing wheels – just as the divisional commander General Dugua roared into the centre, arm raised, shouting from his saddle, cheers following him, *Papa Papa!* And the square of the 1st Division slammed shut: '*Hwa!*'

Caron looked down the lines, sergeants shoving men into the gaps, pulling some further back, six ranks deep, two hundred men abreast on each side of the square. None of them could move against the other and Caron saw them jostling, some fighting. He raised his short-sword.

'*Division…! Division will load and ram! Chargez vos armes!*'

As one, all four walls of the formation brought their muskets to their fronts, ready to load, *Hwa!* The centre was clogged with braid, *chefs de brigades, chefs de bataillons*, all shouting their chain of orders, and Caron's voice boomed over them all, '*Ready to open your priming pans! Ouvrez bassinets! Ouvrez…'nets!*'

The hands of each rank moved in automated unison.

'*Ready with your cartridges! Prenez…'touche!*' He waited just one beat. '*Déchirez! Tear cartridge!*'

The ground began to tremble with the thunder of hoofbeats. He could see the pillar of fire closing on them.

'*Amorcez!*' Prime!

Captain Moiret nudged Caron. 'Achille – *look…*' He pointed.

A lone Mamluk horseman had appeared. He pranced his mount before them, rearing on the low ridge just ahead, the rider spying out the French formations. The sun glinted from every silver and golden stitch on his woven armour, coins, chains, jewels sparkling, his billowing *binish* robe flaring behind, white, translucent. He galloped first to the right, then stopped dead and galloped back to the left. The horse reared, its forelegs kicking in mid-air, and turned slowly on its hind legs in a full circle. Caron heard the cavalrymen behind him, '*Incroyable – c'est magnifique.*'

Caron spat sand and dust from his mouth, took a swig from his water bottle and spat again. '*Magnifique… putain.*' He continrued, '*L'arme à gauche! Cartouche… dans canon!*' *Pour your powder!* The hands tipped the cartridge powder into the muzzles.

'*Balles dans canons!* Spit your bullets, *mes enfants!*'

The 14th, 32nd and 4th *Légère* of the Second Division under General Bon had formed their square and were moving slowly into position, a fortress of five thousand, shuffling through the sand, kerchiefs over their faces, packed tight, counting their paces in rhythmic unison, *un deux, un deux, un deux…*

'*Putain…*' said Caron. He could hear the 'Marseillaise' playing from somewhere. '*Bourrez…!*' *Ram!*

Several in the second rank to his right toppled and fell, one man knocking the other, and for a moment they went like dominoes, a sergeant screaming out, '*Look to your fronts you bloody idiots and ram! Salauds de merde!*'

The answering call came from the Mamluks. Caron heard it shrieking over the sand, carried on the hot breeze. It grew ever louder, sweeping across the scrubby plain. The square fell silent. The men listened.

Murad Murad Murad! Allahu akbar!

Battalion commanders ordered the front rank to kneel. On each side of the square, two hundred men prepared, then took a knee, a tidal wave, breaking on the corners with the guns. '*Putain,*' muttered Caron, and shouted, '*Apprêtez!*' *Make ready!*

As one, the Charleville muskets were levelled and faced outwards, two hundred across, six ranks deep of bristling spikes, now held ready, *Hwa!* They did not have to wait long.

The Mamluk army had spread into a crescent formation, its ranks of chanting footsoldiers and gleaming pavilions topped with glowing brass crescent-moons and globes stretching from the Nile on their right, and beyond the vast French squares on the left.

On the water, seven Mamluk gunships moved downriver towards the French riverboats, closing the distance to a great bend in the Nile, hugging the shore and the broad mudflats to bring their cannon within range of the French squares. The men aboard waved their swords overhead, their voices calling across the sands. The battle of Shubra Khit was about to begin.

Murad rode at the head of his cavalry. The dust clouding all around them, they darted first to the right, then to the left, following Murad's every move with effortless ease. When Murad saw the French squares, his face creased into confusion, and he recalled the words of Ali Qarim, who had passed on Hazzard's warning.

'What sorcery is this,' he murmured, 'that they conjure castles from the sands...'

One of his *sanjaq* lords cried out, '*It moves! It is a fortress of men!*'

Murad reached to his left hip and drew his sword. 'Then their walls shall bleed!'

Far to the rear, Sharif Nazir, Hazzard and Cook rode among the sparse cavalry guarding the right flank of the footsoldiers, the vanguard just ahead, Murad Bey a dark figure in the distance. The Mamluk foot units around Hazzard were more like a medieval rabble, with shields and swords.

They watched the French squares advance through a screen of choking dust. They had seen their share of sea-battles, formations of great ships turning in line, and been among them as cannon had sought the destruction of all with random disregard. But this was different.

'*Jaysus shite an' all,*' said Cook when he saw them.

Hazzard rode closer to Nazir and shouted through the drumming of hoofbeats, '*Do you see, Sharif? Now do you see?*'

Sharif Nazir stared in awe. '*They are as castles, with walls of spikes...*'

'*There are six ranks, Sharif! Each rank will fire a volley, over two hundred muskets at once,*' shouted Hazzard, '*then another and another!*' He drew closer and they slowed slightly, 'The cavalry will be destroyed! Murad must use the guns from his boats! Tell Hasim Bey! The cannons on the boats *must be aimed at the squares* – it is the only way!'

'But *Hazar-effendi* – you may only observe! Murad spoke it so!'

Cook called back to him, 'They'll be cut to flamin' *ribbons!*'

'Murad is the greatest warrior in the world!' cried Nazir. 'You shall see!'

'*Christ above…*' Hazzard looked again at the antiquated horde around him. At last he understood Ali Qarim's concerns for Cairo. '*He'll kill them all.*'

On the Nile, the Mamluk flagship reached the bend in the river and sighted the French flotilla, which Perrée had believed would make such a useful viewing platform for the *savants* and civilians. The Mamluk ship fired an opening round, the burst hurling a fountain of spray and great clods of riverbank mud into the air. The Mamluk footsoldiers cheered. It was the signal they had awaited.

Nazir called out, '*Hazar-effendi!* We go to Hasim Bey! *Now! Ride, ride!*'

Cook hauled on the reins and Hazzard followed, the Arabian horses leaping forward. 'God, *God, God!*'

Scimitar

Murad raised his sword, calling over the thunder of hooves, '*Ya saif ... Ali...!*'

The cavalry kicked their heels in and charged the French squares. They curved towards the Nile at full gallop in a sweeping arc, the army of footsoldiers far behind, calling on the sword of Ali to lend them power, *Ya saif Ali...! Murad Murad Murad! Allahu akbar!*

Amid the clamour of the charge, his vision blocked by the dust and sand and riders before him, Ali Qarim rode at the head of his own contingent behind Murad. As he spurred down the sloping fields he touched the pistol at his waist, now a protective talisman, a memory of Hazzard and their strangely entwined fates, and intoned under his breath, '*Martimar, Londan...*'

He brought the worn leather of the reins up to his mouth under the silk veil and clenched them between his teeth, tasting the familiar salts of polish and sweat. His black mount, Selim, felt the change, his eyes rolling back as Ali Qarim drew his new London pistol with his right and another with his left, a French Boutet, an irony which made him smile. The amir ahead called the order.

'*Break!*'

The charge split into its troops and the first French formation came shuddering into his view. He fired one pistol then the other, tucked the Mortimer away and threw the Boutet over his shoulder, and drew two more, long-nosed Turkish wide-bores. He fired one then the other, the blast of white powder blossoming then whipped away on the wind, and he threw those over his shoulder, spent.

The French squares stood before him, three, four, five of them, spiked castles of men shaking, tilting in the narrowed vision of his black silk mask. *Selim*, he thought, *now*, and the horse sped onward. He bit down hard on the reins and drew his two great curved scimitars from their scabbards on each hip, holding the blades high and out to the side as the first commands of the French began to rise to his ears.

'*Premier et deuxième rangs…! En joue!*'

The first and second ranks presented arms. Caron watched the Mamluks come and called out good luck to his men, '*Bonne chance, mes enfants…*'

The battalion commander screamed out.

'*Fire!*'

The first volley appeared to Ali Qarim as a long bursting grey stormcloud, as four hundred balls of lead tore into the vanguard of cavalry. Then the corner field-guns barked, spraying the field with grape-shot. The Mamluks flew from their saddles, their whinnying horses crashing into the sand, legs shorn away by molten razor-sharp shrapnel.

Ali Qarim thrust first with his left knee then his right, and Selim responded at once, dodging, leaping, and he shouted '*Hat hat hat!*' Selim jumped a fallen horse and its rider, and in that moment exposed his broad unprotected belly to the second volley of the next two ranks of four hundred men.

'*Fire!*'

The horse turned, twisted, crying out, and Ali Qarim felt half a dozen hammers rapping at his armoured chest and arms, shredding his robes, and he was knocked backwards, the wind blowing from his lungs as he parted from the saddle. His swords still tight in his outstretched hands, he struck the ground and rolled, a passing hoof catching him, kicking his thigh and the sun burst in his eyes as he rolled again, the clouds of dust too thick, the whip and whine of French bullets thudding around him.

'*Fire!*'

Always that word, again and again, and he lay for a moment, trying to breathe.

'*Tiens! Vous là!*'

He lifted his head. Only a short distance away was a startled French soldier at the corner of the square by one of the guns, a kerchief tied round his mouth, pale eyes wide, white dust powdering every inch of him. He stared at Ali Qarim, his hand shaking the man beside him, his outstretched arm pointing as Ali Qarim rose up and fell. One man took a hesitant step forward but another yanked him back, shouting at him, and Ali Qarim stumbled again and fell.

More riders swept in, hurling deadly *djerid* javelins, and one soldier fell with a cry in the tumult. Ali Qarim dived away as a horse tumbled, rolled and righted itself and he threw himself upon it, reaching for the empty saddle. The horse bolted, Ali Qarim riding, riding, the swords heavy as he guided the beast directly towards the next square. *This much*, he vowed, *I will do*. He readied his swords.

'*Allahu akbar.*'

He heard a voice calling, *Sheikh Ali!* and he swung the horse round in time as a sharif's troop galloped past, the sharif reaching out and pulling him along and away, out of danger, as yet another volley burst upon them.

At the front corner, Pigalle hauled round a cannon by himself and shoved in the grape-shot bag for the artillerymen, roaring madly every time it fired. Caron looked out at the sands littered with the Mamluk dead. 'They ride in, they ride out, trying to pull us after them...'

'It is slaughter...' gasped Captain Moiret. 'Why can they not see...?'

It is usually so, thought Caron, *but not so complete.*

Caron saw the stream of cavalry ride off then return in a long curving arc once more. 'It is a madness. Here they come again...'

On the Nile seven oared Mamluk ships surged towards the French flotilla, their Greek and Turkish captains striding the decks, raging at them to row faster, ever faster.

Three French gunboats pushed upstream in line, an oared galley abreast, its pace faltering when it saw the Mamluk advance. They had kept to the centre of the river to avoid the shallows – it was so low now that it narrowed to 250 metres across, but the waters spread out at the bend before them – now blocked by Mamluk ships.

Citizen Monge, Bourrienne and Commodore Perrée stood on the command deck of the *Cerf* at the rear, Perrée looking ahead through his scope, aghast at the approaching peril. He shouted across the decks of the *chebek*.

'*All hands to the guns! Civilians to the stern!*'

He glanced at Monge and Bourrienne. '*Messieurs*, if you do not have a sword,' he said, 'it would be best to find one.'

The Mamluk ships opened fire, pounding the first two gunboats, sending aloft spouts of water, several rounds hitting the decks. French troops tumbled into the water, some crewmen diving overboard and swimming to the second gunboat or making for the *Cerf*. Bedouins rode up and down the shoreline taking shots with their carbines while prepared Mamluk field-artillery crews dragged cannon into position and began to open fire.

Hazzard and Cook reached the right flanking wing of Hasim Bey. The Mamluk infantry stood in loose ranks. Far to the front the bey watched the battle of the squares from relative safety, surrounded by a personal escort in flame-red turbans.

'The cavalry is being shot to *pieces*,' muttered Hazzard. 'He's *got* to turn the river-guns on the squares...'

As he spoke a cannon on the Mamluk flagship roared and the *Cerf* took a hit, but the men who rushed to the bows and beat out the flames were not French sailors or Egyptian deckhands – they were dressed in topcoats and cravattes.

Hazzard felt in his saddlebag for his telescope. 'It's the scholars, the damned *savants*,' he said. He recognised the elder statesman among them, Gaspard Monge, whom he had met aboard *Orient*. 'My God – Bonaparte brought them into the battle...'

'Who are these men?' asked Nazir, drawing in beside him, taking the telescope to see. 'They are not warriors...?'

'No, they damn well are not,' said Hazzard.

The first French gunboat was soon overrun by Mamluks and Greek mercenaries. Several of the French soldiers threw down their arms and thrust their hands in the air. A Mamluk snatched up the nearest and held him to the mast by his hair. Another swung his scimitar. The decapitated body dropped amid gouts of blood, the twisted, open-mouthed head kept in place, and they laughed, the Mamluk waving the sightless horror to his comrades. They promptly beheaded the other captives, lifting the heads by the hair and shaking them at the *Cerf*, laughing, before tossing them into the Nile.

Cook and Hazzard watched. They had seen worse in the battles for the Karnataka, with Mysore, between Rajahs, between Marathas and Mughals. But this made it no easier. Nazir lowered his telescope, evincing no celebration.

'*Bloody savages...*' murmured Cook. 'Whose side we on...'

The next gunboat fired, salvoes pounding the Mamluk flagship, more of the Greek sailors diving into the water and swimming to board the French ship. Soldiers fired their muskets, trying to pick off the sailors before they boarded but were overwhelmed, slaughtered by swinging axes and swords. They heard the cries and shouts as the French tried to escape – and something else: the screams of women.

'Good God...' Hazzard raised the scope once again to the river. One of the gunboats was swung round by the current but still the transport barges behind came on, filled with *savants* and civilians, those same men and women he had seen on the *Orient*, in utter helpless panic. Hazzard tugged at the rein. '*Nazir, to me...!*'

They rode round the head of the formation to Hasim Bey, and found a portly bearded man in a turban, watching, slumped in his saddle. Mamluk spearmen formed a line and kept Hazzard back.

'My lord! Is this *jihad*? Do you call *that* holy? Do you think that *honourable*?'

Hasim did not understand. He gave a shrug and spoke, Nazir interpreting, 'Hasim Bey says it is the death of our enemy, Hazar-*effendi*. He says surely this is why you are here.'

'So that you might do murder to unarmed captives? If you do *this* you can expect no mercy from the French Sultan!'

The bey waved a hand as if Hazzard were an irritation. 'We need no mercy from him. It is he who needs mercy from us. England shall observe.'

More cannons roared on the river and Hazzard's mount whinnied and bucked. 'England shall not bloody well *observe!*' he snapped back. '*Murderous bloody swine...*'

Hasim Bey spoke and once more waved his hand. A platoon of spears surrounded Cook and Hazzard, forcing them to back away. 'We cannot overcome the infidel in *jihad* if we have the infidel in our ranks,' said Nazir pointedly, just as he had warned him in Cairo. '*England shall observe.*'

'I'll be damned if I'll watch this—'

The Mamluk spears were thrust aggressively towards his mount. 'Hazar-*effendi*,' called Nazir urgently, 'you must not force his hand. Already, he says, he is sullied by *kafiri* in his army.'

Hazzard looked out at the Nile, at the cooks, clerks, servants and *savants* battling the Mamluk flotilla. He could do nothing to stop it.

–

'*Mon dieu... barbares, les barbares...*' stammered the aged Berthollet, clutching at Monge's shoulders. 'Gaspard – they are *monsters...* evil, dark monsters...'

'No, Claude,' said Monge, 'they are men. And it is we who attack them.'

'I shall not be taken so – I shall not! My God, my *God...*' Berthollet began gathering musket-balls and cannon-rounds, filling his pockets. 'I shall drown, I shall sink, rather than—'

A cannon-burst knocked them sideways. '*Get down!*' shouted Perrée, pushing Monge and Berthollet back with the others. Flames caught and their hired oarsmen ran from the bow. Sword drawn, General Andréossy screamed orders at the marines as they shot at the swimmers in the water. He saw Monge and called out, '*Messieurs!* Take shelter at once, if you please!'

'Never mind us, General!' cried Monge, then roared to the others, '*Blankets! Sand! Hurry!*' and they charged forward. In their incongruous hats and coats the *savant* scholars beat back the flames, smothering the deck with buckets of sand and Nile water.

'He must turn the squares to support us,' insisted Bourrienne, gasping from exertion. 'He must!' He looked out to the field, at the endless swooping of the Mamluk cavalry, and the inexorable advance of the squares. 'It is the least he can do, rather than leave us to take the brunt of the battle!'

Perrée agreed. 'If he does not move towards us and distract the Mamluk artillery, it is hopeless.'

'Claude! Come with me!' shouted Monge. 'We shall lay the guns!'

'Gaspard, surely we—'

'We once *built* them, so let us *fire* them!'

The oared galley on the west bank was blasted by the Mamluk flotilla, oars flying into splinters, the crew falling overboard, swimming away, crying for rescue. Another heavily laden Mamluk ship moved towards the second French gunboat and men began to leap aboard, some swinging across on lines, swords in hand. The screams shrilled into the air – frantically crowding the stern were Perrée's unarmed passengers, in their coats and in their dresses, the grand spectacle transformed into nightmare as they glimpsed the slaughter awaiting them.

Andréossy ordered the French marines forward to the bows of the *Cerf* and they began firing volleys, clearing the decks of the Mamluk ships as Citizen Monge prepared to fire his cannons. Joseph Fourier ran to implore him. 'Professor, *mon dieu!* Perrée has called the third boat for us! Come with me at once to the rear, *je vous en prie!*'

'Not yet, Joseph! We shall damned well open fire!'

With a strength none of them had before witnessed, the old foundryman dragged the gun back from its place at the rail by himself and shoved in a packet charge. He shouted at the crewmen, '*Load, damn you!*' and Monge took an 18-pound round as if it were no more than a tennis ball, and slammed it in. '*Ram!*'

Berthollet watched, his panic subsiding – until he saw Turks and Greeks swimming directly towards them. '*Gaspard!*'

A volley peppered the surface of the water from further forward, the waves dancing with shot, and the boarders sank into the Nile. One reached the rail but a marine thrust a spike bayonet into his eye and through his skull, '*Ça va, salaud!*' – and put a boot to his face and shoved the body back over the side. Fourier fell to his knees and vomited, then staggered upright with the ram for Monge.

'Now, Gaspard, *come*, for the love of God…' called Fourier.

'Wait, *zut alors*, Joseph!'

The crew ran out the loaded gun and Monge crouched behind it and kicked the barrel into position. '*Ready!*'

A second explosion rocked the boat. Berthollet tumbled to the deck, some of the junior *savants* rushing to his side, muskets in hand, but Monge did not take his eyes off the Mamluk ships. '*Fire!*'

The gunner puffed on his glowing linstock and put it to the touchhole. The cannon boomed. The ball smashed through the first Mamluk ship and took at least a dozen men with it. There was a cheer from the French boats across the river. They reloaded, and the *Cerf* began to bombard the enemy at last.

Perrée called through his loudhailer to abandon the two forward gunboats. The *savants* and clerks scrambled overboard at the stern, some falling into the water, some trying to jump to the deck of the third ship close behind, hands reaching out to catch them.

Sarah and Jeanne were nearly knocked down by the rush of those trying to get to the stern, a *savant* officer-cadet leading them. He snatched at Sarah as he passed. '*Mademoiselle*, please! To safety, I beg of you…!'

Sarah took hold of Jeanne and pushed her into his arms. '*Jeanne! Get to the next boat! Go!*'

'*You first! Vite!*' called Jeanne.

A party of Mamluks and Greeks charged into the troops on deck, French cavalrymen standing line abreast holding them back, their swords swinging – but some of the boarders had swum round behind and tried to clamber over the stern. A hand clutched at the rail beside Sarah and one of the soldiers' wives screamed. Jeanne raged at him, '*Non, vous salaud!*' and snatched up a fire-axe from the deck. She brought it down with all her strength, embedding it in the wood. There was a cry from the water and the man fell away leaving behind his bloody hand.

The *savant*-officer took his opportunity and lifted Jeanne bodily into the hands of another, and she was passed to the third gunboat calling, '*Belle! Belle! Do not leave me!*'

The crippled French ship listed abruptly and swerved towards the river's edge, running aground in the mudflats and heeling over, occupants hurling themselves into the river to get off. Broken lines of French troops fought off the Mamluks as Sarah scrambled to jump over the side with the others but she stumbled, clawing at the rail. She saw a pistol and grabbed it up. A dark shape roared overhead and she pulled the trigger and the man crumpled and fell. Another young officer saw her, took her wrist, '*Come with me!*' and pulled her through the debris of the deck.

A cannon round burst overhead, raining down clouds of splinters and timber. Without thinking, Sarah tore herself away and ran from him – and felt a heavy blow on her back. She flew forward, tumbling over the broken railing, falling head first into the Nile, slowly sinking into the current. She heard the *savants* calling behind her, and Jeanne's voice, '*Belle! Belle!*'

–

Hazzard's mount turned in frustrated circles, its breath snorting through its flared nostrils, eager to move, sensing Hazzard's desperation.

'This is the work of a *diabolus!*' raged Hazzard to Nazir. 'It does no honour to *Allah* or His Prophet! You cannot kill their soldiers but you can kill defenceless women and men of learning, like those of the Al-Azhar! Are you *cowards?*'

The Mamluks began to chatter angrily and shout up at him, thrusting their spears and pikes in their direction, Izzam and Alahum fending them off with their riding crops, shouting back at them. Nazir was horrified at his words. 'Unbelievers must not speak the name of God so, Hazar-*effendi!* It is as saying Jehovah with disrespect and we shall all be put to death for your blasphemy!'

Hazzard would have none of it, and pointed madly at the scene on the river. '*This* is true blasphemy! An affront to His eyes, *unholy, barbarous* and *savage!* And we shall all rot in *hellfire* for it, damn you!'

A cry went up to their left and several scouts ran towards them, Bedouins and Mamluks dragging a pair of terrified Arabs through the sand. They dropped them at the feet of Hasim Bey's horse. Izzam pulled closer to Hazzard. '*Bedu*,' He tapped a finger at his chest, 'Awlad 'Ali.'

Hasim Bey called out angrily to Hazzard, and Nazir said, 'This boy says you know a Frenchwoman! Is this true?'

One of the two ragged *Bedu* was poor frightened and bloodied Yussuf, cowering on his knees, two Mamluks looming either side, one with a raised sword. He gibbered in fear, '*Mes chou-choupettes, al-Aafrit al-ahmar, al-Aafrit al-ahmar,*' he repeated, raising his hands to cover his head, '*Al-Pasha al-ahmar! Non non non...!*'

Then Hazzard saw it, dangling from his wrist. It was his pendant of St Jude.

'*Where did you get that?*'

Nazir looked at him. 'What? You know this creature?'

'*Step back, damn you!*' shouted Hazzard to the Mamluks. He drew the deadly *shamshir* of Ali Qarim. '*'Mshi! Yallah!*'

Cook brought out two pistols and Hasim snapped a command. The Mamluks parted and the scouts retreated from Yussuf and his companion a pace, '*Al-Pasha al-ahmar... al-Pasha al-ahmar—*'

Hazzard threw back his *binish* robe to reveal his scarlet Bombay Marine coat beneath, its gold braid and jewelled Indian orders bright, and the Mamluks backed away at the sight of it. '*I am the Red Devil! Ya al-Aafrit al-ahmar! Ayna!*' Where!

Yussuf collapsed on his face into the sand with relief, '*Milord, milor', I beg...*' he stuttered in English, holding up his open hands again, showing the pewter figurine. Hazzard stared in horrified comprehension.

Sarah. It could only be.

Hazzard felt his chest tighten, his breath coming in short gasps with a sudden rush of fear. He reached down and took the pendant. Lost on his fall from the *Orient*. It was his without question.

'Where is she?'

Nazir was shocked. 'You *do* know of the Frenchwoman?'

'She is not *French*, Sharif! She is *English*—'

'I do not understand, Hazar-*effendi*—'

'An English agent, Sharif! *Where is she, boy!*'

Nazir turned and shouted down at Yussuf. '*Ayna hia! Ayna!*'

Yussuf pointed to the doomed ships on the Nile, the Mamluk flotilla bearing down upon them.

Hazzard looked.

My God.

He turned to Hasim Bey, enraged. 'Stay then, *great Bey al-kebir!* But *England shall not bloody well observe any longer!*' The Mamluk lord jerked back in his saddle with momentary fright, the Mamluks watching wide-eyed as Hazzard tugged at the reins and pulled his horse about, '*Izzam! Alahum! Sergeant Cook, to me!*'

'*Aye, sir!*'

Hazzard's mount leapt into the gallop, Izzam and Alahum after, Cook following. Hasim Bey watched them go with surprise, Nazir calling out 'Hazar-*effendi*!' but Hazzard would not have heard him.

Hazzard could hardly feel the ground beneath him as the Arabian tore across the sand and scrub towards the mudflats at full speed. Mamluk infantry cheered as he rode past them, his scarlet coat bright in the dun landscape, straggling groups of Bedouin raising their muskets, *al-Pasha al-ahmar!*

Guns on carriages, gun-crews rushing towards him then dodging away as he tugged the rein sharply towards the river. *'Fire at the French squares!'* he called. *'Turn! Turn your guns!'* he shouted vainly, then in rough Greek, *'Gyriste ta kanonia sas!'* but still they did not understand and he tried to break through to the riverbank, men-at-arms and squires surrounding their elite warriors, *Where! Where can I go!* He pulled the reins back, the horse whinnying, men waving their swords, leaping aside, *al-Aafrit al-ahmar!* always something *stopping* him, something in his *path*, the horse finding a route, jumping a carriage, *go on, boy, go on*, Mamluks shouting jubilantly, *al-Aafrit al ahmar!*

His *shemagh* headdress flew open, flapping in the wind and he dragged it off, the heat beating on his skull like a hammer. He stood in the foot-irons and leaned forward, *faster*, the Arabian's head plunging, its mane flying, its eyes rolling white as Hazzard charged into the shallows, the water spraying, then up onto the grassy banks again. All he could hear in his mind was the screaming, women's screaming, *Sarah's screaming*.

'*Hazar-effendi…!*'

Izzam was shouting for him but Hazzard did not stop. Unable to keep up, Cook pulled in his reins, gasping, and bellowed at Alahum, *'Get after him! Juldee, damn yer!'* and the Bedouin spurred his horse onward, following Izzam.

Hazzard raced along the riverbank, leaving the Mamluk forces behind, the river battle revealed in full. The Mamluk flagship rammed the French gunboat, shattered galleys drifting, wreckage floating, men on deck pointing, shots whining away behind as he rode. He saw the gunboat and the transports, the scrambling figures trying to get away.

Hazzard judged the distance and without knowing he had taken the decision guided the Arabian to a rise in the riverbank at full gallop. He loosed his feet from the stirrups, one knee on the pommel – *Christ above* – and leapt.

The horse stopped almost dead, and he flew in a sudden silence, turning, the sky spinning – then hit the water flat, his arms flailing, striking out beneath the surface, the robe and boots dragging, Ali Qarim's scimitar bumping against his leg with every kick, the robe tangling and he shrugged at it, *get it off get it off*, his shoulder bursting with pain, and a bright light flashing, *look, look for her.*

He swam hard for the gunboat, put a heavy hand to the rail and hauled himself upward. A French soldier reached down for him and Hazzard called, '*Capitaine St Juste, Batavien!*' It was a cry for help, that Hazzard was clearly no Mamluk, *red coat, yes, but European, Dutch Batavian, better than nothing.* He fell to the deck, a dead weight, the soldier calling to him, *up get up*, fell again, his knee giving way, *weighing a ton*, fire in his ribs, his back, then up again '*Mademoiselle Isabelle—*'

'*Who, m'sieur?*'

'*The women! Where is the lady Isabelle Moreau-Lazare?*'

A bullet whistled past, striking the planks nearby. A Mamluk rounded the ruins of the mainmast and the soldier yanked Hazzard to one side. '*With me, Cap'taine!*'

Three *savants*, two men and a woman running with a physician's bag, collided with them in a panic heading for the stern. More Mamluks, Greeks, Macedonians, and the soldier was pulled off to a bayonet rank, killing two before falling back, Hazzard watching, winded, then looking aft.

'*Vite! Vite!*' the *savants* said, and Hazzard was knocked down from behind, *Turk*, and he drew the sword, *fast*, and swung the scimitar in a rough arc, the steel slicing through a knee without resistance, severing the leg in one clean cut, a scream, a dead weight, a flashing arm, *up, get up.*

A woman helped him to his feet. '*Madame Lascelles, surgeon's assistant,*' she said, and took his hand, pulling him up. '*Go,*' he said to her, pushing them all to the stern, the *saif* blade not finished, flying in a loop to Hazzard's right, a second boarder caught, *shoulder*, a bent-angled Thracian blade dropping to the deck, *and again*, and Hazzard whipped it down and across, a light Talwar, another scream, and the man fell.

M'sieur! A marine helped him propel the small group of civilians through the chaos of fallen rigging, tangled stays, broken spars and oars at all angles. They reached the wheelhouse and a raised afterdeck – it was then he saw a figure in black fire a small screw-barrelled pistol into the face of a boarding Mamluk. The man turned.

Hazzard stared. Jules-Yves Derrien lowered the pistol in disbelief.

'*You*—'

The pistol came up fast and the flintlock clicked, empty, and Hazzard lunged but overbalanced, catching the edge of his wrist with the flat tip of the scimitar and Derrien cried out, dropping the gun as Hazzard crashed into him, dropping the sword. They grappled, arms locking, Hazzard kicking out for his legs and Derrien fell with a shout, trying to clutch at Hazzard's knee but missing. Derrien's scrabbling hands found Hazzard's throat.

Hazzard grasped at his wrists and shouted in his face, '*Get the civilians and savants off, you bloody fool!*'

'*What are they to you!*'

'*They don't deserve to be butchered by the bloody Mamluks!*'

A line of Turks and Levantines clambered through the wreckage of the superstructure, the first raising a half-moon battle-axe high over his head. Hazzard heaved Derrien to one side and burst from his grasp, finding the scimitar and swinging upward wildly, rolling and catching the Turk a blow on the hip, and another across the abdomen. The man retched, falling onto them both, Derrien striking at him with his own blade, missing, striking again.

A hail of small-bore cannon-rounds crashed into the midships shelter by the mainmast and exploded, more of the Mamluk mercenaries falling in the splinters. Derrien struggled upright and swung his sword down at Hazzard's head, driving the filigree knuckle-bow guard at Hazzard's temple. Hazzard ducked away but not enough; light burst behind his eyes and he fell back. Another blast of fire from behind and Derrien stumbled away, reaching the rail – and jumped overboard.

A man in black turban and leather jerkin charged Hazzard with an iron-studded mace – but stopped dead, his mouth open wide, as the mace and his severed hand fell to the deck, the tip of a scimitar bursting through his stomach. He crumpled, revealing Izzam behind, yanking his sword from the man's back, '*Hunehka! Mamliqiyyah! Ha!*' he grunted with satisfaction, flicking the blood from his sword in a spraying arc.

He took Hazzard by the hand and they lurched to the stern, the gunboat rocking with another explosion from the Mamluk flag-ship. In that moment, Hazzard saw Jeanne Arnaud. He recognised her from the *Orient*. She saw him, the sword, the red coat.

'*L'anglais…*'

She ran to him and Hazzard took her hand. '*Is she here?*'

Jeanne knew who he meant but shook her head, distraught. 'I came back for her but cannot find her! You must go, go quickly.'

'Was she wounded on the *Orient*?' Jeanne would not say, her eyes wide and frightened. '*Answer me!*'

'*No!* No, not wounded.'

It was enough.

Alive.

Her little face twisted with despair and she sobbed. 'We should be in *Rosette*…! But came to this…'

'Come with me! *Venez*,' he said. 'Izzam—' taking them both by the hands, he looked at her, '—we jump, or I boot your *derrière* into the river, *comprends*?'

'Ha,' she said with a little laugh, wiping away her tears, 'You must be an *anglais*…'

Izzam looked at the water uncertainly, but nodded, '*Hazar Pasha…*' Another round burst and hit the afterdeck, and the three jumped. The rush of water muffled the thud of cannon and the raging of the battle above. His hands round Jeanne's slim waist, he lifted her up to the surface, holding her safe, her arms tight round his neck. She coughed, her hair plastered to her cheeks, her eyes bright and frightened.

'*Merci, m'sieur,*' she said. '*M'sieur l'anglais.*'

Shouts from the rescue boat, and hands stretched down for her, others reaching for him, *M'sieur, m'sieur, ici!* He lifted her up to them and said, close to her ear, '*Tell her, tell her to find Joseph Hammer of Vienna. Ça va?*'

'*Oui…*' she kissed him and squeezed him tight round the neck a moment, then let go as two cavalry officers pulled her from the water, her eyes not leaving his. Hands reached down for him, *M'sieur, venez! Come!*

Beyond their sight, a thousand yards away, the French infantry squares drew closer to the riverbank, pushing back the Mamluk footsoldiers. The Nile erupted with French artillery fire. The *savants* and civilians cried out, and their rescue boat veered off. Fountains of mud and spray rose from the bank, the barrage rolling across the Nile.

Hazzard heard the splashing behind, *Izzam*, floundering badly, calling his name, '*Hazar…*' a shot and another, and Hazzard swam back to him, catching a piece of shattered timber wreckage, setting Izzam's hands firmly on it for support. '*Hasanan? Eh? Hasanan?*' *All right?* The Bedouin's breath came back to him, '*Shokran*, Hazar Pasha, *shokran…*' *Thank you.*

More rounds howled overhead as Hazzard clung to the broken timbers beside him and watched. He had to reach the rearmost boats, the transport barges, to find Sarah. Clouds of thick smoke belched across the river, the shattered gunboats drifting in the current, one half-sunk, its prow raised at a sharp angle. The *Cerf* emerged from the black curtain, charging towards the Mamluk flagship. French troops opened fire from her decks, shots whistling past, the water leaping, whining off the broken wood by their heads. Hazzard tried to cover Izzam and they swam, kicking their legs to get away, back to the riverbank.

214

A volley of fire boomed overhead and the French muskets stopped, cries of men, some falling into the water. Ahead, on the mudflats of the riverbank, Hazzard saw Alahum and Cook with a group of mounted Bedouin, cheering, waving their carbines in the air, shouting *Kuq! Kuq! Kuq!* Alahum rode his horse out into the shallows, Cook running after, a line round his waist. He dived in.

Cook struck out into the deeper water and reached them in minutes, taking hold of the frightened Izzam, still keeping his hands tight on the floating wood, a broken cask bumping into them, a body drifting by. He tied the line round the Bedouin and the wreckage. Artillery rounds howled above, the crash of flying spray mingling with the rattle and whine of musket-fire.

'*Can you hold him? I've got to get to the other boats!*'

'*You can't! The Frogs are linin' up their guns on the river!*'

He saw Hazzard's face, the blood and cuts, his eyes wide. It was as if Hazzard had not seen him. French field artillery boomed and shells hurtled down, round-shots, howitzers, the water thudding with impacts, sending up grey fountains, the distant crump of a hit on a Mamluk ship.

'Was she here, sir?'

Hazzard's gaze searched the scene on the water. He could not answer. '*I've got to bloody look for her!*'

—

Not fifty yards downriver, Sarah floated gently in the churned, muddy waters of the Nile, her feet kicking against the current, her skirts floating, blossoming, then enveloping her, dragging her down — until she felt the pressure of a large object splash behind her, and hands at her back taking rough hold of her bodice.

With a rush of air from her bursting lungs she was pulled choking to the surface. She coughed and retched blindly, her hands finding the arms of her rescuer, her world a blur, bobbing in the water. She looked up and saw the side of a small boat — then the deep, staring eyes of Jules-Yves Derrien, leaning over the side, reaching out to her.

'Take my hand.'

She nearly screamed, but could not.

'Isabelle. Come.'

With the help of two men, she reached the gunwale and fell in, tumbling against a number of sacks, coughing, wheezing, her throat burning, bringing up water. A soaked marine, evidently her saviour, looked down at her, *Ça va, ma belle?* and several tattered *savants* gathered round her with concern. One held her wrist, taking her pulse, a doctor. *'You are all right now, mademoiselle, do not distress yourself.'*

Sarah looked about, their faces unfamiliar – something was wrong. The boat was filled with sacks of meal and grain, heaps of rope and boxes of French stores – it was a trading *felucca*, not the rescue gunboat, and it was turning away from the French flotilla.

'Where are we going?'

'We are going to safety, *mademoiselle*,' said Derrien patiently, 'to Rosetta. Downriver.'

Derrien shouted over his shoulder in Arabic to make sail, *'Abhur!'* The Egyptian rivermen jumped to it, hauling up the lateen yard to make sail. The canvas caught the Nile wind and billowed.

'No...' She looked at the other passengers. *'Jeanne!* Where is Jeanne? *Jeanne! Jeanne!'*

–

The *felucca* glided slowly into mid-channel, the blasts from the artillery echoing in the distance, the thick fog of smoke drifting. For the briefest moment the wind picked up, the charred clouds parting, revealing a grey darkening sky and the river beyond – then Hazzard saw them.

'Jory.'

He saw the *savants*, and the marines – and the figure beside her. It was Derrien.

'*Jaysus,*' Cook kept his head down. '*It's him…!*'

'*Oh my Christ.*' Hazzard could not bear it – the sight of her, at last, but with Derrien. She was looking out across the water, straight at them, calling for Jeanne, no sign that she had seen them. Her gaze moved on.

Hazzard shoved off violently from the wreckage to swim out into the current but Cook took firm hold of his arm. '*No—*'

'*I've got to—*'

'*Look at her, sir, just look.*'

Five marines sat guard, watching the river, muskets and bayonets held ready. The *savants* spoke with her, comforted her – she was not a prisoner. She was one of them.

'If she sees you, sir, that bastard'll know she's one of *us.* And he'll *do* for her, no mistake.'

Hazzard watched. '*How* is he here… *how!*' Derrien had his back to them, looking away from the flotilla, from the battle, looking downriver to his destination. Hazzard tried to pull away.

'Sir…' urged Cook, '*he mustn't see.*'

'*Damn it, Jory, I'm going to kill him! Bloody kill him!*'

Cook dragged him back to their cover and Hazzard thrashed about until, at last, he hung still, quiet, defeated, and put his hands on the timber wreckage. He knew Cook was right. If he swam out to them, the marines would pick him off or bayonet him. Worse, Derrien would take his ultimate revenge on him – and kill her before his eyes, before he had the chance even to climb into the boat. She must have no connection to him, none. If Derrien divined the truth, especially after his escape from the *Orient*, she was lost, condemned.

Hazzard put his forehead against the flotsam, his anger draining silently into the Nile. He slid behind the floating timbers, the tangled lines, watching her, her hopeless expression, her shape slowly receding, her shivering body, her head now hanging low in resignation. Wisps of smoke slowly shrouded her.

'Got to let her go, sir…'

Hazzard could hardly think, for his anger, his fear, his pain. He let her be taken, for her own good.

But the scene was abruptly obliterated from sight. As the *felucca* pulled away in the downstream current, further upriver the *Cerf* drew alongside the Mamluk flagship just beyond the riverbend. The former Inspector of Foundries Gaspard Monge finally had a clear line of sight, and loosed a broadside of his guns. The cannons roared, and one of the iron rounds struck home, hitting the Mamluk powder magazine. The ship blew itself to pieces.

Nearly everyone on the last French gunboat was knocked off their feet by the explosion, the Mamluk gun-crews and Bedouins on the banks of the Nile thrown flat. Hazzard felt the percussion, the shock of the river as the blast-wave lashed the surface.

The French on the *Cerf* cheered, Monge, Fourier and Berthollet and others, saved, ecstatic with relief, pointing, waving their hats – as the sky filled with the slowly whirling corpses of mutilated Greek and Mamluk soldiers and sailors, gently turning end over end, then falling, splashing one after the other into the Nile, some limbless, some headless, so much macabre flotsam.

Hazzard felt the drag of the shallows, the reeds, stones and mud clutching at his legs, Izzam finding his feet on the river bottom. Within a few minutes, Alahum and Cook's Bedouins were pulling them in, and they staggered through a stand of tall rushes, collapsing onto the mudflats.

The shell of the flaming Mamluk flagship listed and settled, the smoke sending a pungent cloud over the battlefield, the blast stunning the Mamluk cavalry to a standstill. The Mamluk artillerymen abandoned their guns on the Nile and fled, the footsoldiers falling back.

Further distant, Murad looked over Shubra Khit, over his dead, over the spiked castles in the sand. The enemy had not been tempted to break. He called for retreat.

'*Al-Qahira…*!'

Murad Bey raised his sword and the remaining five thousand horse swept away, a flock of swooping birds, pausing briefly to gather, then galloping off, the remnants of the foot-army following.

Alahum dropped down next to Izzam, and the pair stared mutely across the scene. Izzam wrung out his *keffiyah* headdress, his tightly cropped curls glistening and wet. Alahum shook him by the hair and laughed. The other Bedouins handed them food and goatskins of water, repeating their names in awe, *Kuq, Hazar.*

Cook said, 'Sir, may I present the warriors of the Beni Qassim clan...' They bowed and touched their fingers to their hearts in greeting. Cook tipped a goatskin up to his lips and drank. 'Bloody lunatics, the lot, just the job.'

Hazzard stared at the water, burning debris still falling as the flames crackled on the flagship.

'I could have had Derrien...'

Cook looked downriver through the tall reeds. The *felucca* was almost out of sight, the figures indistinct in the smoky haze, the faces pale dots among the lengthening shadows of twilight.

'What now, sir? Alex? Rosetta?'

Hazzard thought of her, the Nile pulling her away from him. The further from him she went, the safer she was.

Let her go.

'Can't go home, Jory,' he murmured. 'Can't go anywhere. No ship, no fleet. May as well be at sea with those bloody barrels again...'

The French drummers began to pound slow and steady. The castles of men wheeled ponderously, their grunting rhythm reaching them on the wind, *un deux, un deux, un deux.* They began to march southwards across the landscape in the failing light.

'Cairo,' said Hazzard. 'Bonaparte wants Cairo.'

Cook looked downriver, towards Alexandria and Rosetta, then upriver at the French boats, still heading south for the capital. 'We can't save 'em, sir.'

Hazzard watched the formations move through the sand, kicking up dust, so many giant preternatural beasts. He thought of Murad. The fortress walls remained unbroken. They had not yet been made to bleed.

'Got to try...' said Hazzard, struggling to his feet, '...because I promised Ali Qarim.'

Al-Qahira

The people of Cairo had awoken in the hope that Murad had been victorious, and had stopped the French demons from drawing ever closer – Ibrahim had said they would feast with their talons upon the flesh and blood of the righteous. But on that Sunday, the first day of the month of *Safar*, news of Murad's defeat reached the city. Yet, still, with the coming of dawn the call to prayer of the *muezzin* remained the same, drifting high above their fears, that God was great, and that all should come to praise Him. Hazzard heard it, and took some comfort.

He and Cook waited in the cloistered courtyard of the Al-Azhar Mosque, its elaborate arches punctuated with still smaller arches within, decorated with geometric or floral ornament. It had a cathedral silence, and Hazzard retreated into it, trying to lose himself and quell the tyranny of his thoughts. A fountain tinkled, still audible though Cairo was in turmoil beyond the mosque's high walls.

Leaving Hasim Bey to his bodyguard, Hazzard and Cook had made good time back to Cairo with Sharif Nazir, Izzam and Alahum – and twenty-five men of the Beni Qassim, the fierce clan of Bedouin who guarded the flanks, threatening any stray Mamluk who dared challenge them. None did.

Confused reports of the Red Devil defying Hasim Bey, trying to direct the guns at the French squares yet fighting Greeks and Turks on the boats, had mingled with reports of his saving women from the river, fighting the Frenchman in black, and his Beni Qassim shooting down French soldiers. The Beni Qassim praised him, and would not move from his side. This was proof enough to Murad Bey, who had heard his warning of the castles of men.

Masoud appeared at Hazzard's elbow. 'Hazar-*effendi*? The bey will see us now.'

They sat on cushions on a dais in a library lined with large books stacked flat on tall, ornate shelves, a low table in the centre, servants setting out coffee, water, fruit, and minted tea. A breeze blew in from tall arched windows, diaphanous silk curtains floating gently. Across the table sat Sheikh al-Jabarti and Muhammad Bey al-Elfi. Muhammad Bey was a quiet, thoughtful man, with an elegant jawline beard and trimmed moustache beneath a long white *keffiyah* headdress, topped by a golden *iqal* circlet. He had led a troop of cavalry against Desaix before Shubra Khit, but for all this, he had the placid bearing of a spiritual *imam*.

The pair watched in benign silence as their guests took refreshment, and then did so themselves. Once they were satisfied, Muhammad Bey asked, 'I understand you have knowledge of the ancient world here, Hazar-*effendi*. Have you studied in the East?'

Hazzard thought of Hammer. He must have briefed some of the beys. 'I was fortunate to know one who did, sir.'

'It is said Egypt holds a special place for you,' said Al-Jabarti.

Hazzard nodded, still far-off. 'I am a student of history, Sheikh, yes.'

'In conversation with me, the Herr von Hammer has said you know much of our science, of the works of scholars on the strange writings we see everywhere.' He gave a self-deprecating smile. 'It would be more than I know of, quite certainly, yet I am fascinated...' Muhammad Bey watched him, aware of some torment hidden from his gaze. His conversation was a distraction, as if discussing the weather. 'The stone idols here are magnificent, are they not? They speak of times long past, indeed, long forgot – as all times of men will be.'

'I have studied them, sir, yes,' said Hazzard quietly. 'Many years ago.'

'It is at times most difficult,' the bey added, 'to discern the true Egypt from among the new religions. Christianity, Islam, the Copts, and the Gnostics in their caves. Which, indeed, is the Real, and which the Unreal?'

Hazzard's shoulders burned with fatigue, his hands still raw with blisters from riding, from wielding Ali Qarim's *shamshir*. He could still see the Mamluks throwing the severed heads into the Nile.

Hazzard must have been silent for too long, for Muhammad Bey leaned forward and said gently, 'Hazar-*effendi*, a people fighting for their lives, so it is understood by wiser heads than mine, cannot be held accountable,' he said, 'to the normal laws of civilised men.'

Hazzard considered this but said nothing. Muhammad Bey al-Elfi sensed his unease. 'But, these stone relics teach us, do they not, that all civilisations must come to an end. Despite our laws. So. What will come to us, Hazar-*effendi*, should the French be victorious at Cairo?'

Hazzard took this to be more oblique conversation than anything else. 'The French Sultan will occupy the city,' he said dully, tired of avoiding the truth. 'He will make himself supreme ruler. And kill any who resist.'

Al-Jabarti asked, 'And what of the true faith?'

'He has none, apart from himself,' said Hazzard. He thought of Malta, the gardens, and the man behind it all. 'He will adapt, Sheikh. Copt, Hebrew or Muslim, it will make no difference so long as he can command. He is a scholar, a friend to science, if it serves his purpose. He will treat the Al-Azhar with tolerance.'

Al-Jabarti seemed doubtful. 'How strange. An Unbeliever who looks well upon Islam. Do you, Captain?'

Hazzard simply stared and Muhammad Bey nodded to a servant who handed Hazzard his untouched cup of mint tea. '*Effendi?*'

Hazzard took it and drank. His hands shook so much he nearly dropped the cup to the table, but the servant caught it expertly and set it down.

Muhammad Bey regarded Hazzard for a time, then spoke. 'You carry a great burden, Captain. This thing that the French work against Egypt – it is not your responsibility alone. It is God's will.'

'I could have prevented it.'

On board the Orient.

Quickmatch.

'I doubt that very much. You have good intentions, but are not the father of a lost little people, truly. Hasim Bey speaks of your disobedience,' he replied. 'He also speaks of reckless courage. My lord Murad and the other beys, however, understand the English better than some, so it is said. As I too have had the pleasure in the past – their benevolent view of all foreigners as unfortunate, misguided children.' He smiled. 'But above all, I believe, the English have a love for the just cause. Are we a just cause? Is that why you fight against God's will? To save all this?' He waved a hand at the room, the mosque, at Cairo itself. He leaned forward, earnest. 'What is it that you truly seek in Egypt?'

Hazzard could feel Cook's eyes on him, Masoud waiting in tense devotion. Hazzard had no answer. He thought of the pyramids, the Father of Terrors, looking out, silent.

Justice? Vengeance?

Duty? To whom?

Muhammad Bey gave that curious tilt of the head Hazzard had seen in Ali Qarim. 'You do not merely seek vengeance, I think.'

I have such dreams, Mr Hazzard.

Because vengeance would not bring back lost time: the time before the battle for the Cape three years earlier, his bloody duel to the death with Harry Race, amid the barrage under those thunderous flaming Cape skies – or the time before Sarah had joined the ranks of the Admiralty spymasters – before all of this had begun. He wanted, needed, something more, something to protect this timeless place, protect his own timeless self, from the machine that came upon them, the machine leaving time crushed in its wake.

But his only recourse lay in subterfuge and trickery, the way of the Admiralty. *How very fitting.* Merely considering his scheme made disaster seem all the more likely, somehow manifesting an evil, elevating it to inevitability.

'I need the scribes of the Al-Azhar to draft a letter for me,' said Hazzard. 'To shatter the dreams of the French Sultan.'

–

Thousands of troops awaited the return of Murad, who still resisted the French, village by village, on the retreat southward. Still the numbers grew: the sheikhs came from Middle and Upper Egypt, Bedouin from beyond Lake Moeris and the Sinai borderlands, the Bili, al-Huwaytat, al-Sawalha and al-Habayba, all had come, answering Ibrahim and Murad's call to *jihad*.

Hazzard and Cook rode the perimeter of earthworks near Embabeh, ramparts heaped before dug-out gun emplacements, the batteries covering the north road, the only road the French could use to approach Cairo – the aim was for these to meet similar works stretching from Bashtil and Giza under Murad's command, but they had not seen much evidence of it beyond the distant watermelon fields, but Hazzard was impressed: the batteries would be a surprise for Bonaparte, and deadly to his infantry squares.

Embabeh was an ancient outpost, little more than a market-place for camel-trading, barely a mile from the river and a short ride to the northwest of the capital on the other side of the Nile. From what he could see, Hazzard recognised it could be Cairo's last hope. He looked across the Nile, over the Isle of Rawdah and the deserted fortress mansion of Ibrahim; the high walls of the great city darkened in silhouette as the sun climbed steadily behind. He looked at Cook. 'Ready?'

'As I'll ever be...'

They rode back for a conference with Ibrahim Bey, who was inspecting the defences. Masoud at Hazzard's side, they gathered with Sharif Nazir in a forward campaign tent with a number of Mamluk beys they had not yet met. Izzam and Alahum and the men of the Beni Qassim ranged about, suspicious of the Mamluks, watching, but taking their lead from Hazzard. Many kept a hand on the *khanjar* daggers at their waists, not trusting any of them.

Ibrahim Bey entered the tent, power emanating from every controlled gesture, the Ottoman Pasha, Abu Bakr following, in full Turkish court dress, complete with entourage, his courtiers keeping a safe distance from the Bedouin, the other beys bowing deeply. They approached a folding table covered with maps. Despite the wishes of Ali Qarim, neither was pleased to have Hazzard question the grand tactical plan.

'This is His Excellence,' said Sharif Nazir, introducing Hazzard, 'Abu Bakr Pasha of the Sublime Porte. Governor of Egypt,' he said with a note of warning. 'He is confident of victory.'

Hazzard bowed to the frigid countenance of Ibrahim Bey and the somewhat pale and sickly pasha. '*As-salamu aleikum.*'

Ibrahim replied with curt disdain. '*Wa aleikum as-salam...*'

Nazir began. 'Since you do not trust us to work it correctly, Hazar-*effendi*, I shall explain...' He pointed at the Ottoman map, its Turkic and Arabic notations incomprehensible to Hazzard and Cook. 'Here is Cairo. And here, at Ouardan, the French have already passed through. This night they will come soon upon Omm-Dinar, here, to the north. We attack them always, when they drink at the Nile, when they place their sentries, but still they come, a swarm of locusts. All the towns are taken to the French – any that resist are burned, the people put to the sword.'

Hazzard tried to focus on the map. He was tired, bitter, withdrawn. Cook watched him carefully. 'And Omm-Dinar is the last village before Embabeh and Cairo.'

'Yes.'

'On this side of the Nile.'

'Yes.'

It was too much. Hazzard wanted to give up, his advice come to naught. He glanced at Cook and they both saw the terrible flaw at once. The great artillery emplacements that the authorities were so busily digging were, to Hazzard, on the wrong side of the river.

'This plan,' said Hazzard with some control, 'is unwise.'

Masoud was disturbed by his certainty and that he would have to translate his displeasure. He duly interpreted, bowing his head in abject apology to Abu Bakr and Ibrahim.

'We have no need of your great opinion,' retorted the Ottoman Pasha loftily, 'the opinion of a *kafir*.' His glance flicked over Hazzard's robes and the red Marine tunic beneath. 'Victory shall be ours, and not yours, England. On this day, England *will* observe.'

Evidently all had heard of what happened at Shubra Khit.

'Yes,' said Ibrahim. 'We can defeat the blasphemers ourselves, Hazar *al-hakim*.'

He used the sobriquet of 'the wise' with irony, and even through the intervention of Masoud's translation Hazzard felt the utter contempt of the nobleman. Izzam and Alahum looked on murderously, Izzam slowly putting a thumb behind his teeth and flicking it at them, then apparently stroking his beard. Hazzard pretended not to notice.

'Why then is it unwise?' demanded Nazir.

'We're on a lee shore,' said Cook, as if it were obvious. 'Fighting to windward while being blown onto a ruddy cliff at our back. Bloody mad. We'll break up on the rocks.'

Nazir still did not understand and Masoud was lost by the naval idiom. Hazzard explained, 'The French will come first to Embabeh, on the west bank, and need to cross the Nile to reach Cairo, on the east bank. Very well. Let them try. Cairo can be a fortress, the Nile its moat, its protection. Bonaparte will not want his disciplined formations thrashing about in the water – they will be helpless. Let them try to cross the river, *then* pound them with the guns on the Bulaq side of the Nile, not Embabeh. Their castles of men will fall apart and be destroyed.'

Nazir looked puzzled. 'But if they are in the Nile, it will be too late.'

'No, Nazir, they will be trapped in the water. If we fight with the river at our backs, there is nowhere to retreat and regroup. *Nowhere*. The Nile will become our enemy. If the French rout

Murad's army on the Embabeh side of the Nile, any survivors will have to run into the river to escape, and the French will slaughter them. Bonaparte will then cross at his leisure, in safety, facing no further resistance.'

'There is my own army,' said Ibrahim Bey, indicating a spot on the map. 'We encamp here, at Bulaq, on the other side of the Nile, to meet any who come. So. Thus shall we spring the trap, and confound them, and be victorious.'

Cook pointed at the map and murmured to Hazzard, 'Look. It's just desert behind him… He can run all the way to ruddy China…'

Masoud stopped translating. Nazir glanced at Hazzard as Ibrahim looked on with suspicion, unable to understand the English. 'You do not trust him to fight?' asked Nazir.

'No, I damn well do not,' said Hazzard pleasantly with a nod, to reassure Ibrahim. 'His plan puts his greatest political rival, Murad, and his cavalry, on *our* side of the Nile facing the French alone, while he has an escape route clear to Damascus. If Murad is killed, he would become ruler of the *diwan* and Egypt.'

Nazir kept his eyes low as if studying the map. 'That would truly be unholy and wicked…'

'You know his past better than I.'

'Can we blow the bridges?' asked Cook.

'That will save the city, yes?' asked Masoud. He began to translate once again for Ibrahim Bey and the pasha, who affected boredom, as if all such plans were in hand.

'Surely the bridges can be used for our army to retreat as you say,' said Nazir.

'Yes, but if the French outflank Murad, and reach the river first, they will then use the bridges to cross the Nile to the city.'

Ibrahim laughed at Masoud's translation, and Hazzard's fears, but Nazir's confidence was shaken and he grew angry. 'How do *you* know of such things, oh wise Hazar *al-hakim*?' He threw down his pointer. 'Are you now the great general as well?'

'Quite so, Sharif,' said Ibrahim Bey. 'Who is amir and pasha here indeed.'

Hazzard swallowed his anger, 'I do hope someone is my lord, because the French will use the Nile as if it were the sea, and push your forces into it.'

'That is *not* an argument,' Nazir snapped back. Masoud quailed at his translations, his eyes closed, whispering to the pasha.

'I am not here to make bloody arguments, Nazir,' retorted Hazzard. 'I am trying to save your city. If you lose Cairo *you will lose Egypt.*'

'You are but an English officer of the sea!'

'Indeed,' chorused Ibrahim Bey.

'We're Marines,' said Cook with finality. 'We know guns.'

Masoud translated, his voice murmuring almost in prayer, bowing his apologies to the bey and pasha.

But Ibrahim Bey snorted and almost laughed. 'They are not so many, these French blasphemers. They came long ago, and were thrown back. They shall run for their lives once again. As do all Unbelievers.'

The pasha sniffed and added, 'Yes, and England shall prove the great liar.'

'How'd you like that turban stuffed up your arse, Baboo,' muttered Cook with a smile. 'Translate that for the little shite.'

Masoud blanched and stayed silent. Ibrahim Bey's face was a mask, giving nothing away, but the pasha looked pleased with himself.

'I pray I am wrong, my lord pasha,' said Hazzard to them, 'but I know this man, the French Sultan. He is the reborn Julius Caesar. When Caesar came to Egypt, he was not thrown back.'

Masoud translated. Ibrahim and the pasha smiled with well-concealed incomprehension and turned away with their entourage, Izzam and Alahum stepping back, the Beni Qassim bowing low and retreating.

Afterwards, they rode out to the gun emplacements, Nazir irascible as ever, Hazzard fearing the worst for seeing the battle plan. The earthworks were extensive, a great barricade of heaped ramparts from the edge of the town overlooking a broad flat plain perfect for Murad's cavalry. He could see Murad's thinking and it afforded him some hope. However, the valley was also the perfect battlefield for Bonaparte's army.

The labourers had dug separate gun-pits behind their ramparts in front of the now deserted adobe houses of Embabeh. The new batteries had been well sited, facing the northwest, providing overlapping fields of fire across the north road and broad, open ground either side, amounting in total to possibly sixty guns – equivalent to the broadside of a large First-Rate ship of the line, thought Hazzard. But, in each pit were a number of different field-pieces, some small-bore cannons on wheeled carriages.

'What's this?' asked Cook. 'Wouldn't hurt a mouse.'

'They are *darbzen*,' snapped Nazir, 'battering guns. Very effective.'

'But you've dug them in,' said Hazzard.

'What of it?'

'They have carriage wheels, Sharif – they are meant to be mobile guns. As the enemy moves, so one moves the guns...' Among them were also three giant ten-foot Ottoman siege bombards, the size of a gaping 68-pounder carronade. 'And those are utterly *immobile*,' he added, 'and should be mounted on a fortress wall.'

There was a short, vigorous Turkish officer in command of the operations, the long tassel on his tall fez swinging wildly as he swatted at his crews with a stick, swearing in thickly accented Arabic. '*Izree, izree, yollah!*'

'He is an *Osmanli*, Hazar-*effendi*,' said Nazir. 'A Turk called Russuf, with the rank of *Yuzbashi*, a captain of artillery. He is a proud man, and knows his science.'

'Science be damned, Nazir. If you dig these into the ground, we'll have to use a company of foot to defend them.'

Nazir turned on him. 'Muslim science was inflicted upon Christian armies with great success for *centuries*—'

'And look at you now! Reckless heroism does not win battles!'

The *Yuzbashi* captain waved them away, irritated at the interruption of his task. He put his thumbs in his generous belt and brushed his long, curling black moustaches. He called out something and Nazir translated. 'You see? He says they shall roar like the lion. Ha.'

Hazzard looked out at the terrain. It was wide open. Despite Murad's strategy and the fields of fire, the French squares had more than enough room to manoeuvre, separate and split into battalions or storming companies. The only obstacles were large clumps of palm and ancient broadleaf trees. It was suitable cover for the Mamluks – but could be used against the gun positions by French light infantry.

'And we have these also,' said Nazir, indicating what appeared to be a cavalry unit trotting towards them. '*Shayalaz.*'

The troop of cavalry turned out not to be horses but camels, each with small artillery pieces. The guns were no bigger than a murderer swivel-gun from a ship's rail – a light cannon firing a one- or two-pound round-shot, its ancient bronze casing oxidised to a dull verdigris colour. Its peculiarity was that it sat mounted on a tripod, not on wheels or a carriage, but on the backs of the camels.

'*Jaysus shite,*' murmured Cook.

'You must be joking,' said Hazzard. Even Izzam and Alahum and the other *Bedu* approached one of the beasts with some amused curiosity. Alahum asked the driver how much it cost.

'Watch.' Nazir gave the nod to the troop commander.

One of the riders called for a footman, who came at the run and lit the end of his long linstock taper with a tinderbox. Holding the wick aloft, the rider whacked the camel with his switch and it roared, shambling off into a fast trot. As he went, the driver pointed at a whitewashed mud hut fifty paces away. After some time, he turned and began his attack at full gallop. At the last moment the camel veered off and the rider put his taper to the gun's touchhole. It fired with such a percussive bang that it startled the horses and Cook nearly fell from his saddle. '*Christ Gawd Almighty*—'

Reappearing from the cloud of white smoke the camel trotted past, roaring in victory, the rider beaming and waving. The hut door, doorframe and a considerable part of the walls either side had been obliterated.

'Good God...'

'It can hit a target at half a *parasang*, a league,' said Nazir. 'With all of these guns, we can stop the French Sultan.'

Hazzard looked at Russuf's *darbzen* and the heavy bombard cannons. 'You will make him withdraw temporarily, perhaps, but not *stop*. We'll need at least a company of foot to support the guns, to be under Sar'nt Cook. The Albanians, Levantines, anyone, as long as they have firelocks.'

Nazir refused. 'Never. *Never*. The *Albani* are the sultan's personal guard and must be employed for the defence of the beys—'

'Sharif Nazir, you will give me support infantry or *lose the guns*.'

Nazir tugged at the rein of his horse. '*Always* you contend! Always! You are more quarrelsome than a *wife!*' He threw up his hands and rode off, furious. He shouted over his shoulder, '*Always, English!*'

Within the hour a company of Albanian Ottomans marched in, a small, stout Turkish sergeant-major at their head. They wore the fez and embroidered jackets of the elite Janissaries of the sultan's royal guard, and carried bent-bladed *yataghan* swords and long Turkish miquelet flintlocks. They halted with a snap.

Cook climbed out of Russuf's gun-pit, where he had been helping site the *darbzen*. The sergeant-major saluted him as if he were King George himself.

'*Kuq chavus!*' he declared. '*Kuq Sirjunt!*'

Cook looked at them and muttered. 'By all that's holy in Bristol...'

Cook tried to drill them in volley shooting, the miquelet much as any other musket, the chief difficulty being its length and the men's comparatively small stature – it took longer to load and ram because it was difficult for them to reach the muzzle easily, quick though they were.

Unwilling at first to break with their own tactical style and adopt rigid Marine ranks, within three volleys they could follow

Cook's parade-ground English commands, Alahum demonstrating, shouting in Arabic. Their only other hurdle thereafter was the urge to throw down their muskets once fired and attack with their swords.

'They pick it up quick,' said Cook to Hazzard as he looked them over, 'but their names are all Greek to me...'

'Albanian actually,' said Hazzard, glancing at the sergeants in front of their platoons. 'What rank are they? Officers? Warrants?'

'Oh, er, that's Fee, sir. Sergeant Fee.'

Hazzard frowned. 'Fee?'

Sergeant Fee cracked to attention and beamed back a ferocious smile. A gold tooth sparkled.

'Yessir.'

Hazzard indicated the next. 'And him?'

'That'll be Fie, sir.'

Hazzard looked down the line at the remaining two. 'Don't tell me. Fo and Fum...?'

'Sir. Well...' Cook shrugged. 'Works for them.'

–

At dawn the next day the Embabeh camp was jarred into action – Murad's fighting retreat had been beaten back. A cry went up and riders came galloping through the camp, squadrons of Murad's cavalry returning. Most had gone further west towards Murad's lands at Giza, but some had come to the capital. Hazzard saw the first of the wounded come in, slung over saddles, dragged on litters by other riders. He knew there would be many more.

The horses kicked up dust and sand as they came to a halt and the wounded were carried to shade under the trees, filling adjacent farmyards, physicians from the city attending them. Their battle-lines now clogged with wounded and retreating cavalry, Hazzard knew they would stand no chance if the French came hard behind them.

One of the Beni Qassim rushed over, and Masoud translated. 'Hazar-*effendi*,' he said with concern, 'Ali Qarim Sheikh...'

The Bedouin led them to the tent where Ali Qarim had been taken. He was lying on a couch, servants rushing about him, removing his shattered armour and robes. The black veil was gone, his half-burnt and blackened face now twisted with pain. Nazir looked down at his brother, who stared as if dead, murmuring, '*Selim... Selim—*'

'Have you any brandy?' Hazzard demanded of Nazir.

'Spirits? Of course not,' he retorted, 'only the physicians are perm—'

'*Find some!*'

'Sir,' said Cook and offered him a hipflask. 'Tastes like saddle-rub anyways...'

'No!' said Nazir, holding his hand away. 'It is *forbidden—*'

Hazzard pushed him off. 'Forbidden by Man, Sharif, not God.' He trickled some onto Ali Qarim's lips and he coughed, gasping, his tightening hand taking a fistful of Hazzard's robes. 'Sheikh, you are wounded.' The frustration of the language was too much and Nazir simply stared down at him, shocked at seeing his brother in such a state. Hazzard snapped at him, 'Nazir! Masoud, *come on!*'

Masoud translated Hazzard's words, crouching beside Ali Qarim. 'He says, I am no *jihadi*, a holy warrior,' reported Masoud. 'He says he has not the courage for it.'

'Christ...'

Ali Qarim whispered again and Masoud mouthed the words as he spoke, then relayed them. 'He says you spoke the truth, *effendi*. Spikes, moving castles of men, rising from the sands, with muskets like a boiling cauldron... The golden sultans stood fierce in the centre... and their guns poured fire upon us.'

Hazzard nodded, recalling Shubra Khit, the squares, the cavalry riding in and out, the endless volleys. Nazir listened to his brother.

'They steal, says the sheikh... food from the houses... daughters from the families... killing all, even children...'

Ali Qarim whispered something to him. Nazir looked at Masoud, confused. 'Weapons... of the *fellahin*, says the sheikh...? What does he mean?'

233

'Arms?' suggested Hazzard. 'Give them arms?'

Ali Qarim put a hand on Masoud's arm and repeated it.

'Yes, yes,' said Masoud, 'he says to *arm* the people, the people of Cairo...'

Nazir added, '...Or they will suffer greatly.'

Nazir protested to Ali Qarim in rapid Arabic, but the sheikh gave a dismissive reply. Nazir rose from the bedside. 'See your influence, Hazar-*effendi*. To arm the peasants! More blasphemies and madness...'

The sheikh sighed and his eyes closed. The servants began to cut his robes away just as a trio of doctors in the white turban and robes of the Al-Azhar entered.

'Will he live?' asked Cook.

'I know not, *Kuq*,' said Nazir. 'His fate is written. It is the will of Allah.'

Masoud asked, 'But why arm the *fellahin*? What can they know of battle that Murad Bey does not?'

Hazzard looked out at the elite Mamluk cavalry and a unit of Ottomans, watching dumbfounded at the numbers of wounded, their officers bewildered. 'He wants men who have something to fight for. It is their city. Masoud,' he said, 'go back to Cairo. Tell the other beys, tell Muhammad Bey al-Elfi and Sheikh al-Jabarti, the *imams*, and Al-Charkawi at the Al-Azhar, to rouse the people of the city. Armed with anything, sticks, clubs, stones, I don't care. Get them out and in front of the gates. And be sure they know these are the wishes of Ali Qarim Sheikh. The sight of them might slow the French or divert Bonaparte's attention.' He looked at Nazir. 'How far away are the French?'

'They have Omm-Dinar,' said Nazir. 'Two hours' ride.'

'Five divisions of five thousand, advancing slowly in squares... we have time. Masoud,' he said, 'Ensure that the families are in the citadel as I requested...' He paused a moment and remembered a moonlit night on a palace landing, and the fire in a pair of almond eyes, '...as well as the lady Nafisa and her followers. Protect *Signor* Rosetti, the Viennese Consul – you must now be Herr Hammer's replacement, and become the Consul's adviser. Sharif Nazir is an experienced warrior and he can ride with the army, but your task is just as important.'

Masoud was at first disappointed at this perceived rejection, then realised the gravity of his task. 'I shall do this thing, Hazar-*effendi*, in your name, as you wish. I shall bring out the people.' He took Hazzard's hand. '*Rabbena ma'ak*, Hazar-*effendi al-hakim*,' and Cook's, '*Kuq-effendi al-bahadur*. May God be with you both.'

Hazzard watched the young Alexandrian go. It had been Masoud, he realised, who had drawn him back to the shores of Egypt – and he was grateful. But he had little hope. Within hours, riders returned from Omm-Dinar. The French were coming.

–

Murad's horsemen charged across the valley, some engaging in contests, leaning from their saddles at the gallop to pluck objects from the ground as they passed amid cheers. Others rode in short gallops, arms outstretched, to practise or prove their horsemanship, preparing their mounts for what was to come.

Hazzard's advice had been ignored: Murad would face the French on the western shore alone. The Embabeh batteries and camel artillery were all they had to hit the French squares before they reached the Nile. The waters of the ancient river drifted by, as it had done before Ramses, thought Hazzard, and would for ever – and into his mind he felt the insidious trickle of the Mamluks' fatalism: *Insha'allah. God willing. It is already written.*

They rode through the lanes of Embabeh, past the batteries, aware of the new crackle of fear in the air, everything done quickly, without conversation, no laughter, only terse greetings or calls to steel the men's shrinking hearts. As they rode by, *Yuzbashi* Russuf spread his arms wide and shouted *Hazar Pasha! Kuq Chavus!* and the men cheered – because their captain knew the exotic foreigner who had foretold of the castles of men rising from the sands, the devil in red. Surely, they believed, this was a good omen.

Izzam and Alahum guarding the approach from the road, they descended the riverbank into the trees and splashed the horses into the water, giving them a final chance to bathe and drink. Bulaq lay just across the water, and they looked across at Ibrahim's army, ten- to twelve-thousand strong, waiting on the eastern shore, blocking the northeastern route to Cairo – a wise precaution, but quite useless, thought Hazzard, the men wasted.

A messenger galloped past on the road, saw Izzam and Alahum, and came to a halt. 'Hazar Pasha?' Izzam called down to the riverbank and pointed.

The courier handed Hazzard a note. 'Muhammad Bey al-Elfi, *effendi*.'

Hazzard took it. It was in magnificent swirling Arabic, English penned underneath, from Masoud.

> *Thus says Mahomet Bey al-Alfi to Captain Hazar al-hakim: so it may be written, one day, that we stood to defend our own. God be with you.*

He handed it to Cook. He thought it a wish of good luck, or perhaps more of a goodbye from the already vanquished. But he was wrong. Cook looked upriver at the city. 'By Davy's locker. Would you ruddy look at that...'

The open gates of Cairo became crowded with people. More, then still more emerged. They poured out of the city, men, women, children, calling, shouting, some with sticks, spears, some with swords, others with nothing, picking up the rocks that lay before them, captains of the army calling to them, *Allah!* And their answer, *Ou-al-akbar! Allah! Ou-al-akbar!* There were *fellahin*, merchants, some in fine clothes, some in tatters, some half-naked, others on donkeys, in carts. They swelled the eastern shore of the Nile, blocking the gates. Their numbers dwarfed Ibrahim's army of footsoldiers. Once assembled, a single officer cried out across the Nile, '*Allahu akbar!*' The consequent roar echoed across the valley.

'Masoud did it,' said Hazzard, feeling a glimmer of hope. 'They've called out the bloody militia. Now we have a chance.'

Then Hazzard heard the first shots. Sharif Nazir appeared at the gallop, and stopped at the top of the bank, his dark face half-hidden in the shade of the overhanging trees.

'*Hazar-effendi!*' he called. '*The blasphemers come!*'

They rode back up the bank and through the empty streets of Embabeh, among the artillery crews running for their guns. They passed a trail of straggling villagers, a family, a lone mother, bare breasted in a torn gown, a naked child in her arms, all led by a long-bearded Coptic priest, all running, fleeing for the river.

Izzam and Alahum close, they trotted past the gun emplacements, the crews alert, listening. They heard the flat percussion of approaching artillery. The ground shook.

Cook cocked an ear and listened. 'Howitzers.'

They watched the open ground before them, across the valley. The Mamluk cavalry had gathered into troops and squadrons behind their sheikhs and amirs, their horses stamping. The first intrusion came, a howling rush of air, one shell, turning on a high, lazy trajectory, shrieking down and striking with a deafening thud, sending up a fountain of earth. Then another, and another. The field began to erupt before them, the descending whine of rounds, the jarring crump, spouts of sand and soil bursting high into the air.

Without looking, Cook handed a folded slip of paper to Hazzard, and Hazzard did likewise to him, an old ritual. They put the wills into their inside pockets.

'In the event.'

'In the event, aye, sir.'

Units of Mamluk cavalry tore through the camp behind Nazir and drew up nearby, in front of the massed ranks of artillery and foot. Hazzard looked behind him. The Bedouin of the Beni Qassim, the Albanians and Egyptians all stood ranged behind, looking to Hazzard and Cook, waiting. Teams of water-carriers moved swiftly through the ranks with a cup, each man taking a swallow, none too much, though some could not.

Hazzard put a hand to the scimitar of Ali Qarim. He thought of Sarah, of green Suffolk, an alien universe in this place of stone gods and dust, thoughts clouding purpose. Cook shot him a glance.

'Sir,' he said, 'if she's in Alex or Rosetta now...'

Then she is safe.

'Yes,' Hazzard drew the sword.

Automaton.

Ships in line, open the ports, run out the guns, drums beating to quarters, master to the helm, bo'sun to the mainmast. He looked about. It was no different here in this dry, dead place full of fear and hope. His heart banged in his chest. The heat was all consuming. The ground quaked to the booming of the French guns.

'Foot to the flanks,' ordered Hazzard. 'Stand by, all guns. *Company!* Make: *ready!*'

Cook drew a broad-bladed Turkish cutlass, transferred a loaded pistol to a holster on his saddle and conveyed the orders, roaring out '*Make ready!*' Nazir did likewise in Arabic, *Yuzbashi* Russuf screaming at his gun-crews in Turkish.

The company had swelled to nearly a battalion, and dispersed into its positions, Sergeant Fee's company running for the right flank of the gun-pits, Sergeant Fum the left. Cook rode through them. '*Open order! March!* Front rank: *kneel!* Make *ready!*'

The ground heaved and burst before them, ranging shots raining down. Murad's cavalry kicked up a cloud of dust far ahead, *Murad Murad Murad! Allahu albar!*

Hazzard looked left and right. '*Marines will form line!*'

It was an old habit, for both of them, from the decks of countless ships and countless duels at sea, but Cook obeyed and drew his horse closer, his voice bellowing out over the heads of the Egyptians and Turks, '*In line! M'rines, clear aye!*' Izzam and Alahum followed suit, and the Beni Qassim moved in behind, ranks of horsemen, scimitars in hand.

Hazzard shouted to Cook over the cannon-bursts, 'We man the guns, but no more. Broadsides and blazing, that's it, no bloody heroics, and the first sign of a turn you get back across that *damned* river just as I shall, clear?'

'Clear aye, sir. And you're a bloody liar an' all too.'

Cook kicked his heels in and cantered back to the middle of the battery and the ranks of Albanian Janissaries, reaching down, shaking the hands of his four sergeants, and they shouted '*Kuq Chavus! Kuq Chavus!*'

Hazzard looked out at the endless shell-bursts. Earth flew up, casting vast sudden shadows. Thoughts of eager Lt Wayland and the men on Malta, Rivelli, killed in Naples, Emma Hamilton, her touch, and the scent of her lips, so close – of Jeanne, of Sarah in the *Orient*, holding her tight. And thoughts of all those falling beneath the wheels of the juggernaut now approaching, driven by Derrien, by Bonaparte, and his damnable self-assurance.

I shall burn his dreams to the ground.

Her face at the rail, the look of a broken doll as she was hit, her hand reaching out as he fell from her, endlessly falling into nowhere.

She is alive.

To protect her, to save her, he recognised, they had to defend Cairo and force Bonaparte into retreat. He knew this would never happen. But Hazzard could admit no further deductions. He knew now what his mind must do, as it had done so many times before. He let the rage come.

How dare they. How bloody dare they.

This time, he determined, he would correct his error on the *Orient*. He would cut off the head of the serpent and damn the consequences.

Through the cover of the palm thickets by the edge of the field on the north road, he saw the first signs of movement – the bastion of a square fortress, a field-gun at its corner, its wheels rumbling, squealing, and slowly, inexorably, they came into view: ranks of men six deep, in blue, in grey, in green, five thousand bayonets pointing outwards, and their slow, heavy, chanting march – *un deux, un deux, un deux.*

Caesar has come to war.

'*Enemy in sight!*' Hazzard called. '*Prepare to engage! Awlad 'Ali! Beni Qassim!*' and they cheered. *Hazar Pasha! Hazar Pasha! Kuq Chavus, Kuq Chavus! Al-Aafrit al-ahmar!*

Murad Murad Murad! Allahu akbar!

Hazzard moved his horse forward one pace.

The only battle that matters…

Never stop.

Never give up the boat.

The shells rained down. He found himself shouting, screaming, the sword high. Riding across the line, he spun the mount and went out alone, calling across the field at the advancing army, a lone voice raging at a storm, '*Bonaparte! By all that is holy in this ancient place, I swear I shall die hard this day e'er I die at all!*' He raised the scimitar and looked back at the Ottomans and Egyptians behind. '*Ya saif … Ali!*'

They roared back, '*Ya saif Ali! Ya saif Ali! Allahu akbar! Allahu akbar!*'

Hazzard was ready. He would man the guns and defend Cairo, then ride the field, find Bonaparte, and kill him.

Pharaoh

Bonaparte led the general staff in a loping trot behind the squares. Berthier and the others watched him as the squares entered the head of the valley. He looked through his glass at Murad's horsemen galloping to and fro, cheering each other, darting in for attack, then dashing away.

'It is quite unbelievable,' said Bonaparte. 'They are still on this side of the Nile...'

The 2nd Division under General Desaix advanced first to the south, opposite the city, far to Bonaparte's right, Reynier's division guarding its left flank. The mobile fortresses moved like armoured creatures across the landscape, the men's steady chant bringing unity and a nameless terror to the people's army on the far shore – the citizens of Cairo began to scream, the women ululating, some running back to the closed gates.

'*Silence!*' called the sheikhs and amirs. '*The Prophet waged war without the sound of dogs baying and screeching!*'

Murad's cavalry raced in turmoil, a swarm of bees in apparent disarray. Bonaparte looked out at the pyramids in the distance beyond Murad, to Giza, the dunes rolling like waves on the sea.

He looked upon his army. 'Divisions to advance in echelon. Squares to engage.' He raised his eyeglass and watched, a murmur of satisfaction to Berthier, 'Forty centuries of history look down upon us, Berthi. Make them count for nothing.'

The command went up: '*Divisions en échelons! Vers la droite – marchez! Right wheel!*'

Desaix's square of five thousand turned to the right, the dust rising as they chanted their pace, *un deux, un deux*, and marched straight for Murad, Reynier's square moving in support. Within moments the disorganised mass of Mamluk riders became an angry swarm in a crescent attack formation.

Murad raised his sword. '*Ya saif Ali…!*' and the answer came back just as before, *Murad Murad Murad! Allahu akbar!*

The Mamluk horse swept down upon the French squares, obscured for a moment by lines of palms before arcing towards them, and drew within fifty yards before the first volleys exploded.

'*Fire!*'

The Charlevilles cracked with a clapping detonation, clouds of grey smoke erupting all along the line, then bursting with a second volley. The Mamluk vanguard fell, so close to the blazing muzzles that some riders burst into flame, the musket balls carrying with them the burning wadding from the barrels, setting their silks alight. The screams echoed along the riverbanks.

The stream of horse dodged away from Desaix's square to the right, towards Reynier's division, and were at once caught in a crossfire as both squares loosed a third volley upon them, and a fourth, and a fifth, and a sixth, the Mamluks dragged through the dust-cloud of flying hooves and slaughtered horses, crushed, trampled, their bodies bouncing to the earth, the silks aflame. They fell in their hundreds, troops riding in to loose a storm of *djerid* javelins, then riding to escape, regroup and attack again and again, never tiring.

General Dugua's 1st Division square moved faster, doubling towards Embabeh and the Nile to cut off the Mamluk cavalry from the city. Obscured by stands of twisted acacia and tamarisk, they had not yet seen the Ottoman batteries. Hazzard watched them approach.

'*Stand ready the guns! Wait for the command!*'

Cook bellowed at the crews, '*Stand by your guns, you bloody beauties!*'

Yuzbashi Russuf shouted overtop, '*Hazir!*' Ready!

The Albanian footsoldiers had begun chanting a deep, repetitive Turkish battlecry, '*Vur un, vur un, Allah Allah Allah!*' Smite them, smite them…

Izzam snatched at Hazzard's shoulder and pointed. 'Hazar Pasha – *innahu al-Sheikh!*'

They turned to see a squadron of horse appear between the whitewashed houses behind, riding up from the river road. At their head were an amir and two sheikhs, white robes blowing like gauze. In their centre was Sheikh Ali Qarim.

His movements were stiff, his face once again the impassive mask. The amir stopped by the southern battery, too far for Hazzard to call, but Ali Qarim looked from left to right, then saw him.

'God help him,' said Cook. 'He won't make it out of there this time...'

Hazzard looked back at Dugua's advancing square. It was still out of range of both musket volley and cannon. He wanted to ride to Ali Qarim, to stop him, to save him from himself, but knew he could not. He watched as the amir drew his sword and cried out, '*Allahu akbar!*'

Allah Allah Allah!

The amir's column sprang forward and charged at full gallop. Ali Qarim inclined his head in Hazzard's direction, a brief bow, then followed, his men close behind. They swooped straight past Dugua's square, taking a withering fire from the unprepared French infantry, and into the centre of the killing field. The amir was soon hidden by flying dust and sand.

Ali Qarim rode into a fog of dust and smoke, his hands heavier than ever before, wearier than he could ever remember. '*Martimar, Londan...*' He touched the Mortimer pistol at his belt, saved from Shubra Khit, and thought of Hazzard. This time, they would make the castle walls bleed.

The scene before Ali Qarim's eyes became a juddering torrent of sand and blurring shapes, with fleeting moments of clarity as the wind parted the haze of gunsmoke. He drew the Mortimer and fired. His lone bullet struck – among the first castle he saw a man fall. He saw one of the French sultans on his horse, a ferocious, dark, heavy man, armoured with golden plates upon his shoulders, a sword in hand, *sultan*, he thought, and heard the word he now knew so well.

Fire!

His troop racing beside him, Ali Qarim drew his Turkish carbine from its saddle holster and fired into the French square as their volleys exploded. The man beside him vanished as if plucked away by the wind. A group of mounted spearmen thundered past, launching their javelins at the squares, nearly all falling in a cloud of musket-fire, their cries left behind in the gallop, the eerie howls of aggrieved spirits.

He dropped the carbine into its leather bucket holster and put the reins between his teeth. He thought of Selim at Shubra Khit, but the bay beneath him was just as fearless, just as trusting. He drew his two swords, their steel singing. Just ahead of him, the amir curved to the right and charged directly at the square.

The first horses leapt the hedge of glittering bayonets, their bellies exploding from the musket-fire, their weight carrying them straight into the French lines, and screams filled the air.

Ali Qarim's bay dodged and flew to the right, nearly unseating him, and in that moment he saw a French soldier at his left, out of his line. He swung the scimitar down with a flick and the man fell. The horse was bolting, its eyes rolling. He felt an unholy wind blow in from the desert, as if from the Father of Terrors. It covered the world with sand and smoke – then just as suddenly cleared.

Before him were six ranks of the 1st Battalion of the 9th *demi-brigade de bataille* in General Reynier's square, surprised, their bayonets rising in a spiked hedgerow to face him as he emerged from the sandstorm, the two scimitars in his outstretched arms. He was alone.

'*Allahu akbar.*'

The front two ranks raised their Charlevilles. *En joue…!*

'*Allah!*'

His cry soaring out and taken by the wind, he heard no more, the horse leaping the first three rows of bayonets.

The blurred faces of frightened men passed beneath him, some shrinking away, closing their eyes, their bayonets dragging at the horse's underside, its whinnying screams sharp. His leaden arms swung downward, the Damascus steel of the scimitars irresistible. Six severed musket barrels and their fixed bayonets floated up around him, with them a hand, a sliced leather shako cap with its brigade plate of two crossed banners, his only sensation a weightless ease, and he was satisfied.

Allah...

The dying horse crashed down upon fifteen men and carried another ten with it, turning end over end, a flailing battering ram more effective than artillery. The ranks flew apart and several mounts of the 4th Horse Artillery collapsed, legs thrashing. The ranks closed fast, *Réformez, vous salauds!*

Ali Qarim lay helpless, his legs trapped beneath the horse, his old wounds open, his arms dead. Bayonets were thrust into him again and again, '*What kind of man does this, what kind of man,*' someone repeated in sobs as he stabbed downwards and Ali Qarim felt nothing after the first pounding blow but a warmth and a wish he had said goodbye. '*Martimar... Hazar...*'

At the Embabeh line with the artillery company, Hazzard waited as the square of General Dugua drew nearer – but then it was joined by another: the division of General Bon paused, adjusted, and wheeled in their direction as well. When he could hear their shouted commands he raised his sword.

'*Ready...!*'

Yuzbashi Russuf shouted to his crews to stand by, '*Estaaeed...!*'

Hazzard swung the sword down, '*Fire!*'

As he promised, Russuf roared like the lion: '*Edrab!*'

The four batteries fired a massed salvo, the equivalent of a warship's broadside. The blast of shot burst through the fog of white gunsmoke and shredded the leading ranks of Bon's square. Round-shot, langrage, and chain-shot smashed into the closely packed French ranks, the infernal rain of whirling iron carrying away dozens at a stroke. Hazzard swung his sword again.

'*Fire as they come to bear! Fire!*'

A second salvo blasted the corner of Bon's formation, peppering the gap between the two squares with fountains of earth, catching Dugua's division and sweeping away two ranks of the 25th *demi* in a flurry of flying limbs. Battalion commanders screaming out, Bon's square pulled back.

As they withdrew, the heavy Ottoman bombards roared, and the earth shook, shrouding the scene in white smoke, the noise so terrible Hazzard's mount nearly threw him from the saddle. The packed shot of the cannon removed heads and an entire corner gun-crew from Bon's square. The batteries cheered, *Russuf! Russuf!*

But one of the heavy guns had recoiled more than fifteen feet, tearing itself from its antique mounting. The artillerymen rushed to lift it back into place, Hazzard shouting '*Reload! Jory!*'

Cook was already dismounting to help. '*Got 'em, sir!*'

Some of the Albanian troops following him, Cook dived into the gun-pit among the gun-crews and they heaved the stricken cannon upwards, *Yuzbashi* Russuf beating at them with his stick. '*Come on, lads, damn ye!*' roared Cook as he lifted the gun by its thick trunions. A squad of Albanian infantry shoved the carriage underneath and they dropped the gun in place, a huge Turk clapping him on the back, '*Kuq guchlu!*' The Albanians cheered, *Kuq guchlu! Kuq guchlu! Mighty Kuq!*

They loaded and rammed and *Yuzbashi* Russuf gave the order. '*Edrab!*'

The guns blasted once again, the thunder of the reports raising cheers among the troops on the eastern shore as the French fortresses flew apart and their unstoppable advance faltered. The walls had begun to bleed.

They are men! They are men!

Vur un! Vur un! Allah Allah Allah!

Bon's division swung off to the left, drums rapping double-time, the boots of the fortress ranks fouling on the dead, dragging the wounded to the interior, reforming, earth and sand bursting all around them.

'*Ye' did it, boys!*' roared Cook, and they raised their arms high. '*Allahu akbar! Kuq guchlu!*'

The other squares drove the Mamluks away from the river and the city, horse and foot riding over the fallen, the smoke and stench of burning corpses blowing across the field on the hot desert wind.

The front ranks of some squares were already looting the bodies of the Mamluk dead. An elderly Mamluk with long white beard galloped out to challenge them alone, driving the looters away with his sword. He rode back and forth before a square, but no volley came, no shot fired.

A mounted French officer charged out of the formation, sword drawn, and clashed with the old man. But the Mamluk scimitar beat away the Frenchman's attacks and nearly knocked the younger man's sabre from his hand. The officer made another pass and struck his aged opponent from his seat. The Mamluk fell. There was a cheer from the square.

Bleeding from a cut to the head, the old man pulled himself along the ground, towards the officer's horse, swinging and slashing at its legs with his scimitar. No matter where the officer tugged his mount, the old Mamluk crawled over the bodies in the field, trying to slash at the horse. The officer shouted down at him '*Ça suffit alors! Enough! Vous êtes fou! You are mad!*' He tried to strike the old man with his sword but the Mamluk was too low. A squad of infantrymen ran from the front lines instead, and battered the old man to death with their muskets. They then ripped the robes from his body and waved them in the air in celebration.

Hazzard had witnessed it all. '*By Christ I shall have them for that. I shall bloody well have them...*' He kicked his heels in, '*Izzam! Alahum!*'

Izzam and Alahum behind, Hazzard galloped down the road, keeping pace with the French squares as they passed each Ottoman battery. '*Fire as they come to bear! Edrab!*' – the *darbzen* sounding their flat, percussive bark.

The French artillery began to answer the Embabeh batteries. Their muzzles were levelled to a flat trajectory and fired point-blank, rounds whistling past, crashing into the mud houses behind. The town shook, the rubble cascading into the streets, stray inhabitants running for the river. A second salvo struck near a battery, the whitewashed mud and brick collapsing onto the gunners dug in beneath. Hazzard jerked the reins round to dodge into a side-street, but a round-shot crashed into the road behind him. Hazzard's mount slewed to one side and he was thrown, the horse bolting.

Alahum turned back for him. '*Hazar Pasha!*'

The dust choking him, Hazzard rolled, a roar in his deafened ears. Alahum dismounted and ran to him, pulling Hazzard to his feet, dragging him out of the street. Even amid the fury of the cannons, Hazzard heard the sharp crack of a single pistol-shot.

Alahum threw his arms out to the sides, his back arching, and he looked round for his cousin, '*Zam…!*' He fell forward, one hand reaching behind as if to feel the wound in disbelief. When he found it, he stopped moving and lay still. Hazzard shook him, '*Alahum!*'

The shattered road was crowded with villagers fleeing the bombardment – but at the far end appeared two French cavalrymen, the youngest of them holding a spent pistol in his extended hand. Cook and Izzam came to the head of the road, Izzam jumping from his saddle, '*Alahum!*'

The villagers swarmed towards the Frenchmen and they backed their horses away, drawing their sabres. They beat down at the hands reaching up to them and began hacking at them. More shell-bursts, rubble crashing into the street, the dust clouding about them as the horsemen tried to ride through the running mob, trampling them, one screeching warhorse knocking down an old man, its iron shoes stamping, crushing, a woman tangled in her *kaftan* ridden down and trampled, a running child cut almost in two by the panicked aimless swings of the horseman's heavy sabre.

Hazzard could hardly breathe, the heat and rising dust suffocating. The guns had not been enough, the fifty French dead and maimed blown from the advancing square nowhere near enough: now he wanted blood. He dragged his scimitar from under the weight of rubble beside him and stumbled towards the cavalrymen, raising the blade over one shoulder as if it were his old Mughal Talwar. '*Vous là! Tiens!*' *You there!*

The Frenchman saw him. Hazzard called to him agaun.

'*Moi, je suis soldat! Come fight a real bloody soldier if you dare!*'

The rider kicked into a canter and charged him, leaning over to his left side to catch Hazzard with his sabre. As the horse closed, Hazzard dived across its path and swung the scimitar in a tight arc behind him with all his strength.

The foreleg of the horse struck him like a cannon-round and knocked him tumbling. He crashed against a wall gasping for air – but the razor-edge of the Damascus steel had bitten into the hamstrings of the horse's right fetlock and the animal collapsed, calling in pain. Hazzard could see the Frenchman's enraged expression as he sank past. In the next moment the man's head snapped back and his throat opened in a fountain of red as Izzam decapitated him.

The second horseman pulled up so sharply his horse skidded and fell backward onto its haunches and he was thrown to the ground not yards from Hazzard and scrambled to his feet.

Hazzard gripped his side, *ribs*, raised his guard, the Frenchman raising his sabre fearfully, the scimitar crashing down onto it, and he sliced under its ornate cup, throwing the man backward, '*En garde alors! Come on!*' shouted Hazzard. The boy struck again and Hazzard thought briefly of Wayland, then dismissed it, and whipped round, the scimitar blade flying from the horseman's hip to shoulder and back down again, opening his trunk. Belching blood, the boy fell, his eyes bulging, hands clutching at his midriff.

Izzam leapt upon him, striking his curved *khanjar* dagger again and again into the man's face, smothering his screams, cursing him, a squad of Albanians joining in, stabbing down with their bayonets until nothing but a sightless skull and carcase remained.

His vision no more than a tunnel through a cloud of dust and smoke, Hazzard found his horse and threw himself at the saddle, his bloody scimitar still in hand, only one thought in his mind, *Bonaparte*, and charged into the field.

Cook called after him but Izzam ran behind, crying out, '*Kuq! Kuq!*'

Cook gave up his horse for him. '*Go! Be after him, lad!*'

The Bedouin kicked it into immediate full gallop in pursuit. '*Hazar!*'

As Hazzard streaked past the Mamluk footsoldiers, cheers went up, '*Vur un, vur un! Allah Allah Allah! Al-Aafrit al-ahmar!*' But Hazzard heard none of it. He felt the earth pounding beneath him and the tied white *shemagh* of the *keffiyah* headdress low over his eyes, crushing his skull in the consuming heat. His *binish* robe flew behind him, his hands slick and red with the young Frenchman's blood, his Marine scarlet sleeves bright in the corner of his eye, not seeing them, not knowing if he were running or charging, *no more no more – Bonaparte!* From his lips emerged inarticulate cries as he shot into the thunder of the field, shouting at the storm, raging against the wind and sand.

French infantry at the rear of a reforming column scattered, their bayonets rising to meet him, a startled general in the saddle, his horse rearing, officers reaching for him in protection, but Hazzard ploughed through the rearguard, the scimitar biting, a cry dying far behind him as he rode past another line of looting infantry, the men still with their backs to him, and he hacked as he passed, '*Cry God for mercy, damn you all!*'

Two more fell, and he heard an insistent voice calling, *Hazar! Hazar Pasha!* always calling him, the gallop furious, the wind hot in his face, *is this where you fell, Ali Qarim, was it here?* and the squares rose up before him at drunken angles, one to the right, one to the left, *God God God! Damn you! Damn you!* French infantrymen in the field, four, five, six of them, looting, *fools*, and he brought one down, the blade feeling nothing, something soft, another cry, and the horse roared round in a sharp curve – *Bonaparte, I will have you for this...*

The dunes of the distant desert swung in dizzying parallax, *al-Sahraa, effendi*, and he lost his bearings, the squares too big, too confusing, Mamluk riders veering off, blooms of muzzle-flashes, an inferno. At the centre of every square a knot of generals, staff officers, screaming, pointing, every one a Bonaparte, yet none, every one a sultan ruling his own domain, *Bonaparte...*

In the distance he saw them, watching, and he slowed.

Pyramids.

Izzam drew alongside him, his voice almost quiet, a lull for the furies of his mind, *Hazar*, and volleys burst. The Bedouin rode him out and past a square, puffs of smoke moving along a rank, too slow, and he realised where he was, *Christ, what are you doing what are you doing...*

Galloping across the ranks of a square, men pointing, *Là-bas! En joue!* Then gone, dust, sand, *watch the rocks*, palms, shade, Nile – *Nahr al-Nil, effendi* – shaking, leaning, slowing, *Hazar-effendi, Hazar...*

They slowed, *yes, the shade*, the horse tossing its head, trotting, walking. They drew to a halt. He slumped forward onto the horse's hot neck. His now burnt and bloody *shemagh* headdress hung down raggedly over his neck and face, the heat beating at him. He closed his eyes as if to sleep, or hide. The scimitar, its ivory grip, his hands, all were dark with blood and caked with sand. His *binish* robe hung in blackened shreds, the left sleeve of the scarlet coat ripped open, the brass and braid torn away. Pain flooded into him and he wanted to drop.

God. God rot them all. Lewis, Melville, Bonaparte, and Nelson – rot with them, anointed tyrants all... in everlasting damnation, your petty kingdoms-come, for nevermore, for dust, for nothing, and pass from here on the wind.

'Hazar Pasha...?' It was Izzam. He was frightened of the spirit that had taken him, as was Hazzard.

Hazzard nodded, looking up. '*Hasanan, sadiqi.*' All right, my friend. '*Hasanan...*'

Sergent-chef-major Achille Caron dashed to the next stand of palms, pistol in hand. Rossy hurried up beside him at a crouch. The battle was in full cry and the *Alpha-Oméga* platoon was on the move. A band of Mamluk horse galloped past on the track, '*Ilal amam!*' not seeing them in the depths of shade beneath the trees.

'As we all have the natural instincts of the true soldier, *Chef*,' whispered Rossy, priming his Charleville with quick, deft hands, 'that is, to do as little as possible, unless anyone is watching...'

'Very wise, yes, Rossy...' agreed Caron. He waved Pigalle and Antonnais forward and they ran ahead and ducked into cover, St Michel following with his Austrian rifle.

'Why then, I must ask, are we performing this little bit of heroic madness, *Chef*?'

'Our lust for glory, Rossy, *mon brave*, our duty to the beloved Republic, and to take these *merde* batteries before they pound our arses into the ground...'

'Not *our* arses, *Chef*, but the arses of the 25th and 2nd *Légère*. And they should not matter, not being fine arses at all.'

'*C'est vrai*,' said Caron, 'It is true. *Come.*' They ran onward, passing the others and crossing the track to a whitewashed mud house. Caron waved the others to follow.

There were twenty of them, the *Alpha-Oméga* of the 1st Company, 1st Battalion, the 75th. The rest of the Invincibles fronted Dugua's square, pulling out of range. A hundred yards from Caron lay the gun-pits and the remnants of ancient Embabeh. They could see the muzzles of the guns, the blooms of smoke as they fired. Rossy grasped Caron's sleeve.

'*Chef*. We cannot. I know the *capitaine* is in the square, but this is open ground.'

Caron nodded. Rossy had meant Captain Moiret. 'Do you think we are like the 25th? *Putain*. We shall do as all wise and treacherous men, and go over there, and come quietly from behind.'

Keeping to shade and cover, they darted far to the left, into the unprotected roads leading to the river.

–

Hazzard watched as the end came. Losing too many men, the Mamluk cavalry pulled back, Murad leading them off to the south in full retreat, a French square in steady pursuit.

Ahead, the Nile was clogged with men, running, swimming, plunging in and making for the opposite bank of Bulaq. Hazzard saw the red and white banners of the Ottoman Sultan flutter and snap in the hot wind – then the eastern army broke. Without engaging the enemy, Ibrahim Bey and the Ottoman Pasha Abu Bakr turned their horses at full gallop and rode away. Sheikhs waved their fists and called after them, cursing their name, then turned to the river to rescue their swimming countrymen from the water, elevating the guns to fire across the river and support Embabeh.

'*Sinai…*' muttered Izzam, watching Ibrahim Bey, muttering their likely destination. He spat.

But breaking from Murad's Mamluk cavalry in a tight arc came an unexpected sight. It was a troop of horse.

'*Innahu al-Sharif!*' cried Izzam and pointed.

An arrowhead of galloping cavalry churned the dust into a broadening cloud, at the head, Sharif Nazir, sword drawn, calling his orders, keeping them in formation, speeding the charge ever faster, trailing a whirlwind of dust in his wake. Behind him came charging mounts and the *shayalaz* mobile camel artillery, their small deadly guns puffing smoke, their sound reaching their ears moments later, no more than a muted popping in the distance. Hazzard watched as Nazir dodged the formation along the wall of a French square, the disciplined ranks falling in clouds of packed *shayalaz* grape-shot, the camels braying in victory.

But the inevitable response came: a single volley burst from four hundred French muskets and the attack disintegrated into a writhing mass of dead and wounded. Of Nazir there was no sign.

Hazzard looked away, head down. *And thus, the princes of Egypt fell before them*, because they were right, he decided, it was written. Perhaps the sooner he accepted this the better.

From the timeless wastes of stone and gods came the wrath of Ptah Himself, angry clouds of dust and smoke swept away by an unseen hand, a sandstorm blown from Giza, whipping at their faces and stinging the skin. Izzam tried to shield Hazzard and they buried their faces in their *shemagh* headscarves. But Hazzard looked numb, lost, dead.

Izzam shook him awake. '*Effendi, Embabeh, Kuq...*'

Hazzard blinked and nodded. '*Yes, Embabeh, Izzam – Embabeh...*'

Izzam led the way and they galloped. The battle for Cairo, and Egypt, seemed lost, the grand manoeuvres of armies descending into individual acts of savagery. As they rode into the maelstrom of sand, faces materialised in the storm, then dissolved, shadows in the whirling dust, some crying out, running, leaping aside, somewhere drums rapping. A Mamluk as tall as Cook facing a charging French cavalryman dived for the horse's forelegs, clamping his massive arms round it, the hindquarters of the beast rising up and over his back in a somersault, the rider launched screaming into the air – then abruptly impaled in mid-flight by two Mamluk spearmen.

'*Jory!*' He would hear no answer, Hazzard knew that, but still he called. '*Jory!*'

Embabeh lay ahead, but only some of the batteries were firing. The left flank company of Albanian Janissaries stood in ranks, their sergeant shouting at them, one volley, then another. A shell burst and the sergeant fell. His troops broke formation – but they did not run: instead, they attacked. Some brandishing their long miquelet muskets and spike bayonets, others waving their *yataghan* swords, they charged into the blast of French artillery without fear, Cook's voice roaring over it all, *Get back in line!*

Struck by two volleys and French field-guns, the Albanians were cut down in minutes. The survivors stumbled on, some reaching the first row of bayonets, taking two men with each swing of the *yataghan*, but the others fell back. The right flanking company had also been turned and routed. The guns were next.

Sensing victory, Dugua's square broke formation, the battalion commanders screaming out, '*Dans l'ordre des colonnes! En avant!*' *Column order! Advance!*

The front ranks charged, streaming down in a cataract of grey and green uniforms, overwhelming the batteries. The fleeing Albanians were clubbed or cut down without mercy, the fleeing conscripts bayoneted as they ran, the French troops at last released from their tight formation discipline, enraged by their defiance.

Izzam's black robes flapped ahead like wings as he rode through the slaughter, Hazzard following, the brightwork of Izzam's sword gleaming in the howl of the sandstorm, the desert come to the Nile in its displeasure.

The pair burst through a platoon of white-coated French grenadiers in tall mitre headgear, *Aux armes! À droite…!* Hazzard dropped his sword-arm and the bloody scimitar cut through wool, leather, skin, bone, and a man fell, his hands clawing at his head. A bullet caught the saddle, once, twice, unseen blows smashing into Hazzard's right leg, *hit*, and he fell across the horse's neck.

'*Jory…*'

He saw *Yuzbashi* Russuf fighting off three men, a fourth sinking his bayonet into his chest, and the Turk gasped, his giant Turkish *kilij* crashing down, cleaving his killer almost in half as he fell by his guns.

Izzam made his final leap over a gun emplacement into a knot of French. A grenade exploded, and he was thrown from his saddle, Hazzard losing him in the dust as the sand and wind whipped in. '*Izzam!*'

A soldier dived on the Bedouin but was cut open by his whirling scimitar. Hazzard jumped his mount into the pit, his hand reaching for him. '*Izzam – isri! Yallah!*' Izzam leapt for him but was snatched backwards into the pit. '*Hazar!*' He swung his sword in a tight circle as he had seen Hazzard do, and took another head, but Izzam of the Awlad 'Ali was at last brought down by a musket-butt and collapsed. '*Izzam!*' cried Hazzard, but helpless, too far from him, and drove his sword down into a French shako, then saw Cook.

He had one man by the throat, '*Come on, ye bloody mollies!*' He swung him up and over his shoulder, snapping the neck, throwing the body to one side, skittling another. Caron saw him and called out 'Anton! *Les jambes!*' and one of them dived for Cook's legs, Pigalle swinging a Charleville musket overhead. Cook kicked Antonnais away with a boot to the chin and the boy flew back with a cry. Pigalle lunged for the big man. Cook ducked the blow, put his head down and charged him with a roar, doubling the giant over, lifting him from the ground, and dropping him. The huge Pigalle bellowed as he fell and rolled, crushing a fusilier and a Turkish gunner. Hazzard swung his mount round, and Caron recognised him.

'Rossy! *L'anglais!*'

But Rossy could not reach him, and Hazzard was knocked from his saddle by a grenadier, a bayonet rushing down at him – he rolled against the man's shins, the tip of his sword stabbing upward, biting, and he thrust the blade from thorax to throat, twisting the grip, *For Izzam.* A gout of blood and a scream and another shadow, bared teeth flashing, wide eyes, and Hazzard shoved a hand over the face and *cut* as he withdrew from the grenadier's body, the rage feeding on itself, giving him strength. *For Alahum.* He felt Cook's hand on his collar, hauling him up, but still he swung and *cut* and another fell, a Charleville flying to pieces.

'*Out of it, lad!*'

'*Not yet!*'

The scimitar flew up and a face split apart, *and turn*, and cut *down* on the other side, a wild ferocity gripping him, *for all of them*, until Cook grabbed him hard. '*Now, damn ye!*'

They ran, stumbling out to the road towards a stand of trees, Hazzard dragging his leg, Cook half-lifting him, the pair of them limping, struggling, the Nile just visible through the rubble of a shattered house. '*Just – reach the river…*' gasped Hazzard, and he looked across the blue waters, whipped into waves by the sudden storm. As Ibrahim's army ran for the open desert to the northeast, the people had turned for the gates of the city, their cries filling the air.

Cook's voice was dull with exhaustion. 'Time to bloody scarper with the wind…'

Salvoes rushed overhead, crashing into the water, into the fleeing Mamluks and Ottomans, into the running Turkish gun-crews and the Bedouin and *fellahin* swimming across the Nile. Hazzard heard the barking blasts and knew they were their own guns: the French had turned the wheeled guns of *Yuzbashi* Russuf on the Mamluks.

They loped along the bank, Hazzard's wounds flaring with fire. Mamluk bodies clogged the Nile. French soldiers stood on the riverside, tearing the silk robes and gold from the fallen, kicking the corpses back into the water, some sniping at the swimming Egyptians. One of them turned and saw Cook, but far too late.

The big man charged into their midst before they had a chance to turn. Two men fell. Hazzard made a loose swipe, *too tired*, and the blade jammed in the man's knee, *no more*. He jerked the blade free and knocked away the muzzle of a Charleville, the blast going off too close to his leg, and the powder scorched and he screamed and fell into the soldier, using the curling cruciform guard of the sword to hit his face again and again. '*Have you had enough now! Have you! Have you!*' A hand snatched at his robe and spun him around and a bayonet tip passed his head and he saw the blue water, so close, so inviting.

So this is where.

The robe tore and he rolled and struck out with the sword, *will not go*, as horsemen of the Beni Qassim galloped through them, their scimitars cutting, their voices calling, *Muhammad Bey al-Elfi! Al-Aafrit al-ahmar!* Cook was down, a French infantryman lying dead on top of him.

'*Jory…*'

It was no more than a gasp, his throat burning with dust, his skin bone-dry, heart hammering. The old euphoria overtook him, from sun, from heat, and he fell, and rolled down the bank into the Nile mud, the Beni Qassim looking for him, calling, then riding off in pursuit of the French.

He pushed himself onto one elbow, collapsed, the shade enveloping him. *Cannot see.* Hazzard slid into the Nile, so cold after the furnace of the field. He floated on his back, the shade offered by the trees sliding away slowly, the sun exploding in his eyes. Somewhere he heard Arabic, *Al-Pasha al-ahmar*, and splashing, then nothing.

He let himself go, drifting slowly downriver with the gently bobbing dead and, so he dreamt, safely out to sea.

–

The *Volpone* slid silently towards the port waters of Alexandria. De la Vega had ordered the ship rigged with lateen yards, to give her the lazy slope of a Levantine trader, with looped lines and cargo nets swagged over the rails concealing her gun-ports. All lanterns and lights had been doused and commands were made on the whisper. Once again, *Volpone* was running silent.

At the starboard rail of the quarterdeck De la Vega observed the shore lights through his glass, Wayland and Alfonso beside him.

'The port, she is busy...' murmured De la Vega. 'But I count only one, two... three French frigates. Where is the great fleet?'

Wayland followed De la Vega's sightline through his own scope. 'Two 24s... the third perhaps only twelve guns...'

'Their lookouts, they sleep,' said De la Vega. 'They shall have the bad surprise when your Nelson comes.'

'If that Turk can be believed.'

De la Vega was not so dismissive. 'Ah, those men of the *tartane* boats are never wrong. They know these waters. If he saw eleven great British ships heading this way, then be certain that he did.'

'We should burn the French in the port,' said Wayland. 'Make a signal-fire for Nelson. Teach them a damned lesson...'

De la Vega took his eye from the glass. The boy had changed, there was no doubt, his frustration expressed in the rapping of the walking-stick he now employed as he limped about the ship. The unlucky shot that had taken so little of his calf on Malta had so far left him virtually lame in one leg.

'*Tenente*,' said De a Vega, 'you are impatient.'

Wayland seemed to have lost his uncertain deference. He seemed, after all, not unlike Hazzard. 'Sir.'

'Are the men prepared? Alfonso? *Todos preparados?*'

'*Sí, Capitán.*'

The marines waited on the main deck below, Underhill, Pettifer, De Lisle, Hesse, Kite, Cochrane, Napier, Porter and Warnock. At Underhill's instruction they had put on plain shirts, jerkins, some wore Spanish bandannas or dark turbans in the Turkish style, much as they had in Malta. They checked their weapons, each musket and blade smudged with a coating of dried pitch and boot-black.

Wayland looked down at them. 'Clothes dark, weapons dark.' It was just as Hazzard had promised them on that first day. He turned to De la Vega. 'Men are ready, Captain.'

Volpone caught the onshore breeze, gliding past the Alexandrian coast towards the Nile and Rosetta. After a mile or so, they swung a boat over the starboard rail. Wayland put his stick into the boat and began to climb in.

'*Tenente*,' reminded De la Vega. 'We agreed.'

Wayland stopped, his bad leg nearly over the gunwale of the boat. His face worked in anger. 'Damn it all...'

'We'll find him, sir,' said Underhill. 'Don't you doubt it. And we'll plug a bloody great hole in any Frog as tries to stop us, just like you said.'

They all murmured *aye*. De la Vega tried to reassure him. 'Alfonso comes to return the boat. So, we need an *inglés* aboard *Volpone*, to tell Nelson not to shoot, *sí?*'

Alfonso regarded Wayland with his dour eyes. 'I leave you the *Volpone, Tenente*, while I take them. For no other man will I do this thing.'

Wayland looked over at Handley, standing off, watching. 'Aye. *Entiendo.*' Wayland let go of the boat and hauled his leg back to the deck of the *Volpone.* He leaned on his stick, the pain from the manoeuvre evident to all, and nodded to Alfonso. '*Estoy honrado.*' *I am honoured.*

'And your Spanish, it comes better,' said De la Vega.

Wayland then looked to the Spanish bo'sun. '*Señor Carlos, si te gusta*, lower away, *por favor.*' They smiled at his very British 'if you please'.

'*Si, señor el Tenente.*'

The big bo'sun gave the order. The crew worked the boom lines and lowered the boat hand over hand, Wayland watching the dark faces of the marines sink below the level of the rail and down to the water. They raised the oars and began to row for the shore. Handley joined him to watch them go.

'I'd 'ate to be a Frog tonight, sir.'

Wayland made a grunt and stumped off to the quarterdeck. 'Let's bring her about, Handley, guns rammed and ready… I want that harbour kept tight as a drum. Anyone comes out we look them over or blow them to Hades.'

Handley grinned and touched his forelock. 'Too bloody right, sir.'

—

Alfonso had the tiller in the boat and guided them closer to shore. Off to starboard the coast stretched to a headland jutting out to sea to a small rocky island outcrop. On the tip of the headland was an ageing fortress tower rising into the deep blue of the night. Light shone from within, through narrow embrasures.

The squat shape of the old tower was limned in a backwash of light from somewhere bright beyond. De la Vega saw small boats laden with cargo, lanterns swinging at their sterns, possibly from Alexandria, making their way round the promontory.

'To that fort, my friends,' whispered De la Vega, and Alfonso moved the tiller. 'Something is in the bay behind it. *Silencio...*'

'Shallows here, sir?' asked Pettifer.

'Yes, *amigo*, everywhere, the moving sands. But we are light, and I have the long memory. Alfonso, *a estribor...*' *To starboard*.

Alfonso swung them inland and they rowed closer to the shoreline, the surf breaking against shingle and rock, the rhythmic roar louder still as they approached the base of the fort. Alfonso looked up and pointed. The tower had a few small gun-ports, but no guns. A goat wandered through the scrub, grazing. It saw them and bleated.

The tower loomed dark above them, its glowing windows showing few signs of life. On the far side they saw an A-frame gantry standing in stark silhouette, low, dark humped shapes nearby, low crumbling walls concealing something behind. As they rounded the promontory, the source of the distant light came slowly into view. Alfonso stared.

'*Dios mío...*'

Aboukir Bay lay spread out before them, a vast bight from the top of the Nile Delta, its shores curving away and gently back out to sea towards distant Rosetta in the east. There, riding safely at anchor, their lamps gleaming across their busy decks and soaring mastheads, lay the entire battle-fleet of Napoleon Bonaparte's Egypt expedition.

'*Jaysus shite an' all*,' murmured De Lisle. '*It's really here...*'

Cochrane's craggy face glowed with the distant light. '...And lo, the lords of all sin lay before them...'

De la Vega hissed at them, '*Back back back, rápido, amigos, rápido...*'

They began to paddle back into the safety of the darkness. Countless lights winked around them, shining into the night, the waves black, the white surf foaming. They had seen the distant lights of the French fleet at Malta, but not like this: at last, after two months, they looked upon the target they had sought.

261

'I never believed 'em…' whispered Warnock. 'It's like bloody Spithead…'

Behind a cluster of smaller bomb-craft and sloops, the warships rode in line astern, the 74s and 80s, *Guerrier, Conquérant*, and *Spartiate, Aquilon* and *Peuple Souverain*, and the big *Franklin*. Just behind them in the centre rose the largest of them all, the giant 120-gun flagship.

'That's the big bastard I saw Cookie go in, the one they gone an' took the major in,' said Pettifer. 'The *Orient*.'

'That means he's *here*, lads,' said Kite with realisation. 'Cookie an' the major – *both of 'em are bloody here*.'

'Let us pray so, my friend,' said De la Vega.

Behind *Orient* came the *Tonnant*, and still more 74s, *Heureux, Mercure* – at the rear stood the 80-gun *Guillaume Tell* and her own squadron, the *Généreux, Timoléon* and several smaller frigates closer to the shallows and the rising sand dunes ringing the bay.

Supply boats and tenders were dotted everywhere, French and Egyptian, large *djerms, feluccas* and small punts. Crates and nets swung from booms to waiting barges, livestock taken aboard and munitions taken off, labourers hauling cargo up the beaches for the road to Alexandria.

'We have seen enough,' said De la Vega. 'Alfonso, we must come about.'

'But we *got* 'em, sir…' whispered Warnock.

'Too right, Knocky,' said Napier. 'Let's gut one and burn her down…'

'Not yet, y'daft oke,' hissed Pettifer. 'Got to find the major first.'

Underhill agreed. 'The Professor said we've to join Nelson, lads. But I'm for finding the major first, as no one else in this bloody navy will. They'll cut 'im adrift given 'alf the chance and us with 'im if needs be. 'Tis the way of things. He and old Cookie might've signed on for that, but I don't cares for it one bit, as it's not fittin' to be doing that to our major, mad or no, be he Jack or Jolly.'

'*Jack or Jolly,*' they repeated.

'Amen,' said Cochrane.

'Too right, Sarge,' confirmed Kite.

They murmured their agreement. 'Then we can watch Nellie burn 'em all bloody down like it's Guy Fawkes Night. What says the boat?'

They looked to each other and nodded. 'Boat says aye, Sarge,' said De Lisle. 'Let's crack on.'

They rowed back towards Alexandria. Under cover of scrub and stunted trees they grounded the boat on the shingle of the rocky shoreline, past the bay of ancient half-sunken Canopus. Fluted columns stood doleful guard over bare pediments and tumbled stone ruins, the waves washing at them, wearing them down. The marines leapt out. De la Vega followed, but Alfonso stopped him. '*Padre.*'

'Go,' replied De la Vega. 'Take the *Volpone*, find the great admiral *inglés*. Tell him what we have seen.' De la Vega smiled faintly. 'I am obliged, my son, to my duty for my friend.' When he saw Alfonso's disquiet he added, 'They tried to drop a house on me, hm? How can Providence let the *Franceses* defeat me now?'

Underhill made his way through the bushes. Beyond was a featureless desert of dark hillocks, visible only in the reflected light from the fleet and the traffic on the distant road to Alexandria. He held up a hand. The marines sank down in the dark, and he mouthed, '*Locals comin'*…'

From around a bend further ahead a donkey-cart appeared, driven by an old couple. Beside it came two heavily laden mules pulled by two younger men, arguing, one shaking a bag of coins at the other in dispute.

The family stopped when they heard a distant shout. There was a fast thudding of hooves from behind, slowing gradually to a walk. Four French horsemen arrived, light cavalry.

'Jesu, bugger an' blight…' whispered Underhill, and sank down lower, his hand going out to the side and making a cutting gesture in a mute signal: *silence in the boat.*

The cavalrymen bombarded the family with questions in French, pointing back at the bay. One dismounted and swaggered in front of the younger men, his thumbs in his belt, his white gauntlets glowing.

He took the bag of coins from the young man, wagging a finger at him, chuckling. One of his three comrades said something and they laughed, the trooper pocketing the purse. He then poked at the bags on the mules and in the cart.

Underhill pointed at De Lisle and Hesse and raised four fingers, and pointed left. He then looked to Warnock, raised one finger, jabbing to the right, then at Pettifer and Napier, and raised two, then three. De la Vega, Cochrane, Porter and Kite crouched behind Underhill in the shadows of the scrub, blackened blades and muskets ready.

The dismounted cavalryman gave a victorious little cry when he found what he had been hoping for. 'Aha! *Tabac, hein? Oh ho ho…*' He wagged his finger again. '*Vous êtes méchants, oui?*'

The young Alexandrians argued as the elder shielded his wife with a protective arm but the Frenchman drew his holster pistol – just as Warnock stepped out, right in front of him.

'Knock-knock,' he said, 'you *twat*.'

He struck the cavalryman in the neck with his tomahawk with such force he nearly removed his head. Pettifer and Napier burst from behind the other two men and dragged them both out of the saddle, Pettifer putting his knife into the first, Napier holding the other down with his boot as he yanked up his free arm, and stamped on the man's chin, the bone cracking loud. De Lisle and Hesse raced round behind the fourth man furthest from the group, De Lisle snatching the reins as Hesse leapt up the saddle and pushed his knife through the rider's throat, throwing him down the other side. He was still choking as De Lisle dragged him into the bushes. It was over in seconds.

One of the young Egyptians stooped to retrieve his purse from Warnock's dead cavalryman, spitting on the body. The old man looked down at the marines from his cart in fear and confusion as the others appeared. '*Matha turidoon?*'

De la Vega put a finger to his lips. '*Shh, padre.*'

The old man looked puzzled. '*Vooz non ettas Fransay...?*'

Underhill shook his head. 'No, me ol' cockerel, we are not Franssay, we are *al-Ingleezee*, from King Georgie–Sultan of England, Gawd love his mad little socks.'

'*Nelsoun Amir!*' The young men appealed to the old father, '*Hal turid Masoud!*' The son smiled at Underhill. 'Masoud? *Hammer,*' he said, by way of explanation. '*Hammer!*'

Chevalier

Within hours of formal occupation of the deserted palaces of the beys, the aides of the French general staff began to pore over the accounts of the former Mamluk civil administrators – many of whom had been retained by Bonaparte's more astute logistics officers.

Masoud proved invaluable to them. His grasp of Turkish and French smoothed the way of the new government. The patient, helpful young Alexandrian was everywhere it seemed, so much so he earned the wary distrust of other Egyptians. Had it not been for the support of Al-Jabarti and the Al-Azhar Mosque, he might have become a target for his own countrymen.

One morning several days into Masoud's tenure among the Headquarters Battalion at the former palace of Qasim Bey, ADC Desvernois marched into his temporary offices in the rear mews with new despatches. He saw the name of the first intended recipient at the top of the pile.

'*Merde...*' Desvernois called for his corporal, '*Caporal! Venez-ci, vite!*' But one of Masoud's assistants, Firaj, appeared at the door instead. 'Has the courier departed?' demanded Desvernois. 'Gone? Clippity-clop, *yallah-yallah*?'

The little man shook his head at the young officer. 'N-no *effendi...* but toot syit!'

'It's *suite*, for God's sake, *tout de suite...*'

Masoud had heard, and hurried in. 'I take it, Devenwa-*effendi*, a pleasure.'

'Just get it to him before the damned man goes, and get Corporal Battista in here,' he muttered, and without another thought handed it to Masoud who dashed out, calling in deliberately bad French to the quad for the rider to wait, *attennday, attennday!*

But he did not take it directly to the quad. Instead, he ducked into the scroll rooms with the sealed despatch and took up a pen at an open inkwell to write. Once finished, he rushed through the cool corridors past the stables and saw the army galloper in the quad, mounted in the saddle ready to depart, the horse rearing, grooms trying to hold it steady, its rider still dusty from the road, fearsome in his tall leather shako and draped golden braids, roaring angry. He drained a water bottle and threw it empty at one of the grooms, saw Masoud and charged across to him, a black gauntlet thrust out, the horse's iron hooves clattering loud.

'*Well!*' he demanded. '*For whom? Which district?*'

Masoud read the slanting hand on the despatch. 'For the *Général* Damas! At Ouardan! Damas, yes!'

'*Ouardan? Merde alors...*' With a sigh of disgust the rider snatched the document from his hands and stuffed it into his sabre-tache, '*Arab dog...*' before he spurred away into a canter.

Masoud knew the despatch riders were easy targets, and this one would be no exception. Having mastered Desvernois' impatient hand, he had falsely directed the rider to an area infested with *Bedu* bandits: *Ouardan Banlieue, 3ᵉ Bn 7ᵉ Bis Hussar.* General Damas had long since moved on with his dragoon cavalry, but the despatch rider had not known that – no one did, as Masoud had not delivered that particular news to Desvernois, or to anyone. He watched him go without a flicker of compassion, and reflected how very easy it was to play the fool for them. The battle for Cairo had changed the learned scholar and now he felt no sorrow for the invader. When he turned, Firaj was waiting.

'Why do you help them so, Masoud *al-hakim*? They are uncivilised animals...' Masoud returned to the shade of the mews corridors, Firaj hurrying after, his voice a whisper, 'They eat like *pigs*. Meat, meal and *limes* mixed in the *same bowl*. Disgusting. They tread upon the carpets in their filthy boots, and blow their noses on the curtains – they are *revolting*. And the women are worse! Laughing on mules as they race through the markets, calling to their friends, causing disturbance, consorting with the common people—'

Masoud spoke in a low urgent voice, 'Firaj ibn Saleh… you will help them, as I do. Become indispensable, as I do. And thus learn their secrets, as I do – and *help me find him* before they do.'

Firaj looked up at him, frightened of speaking his name. '*Al-Pasha al-ahmar.*'

Masoud did not correct him. After his furious ride across the field of battle, all now followed the Awlad 'Ali and called him the 'Red Pasha'. He strode down the corridor towards a distant archway. 'They say a rogue clan of Maaza took him from the battle. I want the Beni Qassim, the Awlad 'Ali, the Al-Habayba, the Huwaytat, from Maryut, Menouf, Ouardan, Sais, from El-'Arish, everywhere, to seek him out. He is beloved of God, and risked his life for us. Honour demands we do the same for him.' He stopped at the exit, looking out at the steps and garden path to the wall and gates, Firaj catching him up.

'But where do you go, Masoud?'

Masoud was in no doubt. He looked out through the arch and the cool shade of overhanging trees. 'To the Nile, Firaj. To find Hammer-*effendi*. And to find my friend.'

A roar. Izzam.

Izzam!

A camel, he thought. *It is a camel. Izzam had a camel.*

No, horse, he had a horse.

Grit in his teeth and sand and the heat from it, an oven of molten glass, like that airless *abattoir* of Cairo. St Jude's… the lawns, Sarah as he had longed once, as his wife, three children, a townhouse in Cambridge. But India had called and France killed their king.

The king the king.

Swaying.

Damn the king.

A stinging blow across his cheek, fourteen years of age, his Uncle Thomas, the Reverend Hazzard, red-faced and angry, *Never! Never say such a thing, boy! Your father served the king, as did I—*

France. Golden France, the ghost of mother somewhere nearby, and his promise to the Mediterranean breeze, *Maman... I shall be English, Maman, as you wished.*

Burning on his leg. A thousand tons pressing against his thigh and he shouted out, a fire in his bones, then relief, the sound of metal ringing, *bullet,* and another, *second bullet.* A fierce gaze watching him, a surgeon, Al-Jabarti? *No,* and he tried to speak, but could not, the educated face saying, *be still.*

Days passed, dressings changed, Nile breezes. Birds. Ibis perhaps. Ibis everywhere. The ibis-headed god, Thoth. God of science, of letters, of writing, of knowledge. *My patron saint,* patron of the man of letters, the man of straw and his bloody pen—

No, mine is St Jude, Patron Saint of Causes Lost. Laughter somewhere in the dark mind. *Four hundred ships – what a damned good lost cause that was.*

Swaying stopped.

'*Combien? Vous êtes fou, mon cher salaud.*'

You are mad, my dear bastard. *Mon cher salaud.* Very polite. Cavalry officer, talking to someone. On a horse, talking down to men on foot. Hoofbeats riding, riding, and the sands receding, weightless heat, all-consuming *heat.*

Hands lifting him, carrying him – a *Bordelais* accent, and a Norman, he could tell, *Muddy-arse!* They called Normans and Gascons that in Paris, he remembered, *Cul terreux!*

At last the drenching cool of shade, a cloud, a veil over the sun, palm fronds above, and water on his face, hands slapping it onto his cheeks, forehead and chin, a bandage across his eyes and this too gradually soaked with water, evaporating, cooling.

'*Voilà, mon brave. Seulement un petit peu.*'

Just a little bit, and he drank a mouthful, holding it, then swallowing carefully.

'*Oh God…*' he choked. Swallowing nails, his parched throat tight and shrunken. The bandage was lifted from his eyes but the inside of the tent remained a blur, a face gazing down.

'*Bonjour.*'

Hazzard tried to focus. It was a dark-skinned soldier, an officer, long dark sideboards, that weary, ironic Gallic look he knew so well.

'*Moi, je suis Colonel Jacques Cavalier, à votre service.*' *At your service.*

He nodded his head in a bow. Hazzard could not speak his thanks.

'And you are the Red Devil, hm? *El afrit l'akhmerre.*'

Cook lay on a mattress a few feet away, eyes closed, face blistered, lips puffed and cracked. Dead? *Be dead soon, like I am.* Hazzard tried to reach over and put the bottle to Cook's lips but was too weak, could not do it, *embarrassing really, try again.* Cavalier took it. '*Ah, non non non… moment, moment…*'

Cavalier trickled some water onto his fingers and applied them to Cook's face and mouth. 'It is bad, you know, the water, when one is without mind, without *conscience*, hm? One can drown after the desert.'

Two sun-blackened Bedouins looked down from behind Cavalier, baffled by his care for the prisoners. They were dressed much as the *Bedu* Hazzard had encountered when he had met Ali Qarim: *Maaza.*

'Our friends here, they want to sell you, for the ransom, to the next East India ship on the Red Sea. But we found you instead and bought you. Give you proper hospital attention sooner, hm. Better or worse, I cannot say, forgive me but I think it best for you.' He shrugged. '*C'est la guerre.*'

He could hear movement, shouts of men beyond the canvas. They were in a camp. Cavalier handed him the water bottle. 'Messengers have ridden with news of your capture. It is the big day for the colonel here, Lacroix, *un salaud*, hm? Beware.'

Hazzard blinked and nodded, words not yet possible.

Cavalier gazed at him a moment then spoke, lowering his voice, 'My men of the 1st Cavalry saw you ride the field with the sword. I thought I had seen all on campaign but, *mon dieu*, an *anglais* with such skill.' He looked over his shoulder, then back. 'The officers, they fear you. But the men, they respect you. They call you *Milord Mamluk*.'

The tent flap was thrown aside and a major and captain entered with two infantrymen behind, followed by a still more senior officer – white-haired, greying moustache, a pinched, sour mouth, a dark blue coat adorned with white facings, braid and epaulettes – judging by Cavalier's glance, this was the *salaud*, 'the bastard', Lacroix.

'*Chef d'escadron* Cavalier,' announced Lacroix, 'you are still here.' Hands behind his back, he raised himself up on his toes once or twice, a triumphant schoolmaster discovering misbehaviour.

Cavalier remained on his haunches next to Hazzard, his features twisted with humour at a private joke. '*Oui, chef de brigade*, I am. But now I go. Two colonels in one tent is one too many. Though one of us was a – what was it? A paper-hanger for the bourgeois ladies…?'

Lacroix went red. 'How *dare* you.' He snapped a finger at Hazzard and gestured at the two infantrymen. 'Take him.'

Lacroix could have waited but it was clear even to Hazzard he wanted to do it deliberately in front of Cavalier – the soldiers forced their way past him and seized Hazzard. Cavalier protested, 'Colonel, he is recovering from battle. His wounds—'

'I have standing orders, Cavalier,' said Lacroix airily and held out a tattered note. He read it with some relish. '*If captured, to be bound. To be isolated. To be watched. To await interrogation.*' He jerked a hand to the men. 'Go.'

They dragged him outside and Hazzard was blinded, the light bright white, the heat crashing onto him, and he sagged still further. They hauled him to a fence-post by the nearby livestock corral and threw him against it, Cavalier furious.

'*Lacroix!*' he shouted, 'This stands contrary to the laws of arms!'

'I am a soldier, Cavalier, not a grand *chevalier* like yourself. I *obey* my orders.'

Hazzard's torn red coat was pulled from him and the shirt stripped from his back. The two infantrymen stopped. They saw the scars, old stripes of the lash, the sword-cuts. All soldiers knew the marks of discipline. Lacroix had to order them.

'Do it!'

Though hesitant they bound Hazzard's wrists behind him and secured them to the post. His legs buckled and he sank to his knees, the tension on his shoulders pulling his arms taut behind him. His head hanging low, he leaned forward, exposing his back to the beating sun – his only chance, his deadened back, his armour. Hazzard heard a sword scrape from its scabbard.

'You will release him Lacroix, or I will demand satisfaction.'

Hazzard stared at the sand, his thoughts wandering, but one surfaced above the others. *Cavalier… no duel. A marine fated to die a drier death on shore.* His throat rasped, 'Cavalier… non – c'est… fini. Mais… pas pour vous.'

It is over. But not for you.

There was silence around him. Then Lacroix's voice. 'There, you see, Cavalier, he knows.'

Cavalier took a step toward the post. Hazzard heard the click of a lock being cocked – one of the infantrymen, he guessed.

'We are not finished, Lacroix. I will send my second to you with my card, and I will open your tiny heart, if my blade can but find it. But know that you shall die by my hand for this.' Cavalier's sword scraped back into the sand and grit of its scabbard. The cavalryman's boots crunched on the desert stones and stopped in front of Hazzard, '*Suis désolé, mon ami.* Forgive me.'

Hazzard heard movement, a call, infantrymen again, and the muffled thud of fists as they beat the unconscious Sergeant Cook. The trial had begun. Hazzard could see only his own shadow on the dazzling sand before him, the figurine of St Jude, the hanged man, swinging, twisting under his gaze, one way, then back – but his lips were still wet from a bottle given him by Jacques Cavalier, and he would never forget.

Just out of his sight, among the tent-lines, looking on with faces of stone, stood *Sergent-chef-major* Achille Caron and his best men of the *Alpha-Oméga*.

–

Dining by torchlight on the stone terrace of his newly acquired governor's residence in Rosetta, General Jacques-François Menou and the assembled company took in the view of the old port and glimmering sea, all grateful at least for the cooling breeze – while they discussed his heroic role in the capture of Alexandria. Jérôme Bonaparte, brother of the Commander in Chief, helped himself to another glass of chilled Pouilly and said provocatively, 'I hear it took all of two hours, General...'

The ladies tittered, Menou's escort for the evening *Madame* de Roubaix putting an indulgent hand on the general's as he blustered, 'Three, Citizen, *three* hours – it is how I was shot from my horse while leading my valiant troops by God, the fiendish defenders wailing and howling, pelting us with rocks when their ammunition ran out—'

Bonaparte inhaled the bouquet of the wine. 'Which happened, I believe, within the *first* hour...'

There were more chuckles from a number of officers over Menou's protests. At the other end of the table, with junior *savants* Pierre Bouchard, Prosper Jollois and Édouard de Villiers, sat Jeanne Arnaud and the quiet *danseuse* and favourite of the Commander in Chief himself, Isabelle Moreau-Lazare.

Sarah held her head low, her eye avoiding everyone, her food untouched. Jeanne squeezed her ice-cold hand under the table to give her strength.

Derrien had been true to his word and deposited Sarah in Rosetta. She was now billeted with a merchant's wife, a *Madame* de Vitry, and her two sisters in a cramped townhouse, her world shrunken to a servant's chamber in the stifling attics, an iron-framed bed and chamber-pot, the mosquito net slung from the ceiling her only comfort.

Had it not been for the *comtesse* de Biasi she would have been lost. The old lady had sought out and made the acquaintance of *Madame* de Vitry, and found Sarah through deliberate coincidence. They now took exercise together every day in Rosetta, flanked by Citizen Masson and two of Derrien's black-clad *Bureau* men.

Rosetta was the most European of the Delta ports, tall multi-storeyed houses in bright colours, colonnades, covered Italianesque passages to give shade, palms in neat rows, the harbour inlet almost pleasant – and a crumbling medieval tower at the river mouth provided the final picturesque antique effect. The conquering army had been welcomed with applause and a parade. Despite the fine surroundings, Sarah's relief in the company of the *comtesse* had been overwhelming.

'We are being observed so do keep smiling, my dear,' the *comtesse* had told her that first day, 'and try not to change your expression as I tell you that your captain was at Shubra Khit and saved the life of our little Jeanne...'

Sarah nearly fainted on the promenade, the Nile sliding before them, and she grasped at the handrail. '*Mon dieu...*'

'Yes,' laughed the *comtesse*, for the sake of their *Bureau* escorts, 'and we are possibly being watched over right now by our protector, a *M'sieur* Hammer of Vienna, so be reassured. But I have heard nothing of the captain since the battle at Cairo last week. Herr Hammer will find him, somehow.'

Sarah stared down at the water. At last the question she had always wished to ask came forth, '*Madame*, why have you come with the fleet? Why any of it? *Please* – who *are* you?'

The *comtesse* linked arms with her. 'Come, *ma petite*. Do you think I found you in this town by accident? Let us talk of republics and despots...'

She would have fled to the salon of the *comtesse* without hesitation but for Derrien. He was always there, with *Madame* de

Vitry, taking coffee, taking tea, having supper, in the drawing room, answering *madame*'s bland questions: 'And do you both like Rosetta, my dear?'

Derrien would answer as if for Sarah as well. 'Why yes, we find it most distracting.' He was acting, she realised, as if they were married.

The first night after she had snuffed out her candle in her attic room, she had heard a creak on the floorboards outside in the passage. A light appeared at a knothole in the door planks. Then a sheet of her coded notes was slipped beneath the door, the burnt ink betraying her treason. With a gasp she retreated to her bed, and the light was gone, the footsteps passing.

The following night, the light came again. She was waiting. It glowed at the knothole, and she looked out – straight into Derrien's reptilian eye. As if the breath had been sucked from her body, she fell back, a hand to her throat at the thought of his constant, silent gaze – as she slept, as she woke, as she dressed, and the endless fear: *When will they come for me? When?*

But they never did. The following night, he was there again, another sheet under the door, her descriptions of the divisional HQ battalions, to taunt and torment her, to demonstrate that he knew all, and wielded ultimate power over her. On the last night, she saw the diffuse light of the passage glowing under the door. Then brightening, a slow footstep approaching. She watched the knot in the planking. The light appeared. She could bear the waiting no longer, for his rapacious hands upon her or the rough grasp of the soldier dragging her off to death.

She flung open the door, to find the startled face of the thick-necked and wheezing *Bureau* deputy Masson, his bulging eyes wide with surprise.

Before she could say a word Derrien came running, and shoved Masson away, striking him with a stick, driving him cringing and crying out down the stairs. Enraged, Derrien turned and stood in her doorway, face streaming with sweat. She backed away but this seemed to draw his power deeper into the room, and she shivered, as exposed before him as she had been aboard the *Orient*. Derrien stared, his breathing heavy and thick, his eyes ever on her now, and he reached slowly for the latch, and retreated back into the corridor. He slammed the door shut, the key turning violently in the lock.

She closed her eyes, her body shaking. Then his mouth pressed to the knothole in the door as he whispered, '*Mine. Mine alone.*'

She screamed, the torment too great, and hammered on the door until, exhausted, she shrank back to her bed sobbing, gathering the shift to herself as if to shield herself from his madness.

The *comtesse* sat beside her at Menou's table, fanning herself in the heat, the candlelight flickering. She urged Sarah to eat, *Please, anything, my dear.* The young *savant* Propser Jollois watched, and tried to help, with a distraction.

'Perhaps, *mademoiselle*,' he offered, 'you would like to accompany me on a hunting trip in the Delta? Not far, enough to get some birds for the zoologists…'

'For Saint-Hilaire so he claims,' confirmed De Villiers, happy to be eating a large meal at a general's table for a change. 'He tramps about blasting at anything that moves. Very scientific.'

'Will you take me?' asked Jeanne. 'You are almost handsome enough, *mon petit*.'

The boy blushed and there was mild laughter, but Sarah said nothing. As an incentive Jollois added, 'The sun is more powerful than at home – with the dust they say it can cause ophthalmia. You could try my special sun-spectacles?'

Sarah nodded, her raging thoughts miles from the scene, not least because, sitting opposite was her tormentor, Derrien. He spooned his chilled soup carefully.

'If it is suitable, Citizen,' said Derrien on her behalf, 'then perhaps we shall join you. Will we not, my dear?'

Once again, he spoke as if they were man and wife. The thought made her shiver. She nodded numbly.

Jollois mumbled a reply, 'Yes. Yes, of course, Citizen…'

Menou broke in. 'Citizen Jollois down there is one of the finest young engineers in the land, you know.' He turned proudly to

276

Jérôme Bonaparte. 'Listen to their every word, Citizen, listen, geniuses all. Fire engines on the Nile, balloons and sun-spectacles – and heroes of the battle at *Chèvre-chit!*'

'Ahum…*Shubra Khit*, surely, *mon général*,' murmured Bonaparte with a muffled snigger.

'Oh, is it?' asked Menou. 'As you say then, but they were there, on the burning deck!'

'Here here,' said one, and raised a glass and there was applause, the other *savants* silently thanking God they had not been there.

Menou got to his feet. 'But in honour of our guest, the brother of our great Commander in Chief, I should like to salute our finest victory yet. The Battle of Cairo—'

He could go no further for the door banged downstairs. The guard in the entrance hall conferred with a visitor as Menou grumbled, *Who the devil's that*, but Derrien set down his spoon as he heard two sets of boots hurry up the stairs. It could be only for him. The dust of the road still clinging to his cloak, a sunburnt courier appeared, and behind him, Masson.

'And who in devil are you, Citizens?' demanded Menou.

The courier bowed to the general, then saw Derrien. He held out a sealed packet. 'Citizen. This was delayed. They thought you were in Cairo.'

Derrien was already on his feet and moving round the table to take the despatch. Masson murmured to him, '*You have him, Citizen. He is yours.*'

Derrien reread the note several times.

Lacroix, his location, the day and month, 13 Thermidor.

Hazzard.

He resisted showing his pleasure but closed his eyes briefly and took a breath in some small measure of self-reward. The night view of Rosetta's lights winking on the black Mediterranean seemed somehow more pleasant than ever before.

'We shall leave at once,' he said to Masson. 'Ready a carriage.'

Sarah watched them and guessed it was about Hazzard. Her hand gripped Jeanne's and that of the *comtesse*. '*Tell Hammer*,' Sarah hissed, '*tell him.*'

277

Menou was most put out, a stickler for formality. 'Do you depart, Citizen? So abrupt? It is late, past midnight! We should observe the decencies, for the ladies, for our guest of honour—'

'Matters of the Republic, Citizen Governor,' said Derrien with a bow, 'which will now become clear.'

Sarah gasped as Derrien touched her bare shoulder with his cold hand. She shivered beneath his fingers and looked up at him. He met her sapphire eye as a squad of Menou's personal guard marched up the stairs, porting muskets with fixed bayonets, *Who called them up, damnation*, and, to Menou's alarm filed in behind Sarah and the *comtesse*, the Arab servants hurrying out of their way.

'It has been a terrible journey for you, my dear, I know,' Derrien said to her, looking occasionally to Jeanne and the *comtesse*, 'and I tried to keep you close, to *protect* you...' The gathering looked on with incomprehension. 'But now I can at last safely place you under arrest for crimes of espionage against the State as an agent of the British Admiralty.' He nodded at Masson and the guards. 'Take her.'

—

Within the hour Jeanne and the *comtesse* de Biasi were hurrying through the deserted streets of Rosetta, down the cool twisting lanes, trying to avoid the army curfew patrols. '*Come, Jeanne,*' whispered the old lady. '*Vite alors!*'

They hurried down an alley, barely wide enough for a donkey and cart, past scrub trees and palms, and stopped at a darkened doorway. The *comtesse* rapped urgently several times in quick succession. There was no reply. She knocked again. Jeanne's face was tight with fear, and the *comtesse* squeezed her hand.

A light appeared over the wall, a dash of footsteps. '*Oui oui je viens, I come I come—*'

The door opened. Inside was a small ornamental garden court-yard leading to the front of the house, its doors standing open beneath a series of arches. A bearded man in a turban held up a lantern, looking quickly up and down the lane.

'*As-salamu aleikum*,' whispered the *comtesse*, 'Hassan.'

The Alexandrian looked at her a moment, then beckoned them in, closing the door, and rushed off. They heard a few sharp words, running feet, the murmur of voices. A wealthy Turk appeared in kaftan and turban at the open doors. He bowed.

'Hassan is not here,' he said in French, 'it is *Safar*.'

'Then he withdraws,' replied the *comtesse*, 'and shall soon emerge.'

Satisfied with the coded reply, the Turk bowed again. 'Your message?'

'For Herr Hammer. They have *Al-Pasha al-ahmar*. We saw Citizen Derrien receive a note—'

'But what of Belle?' whispered Jeanne in anguish, 'and the *anglais*? Where has that monster taken Belle?'

Hassan interrupted her. 'If they have the Red Pasha, then the Beni Qassim and Herr Hammer will find him, *madame*. When was this?'

'Not an hour ago. A messenger direct from the road.'

The Turk looked over his shoulder and snapped a few words, names and orders, and his attendant ran back into the house. 'We shall track them and inform Hammer-*effendi*. They will not get far...'

'Thank God, *al hamdulillah*. But they take my Isabelle, I know not where, perhaps Alexandria, to a place he said where no one can escape.' The *comtesse* now looked worn and frail, her stately beauty marked by lines of fear, her voice shaking.

The Turk seemed disturbed at the news. 'My dear *madame*, if so, then there is only one place in Alexandria where no prisoner may escape.'

'Not the old fort, or the gatehouses, they are full of troops,' she said.

'No, *cher madame*,' he said, 'this particular prison is on the sea.'

They heard the sounds of running feet, and a hissed call came from inside, '*Al faransi, effendi! Al faransi!* The French!'

Hassan opened the door to the lane. It was clear, but they could hear the echoing sounds of running boots, 'The French come. You must *go*.' He ushered them out quickly and they looked up and down the lane, lost. 'We shall find *al-Pasha al-ahmar, madame*.' He looked grave. '*Rabbena ma'ak.' God be with you.*

He shut the door and the bolt was slammed across. Frantic, the *comtesse* took hold of Jeanne, 'You must *go, ma petite*, back to the house.'

'No, I will not leave you—'

'You *must*, you do not understand—'

She took the *comtesse* by the hand and pulled her along to the end of the lane. When they turned the corner, they found a platoon of French dragoon troopers gathered by an enclosed black carriage. Their officer was interrogating two frightened boys. When the boys saw the two women appear they began to jabber excitedly, pointing at them. The officer turned, '*Vous là! Arrêtez!*'

The *comtesse* stumbled, falling to the cobbled road, Jeanne trying to catch her, '*Ah non – Jeanne, vite, vite!*'

But another squad appeared from the end of the lane, and the dragoons surrounded them, spreading out, muskets levelled. From behind the carriage came Derrien. He raised a lantern, its yellow glare blotting out the stars and moon. He almost smiled.

'How very amenable of you, *madame la comtesse*,' he said, 'to show your hand so soon. Herr Hammer cannot help. He is watched everywhere he goes.'

'You would not dare...'

Derrien considered the point. 'Oh, but I would. Until this night I had only suspicions, doubting how one agent could gather such comprehensive information – I mean my dear Isabelle, of course. I then made the correct deduction. There was no *M'sieur le Conte de Biasi* in France, *madame*, was there. But there was a *Freiherr von Biasi*, a baron, I understand, in Austria.'

'*Va te foutre!*' screamed Jeanne and spat at him. '*Putain de la merde!*'

Derrien wiped a trace of flying spittle from his cheek. 'Oh I think we know who the *putain* is here,' he said softly, 'and our gallant troops will learn it first-hand.' He indicated the carriage. The door swung open, revealing a lewdly grinning Masson, his groping hands holding Sarah, bound and gagged, her muffled screams reduced to convulsive sobs as she saw Jeanne and the *comtesse*.

Derrien's eyes glittered. 'Now,' he said, 'we shall all go to Alexandria. And your new home by the sea.'

–

Caron stood silent between two tents, the bleached canvas either side luminous white in the cold desert night. He had waited until the picket guard had changed. The day patrol had still not returned, and only engineers remained, auxiliaries and walking wounded from several *demis*, the 86th, 69th, *sapeurs*, artillery. Lanterns hung from props outside the command tent, two bored men on guard, one virtually asleep on his feet. But otherwise the camp was quiet, deserted, all in their beds. He looked across the compound towards the mule corral. A scorpion scuttled across the sand and disappeared under a stone.

His slackened bonds still holding his arms to the post behind him, Hazzard lay crumpled on the sand. Once Cavalier had gone, Lacroix had dragged him into his tent twice at least to attempt to interrogate him, but failed, and slung him out again. As evening fell someone had thrown a canvas cover over him. The pack animals milled behind, occasionally braying. There was only one sentry, an overfed corporal of the 25th *demi*, slumped against a shattered adobe wall in the dull wash of a lantern, glugging from a jug of wine and gnawing on a piece of dried sausage.

Caron surveyed the scene and felt a great sorrow overwhelm him. He had worn his coat for nearly thirty years, he reflected. In that time he had carried messages, then powder and shot, then a musket, and eventually the colours. He had fought in different regiments, served two kings, a duke, a marquis, and big-wigged viscount-generals – and now, he thought with distaste, now he served the *petit bourgeois*, men like Lacroix, administrative clerks, insurance men, merchants in brand-new uniforms they had not earned. At least, he mused, the *aristos* had better manners. There had once been a sense of serving something greater than oneself, however false. The Revolution had become that, the new purpose, the new hope, but even that had faded – the murderous *bourgeois* had drained its font dry of all promise. He had once stepped over a stream of blood in the gutter of a Paris street, draining from a guillotine scaffold, and knew at once that hope had died, along with the souls of his fellow countrymen. All the Revolution had achieved, it seemed, as with any coup, was to change the king, several times over.

He looked at Hazzard. He knew Lacroix did not have the courage for this brutality without the cover of an order. And Bonaparte would not have countenanced it. No, this, he had reasoned, bore all the hallmarks of *le diable*: Citizen *Croquemort*.

Rossy and Pigalle emerged silently from the tent-lines and joined Caron, fully armed. They had seen and heard everything the previous day. Cavalier, Lacroix, and the squad from the dung-eating 3rd Battalion of the 25th *demi* dragging Hazzard to the post, then beating Cook. They had not liked that. Cook was the brother-in-arms of their special *anglais*, and they had fought them in the field, each doing their duty. They had more respect for the Englishmen than they ever could for Lacroix. They sided with Cavalier in that regard – but called Lacroix a *con*, instead of a *salaud*.

'I wish to be certain, *Chef*,' whispered Rossy, adjusting the sling of his musket, 'that we do not do this in the name of honour, hm?'

'What a suggestion,' said Caron. 'In any case, I told you all to stay.'

'That is funny, *Chef*.' Rossy did not laugh.

Pigalle looked out at Hazzard, at his head hanging low. 'It is not good,' he said, 'what they do here to a man.'

'No, Pig,' agreed Rossy, 'it is not good. Let us stop them.'

St Michel appeared, his Austrian rifle slung over his shoulder, two full *bidons* of water in his hands. '*Chef.*'

Caron nodded to him, still lost in thought. What he did next, he knew, could destroy him. He no longer cared. He had worn his coat, he decided, for a few years too long.

'*Bon, Micheline. Allons-y.*'

Caron led the way across the compound. They passed the glow of the command tent, the one sentry watching them, the other snoring, then jerking awake. When the guard at the mule corral saw Caron approach he dropped his wine-jug and began to struggle to his feet, still chewing. '*Chef-major*... I was just, I was...'

Caron ignored him and went straight to Hazzard. Where once there had been unbearable heat there was now a chill, even to Caron, and he had not been staked in the open all day like a beast. He set down the *bidon* of water, and threw off the canvas thrown over Hazzard's back. He lay unconscious, his breathing merely a dry wheeze. Caron drew his old Prussian sword-bayonet and started to cut the ropes binding Hazzard's raw, blistered wrists. The guard began to protest, and raised his lamp.

'*Chef?* Lacroix, the colonel, he said no water... I – I have orders not to, but, to – do you, have... any orders?'

Hazzard's hands came free and he rolled forward, Pigalle catching him and setting him upright, his back against the post. Caron opened a *bidon* and poured water onto his hand and patted Hazzard's mouth, trickling a little over his head. His wounds had opened, others had been left untended, dark bruises had spread across his ribs and shoulders. Caron swore. '*Mon dieu...*'

The sentry began to babble, '*Chef,* I – I will get the, the colonel, Colonel Lacroix—'

'*Go then!*' snapped Caron with disgust. 'Get out of here, *vas-t'en, tu idiot!*'

The guard set down his lantern and tried to run but Rossy put up a hand to stop him, then pointed out into the dark. 'Goodness, what was that?'

The man looked and Pigalle dropped him with a fist to the top of his head. He fell heavily to the ground. Pigalle kicked him. '*Con stupide.*' The two sentries by the command tent had run.

Caron nodded to Pigalle. '*Alors, mon garçon.* We take him.'

Pigalle lifted Hazzard, taking one of his arms across his shoulder, his own round Hazzard's waist, and carried him to the tent some twenty metres away. Caron threw open the tent flap. They saw by the light of a flickering candle the vacant bedroll on the floor, Cook lying beside it. The big man's face was livid and swollen from his beating and he shook with cold. Cook's guard, another soldier of the 25th, rose from a stool, puffing out his belly. 'Ehh, *tiens*, what goes on here?' Caron drew his Liège pistol and pointed it in the man's face.

'*Get out or die.*'

The soldier threw up his hands, '*Non, non, Chef!* I beg you – *je vous en prie*,' and dashed outside.

They dressed Hazzard in the remains of the shirt that had been torn from his back and lay him down. Hazzard began to breathe more deeply, then coughed and hacked, his chest rising and falling, his throat rattling. Caron held his head back and Rossy poured water over his dry, cracked lips. Hazzard fought them off but Caron held him tight, until he swallowed and coughed, then drank again.

Caron knelt beside Cook and gave him water as well, holding up his head, and the big man drank, and breathed, sinking back. Pigalle watched, confused, awestruck. 'He is the first to put me down, ever, this *anglais*,' he said in wonder. 'He is truly the John Bull.'

When Caron returned to Hazzard, Hazzard put a hand on his wrist. '*Qui... êtes vous...?*' *Who are you?*

They had never heard his voice. Not clearly – shouting out at Malta, raging with the guns at Embabeh, but not like this. They listened. His French was pure, not *anglais* at all. Caron looked down at him, the grip on his wrist strong, his eyes cloudy but open. He decided Hazzard deserved an answer.

'I am Caron. Of the 75th. These are the *Alpha-Oméga*. Soldiers. Like you.'

Hazzard then relaxed, his eyes closing, his grip slackening, his hand falling back to the bed. '*Merci...*'

They watched him a moment, the breathing returning almost to normal, the wheezing rattle almost gone. There was no doubt they had saved his life.

'*Bon*,' said Caron, breaking out rice rations in a tin bowl. 'You go, all of you. I shall watch over him.'

'In all the excitement,' said Rossy, settling down, his back to the central tent pole, 'I forgot how comfortable these old tents can be...'

Caron looked at him. 'Fusilier Rossy. I gave you the command.'

'You are in fine form tonight, *Chef*,' said Rossy with a smile, closing his eyes. 'Wake me when the bad men come. I wish to see the look on their faces.'

–

They did not have to wait long. Just after dawn there was a distant shot and St Michel peered out the tent flap. Hoofbeats approached and soon they heard horses stamping to a halt by the mule corral, voices raised.

'Company,' said St Michel. 'Two men on horses.' He hefted his rifle and flipped up its ladder-sights. 'I shall get in a good few shots before they come for us. Maybe get the colonel,' he added brightly.

But Caron was having none of it. '*Enfants*,' he said, 'trouble has found us again. Let us shake its hand.' He got to his feet and checked the pan of his pistol, then slammed it shut.

When they stepped out into the cool morning air, they fanned out in front of the tent, Pigalle towering over all, a *sapeur*'s axe in each hand. Lacroix stood screaming at the babbling sentry of the 25th *demi*, and at the empty wine-jug by the bare post where Hazzard had been tied.

Of the two riders in black looking down upon Lacroix one turned and saw Caron. The unmistakable blank stare made Caron's skin crawl.

'*Alors*,' he whispered, '*Le Croquemort*.'

Derrien's gaze took in Caron and his squad and came to rest on the tent. '*Over there*,' he told Masson. Ignoring Lacroix, the pair dismounted and marched towards them.

'*Enfants*, let them pass…'

Rossy was reluctant to do so and readied his Charleville. '*Chef*… I want very much to hurt this one…'

'Be wise, *garçon*. He is the enemy of Lacroix.'

Rossy and Pigalle stood still as Caron cocked his pistol. Derrien slowed and came to a halt.

'We meet again, *Sergent-chef-major*.'

Caron looked back at him. 'Infamy brings us close too often, Citizen.'

He nodded to Rossy who stood aside and opened the tent flap. Derrien stepped in and saw Hazzard and Cook. He glanced at Caron. 'Lacroix?'

Caron nodded. 'Had the sergeant beaten. Tied the *anglais* in the sun. No water.'

Masson bent over Cook, a hand to his neck. He looked up. 'He lives, Citizen.'

'Very well.' Derrien shrugged off his cloak. 'Then Lacroix must be kept away.'

Pigalle crowded in behind Caron in the tent entrance. 'So,' said Caron, 'we save him from Lacroix only to deliver him up to you? I think not, *m'sieur*. I give the word, and you are dead men.'

Derrien glanced at Pigalle.

'And what then of you? And your men?'

Caron did not blink. 'We have been dead men for years.'

Derrien met his gaze. 'You will not win, with me, *Chef-major*.'

Caron did not budge. 'No. But neither will you, with me.'

Pigalle moved forward slightly with a growl. Masson looked up, uncertain.

'I am here to question him,' said Derrien, holding up a letter. 'He is then to be handed to the *général en chef* who seeks recompense for his deceptions.'

Caron took the note and read, doubtful. 'Bonaparte? How can I believe you?'

'Because you shall escort him. After all...' said Derrien, to mollify the sergeant-major, 'he was your prisoner.'

Caron considered his words. They promised more than Lacroix would.

'I do not like him,' said Pigalle.

'Nor do I, *M'sieur* le Pig,' agreed Caron – but he nodded to Derrien. 'Thirty minutes, no more, then we go. My men will be outside.' It was more threat than reassurance.

He turned to go but Derrien spoke, an admonishing reminder, '*Sergent-chef-major.* He is our enemy.'

Caron looked back at him a moment. 'I know who my enemy is...'

An audience had formed, men coming out of the tent lines, some giving a low whistle with applause, one shouting, *Vive le Pig!* Lacroix stormed across the compound towards them, his guards running alongside belatedly, the sentry corporal gibbering, pointing. '*Caron!*' screamed Lacroix. 'What is the meaning of this! You defy my orders!'

St Michel, Rossy and Pigalle formed a protective cordon around Caron and the tent entrance, Pigalle swinging an axe from each hand, Rossy's Charleville levelled at the hip, St Michel's Austrian long-rifle cocked, ready. They stood like rock, unmoving. Lacroix stopped dead, glaring at them.

'You are *all* under arrest! *Traitors! Do you hear me!*' He turned to a staff major beside him. 'Arrest them! At once!'

Hesitantly pulling the pistol from his belt, the *Chef de bataillon* began to protest, 'But, I am sure...'

'*Do as I say!*'

Caron stepped out in front of his men, his pistol hanging at arm's length. '*Chef de brigade* Lacroix, you are not fit to command!

287

Come to this tent by force of arms, and you will be the first to die.' He cocked the pistol.

Lacroix's eyes bulged in disbelief. 'You *what!* You *dare* give me orders!'

'I am Achille Mérové Caron, *Sergent-chef-major* of the 75th *demi-brigade de bataille*, The Invincibles, veteran of the Indies, the Americas, Batavia, the 13th *Vendémiaire*, of Montenotte, Lodi, Caldiero, and saviour of Bonaparte at Arcole.' Caron looked out at Lacroix's officers ranged around him. 'You who do this thing to this soldier, are cowards and swine. Not men.'

Lacroix staggered backwards, his face reddening. 'You *dare* speak to *me* like this!'

'I have seen too much done to my own countrymen in the name of kings, or freedom, or revolution, to let this be done in my name.' He raised his pistol, ready. 'I am Caron, *soldat de France*. And here I stand.'

The audience cheered once again, *Vive le chef! Vive le chef!* Pigalle calling out, '*And I am Pigalle! And where I plant my boot, there shall I not be moved!*'

Lacroix jerked round at the gales of cheering, *Chef! Chef! Chef! Vive le Pig! Vive le Pig!*

'*Stop that!*' screamed Lacroix. '*Stop that at once, I say! Arrest them! Chef de bataillon!*'

No one in the camp moved to help him. Instead, the men of the 25th stepped further back, well out of Pigalle's long reach. Lacroix screamed again for silence as the whistling and jeering continued. Caron remained still, waiting.

–

Inside the tent, Derrien tossed his cloak onto the guard's stool and knelt by Hazzard, taking firm hold of his wet and filthy shirt-front and yanking him forward, whispering viciously into his ear, '*I would have staked you in the middle of the Sahara, Captain*, but I had no idea it was *you*,' he said. 'This so-called devil in red or "Red Pasha" or whatever nonsense these *animals* call you,' he hissed.

'We are not alone so I shall be brief: this time, you *will* answer my questions,' he said with venom, '*because I have her.*'

Hazzard stirred. '*Sarah…*'

Derrien's face lightened. 'Ah yes… of course! How very *English*, I should have guessed. *Sarah…*' He came closer, relishing his triumph. 'Can you hear her name upon my lips? *Sarah…* I can *taste* her even now…'

Hazzard tried to fight him off. '*Mur – murderer…*'

Derrien gripped him more tightly, shaking him, his teeth bared. 'And what of *you*, *Mister* Hazzard? Do you know Bonaparte still calls you that? And the cavalry *loves* you, their gallant foe! Are you French, or *English*? What are you now, Bedouin, or Mamluk? Soldier or sailor? Scholar? *Traitor*? Or *none*.'

Hazzard collapsed, his head heavy, hanging.

'You are *nothing*, you are *adrift*—' spitting out his hatred, sweat pouring from his brow '—a thief of hopes, *Mister Hazzard* – promising so much to them all, and delivering *nothing*.'

Derrien threw him down as if sullied, tainted. He pulled a sheet from his coat pocket and flapped it open. 'Do you see this?' He held it before Hazzard's face. It was a map. He seized the back of Hazzard's head and pushed his face closer. '*Look at it, damn you.* Upper and Lower Egypt as you well know…'

Hazzard focussed on the names, in Roman characters, *Memphis, Karnak, Nécropolis et la route au Memnonium*, faces blurring before him, at the museum, figures bending over the tables, charts, engravings.

'De Toit-Thainville,' said Derrien, 'for Vermiac, years ago. We have been ready for this day for longer than even we have known, and we alone shall open this desert tomb of yours – treasures beyond your imagination, they said, Egyptian kings, *les pharaoens*, hm? While the clever oxen dig their ridiculous canals, their grand works at Suez, *this* is where we shall go, Captain, you and I, to find prizes, booty to fuel the Republic,' he said proudly, 'gold, jewels, proof of the Revolution's indomitability. And you, the expert, the *savant anglais*, will lead us *to each one*.' He shook Hazzard violently.

'And I shall be the man who enslaved *Milord Mamluk*, the great Red Devil – not the general, not *Bonaparte.*'

Derrien had waited so long for this moment that simply killing Hazzard would have left him bereft, devoid of the power he had sought so desperately to wield over him. Instead, Hazzard would become a symbol of his victory, his own personal trophy, paraded before the world.

'And you *will obey*, I know.' He leaned closer and said, '*Because I have her.*'

The breath sighed between Hazzard's lips, a dark realisation creeping into his eyes, '*The savants...*'

'Yes, the *savants*. And *why* should we not? – I said this to Maximilien as they pushed him into the machine to be slaughtered like a beast *and afterwards they let me hold his head. Do you hear? His head.*' In his rage he shook Hazzard by the neck and thrust him violently back onto the bedroll. Masson grew concerned.

'Citizen... they will come back—'

'The case,' Derrien snapped at Masson, who then handed him a bulging leather wallet. Derrien opened a flap, and from a series of pockets inside pulled a small blue bottle. He uncorked it with a pop and put a folded pad of cotton over it, tipping it up.

Masson grabbed Hazzard, forcing his head back, as Derrien clamped the cloth over Hazzard's mouth, Masson pinching his nostrils shut. 'And when I am finished, I will leave you a mindless husk in the sand, a relic from one of your damnable lost tombs—' Derrien relaxed his grip on the pad '—and nothing will remain of you, but a fading memory of dust.'

Hazzard tried to cough but could not, and breathed it in, the fumes of the pad swirling into his mouth and throat, a hissing poisonous mist, his eyes closing, his muscles sagging. He sank back, shivering, and Derrien leaned over him again, barely able to contain the vengeance in his heart. '*You will answer because I have her. And she is mine.*'

Heat. Always heat, thought Hazzard.

Heat had a physical mass, he decided, in that remote corner of his mind where he had saved his fears, loves and secrets, somewhere Derrien would never find them.

The sun leaned upon him, a burning stone, crushing him – then shade, blessed relief – then the sun, vultures circling on high, gliding, silent, searching, and the screams, *no not out there again*, and more fire.

India, Brahmins discussing the elements, *fakirs* standing in hot coals, *I become as fire, Sahib.* Hazzard too had become as fire, and it angered his tormentors, shouts from above, from below, all around, in bitter frustration. Masson's intermittent blows became dull, distant sounds, a madman raging at a closed shop door, demanding to be let in, his blurred face visible through smudged, distorting windows.

Bastard bastard bastard…!

The ghost of Harry Race, cousin, he thought, adopted brother, friend, enemy, so full of hate all those years before at the Cape, *It should have been me to marry her – bastard bastard…!*

Derrien's face, broad as the moon, immense, an enchanter's poison. Sour, vaporous, pungent. Rising, falling, on an ocean swell, calming, their anger growing because it was not working.

Mera naam Lewis hai… yah ek mugal taalavaar hai… India pattern compliments, is that a Mughal Talwar, kunjani kunjani! Ndiphilele enkosi, tata…how are you! Perfect thank you, tata!

Speaking very fast, almost incoherent, schoolroom Hindi and isiXhosa, wide awake now, eyes open, *Harry!*

Harry Race, dead Captain of Marines, slain by William John Hazzard at the bottom of the world, roaring in the bleeding surf.

Harry!

Harry's hand shaking him, *Wakey wakey, the* HMS *William!*

Derrien's mouth opening, a yawning cave to swallow him whole. 'Yes, Sir Rafe Lewis, yes we know of him! Who is Harry! *Who?*'

291

Streams of images, endless whispering, Lewis and Blake, and Hazzard thought, *Yes, I have failed*, and Lord Melville, *Egypt, sir, Egypt, I don't give a damn where they are if I can keep 'em there*, as if drawn by Rowlandson, a king's warrant not worth the ink – and a letter, *Leave them! You cannot leave them to die!*

Letter.

To Nelson.

More laughter. His. A hand slapped him in the face and he felt it. Coming down, breath light and quick. Masson – fighting Masson, *bloody bastard bloody bastard!*

Water on his face.

Caron shouting.

Grenôble, the old stairs, books, *des livres, oui, Kircher, hiero-glyphs, Thoth.*

Englishman!

Lies.

'Lies, yes, all of them.' Derrien's voice urging him on faster. 'Through Hamburg, yes, you told us, your Captain Day and Mr Udney the spy, yes, we know them all now...'

Push, till it stops.

I never stop.

Coming full circle, *strength of ten men*, Masson's face, his bulging eyes open wide in surprise, Hazzard's fist catching him, an old *payattu* strike, *Mahakali...!*

Masson went down, falling against the tent wall with a cry as Hazzard swung from the waist at Derrien, but Derrien caught it and threw him back down.

'What were your orders, 34'18'89? You told us so very much, Room 63, yes, but *what were your orders*? To prevent the invasion? *Then you failed...!*'

Ahoy the HMS *William! Ahoy!*

Harry calling, always mocking – something, somewhere, to do with ships, Nelson's ships.

Nelson.

Time, distance, so forth, timing important, *that is why I sent him there, I, W^m. J. Hazzard Esq. the Exploring Officer in the field, defender of deserts, keeper of gods, pharaoh of dust, I called the Destroyer back to Egypt, back to the House of Ptah.*

Because Bonaparte would never come to this strange new world without leaving a coachman waiting at the corner to take him home again.

Where is the coachman, oh, he is where, waiting here, waiting there, waiting waiting for his fare...?

Aboukir, the great bay.

The coachman, waiting.

A tethered goat. For the tigers' dinner.

Masoud, Muhammad Bey al-Elfi, Al-Jabarti. *Tell me, scribes of the Al-Azhar, did we crush his dreams?*

Derrien looked down at him. 'What? *What of the scribes of Al-Azhar?*'

Derrien broke off at the sound of more shouts, stamping hooves, an enraged officer calling to Lacroix, to everyone, *Where is he!* Marching through squads of shouting men, hurried feet following him. The tent-flap flew open, two *Bedu* in the robes of the Maaza behind, each carrying an ancient Turkish blunderbuss.

'*Be damned, m'sieur!*' the officer shouted down at Hazzard. '*Your Bedouin have killed him!*'

Derrien got to his feet. 'Killed who? Identify yourself—'

The officer looked at Hazzard and Cook. '*Jullien*, Citizen, *Jullien!*' he cried. 'They have *killed* Captain Jullien and massacred his escort!'

'Where? How?'

'At Alqam! He was riding north with fleet orders, and they *threw his butchered body* into the Nile!' He dropped a bloody saddlebag. 'I am Jumard, of the 4th *Légère, taking his place!*'

'Which fleet orders?'

Jumard tore open the bag and held out a sheet of paper, waving it at him. 'These, Citizen! To Admiral Brueys, *countersigned a week ago!* They never reached him! To move the battle-fleet! *It still stands exposed in Aboukir Bay!* The commandant was outraged – and Jullien volunteered to take it himself!'

Derrien took it from him. 'They should have sailed to Corfu...' Derrien read the order to set sail, signed with an angry flourish, '*Bonaparte*'. Then he stared into nothing, past Hazzard, past the camp, the Nile, the glories of conquest, the triumph of their battle in the shadow of the pyramids. He repeated the name, 'Aboukir...?'

Hazzard stared up at him, whispering under his breath.

Derrien looked down at him. 'What did you say?'

Masson watched. 'He is raving, Citizen.'

Derrien knelt over Hazzard and shook him. '*Tell me.*'

'*B'nson... Cr'soe...*' said Hazzard.

Derrien shouted, '*Encore.* Again!'

'He said *Crusaud*, Citizen,' said Masson.

Derrien shook Hazzard again. 'What is it, what is this Caruso? A place? A codename? For what? A counter-attack? Are the English coming to invade?'

Instead, Jumard had the answer. He frowned. 'It is a book—'

Derrien turned. 'Book?'

'Yes, *Robinson Crusoe...*' said Jumard distracted, irritated. 'My son, he has read it in English, for his study...'

'But what is it? What does it mean?'

'*Ah, ma foi*, I do not know!' exclaimed Jumard. 'A man on an island, *alors*, abandoned, his ship sunk, lost, what do they call it, the *shipwreck*, he is, how you say, *marooned*. What of *justice* for *Jullien!*'

Derrien gazed unseeing, the word playing in his mind. 'Marooned...'

'Yes!' snapped Jumard, gathering the contents of the saddlebag together again. 'Left on the barren island with no chance of sailing home, what does it matter!'

As if he had suddenly recognised a train of thought so obtuse, so tortuous, Derrien looked at Hazzard, astonished, and recognised the hand of the British Admiralty. Hazzard looked back.

'That is why Nelson departed...' whispered Derrien. 'You could not find us at sea... so you *wanted* us to land – in the desert... *to be stranded*?' He looked at Jumard, then glanced at the crumpled order in his hands. '*Mon dieu.* I have been guarding the army – *but not the navy.*' Derrien stuffed the order into his pocket and pushed past Jumard to the tent entrance. '*Lacroix!*'

Derrien burst out of the tent to find a state of anarchy – the day patrol at last returned, enraged at the news of Jullien's death, discovering Hazzard's presence and holding him to blame, men pointing at the tent, shouting, their officers at gunpoint. A full platoon of the 25th had Caron and the Alphas at the point of the bayonet, a terrified young lieutenant calling, '*You w-will throw down your arms, Sergent chef-major...! I beg of you! Je vous en prie!*' Captain Lefebvre of the patrol stood beside Caron, shouting, '*The 25th will stand down! The 25th will disperse at once,*' Pigalle was ready to wade into the infantrymen, Caron calling over it all, '*Lacroix, you will reign over corpses!*'

'No, *Chef!*' cried Lacroix in victory. 'First his crimes against the Republic, and now this, our own young glorious Jullien! How can you defend him *now!* Enough of this charade – *bring him!*'

Pigalle smashed three out of the way with a sweep of his sapper's axe and the rest fell back at once, but Caron put out a hand to restrain the big man. It was over. '*Ça suffit, mon fils.*' *Enough, my son.* Rossy and St Michel put up their guns, and the 25th shouldered past, two seizing Derrien, pinning his arms back, '*Non! Lacroix – wait – he has information...!*'

Two men hauled Hazzard to his feet and into the scorching sun, the two Maaza following, a deadly escort, one calling out, *al Pasha al-ahmar!* Hazzard's legs collapsed under him and Caron made a move but was kept back by a pair of bayonets. Six men formed line a short way off as Hazzard was dragged into the heat, blinded, the colours bursting in dizzying array. Two others came behind him, dragging something heavy, Lacroix calling like a town crier, '*...for the crimes of espionage and aiding the enemies of the Republic, you are sentenced to suffer death by—*'

It was Cook.

Each held by a pair of soldiers of the 25th, Derrien and Masson were marched into the crowd of shouting men to watch. '*Lacroix!*'

called Derrien, '*The fleet!* They know of Nelson's plan, his attack! We do not know if they bring *troops* with them! You will *release* him! *By order of the Republic, damn you!*'

Lacroix stopped and turned. 'By whose order?' he scoffed.

'*Mine*, you imbecile! *In this damnable place,*' raged Derrien, '*I AM the Republic!*'

For a moment, Lacroix considered his words. But the threat had no effect. Lacroix laughed. 'Here, *M'sieur le Croquemort*, you are nothing but the sand.'

Hazzard's head sagged and the light burned his eyes, but basic shapes began to take form: Lacroix, a staff officer, and a line of dusty blue-grey coats porting muskets. Murmuring among the men, someone shouted, *Ce n'est pas la guerre, ce n'est pas l'honneur*, and others joined in, some fighting, *Justice pour Jullien!* Captain Lefebvre standing with Caron, a shot in the air from the boy lieutenant, and all stood still. The *Bedu* guides watched, moving away, dark faces swathed in black headdresses.

Cook was lashed to the post by the mule corral, his head hanging low, almost the colour of his coat, thought Hazzard, that blood-red coat he had worn for twenty years.

Jory.

A hand clutched at Hazzard's hair, pulling his head back and his mouth opened. Water was poured in. Hazzard choked, and they laughed, his insides contracting in spasm, and again, more water – he coughed but swallowed, the cascade continuing over his head, across his neck and shoulders and down his chest. He gasped with relief.

'You shall be awake to see what you have done, *Milord Mamluk*,' snorted Lacroix.

Cook struggled at his bonds, but only to get sufficient purchase to stand upright. Slowly he raised his head in Hazzard's direction. Hazzard tugged at the hands behind him and fell forward to the sand on all fours – more laughter, but it was good to be out, on his own, even if beaten to the ground. Someone said, *No, leave him, what can he do.*

He pushed himself up onto one knee, then both feet, the sodden bloodstained shirt hanging loose, the heat a roaring crucible, the air baking iron. He saw the line of men, the officer calling out, *Portez… armes!* and Hazzard made his way slowly towards Cook at the post. *Legs weak*, he thought, and stumbled, *been in a battle, bit sore, yes*, and he pulled himself up then sank again, head hanging, till he heard Cook.

'*On yer feet, boy…*'

Hazzard pushed himself up again, *yes*, his legs, *pas devant les domestiques, yes, not in front of the staff*, but enough to stand, and he reached the dark shape of the big man.

Cook whispered, '*Least not… goin' t'be drownded…*' He managed a feeble laugh and Hazzard fell against his shoulder, facing the line of men, a throb throughout his head, neck and shoulders, light and heat pulsing, matching his heartbeat, thudding in his eardrums.

'*Had 'nough, Jory – just… had enough.*'

'*Me an' bloody all…*' Cook coughed deep in his chest.

The command came.

Apprêtez! Prenez cartouche!

They began to load their cartridges.

'*D'you know…*' sighed Cook through bloated, cracked lips. '*The G in m-my name… tss… it's not f'r George…*'

Hazzard hung there, staring, every ache and pain and stitch coming to life in the heat. 'Jory, is short for George…'

'*No… Not George.*' Cook looked down. '*It's Gulliver…*'

Hazzard dimly registered Cook's words.

'*Ma wanted me… t'see th' world…*'

Hazzard wanted to laugh. 'We did that…'

'*Aye…*'

Hazzard felt the crest of a wave, lightness – just as he had at Giza, seeing the Sphinx, seeing the pyramids, a release, a burden going heavenward. Time would always win.

'Then 'tis a secret, Mr Gulliver Cook.'

'Much 'bliged, sir…' rasped Cook. 'W'd ne'er live it down…'

Someone shouted to come to attention, *Garde… À vous!* and the once voluble troops quietened to watch solemnly. *Very kind of them*, thought Hazzard. The closer the end came, the stronger he felt, a last bid to squeeze precious life from what few seconds remained. Clarity, the tang of salt in the air, the screech of a seabird. He felt the figurine on his chest, bumping in rhythm to his heartbeat.

Cook's voice was no more than a whisper, but Hazzard heard it clear. '*Stand fast th' Marines, sir…*'

Thief of hopes, defender of dust. England shall observe no longer.

Hazzard saw them, a row of filthy, misused toy soldiers, the blue of the sky brilliant above, birds wheeling, Derrien screaming, *Lacroix! Lacroix!*

En – joue!

The muskets came up, ready to fire.

'Stand fast it is, aye, Sar'nt…' Hazzard patted his arm. 'Excuse me…' he said and moved round to stand in front of him.

Cook shouted, '*No! No, sir!*'

But he cried too late to stop it, as one of the Maaza leaned towards the boy lieutenant and whispered, '*Hsst.*'

The boy looked at him. '*Pardon?*'

'*Knock-knock.*'

The Maaza stepped back, levelled his blunderbuss and pulled the trigger. The packed weapon erupted, and the other Maaza did likewise at the other end of the line, '*Bloody have that.*'

The six men of the firing squad were blown to pieces and fell just as the first *Bedu* rider of the Beni Qassim tore past the mule corral. '*Yallah!*'

The staff major next to Lacroix dropped to one knee as if suddenly tired, his severed head rolling through the dust to Lacroix's feet. Lacroix screamed at it and staggered backwards. '*Aux armes…!*'

There came a call in English, '*Hit the bloody deck!*' A rattling volley followed, and another, the men of the 25th falling. A line of galloping horse poured through the camp, the dust kicked into blinding clouds. Lacroix ran. Hazzard fell back to the post and pulled Cook as low as he could as another volley came in from over the heads of the mules behind, which began braying in fright.

Derrien wrested his hands from the two soldiers behind him, spun and shot the first in the forehead with his screw-barrelled pistol, Masson smashing a fist into the face of the other. They ran after their bolting horses.

Hazzard saw Bedouin headdresses float before his eyes and a lopsided grin. The two Maaza.

Warnock, Pettifer.

'*That were right bloody close, weren't it, eh, sir?*'

Pettifer tried to free Cook while Warnock knelt in front to shield them for cover, reloading the blunderbusses. The Bedouin horsemen wrought chaos, *Allahu akbar!* one riding past and pointing at Hazzard, *al-Pasha al-ahmar! Al-Pasha al-ahmar!*

Barely recognisable in his filthy smock and Greek cap, Porter appeared, coming at a run. 'How we doing then, sir? Bit peaky?'

Masoud with his *khanjar*, proud, pleased, exhilarated, cutting Cook free, his shaking hands on Hazzard's shoulders. 'We searched the land for word of you, from Aswan to the ports! As you came back for *us*, Hazar-*effendi*,' he said, 'so we have come back for you.'

The French scattered, Lacroix calling, *Regroup, regroup*, as the Bedouin riders charged through them time and again, tents collapsing, canvas dragging, men running.

Napier was swinging a heavy club, knocking men down like skittles. '*Come on, yew littew daisies!*'

Some of the 25th formed a firing rank but were run down by further horse led by De la Vega, galloping in hard and fast, sword in hand, leaning low to his left, cutting down two, throwing the blade up in the air and catching it with his right, leaning to the other side and taking another. Joseph Hammer followed, and Underhill came in behind on a camel. He waved to Cook.

'*Come, y'auld Methuselah, or must I fetch thy sorry arse out of it meself!*'

'*Amigo!*' shouted De la Vega to Hazzard. 'Come, get him up here!'

Hammer handed down a goatskin bulging with water. 'Drink, my friend, and quickly, *mach's ja schnell, hm?*'

From atop his camel Underhill flung Hazzard a quivering salute. '*Sah! Beg to report Royal Navy sighted and French fleet anchored in Aboukir Bay like cornered rats for the catcher! Officer commanding 9 Comp'ny standing by to lead Nelson straight to the bloody bastards, whence they shall learn the error of their sinful and misguided bloody ways, sah!*'

The words filtered through the thunder of hoofbeats and gunshots, and Hazzard stumbled against Pettifer, Cochrane and Kite and they lifted him. *Wayland. He did it.*

Hazzard was pushed up onto the rear of De la Vega's horse, the Spaniard taking his arms tight round his waist. 'Hold fast, *amigo! Vamanos,*' he said, Hazzard's fingers interlocked so he would not fall, concentrating on that much. The muffled whump of an explosion, *ammunition*, the Bedouin running amok. Infantry were racing everywhere, some heading into the dunes. He stared after them, four men, watching, then turning away, *Caron*? but he could not be certain. Then they were out, riding over the low scrub and dead, dried crops underfoot, the horse plunging and rising, shots fading on the ceaseless wind.

After a time the horses slowed, and he saw the sparkle of water. *Nile*, he thought, *seabirds.*

He slid from De la Vega's waist and collapsed into the leaves all around, *watermelons*, and he thought of Izzam and Alahum.

One of the Beni Qassim brought him another goatskin and they crowded round him for protection as he drank, mad with it, a hand holding his head. *Careful, sir, not too much now.* Hazzard breathed. Every movement was fire, the water unable to extinguish it, but the world came back to life.

'Porter...' he gasped, the bespectacled Yorkshireman before him, '*A liquid... on a pad... made a gas. I brea-breathed it in...*'

Porter looked into his bag, 'An ether, sir, from a base salt, by the sound of it, one of the chlorides, sublimates quickly, steals the air from the blood and the lungs, nasty...' He delved in his bag, looking, and found a thin leather pouch. 'Breathe into this, sir, in and out, slow as you can.'

Hazzard covered his nose and mouth and breathed, slowly, deeply, his heart slowing, calming, his chest opening. De la Vega crouched down next to him. Hazzard gripped his arm.

'*How?*' he asked.

De la Vega shrugged. 'The houses in Malta, they are not so heavy, my friend.' He flicked a glance at the marines. 'But your *muchachos*, they sail across the seas to find you, and *Volpone* found them.'

Underhill on his camel, Hesse, Kite, Porter, Cochrane, Napier, Warnock, Pettifer, De Lisle, all dressed as *Bedu*, Turks and Greeks stood looking down at him. 'Masoud and Mr 'Ammer, sir,' said Pettifer, 'Told us the lot.'

'Shoober Kit,' said De Lisle.

Kite nodded. 'Bloody Cairo an' all...'

Hazzard nodded.

Never give up the boat.

Excited, a Bedouin rider held out one of the notes in Arabic Hazzard had dictated to Al-Jabarti's scribes.

> *In the Name of Allah and His Holy Prophet, all Blessings Upon His Name, the devout are called upon to confound all enemy infidel messengers bound for Alexandria and the ports, and suffer none to live.*

'The Beni Qassim,' said Masoud. 'They knew this was of your doing, and exalted your name. *Nelsoun Amir* is *coming*, he has been seen by the traders, his sails full! You have cheated Sultan *al-kebir* of his victory, Hazar-*effendi*. He has won his battles, *but you have defeated him.*'

The Bedouin called out, '*Al-Pasha al-ahmar! Al-Pasha al-ahmar! Allahu akbar!*'

Bonaparte. Shattered his dreams.

'An' we seen his ruddy fleet, sir,' said Warnock. 'Like Spithead on parade. Be caught like rats in a trap when Nellie gets 'ere, beggin' yer pardon...'

A warning bell echoed from beyond a distant valley of memory.

'Horse... I need...'

Kite and Masoud helped him to stand, every flexion of muscle in his torso a plunging dagger into a flaming sea. He breathed deeply, charging his lungs.

'The despatches... Jullien...'

Must not stop.

With reverence, the Beni Qassim brought his shamshir, *Al saif Ali Qarim Sheikh*, the remains of his scarlet coat, the shredded sleeves almost cut away, covering him in a loose *binish*, every movement a branding iron, but the heat of the air had gone.

'Who? What despatches?' asked De la Vega.

Derrien.

He spared a thought for young Jullien, *do nothing that would blacken our name.* 'Brueys,' he said, 'Derrien has Bonaparte's order – to disperse the French battle-fleet. They must not reach open water – *must not escape...*'

'*Madre de Dios,*' cursed De la Vega, '*Ya basta! Enough!* You *win, sí*? Your Nelson, he is *coming*, he—'

'*Cesár,*' said Hazzard, '...he has Sarah.'

The Spaniard took it in, saw he had no argument. He lowered his head, defeated. '*Madre...*' He looked up. 'Then we get her, *amigo.*'

'Hammer, Masoud,' asked Hazzard, 'How far to ride... to Aboukir?'

Masoud pointed over the dunes. 'Listen...'

'*How far?*'

Hammer answered for him, holding up his hands. 'We are already here, *Herr Major.* Aboukir Bay lies just beyond the salt lake, over these sandhills. You were never far.'

Seabirds.

Not in the desert.
Near the sea.

The idea gave him hope. Then he heard ships' bells ringing.

'Derrien...' breathed Hazzard, 'I've got to stop him.'

Before Porter could take issue with them, the marines helped him into a saddle. They all mounted and Cook climbed painfully onto one of the horses.

'What will you do?' Hammer asked Hazzard, testing the girth strap, putting a loaded pistol into a saddle holster for him.

'Derrien will make for Brueys, on the *Orient*. That is where—' Hazzard took a deep breath, his vision cleared, *so tired*, and he slipped forward then straightened, '—where everything will depend. It must.' Hazzard's words tailed off. He blinked, alert again. 'Pettifer, Warnock, to me, no more. Mr Hammer, Sar'nt Underhill, while we head for the *Orient*, you will take the squad and meet Mr Wayland to rendezvous with us at the bay...' he hesitated, thinking of Sarah, '...if we are successful. Cesár, agreed?'

De la Vega inclined his head. '*Sí, amigo.* But I come with you. We shall catch *el diablo*.'

Hazzard paused, and looked at his old sergeant. 'Mr Hammer, please get Sar'nt Cook safe to the sea...'

'God willing.' Hammer bowed. '*Insha'allah*.'

Underhill rode up next to Cook. 'Clear aye, sir.'

Cook nodded at Hazzard. 'Gimme some rum... an' I'm good as done. Now,' His voice was barely a husk and his face hardened. '*You get that bastard, boy...*'

Nemesis

Captain Benjamin Hallowell of the 74-gun HMS *Swiftsure* peered through his telescope into the glare of distant Alexandria. Stealth and caution had been thrown to the winds: the Royal Navy had returned with a vengeance.

'French transport vessels… a frigate… no, two, *three* frigates… a sloop… good God.' Hallowell shifted his focus. 'And French soldiers hopping all over the *damned* place.' He lowered the scope and took a breath, adding with a rueful tone, 'Just as your Mr Hazzard said all along…'

Hallowell glanced at the tatty pair beside him, the younger, taller man with the walking-stick, a scarred, sunburnt red-brown face, in a torn, stained, cut-off Marine red coat – the other a grizzled ginger scarecrow in a piratical Spanish leather jerkin, a cutlass and pistol rammed in a broad leather belt. 'Well done, sir, my compliments to you both. And my apologies to Mr Hazzard.'

Wayland merely stared out at the French ships. 'They've been sending tenders in and out of the port for days, sir,' he said. 'It proved too shallow for the overladen transports or ships of the line. Those brigs are collecting victuals for the fleet, which is still unloading cargo and munitions.'

Hallowell looked through his scope once again. 'And making merry in the generous amenities of Aboukir Bay you say. So, let us see this chart of yours…'

Swiftsure and *Alexander* had come in ahead of the squadron to reconnoitre the port, the rest further out to sea, streaking head-long for the bay as if they had scented blood in the water. *Volpone* stood a short way off, still the apparently harmless Levantine trader festooned with hanging cargo nets. *Alexander* surged alongside, gun-ports open, keeping a watchful eye.

'And this is accurate?' asked Hallowell doubtfully, examining the chart. It was De la Vega's. It showed Aboukir Bay, the position of the aged fort at the tip of the northern promontory and a simple thin outline of the shoals and hidden sands.

'My concern is this, sir,' said Wayland, pointing at the old fort on the headland. 'My men reported unidentifiable structures and a possible loading-frame at the foot of this tower. With sufficient cannon, this old castle could command the northwestern seaward approach to the bay, and threaten the squadron, sir. I believe they have created a makeshift battery.'

Hallowell glanced at him, impressed. 'And we can trust your Spanish pirates?'

'Let them be Turkish merchants for the log, if you please, sir,' said Wayland.

'Then Turks they shall be...' He folded the map. 'Will you stay aboard and come in with us?' he asked. 'Or do you Special Landing Squadron types prefer going in a tad more doggo?'

Hallowell's vernacular left Wayland puzzled, but none more so than the unexpected title he had used. 'Special Landing Squadron, sir?'

'It's what his lordship dubbed you at Gib, though I rather prefer the "Oddfellows", what?'

Wayland's thoughts flitted momentarily to his encounter with Admiral St Vincent, with Cook and Hazzard, the security and fellowship of the fleet. 'We shall rendezvous with Major Hazzard and reconnoitre the shoreline batteries. Our brief, sir, is to seek out and destroy.'

Hallowell watched him. Wayland was indeed a grim fighting officer. The blushing boy had gone. 'But this battle will be at sea, sir, not on land,' said Hallowell. 'That is where careers will be made, and all anyone will ever remember.'

Wayland looked out and saw *Culloden*. She had lagged behind the rest of the squadron, towing a prize merchantman. A figure on the foredeck surrounded by junior officers raised his hat. Wayland sensed it was Captain Troubridge. He raised a hand. 'Sir Thomas will remember, sir. He was there that night, when we sailed from the *Ville*.'

Hallowell seemed suddenly concerned for the younger man. 'There is no shame in coming home, Lieutenant. You have done more than your fair share. We would be glad of your company.' Months earlier, eager and hopeful, Wayland might have agreed with Hallowell and chosen to stay aboard, dreaming of fame and glory in battle.

Instead he thought only of Nelson approaching a fortified bay lined with French batteries, and had no doubts. 'No, sir, thank you,' he said. 'Let us take the battle on shore.' He glanced at Handley. 'It's what we do.'

–

The alarm bells rang out across the turquoise waters of Aboukir Bay, the first cry echoing down from the lookouts in the tops over a hundred and fifty feet in the air.

'*Enemy sail off the starboard bow...!*'

Seated at his desk in the day-room with the ship's log, Vice-Admiral Brueys stopped his pen in mid-flow.

So. He comes.

He stared at the pages before him. Why had he been writing, he wondered – for posterity? Such presumption, he decided, presupposed a posterity born of victory. Or did he write more out of hope than confidence in survival of this fateful moment – part of him felt more the former than the latter.

To bolster his spirits he made a final entry: *Enemy sighted.* Perhaps he might later be able to render an account of the events that followed, but perhaps not. He set down his pen, and stood. He adjusted his waistcoat, and buckled on his sword.

The air was now alive with the call, repeated from ship to ship, number and bearing added moment by moment, *Three! No, four, five enemy sail, correction, seven, eight...* He stepped out onto the broad quarterdeck of *Orient*, nearly fifty feet across; by any standard she was a giant. An ensign bowed and handed him his telescope. Casabianca stood with his officers looking out to sea at the starboard rail. Brueys joined them. 'Where away, Captain?'

'Starboard bow, *mon amiral*, north-northwest, rounding the headland to come north-northeast. A lookout on the *Heureux* had the honour.' Casabianca looked at him. 'It is the English. It must be Nelson.'

Brueys nodded, the moment they had dreaded, or anticipated, each to his own experience, had finally fallen upon them. The seascape seemed a peaceful rolling blue, bright in the afternoon heat. Brueys raised his glass. Coming in from the open sea, straight for them, a line of ships in full sail leaning heavily with the westerly wind. *Eight, nine, ten*, he counted – then the last, *eleven*? Before his eyes their rough line of battle broke, and they curved in towards the bay, heeling with the onshore wind, topsails, spritsails and topgallants billowing white against the blue, some ships growing in the eyeglass faster than others. As he watched he began to understand their constant change of position.

'*Mon dieu*,' said Brueys, sickened. 'They *race* each other.'

He lowered the scope but could not take his eyes off the sight. 'Recall all crews and shore parties.'

'So recalled, *mon amiral*,' said Casabianca. 'Over a third are ashore for provisions in Alexandria and Rosetta. The boats have gone out.' His voice was taut. 'It is no longer for the captains to argue...' Casabianca sounded resigned. 'We have insufficient men to put to sea and man the guns at the same time.'

Brueys glanced at him. The endless furore with the admirals, Blanquet du Chayla and Villeneuve, and captains such as Du Petit-Thouars had raged for days: whether to put to sea or fortify the bay, Brueys preferring to stay, and mass the guns to seaward. The decision had now been made for them, by circumstance, by Nelson.

'We command the bay, Captain,' insisted Brueys. 'We have the advantage.'

Casabianca did not look away. 'The wind, *Amiral*. We are now trapped on a lee shore.'

Brueys looked off the port side. Of shallower draft, several frigates had been positioned closer inshore, between the shoals and the battle-fleet, to keep them clear of the fleet's massed batteries pointing out to sea. He looked at the nearest, *Sérieuse*, and further down the bay at those in Villeneuve's rearguard, *Artémise*, *Diane* and *Justice*.

'Requisition all frigate crews to man the ships of the line, crews to man all guns to starboard first. That is where Nelson comes. Then captains' conference at once, no exceptions. And reaffirm the order to all, *including* Admiral Blanquet du Chayla,' said Brueys, pricked by the name – his had been the only voice of dissent to their otherwise unanimous vote to anchor in the bay, 'to cable all ships together and *close the gaps*.' He changed his tone and looked down a moment, distracted, disturbed as if by some forewarning. 'And… ensure all passengers go ashore, Captain,' he said. 'Any of the *savants*, ladies, wives. Including young Giocante.'

Casabianca gave a short bow in thanks. 'My son will not go, *Amiral*. He says he is Ensign Casabianca and if I do not go, then he will not go.'

'We need a reliable officer to escort passengers.'

'I had told him so already, *Amiral*,' said Casabianca with a bow. 'But I thank you.'

Brueys nodded sadly, and raised his eyeglass once again, to conceal his sense of doom. 'You must be very proud. As would I, to serve beside such a grand heart…' A grand heart with no knowledge of what was to come, he thought, none. *None*.

Casabianca watched the white-haired patrician as he stood at the rail, looking out, bearing witness to the approach of his own destruction. Though he knew Brueys would direct a fierce engagement until his last breath, he had about him an air of resigned acceptance – that, until now, he had somehow eluded a fate which had at last caught him up.

'It will be a day, *mon amiral*,' said Casabianca, with affection. He bowed and withdrew, to execute his orders.

Brueys looked down across the cluttered decks of *Orient*. There were supplies for the army, buckets of paint and tar left abandoned, the tops were undermanned, the standing rigging sagged, and now Blanquet du Chayla could rage all he wished, for there were not enough hands to man the guns as well as sail the ships out to sea.

But he felt reassured when he looked down the seaward broadside of his great flagship: *Orient* presented sixty guns over three decks, and before and astern extended in line some five hundred more. If only they could get the men *back*, they would blast Nelson into the Mediterranean.

He looked to the front of the line, past *Franklin, Peuple Souverain, Aquilon, Spartiate* and *Conquérant*, to the 74-gun leader, *Guerrier*, her bows anchored near the shallows, the surf on the beach so close he could see the foam. *Guerrier* would stop them, he thought, *Guerrier* would block the path of the impetuous, impatient Nelson.

He then felt a *frisson* of nerves shiver along his spine.

Surely, he thought, no captain would risk attempting such shallows. Not even the English.

Surely.

—

Two mounted troopers of the 20th Dragoons forced a path through the mass of people clogging the road from Alexandria to Aboukir Bay, cursing down at all. Frustrated, they rode out towards the ruins of ancient Canopus onto the coastal track – when a tattered sailor dashed out in front of them from the shoreline brush. '*Messieurs! Messieurs! Anglais! Anglais là-bas! Vite, je vous en prie!*' English, over there! Quick, I beg of you!

The horses whinnied as both men were torn from their saddles, then quick hands clamped their mouths shut, and immediately thrust short cutlass blades through their throats, then held them tight until they stopped kicking. Their bodies were dragged into the bushes.

Handley and Wayland emerged from the trees and took the horses. 'Well done, Purdo,' said Wayland. 'Thought you were a Frenchie there myself. Been hiding your theatrical talents, have you?'

The toothless little sailor tugged his forelock in salute. 'Ta very much, sir.'

The marines all gone ashore, Wayland had taken the decision not to wait for their return but to make a landing with a number of the British survivors of the *Esperanza* that had been taken aboard the *Volpone*. A motley band of gunners, seamen and armourers, they lived up to Hallowell's name of 'Oddfellows' as much as the marines of 9 Company – with the imminent attack of Nelson's squadron, Alfonso agreed, and waited offshore, ready.

Handley helped Wayland into the saddle. 'Sir, the major wouldn't like this...'

'We shall reconnoitre, Handley. We do not yet know the disposition of shore batteries or reinforcements in the bay. French artillery on the high dunes may be able to range on Nelson's attack squadron and we've got to prevent them – *damnation!*' He tried to lift his left leg into the foot-iron but could not. 'Dammit, come along, Handley, get me up...'

Handley bent the limb at the knee and Wayland shoved it into the stirrup. 'Anyone challenges us, I answer. We'll pass as French sailors and their officer. If we find a single gun that can hit our squadron we're going to blow it sky-high, clear?' He had discarded his red coat, which left him in gentleman's shirtsleeves, white waistcoat and pistol-belt – they all looked the part. 'Mount up then, Handley, and let's get on.'

Handley looked at the saddle before him, Purdo holding the bridle ready. 'Well, I – ain't never been on an 'orse before, sir...'

Wayland could not believe it. 'You walk on foretop yards in a gale in bare feet without a line but you can't ride a horse? Just get on it, kick the thing with your heels and hang on.'

Handley clambered up, and Purdo stuck his boots into the stirrups. ''Old on tight, 'Andy, feet in the irons and stand up if it gets bumpier than the *Ville* with you at the 'elm.'

'Well bugger you an' all.' Handley did so and took off so quickly Wayland had to catch him up.

Far off to their left, the sea glowed in the setting sun, the fleet alarm bells echoing across the bay, creeping shadows bringing dread of the darkness to come. Wayland, Handley and the *Esperanza* hands forced their way through gaps in the crowds of soldiers, labourers and traders clogging the road from Alexandria to Aboukir, some heading for the bay, others fleeing from it.

Playing his role to the full, Wayland cursed down at the troops in his path in French, hitting out at them with a crop; a sergeant yelled out at them, *Putain matelots!* and Wayland stuck two fingers up and shouted back as they rode past, '*Va te foutre, tu salaud pompeux!*' *Up yours, you pompous bastard!*

The *Esperanza* seamen laughed, as did most of the French sailors around as well, calling *Vive l'Orient!* They pushed through the low scrub on the side of the road, Handley doing just as Wayland had told him, his legs clamped round the horse's girth for dear life. The dunes of Aboukir rose before them and Wayland chivvied his mount to the crest, its hooves thrashing in the sand, 'Come on, Handley, *dig in.*'

They crested the rise and looked down.

'By God...' said Wayland.

The French fleet lay moored in the bay below, bells clanging all the louder, the shallows teeming with boats, sailors rowing for the fleet, rushing into the water, officers driving them on, soldiers forcing some to obey, others simply running.

Nelson's squadron was closing fast, a thousand yards from the French, a loose line of sail, two leaders jockeying for position, HMS *Goliath* and HMS *Zealous*.

'Bloody 'ell, sir... Frogs've been caught bloody nappin',' gasped Handley beside him.

High dunes formed much of the seawall of the large bay, curving down to the south on their right to Rosetta on the far side. In the centre lay the waiting French line, a floating fortress of cannon, moored nose to tail.

To their left, the headland of the bay curled past the ramshackle village of Aboukir and out to sea, the antique fortress tower at the far end, dim lights winking as the sun faded fast. The top of the ridge along the headland towards the fortress tower looked almost deserted, only a few lines of soldiery now running down to help on the shore. Between Wayland and the fortress tower squatted the makings of artillery positions, guns in place but not yet sited.

'Field-guns...' said Wayland.

Handley looked out to sea. 'Range from here is at least two thousand yards to the Frog battle-line, sir. They'd need a long 32-pounder to hit one of ours.'

The 24-pounder, Wayland knew, was a ship-killer. A 32-pounder, however, could send a ball over two miles and batter its way through two feet of solid oak. But all they could see were a handful of army howitzers and field-pieces, 12- or even 9-pounders. Wayland zeroed his telescope further along the head-land to the fort, which had the best forward position in the bay. Then he saw it, at the foot of the old tower.

'Good God.' He gave the scope to Handley. 'That ammunition. Look.'

Handley refocussed. There was a stack of heavy round-shot at the side of the tower. Two men were rolling one ball to the gates – it was at least two feet in diameter. '*Jaysus alive...*' he said, 'That's not for a 32-pounder, sir – more like an 'undred-weight or a one-fifty mortar.'

'Could a mortar hit one of our ships at that range?'

'If ours draws too close, aye, sir,' said Handley. 'They could lob a one-fifty down a 74's throat with a lucky shot an' send her straight to the bottom.'

By the light of swinging lanterns Wayland saw support troops and several half-finished gun-emplacements – one of them with an 18-pounder naval gun slewed on its carriage. He thought it would be just the job.

Wayland kicked his heels in. '*Come on.*'

Derrien could scarcely breathe. His cravatte was tied tightly over his mouth and nose against the dust and almost choked him, his lungs wheezing as he rode for his life towards Aboukir Bay.

Masson beside him, they charged between landsmen labourers digging wells, raised fists cursing them for their flying dust and soil as they shot through and onward, over scrub and rocky hillocks, the fear tearing at him, *the fleet the fleet.*

He was in no doubt that it would cost his life if he failed. If Nelson crushed or captured the battle-fleet, he would take with him not only Brueys and Casabianca, but Du Petit-Thouars, Admirals Blanquet du Chayla, Villeneuve and Ganteaume as well – but also the expedition's last chance of contact with home. They would be trapped, marooned in the Egyptian desert.

An entire army, lost.

With a twist in his vitals he recalled his confident assertions over the past six months – and now, here it was, the reality: a brutal death awaiting at the hands of the Ottoman Turks, Bonaparte and the *Armée d'Orient* joining the lost souls haunting the Nile.

Because of me.

Approaching from the Rosetta side of the bay, the southern end of the battle-fleet appeared before him on the bright horizon. He saw Villeneuve's flagship, the *Guillaume Tell*, and the *Mercure* and *Timoléon* just behind. Strung out ahead lay the remainder, furled sails a gilded yellow in the dying sun. The dunes in the foreground rose to obscure his view, the few half-complete artillery positions on the ridge summit picked out in silhouette against an opalescent sky. He would have flogged them raw at Valmy for such dereliction: *They have had weeks*, he thought. He could hear the alarm bells.

He and Masson splashed through the salt marshes, scattering flocks of shrieking shore birds into the sky. They seemed to be laughing, endlessly laughing.

'*It is Nelson, Citizen! He is arrived…!*' called Masson.

Derrien pressed on. There was a loud thud and a whine off to his left. Then another to his right. Derrien glanced over his shoulder: Bedouin. They came at the gallop, crossing the marshy wasteland of Lake Maadiyya, letting go of their reins to fire their carbines, their speed and agility inhuman. Behind the first few was a European, and behind him came another. And another. Then he saw it, beneath a flying Arab robe: a flash of red.

No.

Hazzard.

Masson roared out. '*Still he comes, Citizen! Still!*'

'*Separate!*' shouted Derrien. '*Find the Ordinator! I will board the Orient with the orders!*'

'*Yes, Citizen!*'

Hazzard could not feel the ground beneath him, his legs and knees were locked, braced above the saddle like a steeple-chaser on the home straight. The black mane before him thrashed violently as the head of the Arabian plunged and shook with unrelenting power and pace. Pain had gone, become something else, become someone else, an insistent voice lost in the wind, lost to an encroaching numbness. The light of the evening sky was bright, oranges and yellows dying with the sun – but all he could see was Derrien, driving him on: *Must not stop.*

The Bedouin riders ahead jumped the scrub hills and splashed through the water's edge. The horse accelerated, thrilling at the chase, passing the rearmost of the Bedouin who waved him on with shrieks. He saw the broad-backed Masson breaking off, galloping hard to the left, two of the Beni Qassim following, but Hazzard held his course, wanting only Derrien.

The figure in black rode towards a gap in the palms by the lowest dunes. The Bedouins were taking shots at him and Hazzard prayed for a hit. The ground kicked up in spouts as Derrien ascended the soft grassy sand hills.

He heard De la Vega behind him, the Spaniard waving him on, '*Vaya! Rápido, amigo! Vaya, vaya!*' *Go! Go!*

Derrien made the summit, sand flying in clouds, and Hazzard nearly slipped, his hands snatching for the mane, *hold on*, through the marsh, the water spraying, ibis flying up, white and black, omens of Thoth, crying, crying. He was soon charging up the sandy incline, gasping for breath, clinging to the horse's shoulder, shouting to someone, to himself, '*Go on! Go on! Don't fall, don't fall!*'

The hooves of the Arabian exploded through the sand on the crest of the dune, and he hung on, Aboukir Bay spreading before him, the clanging bells banging loud in his ears, shoreline alarms mingling with the fleet's, the French ships magnificent, but trapped, calling out.

Beyond a broad curve of beach small boats dotted the water, crews trying to reach the warships, seizing the barges and punts of merchant traders in the race to get aboard the battle-fleet before Nelson reached them. Hazzard saw the sails. Ten, eleven, twelve ships and a sleek brig – *Hardy*, he thought, in the *Mutine* – a thirteenth making her way round the far headland shoals, the blood-red ensign flaring out behind each, a spear heading straight for the heart of the French fleet.

Nelson.

One of the Bedouin pointed.

'*Nelsoun Amiral! Amir al-bahr!*'

Derrien reappeared below them between the sand hills, his horse trying to make the steep descent, but it lost its footing and staggered and Derrien flew from the saddle. The Bedouin took shots at him again as he struck the ground with a cry and rolled. French soldiers looked up, pointed at them.

Hazzard's Arabian took the sand in leaping strides and he hung on as he gained on Derrien's black figure, stumbling through the soft sand, his head turning to look over his shoulder, eyes wide as Hazzard reached for him from the saddle and leapt.

The impact was worse than he had expected and he caught Derrien's shoulder, lights exploding behind his eyes, rolling end over end down the slope, Hazzard's sword flailing, the curved scabbard biting into his hip. A hand rose up into his face, a small pistol muzzle gaping and a puff of smoke, the crack deafening as the bullet passed his ear. *No, you will not…!*

He reached for Derrien's neck, the dark face now darker as the teeth flashed white in the primal grimace of the animal, and they clawed at each other until his fingertips felt the fabric at Derrien's throat, *cravat*, Derrien's fist struck him again and again, *ignore*, and he twisted, now screaming in Derrien's face, knocking his hands away, locked in the determination to strangle the breath from the creature before him.

'*Non…*' choked Derrien. '*Non…*'

A bullet whined past and struck the stones and Hazzard heard a shout in French, '*Là-bas!*' *Over there.* He saw a squad of sappers, half of them unarmed, some with only picks and shovels. A startled artilleryman appeared. A single shot cracked from behind and the man vanished. Sand burst and a shadow leapt, the thud of hoofbeats behind, the French crying out as the first Bedouin took him with his scimitar. '*Allah…!*'

Derrien tossed sand in the air, and Hazzard turned his face away, blinded, *too weak, too weak for this*, a French soldier roaring before him, his eyes wide, a black stovepipe shako, a pike in hand – there was a shot, and the man's chest burst, and De la Vega rode through them, the horse's hooves crushing his further cries into the sand.

'*Where is she!*' Hazzard screamed, '*Where! Where, damn you!*'

'*Non…*' gasped Derrien and Hazzard knew he had him fast, his forearm on his windpipe, crushing. His right arm around Derrien's neck, he whipped his left across his forehead, pushing him down, controlling him, ready to *twist* and *break*.

'*Where is she, où est-elle! Where is she!*' he grated in Derrien's ear, all he could think of, all he could say, '*Where…!*'

Derrien's arms waved helplessly, a marionette with cut strings as he gazed out upon the bay and the crashing waves, at the battle about to rage, the British ships closing in.

'*Every ship out there will be shot to pieces!*' shouted Hazzard, '*And every wretched bloody man, woman and child you brought to this place will die in it — thanks to you and Napoleon bloody Bonaparte! Now where is she! Let me save her!*'

Derrien struggled, shaking violently left and right, his fingers trying to prise Hazzard's arm free. '*Non… non! I must…*'

Union flags ran up the British topmasts, the white of the Jack bright in the deepening dark. The attack squadron split. Two streams bore down on the French, HMS *Goliath* leading the charge with *Zealous* directly behind, cheers echoing across the bay as the sailors on *Zealous* waved them on, the *Goliath* officers doffing their hats as they won the race, heading straight for the leading French warship of the line, *Guerrier*, positioned so carefully by Brueys, close to the shoreline shoals, where no captain would dare go — except Foley of the *Goliath. Conquérant*, second in line behind *Guerrier*, ranged her guns and opened fire. The battle had begun.

Hazzard shook him again. '*Watch, damn you!*'

Goliath streaked for the bows of *Guerrier*, her sails furling to control her speed, the battleship passing smoothly between *Guerrier*'s prow and the deadly shallows. *Guerrier* stood little chance. As *Goliath* passed *Guerrier*'s defenceless bows, she unleashed a broadside, raking *Guerrier* from stem to stern, the bursting cannon-rounds exploding through *Guerrier*'s gun-ports and the gallery windows, carrying everything in their path, the screams shrill on the evening breeze. Hazzard could not look away. '*Good God…*'

He could see the French captains caught in their boats, shouting orders up at their ships as they were rowed to their commands, Trullet of *Guerrier* shaking his fist up at the decks, '*Return fire! Return fire…!*'

Slowing, *Goliath* swung hard to port, tucking in beside *Guerrier*, putting herself between the French battle-line and the shore. She then fired point-blank on *Guerrier*'s undefended portside. The blasts rocked the French ship, rigging hands falling to the shattered decks, into the sea. Hazzard held Derrien tighter in his grip as they watched the spectacle.

'*When Nelson sailed away*,' grated Hazzard, '*when the Admiralty or the damned War Ministry abandoned Egypt to you and your liberating, murderous bloody Republic, I sent him just far enough, Citizen, to come back. For this. Watch, damn you!*' He shook Derrien, a ragdoll in his arms. '*This is how it always ends for bloody empires! Damn them and damn you and your pride and your kings and banners!*' He began to squeeze. He was beginning to kill him.

For Sarah, for Bartelmi – father, mother, all.

Gone. They are all gone.

Inarticulate sounds emanated from Derrien's bubbling lips as he lashed out in vain. '*Non... pas vrai... pas possible...*' *Not true, not possible.*

HMS *Zealous* followed *Goliath* round the bow of the stricken *Guerrier*, and gave *Guerrier* another pounding broadside. *Guerrier*'s foremast collapsed in a cloud of splinters and there rose a bloodthirsty roar from the bowels of the British ships. *Goliath* passed down the French line and came to rest opposite *Conquérant* and the bows of *Spartiate*. She opened fire once more, pounding the unprepared portsides of the French ships.

'*Where is she!*'

Desperate, Derrien stabbed a finger at the shoreline and the small frigate anchored there, his strangled words barely comprehensible. '*Iss-en...! She is there...!*'

He caught Hazzard's attention, because he had spoken in English.

'*On... a ship...*'

Derrien's meaning became clear to Hazzard only a moment later.

'*What? Where! Which! Dites-moi! Tell me!*'

The third British 74 in the line, HMS *Orion*, approached the bows of *Guerrier* to follow *Goliath* and *Zealous* into the blazing shallows. Derrien's fingers pulled frantically at Hazzard's arm. '*Zabell...! Is-a-belle...!*'

Derrien's free hands waved, the straining fingers extending and contracting, trying to reach out to the ship, to take hold of it. He pointed. '*Ss-Sérieuse...!*'

318

Hazzard saw the lone frigate moored closest inshore. '*That ship? That ship there?*'

'*Ess…!*'

The light frigate had previously been sheltered by the French battle-fleet, but was now at the mercy of three 74-gun British ships of the line. *Zealous* had ignored her – *Audacious* and *Theseus* had cut across the French line and were raking *Conquérant* and *Guerrier*, but *Orion* had swung very close. Hazzard had a memory of Sir James Saumarez at Nelson's table, amusing, benevolent, laughing about his sherry ration.

'*Arr… est'd her,*' choked Derrien, his final confession, not to Hazzard, but to his own uncomprehending mind, '*to k'p her – for mys'lf…*' Derrien slowly sagged in Hazzard's arms, his limbs going limp as Hazzard watched the end, of everything.

HMS *Orion* towered above the diminutive *Sérieuse*.

A boot caught Hazzard in the back and he fell, another horse coming fast, *Geddown, sir!* Warnock jumping, bringing a man down, smashing his tomahawk into his head. Derrien sprang away, gasping, a hand to his throat, another shape, Pettifer, out of nowhere, shielding Hazzard as Derrien's arm extended, his aim wild. '*Petty!*'

Derrien fired a second pocket pistol – a blast of smoke clouded their vision and Pettifer spun, hit, clutching his arm, *buggerin' 'ell*. Warnock and the Beni Qassim grappling with others, De la Vega on foot, taking one with his sword, then two, swinging close and tight like a sailor on a fighting deck. Hazzard tumbled down the slope, sand in his mouth, ears and eyes, until he saw Derrien, running, falling, rising, tearing into the gloom of the beach, shouting, calling, to whom, no one could say – perhaps to Sarah. *Attendez! J'arrive, j'arrive! Wait! I'm coming!*

Hazzard could not hear, a roaring in his ears. Pettifer shouting mutely, De la Vega's face close, kneeling beside him. He saw men with torches lighting braziers on the shore and others running with lamps as the night drew in fast. '*Horse…*' he gasped, '*Horse!*' and Masoud appeared with the Bedouin, one sliding from his saddle. '*Sérieuse…*' he said to De la Vega and pointed, '*The frigate!*'

He tried to haul himself into the saddle but fell, *get up*, and dragged himself up again as the horse set off through the flickering twilight. De la Vega swung his pistol at the others. '*Vamanos, muchachos! Go!*'

Hazzard followed Derrien, running, spinning and twisting through the knots of people, a dark, distant figure among so many, shouting, calling. Above it all, Hazzard could hear the popping of the meagre guns of *Sérieuse*. He knew now what would come, the unwritten rule of naval engagement: if enemy ships of equal size were present, no smaller vessel would suffer attack – unless it fired first. In brave but reckless disregard for his ship, the captain of *Sérieuse* had opened fire on the 74-gun HMS *Orion* of Sir James Saumarez.

'*Oh Christ…*'

Orion placed herself perfectly alongside the frigate, ran out her guns, and fired a single devastating broadside.

Up ahead, Derrien stopped, his back arching in agony as if shot, his hands up to his head, a plaintive cry as he fell to his knees. Hazzard felt the breath rush out of him and he stared.

The massed blasts of thirty-six heavy guns echoed round the bay. The round-shot crashed through the French frigate's hull, shattering its masts, rigging, decks and bulwarks, the cries audible on the breeze. In the space of five seconds, HMS *Orion* had reduced the *Sérieuse* to a smouldering wreck.

Detonate

Wayland and Handley charged along the deserted northern arm of the bay, Wayland jumping obstacles, plunging into sandy troughs and out, Handley and the men of the *Esperanza* hard behind. The fort teetered at the far end, lanterns swinging, the mortar crews hurrying to the rear.

They passed the adobe hovels of Aboukir, the inhabitants clinging together, bystanders to the strange drama unfolding on their doorstep. HMS *Goliath*, *Orion* and *Zealous* had already swung round the bows of *Guerrier*, the British ships so close inshore that Wayland could hear the commands of their marines on deck. The air reverberated to the percussive thud of the guns and the drawn-out tearing thunder of their broadsides, the scene lit by the rising moon and the muzzle-flashes of the fleets. But not all of Nelson's ships had been able to follow.

Handley called out, '*Sir – ships to wind'ard.*' He pointed out to sea beyond the fort. '*Two sail, sir, must be ours.*'

Wayland drew to a halt, the horse snorting and stamping, and he raised his glass. The stone tower rose in the dark foreground, black against the deepening twilight – roughly 750 yards out to sea was a small rocky island, picked out by the foaming surf breaking on its submerged reefs. Two British ships of the line were struggling in the boiling waves, one of them listing, her hull exposed, too high – she had run aground. The other was trying to tow her off, boats in the water, trying to dislodge her hull from the grip of the rocks.

'It's the *Culloden*,' called Wayland. 'It's Sir Thomas – the *Leander's* trying to tow her off!'

From just ahead he saw a flash, followed some while after by a dull boom, then another, the light bright from behind the dilapidated tower. Water spouts erupted in the lee of the island, a hundred yards short of the two ships. The guns at the fort were taking aim at the *Culloden*.

'She's a sitting target...' Wayland drew his pistol and kicked his mount into a gallop, and Handley tried to follow.

Hearing the approaching hoofbeats, some of the French artillerymen at the fort gates turned with no sign of alarm, assuming that any troops ashore must surely be French. One of them waved.

Drawing within thirty yards, Wayland raised his pistol and fired. The waving artilleryman spun and fell into the scrub. The remainder backed away, then ran, one tumbling down the slope to the rocky beach below, the rest making for the gates, *Bédoux! Bédoux!*

A squad of battery support troops emerged, lanterns in hand, some piling into the empty gun position to take cover behind the abandoned 18-pounder. Wild musket rounds zipped through the darkness and kicked up the earth.

Wayland's second shot hit another, sending him falling across the ammunition stack, an NCO crying out, *En joue, en joue*, followed by another volley of rattling shots. Stones jumped around Wayland, a bullet whipping at his arm like a lash, and he shouted out, charging straight for them. The gun-crew scattered as Wayland jumped the rampart wall into the pit and out the other side.

The horse struck the tail of the 18-pounder's gun-carriage and stumbled. Wayland's left knee failed and he fell, calling out, crashing onto the stone and sand. He rolled and tugged out his sword to find an artillery sergeant, a shovel stopped in mid-swing. '*Officier français?*'

Wayland kicked out at him just as Handley rode past, his cutlass taking the sergeant with him. The hands of the *Esperanza* opened fire on the run with their muskets and pistols and drove the remaining French back to the cover of the fort gates.

Jonsen, their biggest gunner, jumped into the gun-pit and pulled Wayland upright. 'You play it tight, sir—'

'Not tight enough…' Wayland reloaded his pistol. 'Are we all here? Eight of us? Right. We are going to *clear* that *bloody* mortar battery and stop them trying to shoot holes in the *Culloden*.' As he spoke another salvo thundered, water bursting out by the island.

Beyond a low stone wall behind the fort they could see four wide-mouthed snub-nosed mortars gaping skyward, stacks of giant rounds by each, the A-frame gantry hoist spotted by Alfonso and the others now swinging a round into a cavernous mouth. Wayland looked at the unloved 18-pounder in front of them. It sat crookedly on an army gun-carriage, its trunions unsecured, but there was a powder locker and a pile of small 12-pound round-shot.

'Handley – can we bring her round?'

Jonsen got it first, and the big gunner's face split into a grin. 'Aye, sir. She's only a baby.'

The huge gun was nearly ten feet long, but Jonsen and Lambert took the weight, lifting the tails of the gun-carriage round, *heave*, and swung the massive cannon on its broad wheels, Wayland waving them on, 'Double round shot, langrage, whatever we have, sticks and bloody stones, load and ram!'

Purdo looked down the muzzle of the cannon. 'She's got a packet down her throat, Jonno! Wad and ball and we're off!'

Purdo rammed in the wadding, and Jonsen took a pair of 12-pound rounds from the heap in the corner and shoved them in the cannon-mouth. '*Ram, Purdy, ye lazy bugger!*'

A musket cracked, and another. The French had emerged from both corners of the fort and were trying to outflank them. But they stopped when they saw the 18-pounder had been turned about, and began to run for the dunes, *Vite, vite!* A renewed salvo of crashing explosions boomed from the bay, and the mortars fired again, spouts of water showering *Culloden*'s small boats. '*Are we clear? Hurry!*' Wayland groped for the firing lanyard of the 18-pounder. He found nothing.

'*Where's the damn line to the gunlock?*'

Purdo looked in the locker for the flintlock firing mechanism. There was none. 'Ain't got one, sir! She's a Frog, see, and needs a pricker and touch to warm 'er up!'

Lambert saw the dead French sergeant lying nearby. 'Here, Purdy—' He yanked the man's bayonet free, 'Use this—' Purdo grabbed it and jumped on the breech, ramming the spiked tip into the touchhole, perforating the powder cartridge deep inside. 'Whitto! Prime!'

Whittaker, small and quick, tossed him a packet charge and Lambert slashed it open, pouring powder down the touchhole. '*Clear, aye!*'

'Handley!' cried Wayland. 'Pistol! No – a musket!'

Handley threw a discarded French Charleville to him. They had no ship's rail to secure the gun, no lines to hold it for the recoil. If Wayland knelt by the touchhole to light it he would be too close to the gun when it went off. He loaded and primed the musket, wadding a powder cartridge down the barrel but no ball, put the long muzzle to the touchhole and stood back. '*Ready, Handley!*'

'*Clear!*'

'*Clear aye!*'

'*Firing!*'

They turned away and Wayland squeezed his trigger. The blast from the musket sent its fire into the powder of the cannon and hit the main charge. The 18–pounder boomed, leaping backward, its carriage wheels lifting with the recoil, its tail smashing down the rickety wattle shelter on one side, digging itself into the ground.

The round-shots crashed through the wooden gates of the fort and blew them to shreds, the wreckage sweeping away several men in the process, a cascade of stone blasting the wall from the corner of the fort, sending the mortar crews diving for cover. They now had a clear shot to the mortars.

'*You done it, sir – it's a ruddy Lloyd's write-off!*'

Wayland primed the musket again. '*Reload, dammit! Langrage double-shotted! Forty-five seconds! Muskets make ready!*'

They had no swab to clear the inside of the barrel – any burning embers could set off a new powder cartridge as soon as it was rammed in. Purdo ducked a look into the dark muzzle, *She's clean!* He shoved in two cartridge bags and Lambert thrust the spike bayonet into the touchhole again to pierce the first packet charge. Purdo pushed handfuls of stones and two loads of scrap metal from the ammunition locker down the barrel, wadded and rammed.

'*Prop her up! Point blank!*'

'*Aye, sir!*'

Jonsen and Lambert pushed stones beneath the tails of the carriage, levering the gun up and forward, until it was dead level for a flat trajectory. Wayland knew that after firing this shot, the cannon could part company with the carriage.

'*Clear!*'

'*Clear aye!*'

Wayland applied the musket again. '*Firing!*'

The 18-pounder bucked, the muzzle velocity from the double-shotted powder and stone so great it cleared away one corner of the mortar battery and the A-frame loading-tackle, sending crewmen flying backwards into the darkness. But their success was short-lived: the naval gun had slewed off its field-gun mount and crashed to the floor of the gun-pit.

They heard calls and shouts from behind. A company of French had arrived from along the headland, infantry, sailors, gunners, sappers, a loose mob of thirty men, moving across the hillocks of scrub towards them as the explosions of the battle in the bay flashed against the dark sea.

Ducking and dodging across the open terrain, they took snap shots as they ran, some occasionally dropping for cover. Bullets bounced and howled off every surface. Wayland and Handley dropped low, Purdo thrown back against the rear wattle wall, dead, the loader, Jonsen, hit in the shoulder, his jawline skinned by a ricochet. '*Handley!*' shouted Wayland. 'Get that gun back on its mount and bring her full about, 180 degrees!'

'*Aye, sir!*'

Bleeding from a gash across his chest and shoulder, Jonsen took up the muzzle of the cannon by himself, while Lambert, Whittaker and the others fought to heft the breech. 'Lay it down, lay it down as she is!' shouted Wayland. 'Damn the carriage! We'll get only one shot.'

They dropped the muzzle across the earth wall of the pit, packing it level as best they could. The calls of the French grew louder, aware of the new danger facing them.

Wayland tore open a cartridge packet and tipped out some of the powder, stuffing it with stones and pistol balls from his ammunition pouch. 'Here! Load with grape and langrage!'

'Grape and langrage, aye, sir!' repeated Handley, taking the packs from him. 'Come on, you dozy lot, or they'll 'ave us! Jonno!'

Another volley rattled around them and they hit the ground. After a beat, Jonsen shouted, '*Loader up! Keep their 'eads down lads!*' and crawled out of the pit on his back, Lambert and the others loosing off single shots from pistols and muskets. Jonsen hooked a cartridge packet into the muzzle, thrusting it down the cannon's throat with his bare arm.

'*Whit! Give us yer ram!*'

'*Comin' up!*'

The bullets kicking up around him, Whittaker slid to the end of the muzzle on his back, put the ram into the cannon's mouth and pushed the powder cartridge in deep, hand over hand. '*She's ready, Jonno!*'

Jonsen took the improvised bag of heavy grape from Wayland and a single 12-pound round-shot. Inching along on his back beside Whittaker, and with a quivering bloody hand, he thrust one after the other up and into the cannon's mouth. '*Stick!*'

The French opened fire with another fusillade. A bullet smacked off the muzzle-rim of the gun and hit Whittaker in the head and he screamed, putting his hands up to his face. He dropped the ram.

'*Whitto!*'

Lambert crawled out of the pit towards him but Handley pulled him back. '*Hold fast, Bert!*' With the flesh at his temple cut to the bone, Whittaker pushed the end of the ram up to the mouth of the gun and Jonsen rammed the load, tugging out the pole and dropping it before dragging Whittaker back to the shelter of the pit. He shouted to Handley, '*Rammed, aye!*'

Lambert thrust the bayonet into the touchhole and poured powder into the channel. '*Clear aye!*'

Wayland applied his musket to the touchhole. The trajectory was as flat as it could be. There would be little chance they would escape the recoil of the loose cannon themselves. '*Firing…*'

The crew dived away from the gun, waiting for Wayland to fire – when they heard a voice in the darkness call out in English.

'*Hallo! You in there, m'sieur!*'

The musket held at arm's length, ready to fire the cannon, Wayland glanced at Handley. 'What was that?'

The French had stopped shooting. Wayland and Handley listened.

'*We wish to parley! You are English?*'

Wayland looked over the parapet wall and saw them in the wash of light from the bay and the fort, a group of soldiers and sailors, some crouching, some prone. But one man stood out, in naval officer's uniform. Behind him was a man in a black coat. It was Masson.

Wayland stood up and looked over the edge of the gun-pit. 'And who by God are you?'

The officer waved an arm. 'I am Lieutenant of the *Ordinnateur Maritime*, and I wish to offer—'

But before he could continue Masson raised his pistol and shot Wayland.

Wayland was in mid fall as Handley caught him, the bullet striking him in the top of the left side of his chest, the blood blooming dark against his shirt as he fell onto the cartridge trunk and dugout wall. '*Oh God…*'

Handley held him down as they heard the officer shouting at Masson, *Coward! Liar! Murderer!* But Masson ignored him and called out, '*En avant!*'

'Easy does it, sir...' gasped Handley.

'*Sword...*'

'Just a mo', sir.' He wiped blood from his eyes, and said to Jonsen, 'Mister Jonno, if you would be so kind... to give it to 'em, right down their *bloody* throats...'

The unmoving Whittaker cradled in one arm, his chest, shoulder and arms torn and bloody, Jonsen took up the fallen musket. '*Bleedin' pleasure, 'Andy...*' He reached up, the long Charleville musket shaking, put its muzzle to the touchhole and fired.

The primer flared, blinding in the dark, and the charge exploded, the gun careening backwards with no restraint, smashing through the opposite parapet wall, crushing the lifeless body of Purdo and two other French dead, spraying its compacted grape-shot over Masson and his advancing platoon.

Limbs were carried away by the blast and some victims flew down the incline, one of them headless, the rest flung off their feet, some into the fleeing form of Citizen Masson as he tumbled and rolled down to the beach, crying out, *Retreat, retreat!*

Handley pulled the bloodied cravat from Wayland's neck and looped it under one arm, across his shoulders and over the chest in a makeshift dressing. 'Well, sir. That was a good day's work... evened the score a bit, I reckon... How you doin'?'

'Hurts like a bugger, 'Andy,' gasped Wayland, and tried to laugh.

Lambert lifted Jonsen onto one elbow by the shattered wheel of the stricken gun carriage. ''Andy,' he wheezed, 'can't move. And we got more visitors.'

Handley looked back into the darkness of the scrub behind them, and saw the shapes of another squad of men running, taking cover, then advancing left and right as they came. He knew at once these were not assorted sailors or artillerymen – they were infantry *chasseurs*.

Wayland stared past Handley, trying to sit up, failing, his voice a gasp. 'Sir Thomas... what of the *Culloden*...?'

Handley looked out into the darkness of the bay. The moon was high, the smoke of the battle drifting across its silver face. The smaller *Leander* had cut *Culloden* loose and joined the battle, but the *Mutine* was making her way to *Culloden*'s side.

The rattle of muskets banged overhead, running feet drawing closer, hoofbeats making the ground jump, the guns in the bay booming, barking, so many angry dogs at each other's throats. But the mortars of the fort were silent. *Culloden* was safe.

'You did it, sir,' he said, 'Mortars out of commission...' He looked out into the night. 'But I think we've 'ad it.'

'*I'd bloody say, lad*,' said a voice from behind in the darkness. 'You babies on shore-leave then?'

Handley looked into the muzzle of a Wayland-Patent Shorter India. It was Sergeant Jeremiah Underhill. Behind him came Kite, Hesse, Napier, De Lisle, Cochrane and Porter – and, drawing up behind, a very bruised Jory Cook.

'Sar'nt Cook...' said Wayland. 'Thanks be to God...'

'You hit bad, sir...?'

'Nothing, it's—' He gasped in pain and clenched his eyes shut – then remembered. 'A man, in black... like that fellow, that Derrien, you once said. Masson, he called him.'

Cook sank down heavily next to him, puffing hard. 'Where'd he go, sir?'

'Down there, Cookie,' said Handley. 'Bastard shot our boy then run off down the slope to the beach, sharpish.'

Ghostly robes flying white in the darkness, the Beni Qassim rushed past, *Nelsoun Amir!* and more shots clattered against the fort walls. One rider wheeled his mount, thudding to a halt. He jumped down and joined them, pistol in hand, his beard dark in the moonlight. It was Joseph Hammer.

'Gentlemen, I suggest you depart before more of our friends arrive.'

Wayland struggled upright. 'The major?'

'*Jaysus shite*, sir,' muttered De Lisle. 'Beggin' your pardon. But you'd never believe it.'

Cook pointed at the raging fury on the shuddering waves before them. 'Major reckoned that Derrien would head for the *Orient*. That's where he'd be right now, sir. In the thick of it.'

Wayland looked out at Aboukir Bay, the battle so close yet so remote. He was seized with a renewed strength. 'Very well... Dr Porter—' He tried to push himself upright but collapsed, gasping. 'Jonsen and Whittaker over there, hit badly, and I – I broke a rib I believe, but can still breathe...'

Porter jumped in beside him first. 'As y'say, sir...' He bent to examine him as best he could, the light flashing off his spectacles. 'Looks good sir, a small ball, went through your waistcoat padding here, but it's not in the wound.' He smiled brightly. 'Must've bounced peculiar, off the bone – so I'll put a wad in til after...'

Wayland took a shaky breath. 'Very good – You and the others get Jonsen and Whittaker up and about, as we're damn well not leaving them here... Kite, you and Handley go pinch us a boat and we shall go in, all of us,' he said, looking out at the bay. 'We'll watch the water, try to find the major, and Captain De la Vega. Agreed?'

Kite nodded. 'Aye, sir. Never give up the boat, eh?'

There was a unanimous *aye*, and Underhill helped Cook to his feet. 'If you're up to it, y'old goat...'

'My lad's down there, mate,' grunted Cook. 'You just try an' stop me.'

–

Sérieuse settled in the water and began to sink, her rigging collapsing, masts toppling, the yards swinging, tearing herself apart. Hazzard slowed his mount, slipping forward onto the horse's neck, something dying inside.

Someone snatched at the reins and hands pulled Hazzard to the ground where he rolled in the wet sand, not caring anymore, the pain in his back and shoulders lancing into him, burning a deep fire, *let me burn, let me burn*, the guns roaring and flashing in the darkness, each impact battering him, condemning him.

Pettifer was first on the scene, Warnock and De la Vega joining him, pistols drawn, men running with the horse, one riding away, others shouting after him.

'*Survivors…*' gasped Hazzard, as if it were something he had forgotten, *matter of habit, sinking ship, hope, always hope*, getting to his feet. 'Must look for survivors…'

A hand grabbed at De la Vega, calling out for help, '*Officier! Officier! What must we do!*' De la Vega spun him round, a pistol to his chin, his eyes staring, his hands out, stammering, '*Non non! Suis de Capitaine Du Petit-Thouars Du Petit…!*' He wore the tailcoat and slouch hat and cockade of a petty officer.

Hazzard lurched over to them. 'Were you for *Sérieuse*? *Quel vaisseau?*' What ship!

'*Spartiate* – I gather more crew…' He backed away, taking in the tattered remnants of Hazzard's coat and robe – it was blackened, stained, cut and torn, the scarlet still bright in the gloom, Warnock and Pettifer in the remains of their dark Maaza *galabeyyah*. 'Which ship are you…?'

De la Vega's French was fast and staccato, '*Capitaine de l'infanterie de marine! De la République Batave!*' snapped De la Vega, then waving a hand at Warnock and Pettifer, 'And our Turkish gunners from Malta! We were attacked by *Bédoux, merde alors!*'

Hazzard hardly noticed, watching *Sérieuse*. The frigate began to break up, sinking slowly into the bay, a roar as the waters burst around her, the holds flooding, bulwarks collapsing. 'Were there women on *Sérieuse*?' Hazzard had spoken in English, then caught himself, '*Prisonnières?*'

'*Comment? How can I know?*'

De la Vega cocked the pistol and Hazzard shook him, weak, an angry drunk in a tavern. '*Think! Répondez! Answer me!*'

'*Sais pas, Capitaine, sais pas!* I do not know! The crew, the gunners, loaders, and the women, to the admiral on *l'Orient!*'

'*Orient?*' Hazzard was suddenly more alert, awoken from a fog. 'You are *sure*…'

'*Oui oui, je vous promis!* It is true! At the demand of *le grand amiral* Brueys!'

The flagship.

When it had been impossible to send them ashore, Brueys had ordered them brought to the safest place he could think of: the *Orient*, 120 guns.

'*Ho there!*' called Pettifer. '*Hard a-nor'east!*' his arm going out, pointing. '*That's him, eh, Knocky? You got im, sir!*'

Hazzard looked out at the bay, the boats, cutters and tenders heaving into the heart of the battle. There, among the boats making their way into the flashing blasts, was a familiar figure.

Derrien.

In the prow of a boat, screaming at the oarsmen to pull faster. It was Derrien without question, heading from the wreckage of *Sérieuse* to the *Orient*.

'He knows... *she's there. He must know!*'

Hope.

'*Boat! Give me a boat, by Christ above...!*' Hazzard staggered, legs weak, unable to connect properly with the stony beach, running for a boat in the surf, anything, De la Vega calling after him, the petty officer following, helping, '*Là-bas!*' *Over there!*

Boat.

A cutter, a swaying lantern fixed to the stern, men gathered round, shoving it into the breaking surf. Hazzard waved at them, '*Attendez! Suis officier! Capitaine St Juste 30ᵉ Infanterie de marine... Vite, pour l'Orient!*'

The coxswain saluted. '*D'accord!* We go to the *Orient* and the *Tonnant, Capitaine!*'

They hit the surf at a run, twelve of them, French, Levantines, Arabs, gunners, sailors, any who would come. Pettifer and Warnock pulled Hazzard along, *get 'im in, get 'im in!* De la Vega took the tiller from the coxswain, '*Tirez, mes vieux!* Pull, *amigos!*'

The swell fought them as they rowed, the thud of cannon-blasts louder, buffeting their ears. Hazzard stood up amidships, riding the swell, the blasts drawing closer, spray flying, the French in the boat looking up at him as he shouted, '*Derrien!*'

The figure in black further ahead whipped round and looked. When he recognised Hazzard he rose up and raged, '*Non!*' his cry cutting across the waves, roaring at the oarsmen to row faster, *faster!*

With every stroke of the oars the battle grew louder, the crash of shattering wood, the savage cries of British gunners cheering every hit. The men in the boat flinched with each blast, the night split by the flashes of the cannon, ever brighter, more blinding, more deafening. Hazzard stared at *Orient*, at Derrien.

De la Vega cried out, 'Men in the water, *amigo! Starboard!*'

Hazzard saw them over the starboard gunwale, struggling to keep their heads above the surface, some calling, hands aloft. '*We can take eight or ten!*' called De la Vega. '*But no more!*'

Hazzard watched Derrien pulling away still further, '*After him!*' as Pettifer and Warnock dragged the men aboard, the long cutter tipping and swaying, the fear on their faces bright, one sobbing, one clawing to get in, their terror at once personal and universal. '*Pull,*' called Hazzard, watching Derrien. '*Tirez! Pull harder…*'

Other boats rowed furiously, the swell heaving with the roll of the great ships, the flash of fire dazzling on its surface, splinters chopping the waves into a boiling spray with every deafening explosion.

Nelson's *Vanguard* streaked in towards the centre to engage the *Peuple Souverain* on the far side, taking fire from *Spartiate* and *Aquilon*, its bows bursting with hits, HMS *Audacious*, *Minotaur* and *Defence* following in her wake. Hazzard saw HMS *Bellerophon* make a lone charge at the *Orient*, dousing sail to slow herself, guns flashing, trying to screen Nelson and *Vanguard*, the water churning all around. Hazzard thought of the hot-headed Captain Darby. Just as HMS *Orion* had done with *Sérieuse*, *Orient* fired a single broadside and Darby's *Billy Ruffian* rocked with the impacts, her mainmast crashing, tearing the foremast with it. Defiantly, she returned fire before drifting on her anchor chain, crippled.

'*Díos mio,*' said De la Vega, crossing himself, 'this is the inferno…'

'*Sir! Orion dead ahead!*' called Pettifer. '*It's Sir James!*' HMS *Orion* was moving down the landward side of the line to batter both the *Peuple Souverain* and *Franklin* – and their overloaded cutter was directly in her path.

'*Cesár*,' called Hazzard, 'make for *Orient!*'

There was no sign of Derrien's boat. It had vanished, somewhere ahead of the *Orion*. The battleships' broadsides were smouldering mountains above them, the *Peuple Souverain* dropping her anchors, the rattle of chain sharp against the endless blasts of shot. *Orion*'s churning bow-wave roared and lifted them, the cutter tipping to starboard, every man tumbling atop another, Hazzard calling, *faster, heave*, the oars wild and swinging, and they rolled back, swept up by the wake and thrown against *Franklin*'s hull, the oars crushing hands and arms, some crying out, some toppling overboard. With *Orion* blotting out the lights from the bay beyond, Hazzard saw Derrien's boat further down the line by the French flagship – but Derrien had gone. Hazzard took up one of the oars himself. They had moments before Sir James Saumarez attacked the *Franklin*.

'*Pull! Pull for Orient!*'

The waves lifted them and they were thrown down into the boat again, just as HMS *Orion* opened fire. They clapped their hands over their ears, some shouting against the roar as the air burst all around them, the blasting percussion maddening, thudding through their bodies as they rowed, screaming to each other, the broadside of *Orion* bright with flashes of fire and clouds of stinging smoke. A blazing cutter emerged from the French line, its contents engulfed in flame, bobbing and dancing on the waves, its light flickering against *Orion* and *Franklin*, cries from the decks above, *Fend off, fend off!* De la Vega shouted and Hazzard turned and looked up: the *Orient* towered above them, lines dropped for the crews to scramble aboard.

Then they were out, hands scrabbling at the hanging lines trailing in the water, the only safety in the storm the largest target on the sea. Some of them had begun to climb when Sir James Saumarez resumed fire not twenty yards off.

'*Get down!*' Hazzard and De la Vega pulled a pair of French sailors back into the cutter and they dropped flat for cover, just as the rounds burst on the nearby *Franklin*'s portside. *Orient* was riddled with fragments and splinters, cannon-rounds crashing into *Franklin*'s hull, staving in her gun-ports, flinging the massive chained shutters whirling into the night.

When the first salvo subsided, the men in the cutter hurled themselves at the ship's side. A hatch on the middle gundeck opened and they called up, '*Canonniers!*' A rope net was thrown out. Hazzard seized the ladder. Scarcely able to breathe, he pulled himself out of the cutter.

'*Marines, to me...*'

Hazzard swung, a dead weight, and struck the broadside, the net shaking with frantically climbing men, two falling past him, and then De la Vega and Pettifer took his elbows and heaved him upwards. He missed his footing, a boot sliding through a rung, and had to pull himself up, Warnock catching hold of him.

'*Sir!*'

Hazzard took his hand and made the last yard to the hatch door, the French sailors dragging them in, *Vite alors! Vite!* just as *Orion* ran out her reloaded guns once again. Hazzard dived on them all, '*Get down!*'

The volley blasted the *Franklin*, and the ship shuddered, debris exploding from the hull waists, the deck alive with running men. It was a crazed warren of wreckage and fallen cargo blocking access to the portside guns, which sat cold and silent. On the starboard side, gunners loaded and fired heavy 24-pounders while barefoot boys clambered over crates and casks to reach the cannon with ammunition, the blast of impacts shaking every inch of the ship's frame, deafening, blotting out their calls, *Munition...! Vite! Poudre, plus de poudre alors!*

Hazzard could see right through the gundeck and its open ports to the approaching British ships now coming to duel with the giant flagship, rounds shrieking through the darkness straight for them.

The marines threw themselves to the planks as the first rounds struck home on the starboard bow. A gun-crew flew backwards as the oak exploded all around them with a flash of light and a cloud of splinters, the gun-carriage swinging, the cannon jammed in its port, a boy crushed beneath it. A shout went up, *Assistance! Au secours!* Hazzard pushed himself up, a young French sailor weeping, a gash by his ear, his face twisted in sobs.

Hazzard dropped to one knee, *up, get up*, and saw De la Vega. '*Cesár! Aft – the staterooms...!*'

They pushed their way through the rubble and knots of running men, De la Vega finding the stairs to the upper decks. '*Aquí!* This way! *Venga!*'

Captain Benjamin Hallowell's HMS *Swiftsure* had moved into the centre of the battle, and now stood off *Orient's* starboard bow, astern of the *Franklin*, and opened a raking fire. The bows of *Orient* thudded with round-shot, crashing through the lower and middle decks into the forward holds. Within moments, HMS *Alexander* bore down on her from astern. Next in line behind *Orient*, Du Petit Thouars in the *Tonnant* tried to return fire, but *Alexander* headed straight for the ever-widening gap between *Tonnant's* bows and the stern of Brueys' flagship. *Orient* was now bracketed by two British ships raking her from both forward and astern. The poopdeck of *Orient* heaved with explosions, her rails and mizzenstays flying to pieces, rigging and yards raining down on the quarterdeck from above.

Hazzard looked across the decks. Gun-crews raced to reload, firing at will, *Swiftsure* and *Alexander* looming over the fo'c'sle and stern, sails blooming white, cannons blazing, *Alexander's* tops filled with red-coated marines maintaining a ceaseless covering fire on the *Orient's* decks. The dead were everywhere, sailors dragging the wounded into shelter, musket rounds peppering the decks, men falling from the rigging, young ensigns shouting to their crews, *Fire, fire!* Hazzard saw two officers standing at the quarterdeck, shouting up at the rigging hands, then vanishing in a cannon-blast, their bodies swept away by an unseen hand as *Alexander* and *Swiftsure* bombarded *Orient* relentlessly.

'To the stern...' gasped Hazzard. 'Day-room or Great Cabin...' He moved aft over a fallen spar to the wardroom passage, his memory of *Orient* now a blur with the *Ville de Paris*, Brueys become St Vincent, thoughts of his Uncle Thomas: *Not to disappoint the good rector of St Jude's.*

Once inside they found shattered panels, smashed bulwarks and doors hanging at all angles swinging from twisted hinges, sailors crowding the stairs, boys carrying men below in hammocks, wounded screaming, crates and gunpowder passing upwards. Another explosion and glass and wood blew in from astern with more cries as *Alexander* struck another blow and Hazzard dropped low. De la Vega surveyed the scene. *'Madre...'*

They pushed through the rubble of the passages. Above, a ceiling sagged, its beams broken, its supporting post gone, the cool air of the night blowing in through smashed stern lights somewhere further aft. Bodies lay half buried in the ruins, and desperate gunners tried to clear the gun-ports of the dead. Some saw them and called, *Aidez-nous alors! Help us!*

Another salvo of gunfire blew in from starboard and they threw themselves down, the fragments and splinters flying. Hazzard knew they had little time. Once Nelson was in position, they would all blaze away. When that happened, there would be no pause, no rest from the barrage.

Ahead, the smashed bulwark gave onto another cabin, a stateroom. A broken desk, a bed up-ended on a shattered frame, castors spinning idly. The smoke had become a fog lit only by the flashes from outside and a single lantern somewhere before them. Another salvo struck, a thunderous repetitive thudding on the broadside and the ship shuddered. Hazzard stumbled onward, hopeless, guessing, '*Sarah!*' If she weren't here then he would try the holds where last they met.

As he rounded a corner in the dark passage, Hazzard saw a woman crouched in a corner, huddled over a small barefooted boy in tattered trousers, miniature naval coat, smudged face, no more than twelve.

'*Sarah,*' he choked, then saw it was not her, but another. '*Jeanne?*'

She was shaking, holding the boy tight. She saw Hazzard but did not move, her bright eyes darting quickly left and right. More rounds began to pummel the broadsides and she screamed, crushing the child to her. They shoved the debris aside to reach her – but a young ensign stepped into view and raised a pistol.

'*H-Halte…!*' he cried.

'*Down!*' Hazzard threw himself to one side as a bullet cracked into the panelling over his head. He shouted back at the ensign in French, '*Fool! To your station at once!*'

'But – I was ordered—'

'*William!*'

It was Sarah's voice, a muffled shriek, almost incomprehensible, and Hazzard lunged forward, '*Sarah!*' – just as the ensign was hurled away by another blast, and Masson stepped into the doorway, a pistol in hand. He was scarcely recognisable, his curled wig gone, a bloody shirt and waistcoat blackened from fire, his face marred by a jagged wound from temple to jaw, one eye a purple mass of gnarled tissue.

A cluster of 32-pound cannon rounds hit the hull below and the floor collapsed in the far corner, a beam giving way, and Masson screamed, clapping his hands over his ears. Whimpering, he got to his feet and aimed wild.

Warnock called out, '*Sir! Mine!*' and fired a snap-shot, the ball smashing through the remains of the doorframe, the splinters and ricochet hitting Masson in the hip. He cried out in pain and fell, the lantern suddenly blotted out as the ship heeled to port and they staggered. Hazzard made his way to Jeanne, the stifling air thudding, crashing in his head, *God God God enough!* He reached the doorway and took Jeanne's outstretched hand, the boy holding out his arms. '*Jeanne…*'

'*She is here – he has her…*' she gasped.

'*Go, quick,*' he said. '*César, take her…*' and De la Vega pulled her past them, hefting up the lad, *bravo, amigo, bravo.*

For a moment, there was silence. Hazzard stood in the doorway, looking into the shattered interior, another anteroom. It was no more than a corner landing to the Great Cabin, where he had dined that night off Malta in the company of Bonaparte and the *savants*.

The guns battered the ship again and the *Orient* shook from side to side, dust and powder raining from above, the walls reverberating, the gunners calling, and the scene burst with light.

A dogleg of passages, a doorway, cracked and collapsing; Masson leaned against one wall, wheezing in pain, beside him, Jules-Yves Derrien, his open lantern swinging. He held Sarah in front of him, her arms pulled behind. On a broken bench to the left lay the *comtesse* de Biasi, a spreading patch of blood on her side. A pool had formed beneath her on the splintered planking.

Hazzard called to her, '*Madame…*'

Derrien jerked his hold on Sarah and she gasped. Hazzard stopped. Again, the guns crashed and the ship heaved and rolled, Masson screamed, stamping his foot to alleviate the fear, the pounding on the hull moving steadily forwards, one hit after another, a gun-port bursting in behind them in a gale of splinters, and they all staggered, wind and spray blowing in.

The ageing countess could barely speak but gasped with some relief when she saw him, '*M'sieur d'Azzard…*'

Derrien was breathing heavily, the small screw-barrelled pistol hanging at arm's length. He had been hit badly, like Masson, his leg bloody, the coat torn and charred, one sleeve ripped open, his wounded pistol arm tied with a bloodstained rag – his invulnerable personal precision gone.

'William…' said Sarah, the dust and soot on her face smudged with tears.

Having found her, Hazzard almost surrendered to his exhaustion, as if finding her were enough, the chase over. He put a hand out to lean on the doorframe. The scene began to slide away from him, his eyes closing and he fought a distant yearning for it all to end.

'*Always, you are there,*' Derrien hissed. '*Always!*'

Spoken in English. Hazzard swayed, *feel drunk*, near collapse. *Ready to drop, Jory, like the Orient, like this old, sinking...* but he managed to speak. 'Let them go...'

Derrien's eyes flicked to De la Vega over Hazzard's shoulder, searching for movement behind. De la Vega nudged Hazzard with his pistol and whispered, '*Vacio.*'

Empty.

'Bonaparte... is *finished*,' said Hazzard. 'Cut off. Forgotten. Just as his enemies in Paris wanted.'

Just as Lewis wanted. Damning Egypt to a new master.

Derrien trembled. Hazzard could not tell if it were fear, or anger. '*I came to this*—' he began, the words shot from his lips uncontrolled '—this *place*... half-French half-*English*man, English *liar* with no king...' He took a breath. 'We came... w*ith the Revolution, and a future for all*,' a hand to his forehead, tired, then in French again, 'At Valmy... I commanded guns, *me, moi-même!* And *I held his head!*' He looked away. '*His head...*'

Hazzard tried everything he could think of. 'The map... I will find the tombs... the treasures, on the map, anything...'

'And what have *you* brought here, *Englishman*?' Derrien looked around him, his eyes roaming the destruction all about them. 'You brought *this.*'

The *comtesse* spoke in English in a sudden rush, 'Find Salah al-Menouf and Hassan Abd-ar-Rahman. The sultan will issue a *firman*, for *jihad*, with Al-Djezzar of Acre—'

'*Silence!*' raged Derrien, and Masson pressed the muzzle of his pistol against her breast-bone and squeezed the trigger. Sarah screamed as the frail body of the *comtesse* bucked, the bullet bursting through her back.

Hazzard shouted, '*Pet! Knock-knock!*'

'*Clear aye!*'

Hazzard dropped to his left and Pettifer and Warnock fired their muskets simultaneously over Hazzard's right shoulder.

Masson's neck and chest burst with the impact of Pettifer's musket-ball, his head smacking back against a post, eyes wide, mouth opening in a cry, his body dropping dead to the floor. Derrien thrust Sarah behind him protectively and raised his pistol, Warnock's bullet driving him back – just as Captains Ball and Hallowell gave their order, and *Swiftsure* and *Alexander* blazed away: in a storm of thunder and iron, the stern and starboard quarter of the *Orient* imploded.

The passage blew in with splintering wood and breaking glass. All were thrown off their feet as the rounds crashed into the flagship, a post flying past, a bulkhead collapsing, Pettifer calling out, and the battleship heeled and rocked. Someone was shouting and Hazzard put his hands to his ears, *get up*, shouting at nothing, everything, pushing a smashed panel away, Derrien's lantern fallen, the crackle of fire, the smell of smoke. '*Sarah!*'

'*Here,*' she said, and Hazzard reached for her and she found his hand as the ship crashed from side to side, the concussion of the guns battering them, his vision catching the scene in flashes, shouting to Pettifer and De la Vega, *Get out! Out out out!* Derrien curled in a heap, unmoving, eyes half-open, and he squeezed Sarah tight, St Jude pressing into his chest, telling him *yes*, this was real, and she sobbed against his neck, '*William…!*'

Another roar of thunder and they scattered, stumbling, falling, the lamplight blotted out, screams from above, from below. Her hand pulled him back to his feet, *this way*, and in the flashing of the barrage he saw Masson and the *comtesse*, dead, the burning debris by the broken lamp flaring in the dark. But for a smear of black blood, Derrien had gone.

'*Where is he!*'

De la Vega pulled him back. '*Vamos, amigo!* Leave him! The devil comes for his own!'

Orient shook and bellowed, a stricken beast in its death-throes, the barracking of the guns incessant. Warnock led the way, French crewmen tugging at them for help as they passed, officers waving them onward to the upper deck, thinking they were crewmen.

A blast struck high above and showered them with splinters, and Warnock went down, Pettifer grabbing him up, and they burst through to the upper deck. French marines crowded the gangways in firing parties, a *sous-lieutenant* calling the orders, wounded lying everywhere, seamen carrying comrades to shelter, others running with lengths of line, some fighting to secure the stays, battling fires, men falling, men jumping overboard.

He could feel the heat on his back and shoulders, and he burned as if alight with flame. Pettifer shouting in his face, *Can't hear... can't see*, his blackened features crazed in a fog. '*Larboard, sir! We got to go over the larboard side! Make for the boat!*'

Sarah screamed at him from somewhere and he felt her hands on his face, shaking him, *can't think*, De la Vega down on one knee, *Cesár!* Hazzard rising, hauling him up, Warnock carrying them past the mainmast, musket-volleys cracking from the British ships and in the fighting-tops. He then saw what he had glimpsed when they had first climbed aboard: buckets of tar and lime.

Fire.

He saw the pale limewash spreading across the boards, meeting a pool of black pitch creeping to the base of the mainmast.

'*Get off!*' he yelled. '*She's going to blow...*'

Hazzard hauled himself up the steps to the quarterdeck gangway, shoving Warnock onward. He half fell, straw underfoot, spilling from split mattresses at the rail, men screaming at them as they staggered past. He could hear Sarah calling, *Jeanne! Jeanne!*

Hazzard could not see Casabianca on the quarterdeck, only a group of officers gathered around a fallen officer, nearby a white-haired figure, lying propped against a cask, his leg shot away at the hip. *Brueys*, thought Hazzard, nearly torn in half, yet still he tried to direct the battle. Hazzard leaned on the rail, and saw Lt Gilles Marais. Marais stared back at him, wide-eyed, unseeing, and Hazzard turned away, a terrible sickness overwhelming him as he thought of Jullien, and their climb into the heavens.

Flame rushed up the mainmast, the pools of lime and pitch catching light, the fire roaring across the decks – the rigging catching like a fuse, the flames rippling along the lines up to those trapped above. A blazing spar crashed down from the tops, men crying out, some falling into the sea in flames.

Hazzard stumbled to the port gangway, Pettifer taking him by the arms, trying to get him to a line, *We got her, sir, we got her in a boat!* but he kept pushing them away. 'Where is she...' said Hazzard. '*Get over the side...*'

He could see boats below, men calling up, urging the crew to jump as *Alexander* and *Vanguard* blazed away, every gun on their starboard broadsides firing at will in an endless pounding rhythm.

HMS *Orion* loomed off the port bow, HMS *Theseus* behind, swinging round on her anchor springs, her reloaded guns emerging, the darkened crippled hulk of *Peuple Souverain* blocking *Orion*'s path. The cry went up: *Sauve qui peut! Every man for himself.* Those climbing down the broadside of *Orient* began to jump. Hazzard saw Pettifer falling from halfway down into the water, De la Vega jumping, Warnock calling upward to him, *Come on, sir!*

Orient began to break up, the blast of the fire blowing men from the rail. Hazzard climbed over on his line, walking down the broadside, the planks bursting around him with fire. He felt only a faint impact, a heavy hand on his back, then weightlessness, as Hallowell on the *Swiftsure* opened fire for the last time.

Falling.

The air burst overhead and he tried to shout but he struck the water, his arms, his shoulders, stiff, useless, his hands like stones. The guns were reduced to a muffled thumping, somewhere far above, but otherwise, there was silence. He could see the bodies of seamen floating gently all around him, some rolling slowly in the current, others hanging, arms out in open embrace, discarded puppetry, nudging their fellows, turning, the glow of the fire and flash of the guns high above illuminating their faces in a weightless underworld.

Drift away... so very easy.

Bursts of light and water above his head, more men diving into the water, some splashing to swim, some sinking. Then one hand, two, *Warnock, Kite*, a third, *Porter*, their swinging fists clutching at him, holding him up, pushing him to the surface, their legs kicking – and the air hit him, roaring, alive, blasting, *too hot*, and he dragged it into his lungs, muffled calls from far off and Cook's pocked and blistered face, '*Got him, lads, move away, away now…*'

There were figures still on deck high above, the fire raging through the rigging, the ratlines ablaze, a fiery web against the smoke, survivors below calling up for them to jump, *sauve-toi, save yourself*, some with their clothes ablaze, screaming, hitting the water, *Where is Sarah?* De le Vega was standing, shouting up in French to Jeanne and the boy, his arms out as if he would catch them. But the boy looked down, then ran back into the flaming destruction, and she followed him, calling his name.

The barrage eased. Saumarez backed HMS *Orion* away, as did *Swiftsure* and *Alexander*, their gun-ports closing, their greater fear now the fire they had created. *Orient* was a blazing corpse, but no one could yet close her eyes and finish her.

Hazzard gulped in the boat, *can't breathe*, a crushing pain in his throat, in his chest, his eyes bulging, and he fought off their help, *can't breathe*. Someone grabbed his legs and up-ended him, the bilge of the boat suddenly in his face as seawater belched out of his lungs and mouth and he retched, his throat tightening, closing, *breathe breathe breathe*.

'*We got him, Sarge!*'

Kite, Porter, De Lisle – they were there, with Hesse and Underhill, Wayland at the tiller…

Where is she?

He was shouting but no one heard him and no one would speak, and all the while he kept shouting, *Where is she!* Cook shook him and pushed him down and he saw, there she was, lying with him across his knees, a faint smile on her lips. '*Here I am…*'

Relief swept over him in a tidal wave as he held her, his head bowed. '*Are you really…?*' He buried his face in her wet hair, holding her tight, as he had done in the Orlop on the *Orient* that night so long ago, feeling her arms around his neck, and he knew all was well – though he could not bring himself to accept it: he wanted to rage at them and their bloody battle, damning Nelson

344

and Bonaparte and his fleet and all of them to eternal darkness. He knew he would have burned down the world just for this moment. *'Sarah... forgive me...'*

She sighed and held him tight and he breathed, *tired, so tired*, running his hands over her, to support her legs, to keep her safe. He then felt the jagged shard of wood that had penetrated her lower back.

No.

'I... feel nothing,' she said, then tried to swallow, and he wanted to stop her as she closed her eyes. 'Really...'

He looked at them all, sitting around him, doing nothing. *'Pull for the Orion! Pull, damn you! Surgeon! Porter!'*

Porter was already at his side, Underhill, Wayland, Kite and Hesse watching, Warnock and Pettifer's smoke-blackened faces downcast. Cook looked on, *Sorry, sir*, and Hazzard could not believe it, would not, and the tears shook him, his breath coming in fits.

'Why did you come?' his voice a strained whisper.

She coughed, almost a laugh. Wayland gripped the tiller, his face white, the boat rocking as Handley helped a few more aboard. Hazzard heard French but registered nothing.

'You promised,' she said, *'An adventure...'*

His numb hands shuddered and he could not stop them, his vision distorted, blurred, fogging. She was pulling further away from him by the moment and he tried to stop her. He put his trembling fingers to her cheek and as he leaned forward, felt that the piercing end of the wood shard had come clean through her front. *'Oh God, no...'*

Porter was saying something quietly to him, his hand on his shoulder, trying to pull him gently away but Hazzard could not hear him properly, *loss of blood, sir, she's just closing her eyes, sir, just tired, falling asleep-like... and she'll be safe away...*

No.

Hazzard rolled forward into a ball over her, held her to him, for minutes, for hours, for moments, and Cook had to pull him off. He heard the murmur of prayer, Cochrane, and the French sailors in the boat.

Someone took a sword from his hand, possibly De la Vega – he had whipped it round and thrust it forward until it quivered at the throat of one of the French survivors, just a boy, praying with his tear-stained eyes tight shut. Hazzard had no idea he had done it. He stared, seeing the curved scimitar of Sheikh Ali Qarim as if he had never seen it before, and then sank down. At that moment, *Orient* exploded.

The blast lit the sky and the ships around with a double clap of thunder, and flattened the water's surface, the surprise on every man's face captured in a white and orange flash. Moments later, the full sound hit them, tilting the boat, knocking them backwards as they clung to the sides, as *Orient* cursed the world with her final defiant act, the decks heaving and bursting into the air, burning wreckage and men flung skyward.

Brueys. Casabianca. Marais.

Jeanne.

The remaining guns of the two fleets fell silent, struck dumb at last. Smoke drifted across the bay, lit by the fires of flaming French ships. *Guerrier* was gone, shattered, surrendered. *Conquérant* had struck her colours, *Spartiate* and *Aquilon* were disabled; *Franklin* and *Peuple Souverain* had struck, and were overrun, hemmed in by British 74s, now pausing in unexpected armistice. The rear-guard of ships, *Généreux*, *Guillaume Tell* and *Timoléon* had watched in impotent frustration, unable to attack, unable to escape the contrary wind. The men in the small boats hung their heads, in sorrow, in relief, grateful for the deafening, woollen silence. The skeletal cadaver of the *Orient* blazed furiously. Everywhere floated the bodies of the dead.

'She's gone…' said Cook.

The only sound was a distant cheer from the British ships, but even this was half-hearted and faded on the wind. The men of 9 Company exchanged glances, then looked away. None were jubilant. Some minutes later, calls came across the waves, from rowing boats, in English at first and then in French, '*This way. Come along. Venez ici. You are now made prisoner, this way, come along...*'

Hazzard saw nothing, heard nothing, but watched the water as it rose and fell, Sarah lying in his arms as if asleep, his fingers toying with her dark curling hair. The oars sat shipped in their locks, untouched. No one moved. Time passed, and they bobbed on the swell, the tide pulling them in, away from the battle.

Eventually they touched the shoals, the boat gently grounding, the gradual stop giving them strange rest, returning them to the earth.

'Sir,' said Cook softly, breaking the silence, 'fleet destroyed. We're done. They get no more of us.'

Hazzard's voice was distant, wandering. 'I have no more to give...' Then a memory recurring. 'I sent you back, with Hammer, and Underhill...'

Cook nodded. 'Found me way back.'

Handley spoke in a quiet monotone, his eyes on Sarah, '*Culloden* grounded on the rocks, sir,' reported Handley, a task to be done. 'Come under mortar-fire from the fort. Riding on a horse, Mr Wayland took a gun position single-handed, killing two... and with surviving hands from the old *Esperanza* turned the gun on the fort, knocking out the mortar batteries. Saved Sir Thomas and his crew. Survivors of *Esperanza* now rejoined the fleet, sir.' He looked at the marines. 'Nine Company recce complete, sir.'

Hazzard nodded. Then, after a moment, 'Well done, Handley. Well done, Mr Wayland... well done, all.'

'Didn't give up the boat, sir,' said Warnock softly, staring down at Sarah.

'No,' agreed Hazzard, 'you didn't...'

On the beach in the distance Hazzard could see a group standing by their horses, others still mounted. *Bedouin*, thought Hazzard. He watched, unmoving.

'*Ahoay!*' came an officer's voice from astern, '*I say there, ahoay!*'

Hazzard saw a gig rowing towards them, then turning, an officer in blue looking out at them, his face a featureless white against the darkness. '*Advance and be recognised! Are you the Special Landing Squadron, 9 Company, the Marines...?*'

Hazzard said nothing. Wayland called back. 'You have found us, sir!'

The officer gave an order to his coxswain and they pulled again, closing the distance between them, but stood off some way to avoid grounding.

'*A message from Rear-Admiral Nelson to one Major Hazzard.*'

Hazzard said nothing. The marines looked from one to the other. De la Vega gave Hazzard's reply. 'He is not prepared to answer at this moment, *señor.*'

The officer replied, '*Very well. Nelson is wounded but recovered, and invites you to dine on Vanguard, sir. Major Tappey of* Vanguard'*s marines is killed and he would have Major Hazzard assume command. Furthermore, the Admiralty requests his presence forthwith for conference.*'

Hazzard set Sarah down gently on the bench seat, and rose slowly, distracted, unhearing. He looked at the water.

'*Major Hazzard, sir?*' asked the officer.

Hazzard breathed, slowly, carefully, staring at the shore, at the waiting figures. 'Volunteers,' he said, with a lost, dead tone, 'to me. Others may report... for orders, for honours, as they see fit...'

Cook watched him, fearing what he might do. Hazzard carefully shrugged off his red Bombay coat and dropped it into the bilgewater of the scuppers at his feet. He looked out at the bay. He did not see the officer, nor his boat, did not look.

'*I said, sir, you are to dine with the captains in victory aboard* Vanguard*! And the men of the Special Landing Squadron are to attend as well. Nelson wishes to honour you all, sir!*'

Hazzard stepped out of the boat and into the shallows. He could feel the soft crush of the water, the pebbles beneath the soles of his boots. He bent down to the side of the boat, but his knees weakened, and he gripped the gunwale for support. He hung there a moment, breathing, then with a last effort lifted

Sarah's body into his arms, and straightened. *She is so very light*, he thought. Porter reached to help but Pettifer held him back. Carrying her, Hazzard waded for the shore, his steps slow and uncertain.

'*Sir? Will you deny Nelson in his moment of victory…?*'

They watched Hazzard, the water splashing around him. One of the Bedouin on shore moved towards the water. It was Masoud. Behind him, Joseph Hammer.

Cook clambered out of the boat, musket over his shoulder, Hazzard's discarded coat in one hand, the great scimitar in the other.

'Marines. To me…'

The French sailors watched as the marines rose from the benches one by one, and climbed out. Wayland gave one of them the tiller, '*Bonne chance.*'

'*You men there!*' called the officer. '*Nelson calls! Do you not answer? Identify yourselves…*'

De la Vega watched as Cook led them in single file after Hazzard to the shore, then got to his feet and followed. The British guns began to bark again, their respectful silence cut short, and what was left of the battle continued – until it too faded in their hearing to nothing but hollow echoes, rapping across the indifferent sands, which stretched far into the glimmering night.

Epilogue – Ankh

They had camped amidst anonymous ruins on the south coast of the bay, slabs of broken glories strewn unremarked across the rocky sands, glowing eerie in the moonlight, the Nile dark and silent nearby. Over the following days, the body was prepared by a group of old *Bedu* women using ancient arts, sealed with *mumiya*, and wrapped in a linen shroud. Masoud recited the *Salat al-Janazah* prayer, the Beni Qassim the reverent congregation. He arranged for a small flat-bottomed barge to take the coffin on the final journey, and filled it with white and pale-blue Nile lotus blossom.

Further fleet boats came and went, some patrolling, some collecting the dead, several at Nelson's insistence trying to find Hazzard and the marines. Hazzard had remained silent until at last he sent back a single demand, and the Navy had acquiesced.

They all waited at the water's edge. The French were in turmoil, miles away, hurrying to fend off a potential landing by the British, many staring numbly out at the smouldering hulks in Aboukir Bay in disbelief. The *Bedu* rode with impunity, harassing their lines, darting off through the dunes and salt marshes. The British battleships hovered with menace, circling, guns run out, ready to bury Alexandria in its own rubble, their stifled rage keeping the marooned French at a distance. Far from friend or foe, Hazzard looked out at the dark sea, the moon a glimmer behind drifting cloud.

De la Vega spoke in a hushed tone at his side, 'So, you did burn their ships, *amigo*, and their thousands of men…' he said, 'as we said. And now we are Cortés no longer.'

Hazzard nodded. 'All for nothing.'

The Spaniard bowed his head. '*Volpone* will always be yours, when you need her.' He patted his pocket. 'Your letter saves me from your admiral and I shake his hand. Cesár Domingo will fight the *Franceses* with your mad King George.' He nodded to himself, confirming a personal conviction. 'France will break her word. And we shall be brothers again,' he said, 'one day. I know this.'

From the darkness of the waves there emerged a single boat, a British cutter, at times catching the silver of moonlight, then hidden by cloud and drifting smoke, its oars swinging, dipping into the black waves.

'Here he comes, sir,' said Cook.

De la Vega put a hand on Hazzard's shoulder and retired with Cook and the others to a respectful distance, leaving Hazzard alone, waiting.

Eventually the cutter ground on the sand and shingle out in the shallows, some twenty yards out. A figure rose slowly in the stern. Even at that distance, Hazzard could recognise him. He stepped out of the cutter into the water, and walked steadily through the knee-deep waves in his long navy coat, then through the quietly hissing foam of the surf. He stopped before Hazzard, a dark silhouette, the moon floating behind. It was Tomlinson, of the *Valiant*.

'Mr Hazzard,' he said. He removed his cocked hat.

Hazzard took a breath, relieved after the waiting. Of all the hardened souls he had ever encountered at sea, there had been only one man he would trust with such a task. 'Lieutenant Tomlinson. Good to see you.'

Tomlinson looked into the funeral barge. 'After dropping you at Cadiz, all these months ago, this was not how I imagined we would meet again, sir.'

'No. Nor I.'

Hazzard looked down at her, wreathed in the blooms of the nation she had tried to save. Tomlinson's arrival had brought it all back, their headlong race to Cadiz, meeting Lord St Vincent,

Troubridge. Markham, Greaves, the *Esperanza*, all. Hazzard was not wholly present, his mind wandering, lost in distant thoughts. He handed Tomlinson a note. 'Minster House... Sible Parva, near Hedingham, in Suffolk. Look for...' His voice faltered and he swallowed. 'Look for St Jude's church rectory and my uncle, to take your rest.' His vision blurred, the eyes stinging. 'And tell her father and mother, I am sorry, I – I was *too late*.'

Tomlinson nodded soberly. After a moment, he looked over Hazzard's shoulder. 'And these are your men.'

Cook and the marines, now in a mix of Marine scarlet and Arab robes, fanned out behind him, watching.

'Yes.'

'I hear they will not leave you.'

Hazzard gazed down at the white shroud. 'No.'

'Most everything I said about you was quite right,' said Tomlinson, looking out at the salvage ships and wreckage in the bay, lanterns playing on the water. 'But by God I don't blame them one bit.'

It was as close to a compliment as he would get from him. Hazzard nodded. 'I thank you.'

They said nothing for a while, each searching their memories, until Tomlinson said, 'Nelson called me out of Gib. Personally. But I was set to run from Syracuse and caught his request early. 'Tis said Lord St Vincent has cleared me to Lowestoft past customs, anyone delaying me to answer to him alone.'

Hazzard thought of Admiral St Vincent, of interrupting his dinner and standing in his day-room aboard the *Ville de Paris* for briefing, dripping onto his 'rather good Turkey carpet' – and how he had offered Hazzard his hand. He was grateful to the old bear, still guarding the Pillars of Hercules.

Tomlinson's voice softened. 'I'm sorry she was in such a place at such a time.' He looked over at Cook. 'The orphan, his lordship wrote, he tried to rescue.'

Cook lowered his head at the memory of the Toulon raid, and the fate of Hugues Bartelmi. Tomlinson recognised Wayland.

'My compliments, sir, and thanks from Sir Thomas Troubridge and Cap'n Hallowell.'

'Thank you, sir.'

'Hallowell says he couldn't be certain it was you, but he saw the French fort firing on *Culloden* and that it stopped most abrupt. He spoke of your marines and said: That's what they do.'

Wayland looked at them, and nodded. 'It is, sir.'

Two of the Beni Qassim walked into the water, intoning a prayer, the barge between them, guiding it slowly out towards the cutter, Cochrane following into the surf, murmuring a Latin dismissal, the marines with heads bowed. The waiting boatmen raised their oars, one climbing out to tie a line and take the Nile boat in tow.

'Be careful with her,' said Hazzard.

Tomlinson put on his hat and extended his hand. 'As if she were my own. Chaplain on *Valiant* awaits her for prayers. I shall seal her safe and carry her home, don't you doubt.'

Hazzard shook his hand. 'The next you'll be collecting,' he said, 'will be mine...'

'We shall meet afore, sir. As sure as God wills it.'

Tomlinson turned and walked out into the water. The oarsmen shoved off, the oars splashing, and Tomlinson climbed into the stern of the funeral barge. They made for HMS *Valiant*, waiting in the distance, her topyards dipped in mute sorrow. Hazzard watched. Tomlinson looked over his shoulder and raised a hand in farewell. Hazzard did likewise, repaying the salute.

After a time, *Valiant* set sail, turning slowly in the current, her lugsails filling and billowing, ghostly in the moonlight. Hazzard continued to stare at the sea for some while, and the marines left him quiet, gathering by the campfire with the *Bedu*. Cook and Masoud joined him.

'Safe home,' said Cook. It was an old palliative from the Bombay Marine, for those lucky enough to be sent back to England – the living or the dead.

Hazzard nodded. 'Safe home, aye.' He stared out at the rippling water. 'I failed you all, Masoud. Forgive me.'

The earnest Alexandrian replied gently, 'You did not, Hazar-*effendi*, no. The Huwaytat, the Sawalha, the Maaza and the Khushmaan, all know,' he said, 'that you came back for us.' He bowed his head in respect.

Hazzard watched the lights of Rosetta, the barges and tenders, the blockade ships, wondering if perhaps it were all written, after all. Flashes of Muhammad Bey al-Elfi, his serenity, the quiet of the Al-Azhar. 'As you did for me, yes.'

When they heard hoofbeats approaching, he did not turn. Out in the half-darkness a pair of mounted Awlad 'Ali came to a halt, calling to the Beni Qassim. After some commotion they led a rider forward slowly, and a horse approached, its hooves thudding softly into the sand. It drew to a halt.

'Mr Hazzard, I presume.'

An educated voice, a gentleman's voice. Hazzard looked round. It was a senior naval officer in plain coat and cloak, an older man, but not by much, at his hip a curved Genoese cutlass, in his belt, a three-barrelled turnover pistol – he was certainly no mere Admiralty official.

'So,' said Hazzard. 'Now comes the price.'

The man looked down at him kindly. 'I believe you have paid quite enough already,' he replied. 'My condolences.'

Hazzard gave a brief nod. 'Thank you.'

'In any case, no one knows I am here,' he continued, 'I rode from Rosetta. Utter pandemonium. Everyone wondering how they shall get home or retrieve their equipment from the bottom of the bay.'

'How did you get through the lines?'

'Rather like you, sir, I speak remarkably good French, but that isn't frightfully important.' He dismounted, handing the reins to one of the Beni Qassim, and stopped before Hazzard and the others. 'Sir William Sidney Smith. At your service.'

'Somehow I doubt that.'

Smith gave a wry smile. 'Quite so.' He glanced at the others. 'And you must be Masoud ibn Yussuf, associate of Mr Hammer. *As-salamu aleikum.*'

Masoud bowed. 'I am, *effendi. Wa aleikum as-salam.*'

Smith looked out at the bay. 'You've been busy, Captain.' He took out a slip of paper and glanced at it. 'Nine ships of the line crippled or captured… two destroyed, run aground, half a dozen frigates captured…' He noticed Wayland. 'And enemy artillery destroyed, survivors rescued… and further unspecified actions, by Unknowns Extraordinary…' He gave them all a brief nod of the head in acknowledgement. 'And very smartly done too.'

'That would be Mr Wayland and the men of 9 Company,' said Hazzard.

Smith nodded. 'The survivors of the *Esperanza* have told us all. They currently rest easy aboard HMS *Swiftsure*.' He cleared his throat and added sombrely, 'I am unaware if you know, but on the French flagship alone, a thousand hands lost. Only seventy rescued.'

Hazzard looked at him. He could see the raging fire on *Orient* again.

'Mm.'

'Du Petit-Thouars of *Tonnant* was blown in half and ordered he be propped on a cask to direct the battle against the *Alexander*, the colours nailed to the mast so no one could strike them once he was dead.'

Hazzard looked away into the night. He had not met Du Petit-Thouars. 'At least they paid.'

'Oh they paid, Captain. Most certainly. Total enemy dead and wounded is estimated at five thousand. Three thousand more captured. But in Nelson's squadron, seven hundred wounded, three hundred dead. No ships lost.' He folded away the paper. 'Apparently a young lady gave birth on the *Goliath* in the middle of it all.'

Hazzard looked at him, anger rising. 'Three of their ships escaped with two admirals.'

'Yes. Villeneuve and Ganteaume. We're after them, never fear. How did you put it? They shall cling to the rocks of Toulon like drowning men?' Smith smiled ironically when Hazzard turned to look at him. 'Yes, I've spoken to Acton in Naples. He was most put out to hear your name again. Damn near choked on his cigarillo.'

Hazzard thought of Emma Hamilton, of the *comtesse* de Boussard. 'Had he helped, none of this might have happened.'

'Indeed. And now we have a problem.'

'Do we.'

Seeing Smith, his uniform, his connection to the fleet, all had revived Hazzard's thoughts of vengeance, of blame, of old resentments. Taking care of Sarah over those last days, these ills had somehow drifted away on a merciful wind, and vanished, becoming nothing more than the faintest whispers in the rigging. Smith had brought them all back.

'Now that the French have access to the Indian Ocean,' said Smith, 'though you have deprived them of a fleet, their army still threatens India.'

Hazzard rounded on him. 'Then their lordships should have thought *wiser* of ordering Nelson to *pull out.*' He turned away, looking out to sea. 'They can all rot in hell.'

'Do you condemn Nelson?'

'Yes, I damn well *do*,' snapped Hazzard, 'because Nelson *let them in.*'

Smith looked down and admitted quietly, 'He is not my favourite. Nor I his,' he said, 'but quite likely he withdrew under necessity, or orders.'

'I know,' said Hazzard. 'I refused my orders. He did not.'

There was a short silence between them. Smith put his hands behind his back, the Italian cutlass swinging, catching the light. 'Then here is something you cannot know: five days ago, a French messenger intercepted Bonaparte on the road to Sinai and told him of Nelson's victory. This fellow looked very much the worse for wear according to my observer – half-crazed, wounded, arm hanging limp, burnt on one side they tell me, coat falling to pieces off his back...'

Hazzard stood dead still. For a moment he could not hear him, his throat tightening, a chill creeping through his blood.

'He claimed he had himself leapt from the flagship *Orient* only moments before she exploded...'

And then he understood.

No.

'And I have since established he is a senior officer of the *Bureau d'information*, their counter-intelligence service.'

Derrien.

'My good God...'

Escaped.

'Bonaparte flew into an unholy rage, but when he was handed one of your Arabic leaflets, and heard that you had not only been seen in the battle aboard *Orient*, but that you had previously been in the custody of this man not hours before—'

'It's *him*,' growled Cook, '*it's that bloody bastard...*'

Hazzard could hardly find the words, could barely speak. '*Where is he...*'

'Bonaparte threatened him with summary execution. The cavalry general with him, Damas or Dumas, I am not certain, wanted to kill him on the spot.'

Hazzard nearly seized Smith by his coat. '*Where is he?*'

Smith was clearly more disturbed by what he still had to relate. 'The fellow swore blind to Bonaparte you had been seen returning ashore and that he would burn every village in the Delta, one after the other, until they gave you up.' He watched Hazzard's reaction. 'And Bonaparte put ten thousand *livres* on your head.'

Hazzard's chest was pounding, '*Good bloody God...*'

A memory of Bonaparte, of Caesar: *I have such dreams, Mr Hazzard... and Fate is with me.*

'So,' said Smith, looking at Masoud, at the Beni Qassim, at the marines, 'what is that charming Room 63 phrase...? Would you like to *get back* to it...?'

Hazzard stared at him, but saw only the splintered decks of the *Orient*, feeling the cannon-rounds crashing into her hull, Masson, the *comtesse* de Biasi.

Derrien holding Sarah tight, his *hatred*…

'She gave you *everything* – *everything* you damn well needed,' cursed Hazzard. '*The entire damned Armée d'Orient and what did you do! What did you do!*'

Nothing.

The words echoed in Hazzard's mind and after a moment he realised he was not addressing Smith, or Nelson, or the Admiralty at all – but himself.

Smith watched him, weighing his words carefully. 'Shall we then let him get away with it?'

Everything Sarah had worked for.

Never stop.

He found himself shaking, facing Cook, Wayland and the marines. He looked back at Smith. 'Is this a briefing? I want maps, contacts, reports, everything you have.'

Smith opened the sabre-tache slung at his side and drew out several folded charts. 'You'll have to be quick about it.' He laid them on the ground by the light of the fireside and knelt, pointing out the key sites. 'Cairo here, the Delta, Rosetta, Damietta, El-'Arish on the Sinai border, Ibrahim Bey's progress to Syria here, very rough, progress of Bonaparte's cavalry half-brigade, and last sighting of your man *here*. As of two days ago.'

'Accurate?'

'Oh very. From a Huwaytat scout.'

Hazzard turned. 'Mr Wayland.'

Wayland stepped forward. 'Sir.'

'Are you fit to ride yet?'

'Yes, sir.'

'Very well. Mr Wayland, Master Handley, plot a course,' said Hazzard, 'for the road to Sinai.'

Handley squatted down by the map, looking it over. 'I'll get us right onto 'is ruddy 'ead, sir…'

'*Amigo*, we must go,' said De la Vega, moving past them to the horses. 'The tide will turn soon.' He glanced at Smith. 'I shall take him to the lines, and he can get us through with his so

358

perfect French.' He jumped into the saddle and delved into a bag, bringing out a heavy bundle. 'Here,' he said, and tossed it down to Hazzard.

'What's this?'

'You will need it more than I, *amigo.*'

Hazzard unwrapped it. It was the Lorenzoni repeating pistol.

'Remember, seven shots only, even for this demon you seek, *loco Inglés,* who fights the winds.'

Hazzard nodded and grasped his hand '*Vaya con Dios.*' *Go with God.*

'And you, *compadre. Volpone* will come when you call.' De la Vega looked at the marines, then at Smith. 'Will you do as this one says, with your little hands-full of soldiers again?'

Hazzard looked at Cook. 'Sar'nt – what says the boat?'

Cook turned to them. 'Well? Answer yer officer.'

Underhill looked round at them all, their sunburnt, smoke-blackened faces: Kite with a raw, livid scar across his cheek, Hesse in white *galabeyyah* smock and jerkin, twin daggers in his belt, Porter clutching his medical bag, broken-nosed Napier, Cochrane, De Lisle, the big Cornishman Pettifer hefting a Turkish blunderbuss, and Warnock with his tomahawk and a newly sawn-off French musket, one side of his face red with burns. After a moment Underhill turned back and grinned. '*Sah* – beg to report, boat says *bloody aye.*'

Smith climbed into his saddle. 'I shall be in support out at sea on HMS *Tigre,* never fear.' He pulled his mount round to join De la Vega. 'Any intentions I should relay...?'

Hazzard looked at the Beni Qassim in the glow of the drift-wood fire, at the broken temple pediments, the fallen columns rolled in the desiccated scrub – and out to sea, where *Valiant* had carried away all he had cherished. 'Yes,' said Hazzard, 'Tell them...'

Thief of hopes, defender of dust.

All she had worked for.

'Tell them I shall hunt down Derrien. That is my price. I shall then drive Bonaparte into the ground, and make him wish he'd never left France.' He pulled his leather sling-holster over his head and jammed in the Lorenzoni. It fitted. 'And when I am done, I shall return to London,' he said, 'and find Sir Rafe Lewis.'

'My dear fellow—'

Hazzard cut him short. 'I am not their man in Egypt. Tell them that much.'

Smith watched as Hazzard buckled on the scimitar of Ali Qarim and headed for his horse, Cook close behind, the marines and the *Bedu* following, as the smoke drifted across the moon from the smouldering remains in Aboukir Bay.

Historical Note

As in Book One, *Napoleon's Run*, the historical events of *Lords of the Nile* actually happened much as described here and, with a few exceptions, most of the characters are real figures drawn from history.

Napoleon's Run details how Bonaparte and his chiefs managed to gather an army of some 38,000 men and a fleet of roughly 400 ships at Toulon in almost total secrecy. There were a few security slips, such as the letter by Dolomieu, the aged and eminent geologist, who had written to a friend that he was considering 'the trip to Egypt' because he'd been promised he would find 'many interesting rocks there' – but otherwise, the Admiralty in London had no idea where the fleet might be headed. After watching invasion preparations at Brest and Boulogne across the Channel, they assumed the fleet was bound for Ireland or England, and consequently acted with lightning speed.

Nelson had been wounded badly in a disastrous attack on Santa Cruz de Tenerife in 1797, losing his right arm, the injury forcing him to recuperate in England – but he was recalled and despatched in May 1798 to Admiral John Jervis, now Lord St Vincent, blockading the Spanish fleet now trapped in Cadiz. It was from here in *Napoleon's Run* that Hazzard set out with his company of Oddfellows, comprising marines from various ships in the blockade fleet, and set off in the captured Spanish brig *Esperanza*. After his battle with two French corvettes he encountered privateer Cesár Domingo de la Vega, who decided he didn't much care for treaties with Revolutionary France, and became a firm ally.

The traditional British enmity for France at this point might seem no different to British enmity for France over much of the previous 700 years, but with the Revolution there seems to have been a difference. It is difficult for us to conceive of the impact the Revolution would have had on the minds of Europeans. When Louis XVI and Marie Antoinette were executed in 1793, the carriage of King George was mobbed in the London streets, the common people banging on the doors and roof, demanding war and revenge. The successive unstable governments of the Revolution were perceived not as mere enemies, but sources of evil, criminals who had usurped power over the people of France. This is not without basis: in a ten-month period in 1794, Revolutionary justice accounted for the murder of some 40,000 French citizens. When the guillotine was working so tirelessly, the gutters of Paris ran with streams of blood. Caron's memory is well-founded: there is a tale of a gentleman and two lady companions en route to the theatre one evening, having to step over this blood, laughing, the man dipping his finger into it and remarking 'Ah, is it not beautiful'. France had become a slaughterhouse. This was the war machine threatening to bring revolt to Ireland and invade England – or Egypt. The only force in Europe left to stand in its path in mid-1798 was the British Navy – more specifically, Horatio Nelson.

Nelson sailed back and forth across the Mediterranean from mid-May to August 1798, hunting for the French fleet. Although it covered some four square miles, he simply couldn't find it, and had no idea of its course or target. After the storm of the 19th May and his repairs in Sardinia, he put in to Naples to seek naval reinforcements; deprived of HMS *Emerald* and *Terpsichore*, which had been blown back across the sea and later gathered off Barcelona, Nelson needed light frigates to scout ahead of his heavy 74-gunners (74s) *Vanguard, Alexander* and *Orion*. Lieutenant Thomas Hardy, captain of the *Mutine* brig, went ashore to make the request but was refused by Sir John Acton, the Prime Minister of Naples, just as Hazzard had been, on the grounds that French forces were in Rome and could attack Naples in reprisal.

Receiving still further reports of Bonaparte's fleet, Admiral St Vincent sent in heavy reinforcements, possibly the most dangerous collection of warships in the world, commanded by aggressive, experienced captains. They were led by Sir Thomas Troubridge, Captain of HMS *Culloden*, and one of Nelson's most respected officers. They moved south from Naples to Sicily, through the Straits of Messina to Syracuse, thereby missing Bonaparte's route to Malta. They revictualled, wondering whether the French intended to attack the Greek islands and Constantinople. It was here that Hazzard and Cook made contact, thanks to the quick-witted fishermen of Ragusa.

Once the French fleet departed Valletta, Bonaparte had word that Nelson was close – though they had no idea how close. There is a report of a British ship detecting what they considered to be a French frigate but which was dismissed as a local trader. In that moment, the two fleets had passed within a thousand metres of each other, neither being aware of the other.

It's extraordinary that Nelson didn't check Malta. One reason might be that he had heard from a passing merchantman that the French were heading to Alexandria (and of course *Vanguard*'s log makes no mention of Hazzard and Cook or their report). Nelson turned his squadron from Sicily and streaked towards Alexandria so fast he completely outstripped the slower French fleet. Meanwhile, the French had diverted northeast, not southeast, and headed towards southern Italy and Crete on a more indirect route to Egypt.

The British arrived at Alexandria some three days in advance of the French invasion fleet. Once again Hardy was sent as ambassador with the *Mutine*, though according to Al-Jabarti, 'a caique' arrived bearing 'Europeans', who later identified themselves as English, looking for the French fleet. Hardy did explain the matter to Kurayyim, the Governor of Alexandria, much as described here, but Kurayyim 'dismissed his speech as mere trickery'. He then expelled the English, telling them to depart 'that God's will might be fulfilled'.

It certainly was. On the 1ˢᵗ of July 1798, nearly four hundred ships of the Republic of France appeared off the coast of Alexandria, the argument still whether to disembark in Aboukir Bay or somewhere safer further along the coast. Bonaparte, ever the tactician, recognised Aboukir Bay as a death-trap, though Brueys insisted it would be easier and faster to disembark troops and supplies (and he was quite right).

As they debated this, they landed men in the port who distributed his Arabic proclamation, which Al-Jabarti criticised so heavily in the *diwan* meeting with Murad, Ibrahim and the other beys. His comments in this scene come verbatim from Al-Jabarti's pen of 1798.

Back at Alexandria, a cry did indeed go up from the *Orient*'s lookout and for a few perilous minutes Bonaparte clutched at Bourrienne, believing Nelson had caught up with them, his words reproduced accurately here. But instead of Nelson, it was one of their own frigates lagging behind from Valletta, the *Justice*, the second sail behind an unknown trader which turned and headed into the distance. With such a near disaster, Brueys concurred that Marabout would be the safest place to land the men.

The landings at Marabout were an utter fiasco. A storm blew up out of nowhere, the ships standing so far offshore in the heavy swell that the men in their jolly-boats were blown back out to sea over and over again, taking nearly eight hours to reach the beaches, weak, seasick, weighed down by their long waterlogged woollen coats. When the first groups landed they were attacked almost at once by Bedouin horsemen, who surrounded some twenty officers and women passengers and rode off with them. One of them was the wife of a Sgt François of the cavalry, who was in Sarah's boat (more of her later). Only five thousand men of the army reached the shore before the landings were cut short.

No artillery made it ashore, nor any horses for the cavalry. Bonaparte had come with Junot and a number of the senior staff, including the one-legged Caffarelli, and forced a night-march on the exhausted soldiers: the only food and water they had was waiting for them in Alexandria. It was very much a matter of 'march or die'.

They arrived at the gates of Alexandria at nine a.m. The inhabitants ran out of ammunition by ten and began pelting the French with stones. By noon, Alexandria had fallen. But not without cost: the great General Kléber had been wounded as was the somewhat less great General Menou. This deprived Menou of the command of a division, but made him Governor of Rosetta instead, a task better suited to his administrative talents. While Kléber recovered, the First Division was handed to the experienced 'Papa' Dugua. The rest of the army was landed, and marched to gather at al-Ramaniyah, Reynier's division suffering the most: they took the desert route along Hammer's dry wells. The men went mad with thirst, some shooting themselves, the Bedouin riding through their lines in sporadic, unpredictable attacks. When the French found Damanhur, many ran straight into the river, some drowning.

The French clashed for the first time with the Mamluks at Shubra Khit, also known as 'Chebreiss', where the medieval tactics of the Mamluk cavalry were met by the disciplined gunnery of the French. Before the battle, a lone Mamluk horseman did approach one of the French squares, and rode back and forth displaying his mount, before riding off – the French cavalry were entranced by his skill.

Moiret, an officer of the 75th 'Invincibles', said in his memoirs that they were instructed repeatedly not to break formation for their own safety. The five divisional squares marched into open battle with devastating results. As Hazzard had forewarned, five thousand men per division formed ranks six-deep bristling with bayonets, and moved across the flat land by the Nile, the Mamluk cavalry charging again and again, unable to penetrate the formations, horsemen falling by the hundred to the massed volley fire of the disciplined French. Although historians blithely estimate casualties to be 'comparatively light', it was an outright slaughter. However, the battle upon the river was even worse.

The Mamluk riverboats and gunships were manned mostly by Greek mercenaries, and it was these who stormed the first French ship, beheading their captives, waving the heads of the fallen at their comrades. Besides their marine and footsoldier escorts, the only threat upon these boats was the group of '*savant*' academics headed for Cairo – crucial to Bonaparte's plan for Egypt.

Bonaparte had brought with him a special Commission of 167 artists and scientists, mostly young men, whose average age was 26, the youngest Réné-Edouard de Villiers du Terrage at only 17, who agreed to take his exams under the tutelage of Gaspard Monge himself once in Cairo. It was these untrained, unarmed scholars who watched the bloodthirsty mercenaries swimming across the Nile towards them, knives in their teeth.

Berthollet really did fill his pockets with stones and weights, ready to throw himself into the Nile rather than be butchered by the Mamluks; Fourier too did beg them to join him and evacuate to the rear boats, and Monge laid some of the guns and fired them himself. The *savants* acquitted themselves as well as any soldiers: in their top hats and coat-tails they beat out fires, manned the guns, helping their fellows to retreat to the gunboats behind, which came up in rescue, and covered the escape of the women among their number.

Although women were 'banned' from the expedition, there were over a hundred among the numbers. As if taking cue from a play by Shakespeare, some had disguised themselves as young men and junior officers, one famously not revealing herself until reaching Cairo. General Verdier's Italian wife was in a league of her own, and was renowned throughout the staff for accompanying her husband into battle. That Sarah and Jeanne were aboard one of the boats would not have been out of the question.

The river battle looked lost until the *Cerf*, commanded by Perrée, made a direct hit on the Mamluk flagship. The explosion was so great, according to eyewitnesses, the sky became filled with the mutilated limbs and bodies of the dead, cartwheeling through the air to fall into the Nile – marked by a great cheer by the desperate French. The battle of Shubra Khit ended. From there, the French advanced on Cairo.

The Battle of the Pyramids (also called the Battle of Embabeh by some) is often depicted in 19th century oils in full fire at the foot of the great monuments, cavalry riding in and out, artillery blasting nearby – and this gave rise to the British propaganda assertion that French cannon were responsible for destroying the nose of the Sphinx. Not so. The pyramids were in fact some 16 kilometres away from the battle on the horizon, but it was so great a victory we can excuse artistic licence; (and research has revealed that a 10th century activist defaced the Sphinx).

Bonaparte claimed in his memoirs that he made the historic comment 'Soldiers, forty centuries of history look down upon you!' But historians such as Herold have often wondered when he could have said this, or to whom, as there wouldn't have been much chance, not having the opportunity to address his troops first: they marched in echelon, advancing toward the city, and found Murad's cavalry once again.

The individual horrors witnessed by Hazzard did indeed happen, Mamluk riders bursting into flame, Lt Vertray fighting the old Mamluk in single combat, and the brave old warrior's brutal death; General Marmont led a column across the field, foolishly unprotected at the rear, but here it was Hazzard who slashed his way through the looting stragglers as he rode, madly looking for Bonaparte. The rage of the division breaking into columns and charging the Embabeh guns is also documented, as was their butchery of the Albanians and Turks, who displayed extraordinary bravery. It seems a suitable place for the heroic end of the devoted Izzam of the al-Kalbi, in his attempt to follow and defend Hazzard, his new lord.

The Mamluk who seized the forelegs of a charging horse is not specifically recorded, but this was a key defensive tactic of the original Varangian Guard of the late Greco-Roman Emperors of Byzantium/Constantinople. Varangians, or Vikings, were one of the several ancestors of the Mamluks, who settled in the region, particularly in the Ukraine and the Caucasus. A particular feat

367

of these giant Norsemen bodyguards was to dive for the forelegs of a charging horse and stop it dead, unseating the rider. It is from men such as these that the Mamluks, and many Egyptians of today, are descended. They later became the deadliest army in the East, fathering famous sons such as Salah ad-din, the nemesis of the English crusader king, Richard the Lionheart. Murad Bey himself was not born in Egypt but in Georgia, though there is some debate whether he was Circassian, but he was sold as a slave himself until he seized power.

However, despite the Mamluks' bravery, and the rousing of the common people who came to defend the gates of Cairo, in the end, Bonaparte's tactics and discipline won the day, and Cairo fell. Seeing the inevitable end, Ibrahim and the Ottoman Pasha rode straight for Sinai, pursued by their army, beginning the long road to seeking reinforcements from Acre, beyond Syria.

Hazzard's capture by the Maaza is not inconceivable, as not all Bedouin tribes knew other clans' loyalties or the grand scheme of alliances, or which Europeans were a threat – perhaps in a way they all were. But Colonel Lacroix was a genuine threat: an administrative paper-pusher and despot who later nearly cost the *savants* their lives and their works – more of that in the years to come. But there is no greater real-life hero of that moment than the gallant Jacques Cavalier of the 1st Cavalry, who defied Lacroix and later saved the *savants* from an uncertain fate – but here with fictional licence he steps into the breach for Hazzard, for honour, and the name of France – as do the men of Achille Caron, the *Alpha-Oméga*.

Bonaparte's triumph lasted only a week and a half, in which time he concentrated on tracking down Ibrahim's army and the remnants of Murad's cavalry – he had, in a way like Derrien, forgotten about the fleet. Despite his earlier orders to disperse the battle-fleet to Corfu, Admiral Brueys had stayed in Aboukir Bay. Bonaparte later claimed he had sent orders on at least three separate occasions, but had received no reply. When he heard the fleet was still loitering, the young and beloved Captain Jullien carried Bonaparte's order personally, with a detachment of the elite 75th Invincibles, and rode to Alexandria. He never made it past Alqam.

To the horror of the French, the men of the 75th had been routed and they later found Jullien's body thrown into the Nile. We can only wonder if some unknown hand had been at work to prevent all messengers from reaching the ports: Hazzard, providing Nelson with the 'tethered goat' for his tigers. Meanwhile, Brueys and his captains argued whether to set sail or cable the battle-fleet in line in Aboukir Bay while they continued to unload materiel. Brueys demanded the latter, and the others bowed to his resolve.

It is a matter of record that on the 1st of August 1798, Captain Hallowell of HMS *Swiftsure* and Captain Ball of *Alexander* went in to reconnoitre Alexandria while the main body of Nelson's squadron headed for Aboukir Bay. In that time, Hallowell logged contact with a Turkish merchantman who provided him with a rough chart of the shoals in the bay – whether this Turk was Lt Wayland and the *Volpone* we can only guess.

It is also a matter of record that Sir Thomas Troubridge's HMS *Culloden*, trailing behind the attack squadron, made the turn into the bay too sharply and ran aground on the rocks of the small island at the tip of the promontory – and came under fire from the small fortress tower on the headland. It was Captain Thompson of HMS *Leander* who turned back to tow Sir Thomas off the rocks – but, try as he might, it didn't work, and *Culloden* remained under fire.

There is no record of 9 Company, or any detachment of marines, assaulting French artillery positions ashore. But it is documented that at some point in the battle the cannon-fire from the fort stopped abruptly. No one knows why. I like to think it was Lt Marmaduke Wayland who saved the day. Hallowell warned Wayland that the battle at sea was all that would be remembered, and he's right. However, true to his duty, Wayland refused to abandon Nelson's squadron to the potential threat of French batteries, and went ashore. As Wayland told Hallowell, and as all marines can attest, 'It's what we do.'

The Battle of the Nile is possibly one of the best documented victories of the Royal Navy beside Trafalgar. The actions of the ships described here are accurate insofar as they assist the story, though much is left out. In the first moments of attack, Nelson's squadron split into separate spearheads, Captains Foley and Hood in HMS *Goliath* and *Zealous* racing each other to be first to hit the vanguard of the French line, Nelson leading a second attack on the centre.

Many have debated whether Foley saw the chart given to Hallowell or whether he simply used his instinct – whichever it was, he judged the distance between the shore and *Guerrier*, the foremost in the French line, and guided the fast-moving 74-gun *Goliath* between *Guerrier*'s nose and the submerged shoals, raking the *Guerrier* as he passed. He then turned sharply and moved down the French line on their largely unprepared portside. He was followed by Hood and Saumarez in the *Zealous* and *Orion* and others. This effectively spelt the end of the French, trapping their static line of battle in a crossfire as more British ships closed in on the seaward side. Each of Nelson's captains anchored opposite a chosen opponent and pounded them for the next four hours until they burned, sank or surrendered. Worse still for the French, there was an onshore breeze, i.e., the wind was blowing from the sea towards the shore, leaving them helpless: they could not escape.

History has not condemned Nelson, the hero of the Nile, for leaving Alexandria the way he did – it has been put down to pure chance, the necessity to revictual driving him on to the Greek islands. However, in so doing, Nelson allowed Bonaparte to land his army and, in the space of just thirty days, conquer Egypt.

The Secretary of War, Lord Melville, the former General Sir Henry Dundas, was the only senior figure at the Admiralty who argued with the First Sea Lord, the Earl Spencer, that the French would try to use Egypt as a springboard to India. Nelson suspected this too. But rather than preventing the French from landing, Melville wanted to leave them to it: he wrote that if a French army were stranded in the desert, at least he would know where it was.

With that in mind we must ask whether Melville played any part in Nelson's departure from Alexandria, or whether it was truly just bad timing. Every passing merchantman seemed to know the fleet was headed for Egypt, yet after that initial abortive reconnaissance of Alexandria, Nelson seems to have doubted their word, or refused simply to wait. Commentators often quote his need for resupply, but given the threat of enemy action, it could be argued that British ships would have stayed on station far beyond the need to revictual – and if need became dire, they would have demanded provisions from Alexandria. Instead, Nelson felt the best course was to sail as far away as possible in the opposite direction to the usual sea-routes that would have been followed by any fleet coming from the western Mediterranean.

History quite rightly remembers Nelson for his courage and faith in his captains – Hazzard's remark that they were the band of brothers to Henry V at Agincourt was exactly how Nelson saw them, 'we few, we happy few'. But Hazzard reminds us that, in his haste, Nelson left a population of hundreds of thousands of poor and wretched to face the firestorm of invasion with no aid whatsoever. All Nelson had to do was wait at Alexandria, and he did not. Whether Hazzard, or an officer like him, watched Nelson burn a sealed order we shall never know.

British sea captains of the period were motivated and aggressive, with arguably the best trained seamen and gunners at their command. Even with his meagre squadron, Nelson would have cut Bonaparte's fleet to pieces, ignoring the guns of the protective battleships and striking straight for the heart of the convoy, blazing his way through the vulnerable transports. The death-toll would have been appalling: tens of thousands of helpless French troops and their supplies would have been lost. It could have meant the destruction of Nelson's squadron, but it would certainly have been the end of the French expedition, the end of any hopes for French Egypt, and certainly the end of Bonaparte. All Nelson had to do was wait. And he did not.

Whether Lewis could conceive of a scheme whereby British arms would 'permit' the French to conquer an entire nation and construct a feature as complex as a canal at Suez – so that Britain could later take it from them – would have been child's play to perfidious Albion and the nameless double-thinkers of Room 63.

Sir William Sidney Smith will join us once again – hero of the Royal Navy and the army, Smith soon took over from the wounded Nelson as senior commander in the Levant. Smith's report to Hazzard concerning the battle is accurate for the time. Only between sixty and seventy survivors emerged from the flagship *Orient* – and a young woman really did give birth on HMS *Goliath* during the battle. Tales abound: a boy of barely ten, a 'powder-monkey', was found sitting on a powder locker, staring, but stone dead, killed by shock. Brueys was standing on the quarterdeck when a cannon-ball crashed through the railing and whipped away one of his legs. Likewise, Du Petit-Thouars, Captain of the *Tonnant*, was cut in half by a cannon-round, but miraculously was still sufficiently conscious to be propped on a cask to direct the fight. The expression 'nailing one's colours to the mast' comes from his determined defiance and devotion to duty.

I would like to think that some marines on the ships surrounding the *Orient* might have seen Hazzard's red coat boarding the enemy flagship and taken heart – there were marines already on the *Peuple Souverain*. When the fire broke out, the British ships redoubled their efforts, bombarding the French flagship relentlessly until their enemy was engulfed in flame. This moment was immortalised in the poem *Casabianca* by Frances Hemans, the famous line 'The boy stood on the burning deck' referring to young Ensign Giocante Casabianca, the captain's son, who supposedly ran to the rail as the ship blazed, and looked down as the crew dived overboard – only to run back into the fire. The prosaic truth is that Casabianca and his son were most likely knocked down much earlier on in the battle. There is a theory that Casabianca set a self-destruct fuse to scupper *Orient*, and prevent her capture, but there is little evidence – just as likely is the theory that the cause was a certain length of quickmatch left unnoticed in the Orlop, set by persons unknown: or as Smith put it, Unknowns Extraordinary – such as a certain Marine Sergeant Jory Cook.

The explosion of the *Orient* was heard in Alexandria, and as far as Rosetta, some twenty miles away. It effectively marked the end of the battle, though several of the French had not struck their colours and surrendered. After a brief silence of ten or fifteen minutes, the British began to fire once again, trying to engage the three ships in the rear under Villeneuve in the *Guillaume Tell*. Owing to a change in the wind, however, these last few ships managed to evade Nelson's line and escape – an escape for which they were later heartily condemned in France despite their attempts to come to the aid of Brueys and the *Orient*. Villeneuve would meet Nelson once again, at Trafalgar.

The Battle of the Nile was one of the greatest victories in British naval history. When the Earl Spencer heard the news, he fainted. The City of London commissioned presentation swords for the captains; Nelson was created a baron, and the Ottoman Sultan awarded him the Order of the Crescent.

Hazzard, however, is the embodiment of outraged British feeling, and he stays, some small part of him claiming the ground for which he, Sarah and a thousand others so dearly paid. Among Nelson's squadron were two hundred Austrian troops, along with at least a thousand marines, and some ten thousand serving sailors – doubtless many Marine commanders wanted to take the victory ashore and finish the job. Instead, the Royal Navy formed a blockade, and kept the French locked up in their new colony on the Nile.

Only Hazzard and his followers remained ashore. What he did next, in his anguish and his hatred for the Admiralty, remains to be seen.

Jonathan Spencer, 2020

Acknowledgements

I would like to thank a number of soldiers, sailors, tinkers and tailors for their considerable help and guidance in the creation of the Hazzard series, including Michael du Plessis, Alistair France, Anthony Gray, John Rawlinson and Willem Steenkamp; linguists Diana Barlow, Ian Tanti, Edwin Galea and Monica Schmalzl; interpreters and transliterators Muhammad Wafa, Essam Edgard Samné, and former Naval Intelligence officer Hassan Eltaher; my editor at Canelo, Craig Lye, and agents Mike Bryan and Heather Adams.

And my father, who told me stories of the desert I will never forget.

Jonathan Spencer, 2020